# Voices from Cold River

Richard Charles Tappan

iUniverse, Inc.
New York   Bloomington

# Voices from Cold River

*This is a work of fiction. All of the characters, names, incidents, organizations, and dialogue in this novel are either the products of the author's imagination or are used fictitiously.*

*iUniverse books may be ordered through booksellers or by contacting:*

*iUniverse*
*1663 Liberty Drive*
*Bloomington, IN 47403*
*www.iuniverse.com*
*1-800-Authors (1-800-288-4677)*

*Because of the dynamic nature of the Internet, any Web addresses or links contained in this book may have changed since publication and may no longer be valid. The views expressed in this work are solely those of the author and do not necessarily reflect the views of the publisher, and the publisher hereby disclaims any responsibility for them.*

*ISBN: 978-1-4401-4106-5 (sc)*
*ISBN: 978-1-4401-4107-2 (e-book)*

*Printed in the United States of America*

*iUniverse rev. date: 5/1/2009*

For my wife, Sally.

# CHAPTER I

## The Virgin's Bath

Mariah told her mother, *yes*, she was going to bathe in the river. An emphatic, even defiant yes for today was the last day of her childhood. No more bowing to Mother's limits. She would demonstrate her independence by plunging into the clear waters of Cold River free and unashamed. Mariah Brandon marched down the dusty path toward the riverbank carrying two large towels. Despite her mother's shouted warnings about the perils of breaching boundaries, Mariah walked on, head up, her black tresses falling loose over her shoulders.

"What if somebody sees you swimming like one of the Rhine maidens?" Sarah called out sharply. "Life is no opera, Mariah," she harped on with Wagnerian fury, sure her daughter was determined to breach all decorum and swim naked as a nymph. For the past few months anger and frustration had colored her tone, but deeper currents of fear occasionally surfaced also. What would become of this female Icarus Sarah had brought into the world? Sarah feared that Mariah was leaving the nest and flying too close to the sun of Victorian convention.

The two-year battle between mother and daughter began in earnest when Mariah completed her formal schooling with graduation from eighth grade. A love of books, encouraged by her mother, had helped her to fly over New Hampshire's mountains to the world beyond. Now her mother wanted her to return to the cage of domestic duty, but the door was ajar and Sarah's beautiful black-crowned bird was about to escape.

"If somebody sees you, we'll never live it down. It just isn't done." Sarah's voice trailed off in resignation.

"Oh, for heaven's sake," muttered Mariah to herself. School was in session and it was harvest time. Chances were slim of encountering anyone at the swimming hole, but it was just that chance that made the adventure all the more alluring. *Enough of worrying what others think; enough of knowing my place.*

Mariah was raised on the same stern lessons that had directed generations of New Englanders along the paths of righteousness of their Puritan forebears. In Adam's fallen world people were consigned to their roles. Some were masters; others were slaves. Men tended the fields; women tended the kitchen. Although they believed Christ's blood was spilled for all, the blood of some of His children ran blue, and blue bloods had a special place in the eternal order of things; their rewards were visible during their lifetimes. Red-blooded commoners who were faithful in their menial roles on earth would receive *their* treasures in heaven. Children learned from an early age that there was a predestined purpose and a place for all of us on earth. True happiness came to those who followed God's will, not your own. Mariah had heard it all at home, at school, at church, but all the pressure to conform had turned the combustible coal of her fiery will into the hardness of diamond.

"You are not to go upstream!" Sarah warned. Mariah disappeared into the bushy cover of the path along the river, adamant that she would swim in the forbidden place reserved for older boys, a mysterious cascade well upstream from the glacial pothole where children and girls swam.

All morning before Mariah's abrupt departure Sarah had vented her steam in the kitchen with four recipes going simultaneously, two assigned to Mariah. The two younger siblings, Florence and Little Moze, were doing their barnyard chores. Freddy, the elder son, had gone to the North Sandwich Store on errands. Bread dough was warming on the stove shelf, pushing up the damp cloths only to be punched down for their second rising; apples coated in cinnamon and sugar stood in a mound awaiting their crust.

"This is the last chance to have my say, so you're going to have to hear it. I'm still your mother and you're under my roof." Sarah had declared a mother's privilege to have her say as she punched the bread dough down with particular vehemence. "A woman who fails to know her place—especially a poor one with nothing to fall back on—will bring a curse down on herself that may haunt her for the rest of her life."

"Know my place. So *this* is my place? The kitchen?"

"Well, yes, that, too, the kitchen is a woman's place, but I mean the Notch, on a farm. Your father and I, and most of our neighbors, we go back five, six generations in this place, and all farmers. This is your home, the place you've always loved."

"But that's not all, is it, Mother? To 'place', I mean." Mariah waved a wooden spoon like a weapon. " 'Place' is also my *station in society*, as they say, and you think I'm being uppity because I don't want to be a cow-milking farmhand wife. That's it, too, isn't it?"

A deadly silence separated them until Mariah whacked down the wooden spoon and let the flour fly. At the table where she was working, a pound cake and a bread pudding loaded with raisins rested in their greased tins amongst flour and utensils. "These are ready for the oven. There. I'm done," she declared. She took the lavender-scented soap her brother Freddy had brought from uptown, found two towels, and headed for the door. The rich sensuality of the French milled soap cleansed Mariah's nostrils of the domestic scents of home cooking.

"Where did *that* come from?" asked Sarah, pushing back errant strands of strawberry blond hair.

Twelve-year-old Freddy, who was eavesdropping on the confrontation at the open front door answered. "It came from Will. I saw him up at Taylor's. He asked me to deliver it directly to Mariah."

"So the groom wants his bride to be *perfumed* for the special day, does he?" snarled Sarah. "Freddy, haven't you got chores to do?" expecting response without reply. Freddy knew this was one of those times to comply without whining or hesitating.

When Mariah arrived at the pothole, she listened for voices; smil-

3

ing when she detected only the call of birds and the rustling of leaves. The only voices she heard were the soft voices of the two branches of the river as they met in a frolicking swirl that had carved out a basin in the solid granite. Although she expected solitude even upstream, she moved stealthily under cover of the thick brush along the bank until she got to the upstream pool where, she had heard, there was a wonderful granite slide, smoothed by eons of water and sand. If only she would dare try it!

But as she broke through thick hemlock boughs, she heard male voices. Farm boys her age or slightly older had apparently using their lunch break from the fields for a final swim of the season. She ducked back behind the branches and tried to calm her racing heart. The young men's hands and faces were brown from a long season of plowing and haying. Sinewy, slippery white arms wrestled in the water with an animal frenzy. Their laughter could not hide the competitive play of dawning manhood. Who could dive deeper or punch harder? Eventually the boys drew themselves up on the warm, smooth rocks in full sun, panting and growing serious as they talked about girls. Mariah could only make out occasional words—she heard some names, including her own. She was tempted to slip into the water and move closer behind some glacial boulders, but she knew she would be discovered. She strained to hear, but the splash of the water down the rocky slide and the buzz of concupiscent insects screaming in the warm sun censored their words. As they stood to dress, she watched intently. Blood rushed to her head, and she thought of Will whose fine body she longed to see uncovered. One more day.

In only a few minutes the boys were gone and the cascading north branch of Cold River was hers alone. She left her clothes hidden under branches and slipped into the cold water. It was crystalline with sunlight reflected from mica on the sandy bottom. As she swam, she thought of Longfellow's maiden "with the meek brown eyes." Mariah's eyes, black more than brown, were not meek, nor did she want them to be. "Her meek, brown eyes in whose orbs a shadow lies like the dusk in evening skies!" She plunged below the surface and burst back into the warm air. "Standing with reluctant feet where brook and river meet, womanhood and childhood fleet." Indeed this was the day when her maidenhood and womanhood met, but there was nothing reluctant about Mariah's feet as she exulted in her flight from maidenhood.

On this early fall day in the year of our Lord 1883 Mariah Brandon slipped underwater again, opening her eyes. "One's-self I sing, a simple separate person. The Female equally with the Male I sing." Truly there was joy in leaving parental authority behind; she could not conceive of marriage to Will as coming under a new authority no matter what others said of marriage. Today, yes, in defiance of Mother and convention, she bathed naked in the river in a place reserved for males. And yes, as a woman with a mind and a voice of her own she would marry Will Dunfield.

William Channing Dunfield ruled the upstream rocks and rapids of Cold River, and was the gold standard in the eyes of the young ladies of Sandwich Notch. Everyone talked about him—whether it was kindly or not—and everyone listened whenever his name came up. Although Notch folks acknowledged Mariah Brandon as smart and very pretty, they were surprised when they heard that Will Dunfield had proposed to her. After all she was just a farm girl from a marginally successful farm—a fine family to be sure—but not the kind of bride they expected on the arm of the up and coming young shoe merchandiser who suddenly appeared back in town in fifteen-dollar suits.

But with all of the attention came gossip. William Dunfield traveled to big cities and was known to frequent saloons, dance halls and theaters. Stories—embellished perhaps—passed from salacious lips to eager ears, from lamppost to street car to train. Coaches and buggies flung dirt at a trot up the Wonnalancet Road into the pristine whiteness of the sleepy town of Sandwich, New Hampshire.

Sarah Sanborn Brandon, a veteran teacher of grammar and morals, let her daughter know that she had heard the stories. Just after Will began courting Mariah, Sarah confronted her daughter with her suspicions about Will. The stories had traveled from Hanson's Livery Stable to the West Ossipee station to most of the farmhouses dotting the valley from Juneau Hill to Whiteface. "I know how people gossip," Sarah told Mariah, "but some of it has to be true."

"Mother, you always told me to ignore gossip, now didn't you?"

"It's different if you end up as the *subject* of gossip, and that is about to happen, isn't it?" Sarah answered with arms folded across her chest. "It doesn't help that he does all that traveling."

"Is there sin in traveling?" rebutted Mariah with too much sarcasm in her voice to be ignored. She received a cold stare.

"You've no doubt heard the stories. I know you have."

"Stories, Mother. He's handsome and has a good job. Curiosity and jealousy. Combine those with boredom and you've got plenty of fuel for gossip."

"I've seen him follow women with his eyes."

"That's a healthy sign," chuckled Mariah.

"Now don't be sassy, young woman. He does it even when he knows people see him doing it."

"They look at him and he looks back. I don't know why it upsets you so."

"*And* I hear that he drinks."

"Oh, Mother, even Daddy has a little…"

"That's not the same. An occasional…well, hard cider's nothing like…it's just not the same as people who go to saloons and you know it," Sarah responded with her thin hand pressed against her cheek.

Mariah left a gap of silence before she spoke. "The Bible," she started quietly and slowly," says don't get drunk on wine. It doesn't say not to drink. In fact at the wedding at Cana, Jesus…"

"Now don't tell me about the Good Book. I know what the Good Book says," Sarah said quietly, but with a sharp edge. "What will happen to the poor widow when Will moves out?"

"Will's given her enough money to hire a couple of hands for spring planting. One more good season and she'll turn a profit even with hired help," rebutted Mariah with evident satisfaction in her defense of the groom-to-be.

That day and the numerous uncomfortable confrontations that had followed led to Mariah's plunge, a new baptism washing away the old life and transforming the old self into a new and better one.

The day was glorious in late September colors. The air was clear; occasional clouds dotted the piebald mountains. White birches, now golden-leafed, scattered their coins of light along the path beside Cold River. Maples were ablaze with orange and red. Mariah wrapped herself in towels and held her soap against her chest, inhaling the fragrance. She closed her eyes and thought once more of Walt Whitman: "Of Life immense in passion, pulse and power...Cheerful, for freest action formed under the laws divine." Here around her, in the rustling, golden leaves and in the murmuring voices of the river were the laws that spoke to her heart.

# CHAPTER 2

## *Proud Crusts*

A mile from the Cold River cascade, Sarah Brandon rolled a piecrust wielding the hardwood rolling pin with military precision over retreating dough. She fumed and muttered, muttered and fumed, talking to herself, and sometimes to her husband. Amos Brandon was in and out filling the woodstove, glad to have something to keep him out of his wife's firing line from time to time.

"Bathing in the river—naked. Preparing herself for that, that Dunfield. I should have known the first time he came over here. A full-grown man courting a young girl like her. Of course, I can see how a young girl could find him…well, attractive in an earthy kind of way, but he has no business…and Amos, you didn't drive him away. Do you want your daughter with a man who's been around like Dunfield has?"

"*Around?* I know he's been around *here* enough," Amos answered lightly.

"You know what I mean." Sarah turned to glare at Amos, but he kept straightening out the wood, avoiding the sternness in his wife's eyes.

"He's not full-growed, for heaven's sake," said Amos. "He's only eighteen, isn't that right, Sarah?"

"No, he's twenty. Could pass for twenty-five. And no innocent country boy, that's for sure."

Amos scratched his head in silence. With eyes laden with sadness, he walked over to Sarah and surprised her with a warm embrace and held on. "Let's pray about it," he whispered. Amos confessed that he had not always done his best as husband and father; he thanked God for each of his children—for a high spirit, courage in the face of trial, a gentle humor to lighten others' hearts, and for a heart for doing what was right. His greatest thanks were for his wife who gave him a family and a home; he praised her fierce protectiveness and caring, and then he asked for God's mercy and peace for the family. When he was finished, he held Sarah until her tears stopped. "Well," he said, holding Sarah at arm's length, something's been tryin' to get into the barn. I got some fences to repair and some boards to nail down better."

Sarah raised her moist eyes and touched her husband's bearded cheek. "My dear Amos."

She recognized she often burdened her own heart by growing a bumper crop of problems in her fertile imagination, then shouldering the grim harvest of her fears alone. Mariah's wedding was now behind her, but Mariah's marriage loomed in the foreground. She struggled to adopt Amos' viewpoint of letting go, but her sense of responsibility was not alleviated by her powerlessness. For the first time in her life Sarah felt incapable of protecting one of her children and equally incapable of renouncing that duty of a mother.

Amos had done a labor of love and turned to a labor of hands. Although he had a gift for the right words at the right time, he was keenly aware when it was the time to leave matters alone.

The mother of the bride fixed her thoughts on her pies. Sarah had a wedding feast to prepare, like it or not. She removed the first two pies from the oven and set them in the pie safe, looking at them with satisfaction. Sarah Sanborn Brandon could role crusts that flaked like mica. The house smelled of apples and cinnamon, of nutmeg and of lemon. The usual smells—wood smoke, mustiness and tracked in animal droppings—fled from her nostrils more easily than Will Dunfield could be driven from her thoughts.

Yet Sarah realized that Amos was right. In truth she knew very little about Will Dunfield. That is, very little from direct observation or experience. Information traveled by the grapevine and that grapevine grew wild and entangled in Sandwich Notch. Could the stories be mere fantasies in the minds of bored farm girls hoping for some excitement in their lives?

Amos and she had gone back and forth on this matter before. *Will didn't get a reputation without some truth behind it…If I was a judge, I'd have to throw your case out of court …don't keep asking me for hard evidence. There's things we just know…What's wrong with givin' him the benefit of the doubt?…turning a blind eye…No it's not …Mariah will raise eyebrows…you can call 'em gossips if you want…Her choice? Yes, of course, but she's only got one chance to get it right…Well, Sai, you took a big gamble on me, folks thought…Don't be silly, Amos. You weren't anywhere near the bottom of the barrel… I'll take that as a compliment!*

Amos did not have the most sterling reputation or much sterling in his pocket when he proposed to Sarah shortly after he mustered out of the Union Army. Sarah had to admit that her family had grave doubts when Amos came courting her. Sarah's grandfather Sanborn called him "Scratch," because he had devilish charm and coal black eyes. Although Amos Brandon had big dreams, Sarah, the ever-practical school marm, gradually turned him from some of his quick buck schemes and disciplined him into the routine and reality of life as a farmer.

Amos made the most of the rocky New Hampshire soil. He did better than many of his relatives and neighbors. Some even abandoned farms they couldn't even sell for the cost of a wagon, and headed West. Twelve years before Mariah's birth, Amos's widowed older sister Bertha had loaded a wagon with essential possessions and joined a party of twenty-five other farmers out of Sandwich Notch. The remembrance of Bertha's departure from New Hampshire came back to Sarah whenever letters arrived from Central City, Iowa.

In the years after Mariah was born in 1868, Amos and Sarah had seen the population in the valley drop by nearly half. White pines began filling in fields that once stretched to the foot of the Sandwich Range. Dozens of old farm houses, paintless and sun bleached gray, stood windowless. In 1840 there were forty farms in the notch; by 1860, only eight remained.

Sarah's mother had helped her struggling family by becoming a mill girl. In the decades before the War of the Rebellion, girls happily left the farm to work in the textile mills. The dam raised on the Merrimack harnessed the power of the river that wound through Manchester, and girls' nimble fingers guided the shuttles flying through the clattering looms for ten hours a day or more.

Even before the war, however, the demand for labor, and the stiff competition, cut into profits, and the mill owners began bringing in foreign labor. First French Canadians, then the Irish. It was no longer decent work or proper surroundings for a Yankee farm girl, and so the "natives," as the Protestant majority called themselves, pulled their girls out of the factories and struggled for survival on their farms, simmering in resentment and fear of the changing world and the foreigners who took over the cities. Sarah remembered hearing her mother sing the mill girls' songs she had learned while tending the looms.

No more shall I work in the fact'ry,
Greasy up my clothes;
No more shall I work in the fact'ry
With splinters in my toes.

Like her mother before her, Sarah worked outside of the home only until a suitable husband came along. Her work, however, was of the mental kind. Sarah was a respected schoolteacher for several years. She left books and chalkboard to marry Amos, and took her place in the home as wife and mother, just as her mother and her mother before her had done. Of one thing Sarah felt certain; her marriage to Amos Brandon was the best decision she had ever made.

"Your father may be a dreamer at times, but he's not afraid of a hard day's work," she said to Mariah in one of her lectures about marrying well. "Bertha didn't listen to the warnings about that loafer Charles, and look what happened to her," Sarah warned. She never admitted to her daughter that there was more passion than planning in her choice of Amos Brandon as the man to share her bed; she also never admitted that she had once hoped for a life with style and grace, just the kind of dreams Mariah dreamed.

Sarah held to her dreams and put off marriage well into her twenties. Her reputation in town, especially among the leading families gave her hope of a marriage into notch society. She joked to herself she might "move up a notch" if she sought a husband from Franconia Notch or Pinkham Notch or one of the other White Mountain notches to the north. But when thirty was looking precariously close, she reconciled to life with a local farmer. In Sarah's eyes Amos Brandon was definitely the pick of the bunch.

Well formed and handsome as a pirate, Amos had a touch of the devil's blood, enough to make him exciting. That he was brave and bold there could be no doubt. His war record attested to that. After being seriously wounded and lying for weeks in a military hospital tent, he returned home only long enough to recover fully and reenlisted for the remainder of the war.

Brave and bold, yes, Amos W. Brandon was the salt of the earth. He paid his bills, kept his stonewalls mended, and walked with his wife arm and arm to church each Sunday. Sarah Sanborn became Sarah Brandon having cast off some pie-in-the-sky dreams for pie-on-the-table ones. The Brandons would never be rich, but marriage to a man like Amos was never humdrum and routine for long.

Amos's devilish side got the better of him from time to time. When Mariah was a little girl, the farmers had a very bad year with potato bugs. Amos's potatoes were spared the blight—why, he never could figure out—but he saw an opportunity to make some money. He devised a concoction of tobacco juice collected from spittoons, a measure of hard cider on its way to vinegar, and some "secret ingredients." He used what little cash they had to buy bottles and cork stoppers, and he went into business the next winter with "Brandon's Potato Bug Remedy." Everyone in town knew for a fact that Amos had a good harvest of potatoes, but all he would tell them is, "I've been experimentin'." In the fall, he started collecting and bottling his disgusting, foul-smelling concoction that anyone would believe would drive potato bugs and just about anything else with a sense of smell, out of Carroll County if not farther.

If it had been poured full strength on potato plants, who knows what benefits might have accrued, but the quantities that it would have taken would have required the population of a city the size of Boston—men, women and children—to chew and spit and save all of the tobacco juice produced in that great metropolis, just to save the potatoes of Sandwich, New Hampshire. So, out of practical necessity and reasonable economy, Amos provided directions to dilute the concoction a tablespoon to a gallon in a watering can. No doubt all but the hardiest "'tater bug" would succumb to the potion if the farmer plucked the bug off the plant and dropped them in the pail, but the diluted mixture sprinkled over the plants did little to arrest the blight. The next season the gnawing critters finally found Amos's fields as well.

At first he advocated making the mix stronger, but eventually he had to admit that the elixir was ineffective "against the kinda bugs we'ah gettin' this yee-ah." This was a puzzling defense since no one could identify various species of potato bugs. Amos had made over a hundred dollars, and he didn't feel the least bit guilty. He was often referred to with a smile as "Tater Bug," but his good nature, his kindly treatment of neighbors, and his wife's good standing in the community brought him quick forgiveness. The third year, the blight of potato bugs had passed, and some even granted that it might be a delayed effect of Amos' secret concoction.

Mariah was especially close to her good-natured father. She also placed her hopes in him to bring her mother around to accepting Will. It wasn't that Amos had a special fondness for Will. Mariah wasn't going to delude herself. Will presumed too much and it grated on Amos at times. The second time Will met Amos, he addressed him by his first name. Although Amos was not one to "stand on ceremony" as he'd often say, this backslapping young man with a powerful grip also told him off-color jokes, and didn't mind letting Amos know that he'd seen a French postcard or two. Here he was courting Amos's elder daughter, a virgin of fifteen, and yet his eyes searched up and down a pretty girl when she got out of a buggy.

After a half hour's peace and quiet, Amos carried a basket of fresh eggs into the kitchen, boots laden with evidence of his barn chores.

"Look at you!" shouted Sarah, sweeping him back out the door and his trail behind him.

He tiptoed back in with clean boots and hung his straw hat on a peg. Lifting a stove lid to add a stick of wood, he let out a belch of smoke that rose like an Indian signal to the ceiling.

"For heavens sakes, Amos, open that damper."

Amos wasn't going to pretend that a belch of smoke was the cause of Sarah's irritability. The time had come to take the burr from under Sarah's saddle. "You can't change nothin' now. Leave it in the good Lord's hands," said Amos pleadingly as he waved away the smoke.

Sarah didn't answer. Amos took her hands and looked into her eyes with a kindly but admonishing smile. Sarah looked back with silent acquiescence before going back to work.

Flecks of ash settled out of the smoke. The cracks and bulges of the stained plaster resembled a relief map of the White Mountains. "Too bad I didn't get to that ceilin' last winter."

"Yes. It's too bad you didn't get to a lot of things," Sarah replied, but her tone had lightened to a shade of humor.

"Well, Will's not marryin' into the family for money, that's for sure," said Amos. "I know what you're thinkin'. I could at least of whitewashed it."

Amos picked up the broom and pointed it at the ceiling like a schoolmaster about to make a point. Sarah turned wondering what he was about to do. "You see them lines runnin' from that bulge there?"

" I've lived with those lines as long as I've lived with my own," responded Sarah with her arms crossed.

"If I was to touch that bulge with this broom, right there where them lines meet, you'd have plaster crusts on them pies."

"So is your point that a little whitewash won't fix our ceiling?"

"That's my point," Amos replied with a wry smile.

"I know your philosophy. If it can't be hidden with whitewash, then don't bother to do anything."

"It's more like this: 'Learn to live with it if you can't do anything about it." Amos looked at his wife of twenty years, still firm and slim despite a few lines of her own, a lady whose dignity and delicacy showed despite years of sun and lye and labor. "You know what I mean, Sai. Please, for Mariah's sake, for my sake, for your sake, try to accept Will. There's nothin' else can do any good."

"It isn't just her stubbornness about marriage. She hasn't learned that a girl must *find* her niche. She doesn't *carve* one out for herself. She thinks she can be what she wants to be. When have we ever heard of a woman doctor or a woman running a business?"

"Lydia Pinkham's Tonic. Cures what ails ya," replied Amos with a grin.

"It may be Lydia's concoction, but I'm sure she doesn't run the company. It just isn't allowed. Mariah doesn't want to hear anything about limits she has to live with. I'm afraid she's going to wear herself out pushing at walls that aren't going to budge."

"I'd be watching out for falling stones if the two of you was pushing from the same side," said Amos with a sideways glance.

Sarah stood in front of the stove, her eyes looking off into space, her back straight and her hands still. "Very well. I get your point, " she said. Amos watched as Sarah gathered up strawberry blonde wisps, touched with some silver at the temples, and tucked them behind her ears.

"Sai, I'm not claimin' that Will's a man of the cloth, but Mariah made her choice…"

Sarah turned to face her husband, a potholder in her hand, as though her hand might burn him if he came too close. "And what business does a fifteen-year-old girl have in making a choice of that magnitude without her parents' approval?"

"I could no more tell Mariah she wasn't gonna marry Will than to tell you that I'm the boss."

"But you *are*. You *are* the head of this household," Sarah said with the strength of an edict. "*I* know my place, Amos, and don't tell me I don't."

Amos couldn't suppress a chuckle at the irony of Sarah's determined argument. Then, in complete seriousness, he walked to face his wife, taking her hands, potholder and all. "I honor my wife too much to tell her what to do."

Softening, Sarah looked down at her husband's sunburned, rough hands. "Wives, submit yourselves unto thy husbands as unto the Lord," she said in almost a whisper.

"Sai, you know I don't want to be the boss. Lots of men quote that verse. They can call me weak if they want, but I go by the verse that comes before that one. 'Submit to each other in the fear of God.'"

Sarah looked into her husband's eyes with the beginnings of a smile. "Submitting doesn't come naturally to some of us."

"Nope, but some are naturals at impartin' the fear of God in others."

"Oh, Amos, really," said Sarah, allowing a smile to break through. "It's hard work being a prophetess," she said lightly, looking off as though she were waiting for a vision to come into focus.

Amos pecked her on the cheek. "Mrs. Brandon, we all have our callin's, and our crosses to bear."

Sarah met Amos in 1862 only weeks before he went off to war. She married him in 1866, six months after he had returned from service with the New Hampshire Ninth Regiment. Sarah laid down school bells for wedding bells. Women were not permitted to continue teaching after they married, a custom of the times that Sarah regretted, but had no power to change.

In the twenty years since they married, Sarah's confidence in Amos Brandon's ingenuity and resourcefulness were sometimes put to a severe test. As fertile lands in the West opened up, McCormack's machines reaped great surpluses of grain and plowed the little New England farms under. The mechanical whirling dervishes, strung to eight or more horses, felt at home on great flat earthen floors of the wide West. New England's little fields bordered in walls of stone and towering timbers frustrated their movement.

Other kinds of whirling machines attacked New England farmers by water. Rivers that once flowed freely, babbling and roaring over rapids and falls, were now confined in chiseled banks, wedded reluctantly to their mill masters for whom they spun and wove, sawed and ground. The rivers in cities just over the mountains had yielded their freedom to productivity. The Cocheco, running through Rochester and Dover to the sea, had exchanged its purity for profits. Its feet of clay, cut from its channel and banks, had become seventy million bricks staring down from factory walls. As the river made her daily walk through the industrial cities, she was stained and fouled by industrial filth, forced out of town like a fallen woman who had dared to show herself in the light of day.

Mariah and Will were going to places where there were perfume shops and saloons, streetcars and burlesque shows. Sarah pictured her daughter weaving through drunken Irish gangs and Chinese in clouds of opium smoke. She would surely be rubbing elbows with anarchists and socialists standing up on boxes in smelly crowds of black-toothed foreigners calling for them to combine in workers' unions. The sins of the Old World—guilds, monopolies, shady intrigue and proletarian slums—had spread across the seas like plague rats into the dank corners of the new urban America. Sarah knew that Mariah loved the notch, but the corrupting allure of the city pulled at her through the charms of one Will Dunfield.

Sarah heard the sounds of the river and knew that the kitchen door was open, even if by stealth. Frederick hoped to liberate a cookie or two from the table and escape unnoticed. It was hard for Sarah to speak sharply to Frederick. Sensitive, and sickly, Frederick almost had to be encouraged to engage in boyish pranks. His angular frame held out promise that he would grow into a hardy man, but recurring bouts of the grippe and croup, and a near fatal case of whooping cough had stunted him, and at twelve he looked to be only eight or nine.

Florence was the proper lady of the house. She never broke the rules, never. She did what Mother wanted, and practiced every stitch or step until it was done with grace. Florence searched *Godey's Ladies Magazine* for fashion and etiquette, and even before she could read, she asked her mother for stories with the illustrations that captured her interest.

Little Amos, affectionately called Moze, approached life with his father's ease. He didn't argue with his mother, but he learned from his father that patience and good humor took the stiffness out of rules.

Sarah's baking was nearly done. The boys eyed the pies and filled their lungs with the scent hoping that at least one pie was not reserved for tomorrow. Florence couldn't wait to wear her brand new dress with the bright ribbon around the waist.

When Mariah came in from her bath, the room was quiet. Moments ago she had been radiant and relaxed; once back in the house and seeing the whole family working together made her feel felt like a squirrel on a high branch ready to make a great leap to another tree. Her father also felt the significance of the moment and didn't have anything to say. They all looked at each other. No one wanted to say that it was their last day together as the family they had known.

The morning ritual began as always: Early chores done, hands washed, Father at the head of the table. A typical family beginning the day in typical fashion, except for a Brandon family custom that set them apart from all of their neighbors. Before Sarah served breakfast and while their tea steeped, Mother asked the children to tell about the book each was reading and to read a short passage that most impressed them. Even little Amos reported on what Mama or Daddy had read to him. Although reading had opened Pandora's Box in Mariah's life, Sarah could not abandon the family custom. As the family bowed their heads to thank the Lord for His provision for the day—and the day to come—Sarah surveyed each face, stopping at last with strong-willed Mariah, her final day as a child at the family table. . Sarah prayed to God that enriching the children's minds—especially Mariah's—had not been a mistake.

# CHAPTER 3

## *School Belles*

Two years earlier, the last school bell that summoned Mariah to the North Sandwich School just before the spring planting in May of 1881. She was thirteen years old and the closing day ceremonies for the spring term inspired only bitterness and resentment until she caught the eye of a young man with prospects for a future she wanted to share.

"Now get in your places!" called the teacher. Boys lined up in front of one door and girls at another. Miss J. Estelle Locke inspected the boys' line that resembled a centipede dropped on a hot stone. "Now, boys, what will Mr. Quimby think if you can't even form a straight line and keep in file when it's time to recite?"

Herman H. Quimby, the chairman of the Sandwich School Committee, had chosen this school among only four others out of the district's twenty-five to visit on closing day. Two sons of the chair-making Taylor family and the Weed's number one son had brought distinction to their school by being accepted at Phillips Exeter Academy. The boys would be praised as the brightest and the best, a credit to the school and the district, and Miss Locke would say nothing to detract from that impression. She had not collected the final installment of her nineteen dollars a month salary, and she desperately hoped to serve as a bookkeeper in the dusty upper rooms of the Taylor Chair Manufacturing Company. The boys to be honored were not actually at the top of their class.

Lunch buckets clattered as the children placed them above their names on shelves in the cloakroom. In the classroom they passed the cold box stove at the rear and proceeded to their seats. The morning would be like any other day at the North Sandwich School; after lunch the community would gather outside to send the eighth graders into the world to find the places God and society had ordained for them. Mariah's sullen face did not escape Miss Locke's notice. The teacher came over to Mariah's desk as the students took out their slates. "Now don't look so glum, dear. I know you'll miss school, but now it's time for you to prepare for life in other ways."

"Yes, Miss Locke." *Prepare for life? Milking cows, plucking dead chickens? I'm already prepared. So it's that or be an old maid like you, is that what I'm preparing for?*

"Walter," called Miss Locke with a generous smile. You are our ranking male scholar…"

Walter rose with an equally generous smile for the teacher and the system that separated him as the cream from the democracy's vast quantity of milk. Miss Locke did not mention what all of the students in the room knew: Mariah was the ranking scholar whether male or female, a student who would close her borrowed books and tie them in a bundle and leave them on the teacher's table as her parting gesture.

"Walter, would you grace the class with the one hundred twenty-first psalm?" Walter Taylor, tall, dressed in fine broadcloth for his final day, recited the psalm from memory. Behind him, through the south windows, Mount Chocorua's stony peak had hooked a cloud streaking east and looked like an awakening volcano.

"I will lift up mine eyes unto the hills from whence cometh my help…"

*He's got enough help without God giving him any more.* Mariah shut her eyes and bowed her head in an effort to contain her resentment. *You'll get help from your daddy who knows people in all the right places.* Mariah thought of her parents. A farmer and his wife; true, a wounded veteran, a valorous, charming, ingenious man, and true, a pensive, complex, well-read former school teacher. But without money, lineage or connections, Amos and Sarah Brandon were like most of their neighbors, gray and unremarkable. They lived on the banks of a river that spoke with the voices of countless anonymous souls whose remains inevitably passed into her channel and into the sea of unrecorded history.

How hard they had worked, and yet there was no money to send sons Frederick or Amos on to high school, no money to gild their beautiful lily daughters for the altar. Mariah and Florence would be presented to Sandwich society—such as it was—without the adornments that the elite could provide. It was families such as the Brandon's that knew what it meant to look to the hills for the Lord's help.

"The Lord shall preserve thy going out and thy coming in from this time forth, and even for evermore." Walter recited the King James Version, the only English translation in use in public schools across America in this year of our Lord, 1881.

Two Catholic families asked that their children be allowed to read from the Douay Version, but to no avail. The Melting Pot was a crucible that fired even the most durable elements into a homogenous amalgam. Americans knew that the Lord spoketh with the silver tongue of King James.

Mariah raised her head and stared beyond Walter at the mountaintop that gleamed in the morning sun.

*When I walk out that door today, I'm going to need all the help I can get, and I know none of it is going to come from the likes of you, Walter Taylor.*

"Now, class, here is your last gem for the term," said Miss Locke. On the board was the memory verse for the day, unusually and mercifully short.

"Only the educated are free."
--Epictetus

Mariah copied down the last of Miss Locke's "gems." The older boys, having recently learned about Louis Pasteur, called the "gems" "germs." As one wit said on the playground, "you can't escape them and they make you sick."

Although Mariah frequently impressed her peers with her insights on the "gems," this day she couldn't force herself to come up with a pithy and positive comment. She knew that she would need a great deal more education to have any freedom, and that education didn't come cheap, never mind, free. If education was so important, Mariah wondered, then why were there fewer than a thousand public high schools in the entire United States? "A high school education will be common by the turn of the century," Miss Locke predicted, "maybe someday even for girls," she added.

Mariah wasn't thinking of *some*day or some other girls. She was thinking of herself now. *Only educated* boys *are free? Only the* free *are educated? And which of us in this room are free to choose the life we want? Walter, don't smirk at me, you with your rich daddy. You'll go to Europe for a final geography lesson, won't you? But I'm the one who knows where the Carpathian Mountains are, aren't I?* Walter Taylor could almost read Mariah's mind. He turned his eyes from hers and to an open book in front of him.

"Well, children, who will be the first today to comment on the wisdom of this ancient Greek philosopher?" asked Miss Locke, seemingly oblivious to the fact that her education had not freed her from poverty and spinsterhood, Miss Locke tapped her ruler into her palm apparently preparing to extract insight with physical punishment. "You younger children listen carefully," she said as she stalled for time while the older children stared at their desktops. "Well?" she barked. "I'm sure several of you can come up with something intelligent to say," her eyes flashing behind gold-rimmed spectacles.

*Go ahead, Walter, say something.* Mariah glanced across the rows to the boys' side of the room. Mariah was seldom the first to speak. Deference must be shown to the boys, especially those who had different clothes to wear each school day. She was seldom the first, but she was never at a loss for words. *You're going to Exeter; I'm not. Your daddy has a closed carriage and indoor plumbing. Go ahead; tell me how free you're going to be after your daddy buys your education for you.*

"All right, Ed," said Miss Locke with a smile as lanky Ed Paisley stood by his desk. "The ignorant are slaves to nature because their minds have not been trained. Trained minds are conquering nature. Morse, Edison, McCormack, Watt. That's the freedom that education provides," Ed sat down, smug-faced.

"Very good, Ed. Yes, indeed, education can free mankind from the limits of nature," affirmed Miss Locke.

*So, Miss Locke, if you had taught the slaves, would they all have thrown off their chains without Mr. Lincoln's war?*

Mariah began to steam with a pressure that nearly brought her to her feet in anger. *What about your father, Eddy? I doubt that he can read the fifth McGuffey, but he built a mill on the north fork of the river. Five men working for him, and now a son going to the academy, and your father as ignorant as dirt. Go on. Tell the little kids here how illiterate sweat labor bought you your freedom.*

"Let's give Ed a round of applause for that insight. Yes, education can give us freedom from the limits of nature. And how else can education make us free?"

One of the Marston twins stood up. Eliza was only eight and hardly bigger than a five-year-old. She stood barefoot in a patched gingham jumper. "If you're smart, and you know how to read good…"

"Well. Read *well*," said Miss Locke.

"If you read well, you can know what is right and wrong better. You can read the Bible and you'll understand better how to be free from sin."

Miss Locke surveyed the class, especially the eyes of the older students. She paused with a brittle smile. "Thank you, Eliza."

An uncomfortable silence fell. Mariah looked around the room. *Were they all going to let this little waif with a sickly widowed mother believe that moral uprightness was the sure product of education? Were the moguls of industry, the politicians and the financiers—J.P. Morgan, Rockefeller, Boss Tweed—pillars of virtue because they could read* the Wall Street Journal *without stumbling over words like "acquisition and monopoly"?*

Mariah stood. "Eliza, a good education can give you all kinds of other words to call things other than sin. You know how someone can call stealing "borrowing"? Well some people learn many new words from their reading to call things, and sometimes things that we call 'sin' they call something that isn't sin." Mariah's bitter irony passed over the heads of nearly all of the students except for those who knew the moral freedom that wealth and privilege could provide.

"Yes, education can be used for selfish reasons, Mariah," said Miss Locke with an arched brow, "but people who are truly educated in great books and great thoughts can only be the better for it, and the freer. You may sit down, Mariah."

"Oh, we didn't applaud for Eliza-—or for Mariah—for adding to our understanding," added Miss Locke with a tense and tentative smile. There was a polite round of clapping that dispelled the tension in the room. The school routine continued as each student worked silently. Miss Locke asked Mariah to assign three eight-year-old girls to read the fifty-seventh lesson in McGuffey's *Second Eclectic Reader.* "Since this will be their last lesson for the year, I think one of them in particular needs the lesson," said Miss Locke, "a lesson girls need before they get to your age. I note, Mariah, that you have plenty of male admirers so I have no fears for your future."

Mariah let the comment pass without a response. *So that sums up a girl's education? All she really needs to know is how to attract the boys.* She went to the bookcase and took the second reader back to her desk. Lesson 57, "The Greedy Girl." Words to learn: dined, gaily, glutton, greedy, tempers. "Laura English is a greedy little girl. Indeed, she is quite a glutton. Do you know what a glutton is? A glutton is one who eats too much because the food tastes so good."

Mariah glanced across at the three girls who were passing notes and making eyes at each other as they waited for their lesson. It was clear to her that little Hilda, the chubby only daughter of the Hanson family was the target of Miss Locke's lesson. The Hanson's had lost three children to childhood diseases. Hilda was the only one of four to survive, the joy of the Hanson's lives.

Mariah felt a pain course through her body. She flipped ahead to the next lesson. "A Place for Everything." Words to learn: Comfort, ashamed, thimble, offended, depended. "Mary: I wish you would lend me your thimble, Sarah. I can never find my own." Mariah smiled to herself. Here was a lesson that could help without hurting. She looked at Miss Locke sitting at her table dispensing correction to all who needed it. *I'm sure you meant Lesson 58, Miss Locke. You certainly wouldn't have wanted to shame that sweet little girl in front of her friends, now would you? A place for everything. That's a lesson that we can all benefit from.*

As the morning wore on, the classroom became stuffy. Mariah asked to open the window. Below in the bright sun of the verdant day she saw a young man unloading chairs from a wagon. This young man had not been seen in town for several months, neither at the Grange or in church, and his absence had taken a lot of the excitement out of life for many of the girls of Sandwich. This young man knew of many of the hearts he set a fluttering, but not all. He and Mariah had never met.

Mariah stood at the open window, still and focused as a cat in wait for its prey. Dressed in her new cotton skirt of robin's egg blue with white blouse and lace collar, Mariah revealed a transformation from girl to woman with her tiny waist and full bodice. Her features could not escape a young man's notice once Mariah had his attention. She lifted the heavy window slowly to prolong the moment. *Look up! Look up!* The young man did not turn his head. She let the open sash come down onto the propping stick with enough of a thud to be noticed. Mariah exploited her dark features and shiny raven black hair with just enough of a cant of the head and arch of the brow to acknowledge without being forward.

He set down the last chair and looked to the open window. Their eyes met. *He likes what he sees, and so do I. He smiled. He nodded.* Mariah returned the nod and smiled. *Lips closed. Don't be forward. There. That's enough; now back to my seat. I've got to talk to him after all the falderal is over.* Mariah had never been introduced, but she knew this young man's name. She had repeated it countless times hoping that one day she would get a chance to lay her eyes upon him, and now there he was in the flesh—William Channing Dunfield.

The chairman of the school committee sat behind a podium on the center of the porch. He, Miss Locke, a lady from the Daughters of the American Revolution, and the minister of the Congregational church sat in the shade; the children and what parents and townsfolk came for the ceremonies sat in the sun, some ladies under parasols or umbrellas.

"The Town of Sandwich has spent hard-earned dollars to provide you an education, but it is up to you to use that education to make your lives better," said Herman Quimby. Mariah sat in the front row next to Betty Grant, the other girl in the eighth grade. She looked to the left and to the right. "Are you looking for your folks, Mariah?"

asked Betty, a pretty blonde with ringlets cascading down her neck under a brimmed straw hat.

Mariah said, "yes" so unconvincingly that Betty giggled into her white glove. "Well, your folks are two rows behind you, and Will Dunfield is one row behind them on the far right. I wouldn't look now. He's looking this way."

"...you have a right to pursue happiness in the great country, but you don't have the right to get it. This town, and this country don't owe you success," said the superintendent. The older folk sat in the warmth of the sun looking across fields that hadn't been plowed in two decades. Of the nine mills that churned with the roaring waters of Cold River in the 1830s and '40s, only four were productive and marginally profitable. Success was unlikely to be found for young people in Sandwich, Mariah thought, no matter how much education or firmness of character they possessed.

"Look," said Betty. Just as Mariah turned, she met Will's eyes once again. She pretended that she was looking for someone else, but the recognition in his eyes erased the pretense and he winked. He winked! No boy had ever winked at her, especially such a beautiful specimen as the square-jawed Will Dunfield with the jaunty sideburns and the bright green eyes.

"...and there are too many people in this country who, in the name of charity, want to tinker with our government and make our neighbor's business our business. It is your duty to take care of yourselves and to make sure that no one else has to take care of you."

"I think he likes me, but I'm only thirteen," said Mariah quietly. Her smile dissolved to a frown.

"You look older, Mariah. My mama said you're an early bloomer. I'm glad we're sitting in the sun. Might speed things along for me!" whispered Betty with a smirk.

Old Beulah Northrop approached the podium wearing a black crinoline long out of style.

"Miss Havisham in black," whispered Mariah to Betty, referring to the lugubrious old maid in Dickens' *Great Expectations*. Beulah was protector of musty records, mourner of the fallen, announcer of memorial gifts, and plenipotentiary overseer of all things dead or nearly so.

"This year marks the loss of three more veterans of the Grand Army of the Republic, men who served like the heroes of the Revolution to protect the blessings of liberty…"

"Mariah, Will's signaling to you."

Mariah turned her head ever so slowly so as not to attract any attention during the prolonged maudlin solemnity of the warble-throated matron who was about to announce awards for top scholars. Will mimed a cup tipped to his lips and pointed toward the tables stretched out at the rear of the assemblage. Mariah nodded once and turned her head back just in time to hear her name called out as the ranking scholar. She went to the steps for her certificate as top scholar and a packet of needles and multiple colors of thread. "These will help you continue your education in the domestic arts," said Mrs. Northrop who dismissed Mariah quickly with scarcely enough time for Mariah to catch the eye of her proud parents. She did not chance a glance in Will's direction.

Tedious minutes, infuriatingly long minutes, passed as Mrs. Northrop, Mr. Quimby and Miss Locke lauded Walter Taylor and Edward Paisley—called "the other ranking scholars" rather than second and third—"how clever with words, how good with figures…"

"Yes, Ed is especially good with female figures," whispered Betty. "I went behind the schoolhouse with him once. He's a good kisser." Mariah was too embarrassed even to look at Betty and pretended she had not heard the remark.

'…next year at Phillips Exeter Academy and no doubt on from there. I wouldn't be surprised if he went to Harvard College," said Miss Locke.

*And our ranking scholar, our number one scholar, who was one of only ten students in the entire district to take philosophy and rhetoric, where will she be going? Well, she will be returning to her parents' farm on Brandon Loop to improve her sewing and cooking, and she will try not to get sunburned out weeding the garden so that she can attract a farm boy who'll be too busy at the table eating to utter more than five words in a row, and that's good enough for her because she's nothing but a poor farm girl, isn't that right, Miss Locke?*

After an admonition to parents to provide pencils and pens for the very first day of the fall term—"writing has not progressed as much as we would like because many students do not come prepared"—Mr. Quimby closed the ceremonies for the spring of 1881 and sent eighth graders into a society of theoretical equality and opportunity and parents to a cornucopian table of delights with a trumpeter and drummer playing "Columbia, Gem of the Ocean."

Mr. Quimby descended the steps and shook the hands of the eighth grade boys. When he got to Betty and Mariah, he patted their hands rather than shaking them. "So here are the lovely young belles of Sandwich," he said with an admiring smile. "Lucky the young men who win your hearts."

"So that's it?" said Mariah to Betty. "So has your education made you free?"

"Not me. Sounds like I'm going to the highest bidder," said Betty with a sarcastic smirk. "Wasn't that the most disgusting thing you've had to listen to? You go that way," said Betty with a nudge, " and I'll go this way. Good luck."

Mariah met Will at the table. He held out a glass of punch for her. "Here's to your future," he said with a clink.

*My future? I haven't been looking forward to my future, I'm sorry to say.* "And to yours. We've heard you've gotten a good job with the Wallace Shoe Company."

Will's smile showed off dimples in the shadow of his beard. "My mother never had the money to send me to Brewster, but I'm doing all right for myself with the little education I got, I guess. Besides, if I went back to school now, they'd all think I was a teacher."

Mariah suppressed a smile. *I'd sure pay attention if he were my teacher.* "So you'll never go back to farming?" she asked.

"No. Absolutely not." His eyes narrowed and he leaned in to whisper in her ear. "I'm good with numbers and even better with words, and I don't sound, look or smell like one of these shit-kickers." He was close enough for her to feel his warm breath. Mariah's laugh brought back his smile. "Nope. I'm living in Rochester now."

"Isn't it kind of lonely living by yourself?" Mariah asked. She was on a fishing expedition about just how alone Will Dunfield was.

"It is kind of lonely, as a matter of fact," Will responded. He held her gaze and his jaw muscles flexed.

Mariah looked down the table. She and Will were the object of attention of the other "ranking scholars" who found Will's physical presence and social assertiveness intimidating. He was a full-grown man and they were boys even if they came from a social station far above the Dunfield's.

"It galls me to think that they can glide through school and then step into daddy's business…"

"Or get set up somewhere else with daddy's connections," said Mariah, adding bitterness to Will's gall.

"I like you when you get mad," said Will with a quick laugh that relieved the negative mood. "Your eyebrows send messages. You know that, don't you? You'll never have to shout to get attention. Beautiful arching brows and beautiful dark, dark eyes." His hand started toward her face, but stopped discreetly short of a touch.

"I'm only thirteen," said Mariah with downcast eyes, feigning modesty.

"I know, but so what? Would you mind if I came by to visit?" Will asked.

Mariah remained speechless, flustered at the suddenness of a dream coming true. "I…I…"

"Mariah," called her mother. Sarah Brandon had watched her daughter linger just a bit too long with a young man she knew of, but didn't know. In a moment she was at her daughter's side, closely followed by Amos who was much more relaxed in Will's presence.

"You're Will Dunfield," said Sarah somewhat too abruptly, almost to the point of rudeness.

"Yes, Mrs. Brandon. You know my mother out on Juneau Road."

"And so I do," she said with ambiguous expression. Everyone in town knew the Dunfield woman who claimed to be a widow long before her missing derelict husband was declared legally dead. "I understand you're a traveling salesman now. I hope someone's watching over the farm."

"As a matter of fact, Mrs. Brandon…"

"That doesn't concern us," said Amos. "We just wish you great success at your new job and I'm sure your mother is proud."

Sarah did not look entirely pleased by Amos' compliments. "And now I think we'd better be going, don't you think, Mariah?"

"I'm done thinking, Mama. School's all over for me," said Mariah with an expression masking sarcasm as humor. "If you and daddy are ready, what's there to think about?" Sarah gave her daughter a disapproving look. *We'll talk about this little exchange later,* her stern expression said.

Amos and Sarah started for the buggy. Mariah stayed behind for a moment. "We'll find a time to talk again, but don't come to the house," said Mariah. Will nodded, but frowned. They parted with understandings and misunderstandings in equal measure. This would not be an easy stream to navigate, especially with a rock like Sarah Brandon in the main channel.

Amos stopped the buggy just as they were about to pass Miss Locke who was walking back toward the school. "Congratulations again, Mariah. Your parents can be very proud of you."

They drove on in silence. Mariah imagined Miss Locke collecting the books and washing away her last gem from the board: "Only the educated are free."

They passed the Taylors and the Paisleys, the Weeds and the Hansons, and finally Will whom Mariah acknowledged only with a subtle and quick wave.

# CHAPTER 4

## *Child Bride*

"**G**od has given us a perfect day," Amos said to Sarah as he stopped the buggy to admire the scene. The Free Will Baptist Church of North Sandwich gleamed in pure white, its Greek Revival simplicity framed by rich autumnal maples and birches. Sarah Sanborn Brandon accepted the arm of a Dunfield kin with a wan smile and took her seat in the front pew. Amos watched from the back of the room as a weary choirboy pumped the bellows of the organ through four verses of "Rejoice, Ye Pure in Heart," his heart surely pumping as hard as his arms. The ushers beckoned Amos out of the sanctuary and closed the doors. The entry way grew hushed. Mariah descended the stairs from the second floor; she was so radiant in her silken gown that Amos was speechless. He kissed her cheek and stared at her with moist eyes. "How could Sai not share Mariah's joy?" he thought. "If only Sai could let go."

The organist saw the doors open and called the twelve-year-old back to duty. Amos could barely make out what Gertie was saying to the boy. "Come on, Abner," he thought he heard her say. "Keep pumpin'. The bride's comin' in a girl, and leavin' a woman. It's our job, son, so let's do it right." A ripple of laughter was followed by an organ fanfare.

Mariah was dressed in ivory, gleaming in a halo of afternoon sun. Little sister Florence marched down the aisle scattering marigold petals sufficient for a hen-pecking frenzy. The ancient fiddler scratched out a rustic processional as close to the tempo of the organ as he could manage without a hand free to hold his ear trumpet. Amos tried to take it all in while moving in an artificial, measured step.

"Don't she look like an angel from glory?" cackled the toothless Maudie Hessler, stunned at the sight of a village girl suddenly transformed into a lady of fashion.

"Such grace for a modest girl," said Deaconess Taylor to her nephew Daniel. The privileged boy condescended to make the trip home from Phillips Exeter Academy for the wedding of a poor cousin.

The deaconess looked to the groom's side of the church that was embarrassingly sparse. There in the front pew sat Mrs. Dunfield, cruelly called the "Silver Widow" by some in the valley, not because of her hair which was more salt and pepper than silver, but because her husband had abandoned her to stake out a claim to a silver vein somewhere in the Rockies of Colorado and had never been heard from since. Those who didn't mock her pitied her, like a character from Dickens too long acquainted with woe. She sat with her eyes fixed on the altar. She never looked back at family or guests. Amos wondered what she was thinking when she looked at the gilded letters carved into the communion table: "In remembrance of me."

Three pews behind Mrs. Dunfield, her elderly Aunt Hilda set out her lacey handkerchief to receive the tears she was working herself up to shed. "Lydia's gonna sing," whispered Hilda to her neighbor. "I always cry when Lydia sings." The sight of the pretty bride and handsome groom, and the sound of the organ prelude triggered Hilda's flood, turning the solo into an unintended duet. The minister frowned Hilda into smothered sobs.

Lydia Ludlow was a veteran of the Baptist choir whom all the elder townsfolk admired for the beautiful soprano voice she used to have. The homemade violin's quivering vibrato matched the soloist's breathy strains and reached pitch with similar irregularity. "O perfect love, all human thought transcending, lowly we kneel in prayer before thy throne." The bridal couple wanted to kneel, but the minister told them that he would not hear of it. Literal interpretations were reserved for the Holy Writ, not for hymns and poems. Only Papists and high church Episcopalians knelt in church.

Maudie moved her gums together and apart, mouthing the words of the hymn. Whatever anyone in the pews had heard about Will Dunfield or felt before entering the gothic arched doors was temporarily forgotten in the fragrance of youthful beauty profiled against the minister's black robe.

Amos watched Mariah who fixed her idolatrous gaze on Will. "O perfect life, be thou their full assurance, O tender charity and steadfast faith." The groom turned his eyes from the soloist's waddle to his bride's silken bosom. Amos ignored the focus of Will's eyes. Sarah did not. The bodice of the gown was beaded like an open treasure chest. "Of patient hope and quiet, brave endurance, with child-like trust that fears not pain nor death." Patience. Hope. Child-like trust. And a creamy, soft bosom.

The reverend pronounced William and Mariah Dunfield man and wife, the groom pledged to honor, the wife pledged to obey, and the wedding ended with the till-death-do-they-part, let-no-man-put-asunder benediction and a kiss with enough motion and duration to prompt the minister to signal for the recessional post haste.

As Sarah walked with the bride into the reception hall, Amos and Will stopped in the men's parlor to ready themselves for the phalanx of witch-whiskered old ladies anxious for kisses. "Well, son," he started awkwardly, "what's the farthest Wallace is sendin' you these days?"

Will took advantage of the sudden familiarity by patting Amos on the back. "You know, I haven't been called 'son' in a dozen years."

Amos pulled at his celluloid collar. He had no intention of commenting on Will's father or lack thereof. He felt much more comfortable talking about shoes and Will's growing sales territory.

"I went all the way to Hartford once. They might send me to New York to open up the market, but my territory is supposed to be Boston to Portland." Will reached into his inside breast pocket and slipped out a flat silver flask, unscrewed the cap, and took a mouthful. Amos pushed the door closed in a hurry. "This is a Baptist church, Will," he said with the expression of a novice bank robber.

Will smirked at his father-in-law's discomfort. The groom looked in a mirror and swirled another mouthful of whisky. He patted down an errant lock of chestnut hair and raised his cleft chin in self-admiration.

"You know, Dad…" Amos' eyes widened. "Should I call you Dad?"

Amos hesitated. "How about stickin' to Amos? You shout 'Dad' in a crowd and half the men will confess to that name."

"Amos it is, then. You know, Amos, this suit here cost me over fifteen dollars." Amos seldom had fifteen dollars in his pocket at one time.

"Should I say I'm 'suitably impressed'?" joked Amos who was relieved to have the opportunity for humor to break the tension. Will smiled and nodded, acknowledging Amos' witticism. "Mariah's good cookin' could bust them buttons inside of a year," Amos said with a forced laugh as he did needlessly preened cuffs, tie and sleeves.

"Nope. I'm not going to get fat. My hands may be soft, but just feel that arm."

In the setting of the church, on his daughter's wedding day, with the man who would soon take his daughter to his bed, Amos found the common male custom of showing off one's manly strength a little uncomfortable.

"Come on. Give it a squeeze," said Will, "if you can."

"Feels like you've been liftin' barrels, not just flasks," Amos said with a laugh as he took the whisky from Will's hand and lifted it to his own lips. "Not often *this* arm gets exercised with real liquor."

Will took the flask back with one hand and squeezed Amos' bicep with the other causing Amos to recoil. "Not bad, for a man of your age. A little more of this stuff wouldn't do you any harm; just might make you a little more relaxed with the ladies."

"It doesn't always pay to be too relaxed with the ladies," said Amos in his small voice. He walked to the window where a golden-leafed branch brushed the panes in a sudden gust. "Just so's you know, Sai keeps me away from temptin' spirits better than a tent meetin' preacher." Amos turned and walked toward his son-in-law, cupping his hand in front of his mouth to check his breath and running his hand over his beard for telltale droplets of liquor. "She don't classify hard cider as an intoxicatin' liquor, thank God. If she ever saw a bottle of the real thing in my hand…" Amos shook his head at the thought of punishments corporal and capital. "Here, one more swig, then you better put that away." Amos' eyes darted furtively toward the door as he heard voices approaching. He waved off the flask and shook his finger to stop the flask's progress to Will's lips.

"You men's needed out he-ya," the organist called in her Yankee twang. "We don't want the food growin' cold, now do we, boys?"

"One more?" implored Will. "After all, this is my wedding' day,' he said. "This doesn't happen but once in a lifetime." Will reached into his pocket and took a final swig, then reached into another pocket. His hand emerged with what looked like two tiny twigs. "Cloves. Chew 'em up," he said in the imperative. Will slapped Amos on the back again.

As Amos reached for the doorknob, he spoke softly without looking at his son-in-law. "Will, remember, Mariah thinks she's all growed up, but she don't know much about a man, if you know what I mean."

"She's innocent, but high-spirited and daring. I love that about her," said Will. "She's anxious to see the world. I don't think she's reluctant about…"

"All right, all right. Being she's my daughter I felt I needed to say something." Amos reddened and was anxious to change the subject. "She doesn't find much excitement in farming, that's for sure. She's told us that enough times. But what I don't really understand is what she *does* want. I hope she wants a family 'cause there's not much choice in that matter."

"Sure she wants a family. Both of us would love a crop, but Mariah and I have other ambitions. She's got her own ideas about what a woman can do. Can't do any harm if she tries. Once we have kids, well…"

"So you don't have any better idea what she wants than we do."

"She's only fifteen."

"And you're twenty going on thirty and you've got the world figured out, I 'spose."

Will turned and stared without smiling. He felt sudden and unexpected sharpness in Amos' tone. "We just don't want to be your typical New Hampshire farmers, that's all."

"There can be worse things than *typical*, you know." Amos met Will's eyes with a look of resentment. Did his life, and Sai's, and others that populated the notch count for nothing because they were "typical"? His feelings registered on his face in an uncharacteristic grimace.

Will broke the uneasy silence. "Now don't take me wrong. You've done pretty well, and you've made a good home for your family." Amos's stiffness told Will that his patronizing tone only made matters worse. "Mariah loves both of you very much," Will added with a forced measure of enthusiasm, "and I sure know she loves me. To have a girl love me, not just want me, and love only me, that gets me fired up."

They opened the door to the fragrance of roast meats and the sound of joyous laughter. Amos made his way to his wife's side. Sarah was working as hard to raise her spirits as her husband was in subduing his own. "Everyone talks about Will," said one town gossip, feigning a compliment on the groom to the mother of the bride—she paused, then alluded to his looks and his success in business, her eyes fixed on Sarah like an angler about to hook a worm.

"Thanks for telling me what you've heard, Agnes," said Sarah with a forced smile. "I'm so busy with my work that I don't seem to have any time to pick from the grapevine."

"I'm sure you don't," said the self-righteous old gossip that mirrored Sarah's forced smile and moved on.

Mariah took Will's arm and moved from one group of guests to another, receiving smiles and kisses regally. It was her day and her mother was deferential; nothing could have brought her more joy except for the prospect of a lifetime with the man she loved.

Amos watched furtively as Mariah and Will greeted guests. Will had made his escape from the routines of tilling and toiling two years earlier, and had assumed the role of a local boy who had scaled the ladder to its utmost round. He smiled down on admiring women receptively, and on old men and little boys. It was men of his own generation or slightly older that generated in Will a different expression, one of superiority, one of challenge. Amos recognized that Will had not forgotten the base degrees by which he did ascend. He was letting others know, especially other young men, that he, unlike them, was not typical.

Amos grew tense as Will approached. He patted Sarah's arm and whispered in her ear. "Remember, Sai. It's more blessed to give than receive. Give him a little warmth, now, will you?" Would she offer Will a perfunctory kiss, at least, or would she merely take his hand? Amos initiated a kiss on Mariah's cheek and a tender hand on Will's back. As Will leaned in for a kiss from his mother-in-law, she turned her cheek. He gave her a minimal peck and a nod. Amos squeezed Sarah's hand hard enough that she winced.

"Amos, for heaven's sake, what are you trying to do? Break my fingers?"

Having greeted all of the guests, Will and Mariah arrived at the table set for the bridal party. Sarah had placed Amos to her right, next to the groom. She nodded to Will and Mariah to be seated first; she smiled politely with her lips closed. The ceremonial tasks behind them, the family was free to eat and the guests were distracted by food and music.

Two hours after the reception, the afternoon grew gustier. The wind stripped the trees around the Brandon farm of many of their leaves; some guests had left early, fearing what westerly winds might portend. Sarah and Amos, holding their hats, helped the bridal couple load a trunk onto their rented buggy.

Sarah handed Mariah a stamped envelope. "Could you have your picture taken in Rochester, and put one copy in the mail for your Aunt Bertha? She'll show it off to everybody she knows in Central City."

"That's near a dozen folk," said Amos with a chuckle. "Will, my sister's lived out in Iowa since '56 and still has only two families in a three-mile radius. I think our letters keep her sane."

"Whose letters?" added Sarah.

"Well, I dictate some." Sarah gave him a skeptical glance. "I said 'some'. Now, Will, there's a lesson for you."

"What's that?"

"Why, don't try to dictate to your wife," said Amos, drawing out his words in a nasal twang as he patted Mariah's knee playfully.

Will and Mariah wound their way down the road and were finally obscured by dust. The late afternoon sun brightened the fall colors across Sandwich Notch. As Mariah and Will passed out of sight through the notch to the dark side, Sarah closed her eyes and accepted Amos' encircling arm.

"She's gone like a windborne seed."

Sarah opened her eyes and pulled away from Amos. "What?"

"Like a windborne seed, Sarah. That's the way I see it."

"And some fell among thorns; and the thorns sprung up and choked them."

"Oh, Sarah, don't spoil this day by assuming the worst. I'm a farmer, so I keep my thoughts on good seed and good soil."

"That's all well and good, Amos, but a good farmer doesn't ignore the weeds either."

"Sai, you weed when the plants are young and the roots shallow, but when the seed takes hold, you let nature take its course, and that's Gospel, and that's all we can do. Mariah's in God's hands..."

Why couldn't she have gotten interested in one of the other boys here in town?" Amos pulled her close as they looked east as the sun lighted up the granite peak of Mt. Chocorua. "Wasn't she warming up to Nathan Ambrose once? He works hard at the lumber mill, and I understand he saves his money. Clean-talking, doesn't drink..."

"The problem was his ears."

"What?"

"His ears. Now admit it. It's the first thing you notice about Nathan."

"There are a lot more important things to consider about a man than his ears. He's really not a bad looking fellow..."

"With a hat." Sarah could not stop herself from laughing even though she tried. They stood for several minutes in the clear fall air with the distant sounds of the river as a lullaby to all sentient creatures to put aside the work and worries of the day and be at rest.

Amos touched her cheek. "We'll both lose our hats if we stay out much longer. I'll go build a fire." Sarah stood like a sentinel over the stillness of the valley, the last rays of the slanted sunlight coming over the western peaks. "You know, dear," said Amos as he looked straight ahead, "Will's lived in this valley all his life, and since he's put a razor to that famous face of his, we've heard stories, but you know, nobody's ever seen a hussy on his arm. Nobody's come up with a single name. Boys jaw with boys and treat imagination like fact. And girls are worse.

You know that. The gossip is just more believable with Will. Let's not worry ourselves 'cause folks amuse themselves with dime novel talk." He gave her a moment to think, but her expression didn't change. He covered her hand and patted it. Amos was always patient. He'd give his words time to sink in.

"Amos, when I married you, I knew the kind of man I was getting." She gently stroked the back of his right hand where the bullet wound from a rebel sniper was still noticeable after twenty years."

"And you married me anyways; now what does that say about your judgment?" Amos retorted with a chuckle.

"A brave man, a man I could always trust," said Sarah with emphatic seriousness. Amos kissed the back of Sarah's neck and held her tightly against him.

"And you took a file to the rough places," said Amos softly in her ear.

"Oh, you silly man. I love you, rough places and all. We've been together through good times and bad. When it really counts, we don't let each other down. I don't know what I would have done if I'd been your sister. She never realized what kind of man Charles Taylor was until it was too late."

Amos looked down the darkening road in silence, the same road of hope his sister Bertha had taken nearly a quarter century before.

# CHAPTER 5

## Letting Off Steam

From West Ossipee to Sanbornville Mariah's head rested on Will's shoulder as the "Harvest Special" looped its way along the margin of Duncan Lake destined for the state's biggest fair. The newlyweds stirred occasionally from their attentions to one another as scenes of particular interest sent murmurs and movements among fellow passengers. An overturned farm wagon lay at a crossing, its burden of hay piled too high for the weathered wheels and axles to bear. The driver, a raisin of a man, sent dust flying from his tattered clothes. He flapped his hat against his trousers, stomped and cursed, his words censored by the clanging of the engine's bell. The belching and chugging of the iron horse triumphantly pronounced the Age of Steam to the farmer and his stymied beasts of burden.

If I'd done what my mother wanted, I'd be like him someday," said Will. " I'd be swinging a scythe and driving a team dawn to dusk and never making a dime."

"Don't you feel a little sorry for him? Things like that happen to my father sometimes, but not with dozens of people looking down on him," said Mariah.

"Yes, I s'pose, but he's a fool like all the others who are hanging on.

They can't compete with the West. The railroad's seen to that. Produce can make it back East in a couple of days now. Big operations, modern equipment. That's what it takes."

"Yes, I know," sighed Mariah. "You don't have to keep reminding me." Mariah pictured her parents overturned and spilled out before the steaming engines of the new American bigness. She looked into her interlaced fingers, an expression of sadness and guilt passing over her for looking down in her own way on her parents' world.

"Mariah, don't worry about your folks. Your father is clever and your mother's smart. They'll manage." He patted her folded hands.

"I want to do more than manage," said Mariah. "That's all most people ever get to do is manage. I want to be able to decide what I'd like to do with my life."

For a moment Will looked hurt. "Aren't we gonna decide together? I mean I'm in business and you'll manage the house…"

"Manage the house? Is that all?" surprised at Will's sudden traditionalism.

"Well somebody's gotta keep the place up and take care of kids."

"What if I want to run a dress shop or…"

"Of course. I'd like to see you do whatever you want. But once you have kids, you'd need hired help to take care of the shop and there go the profits."

Mariah looked down, once again feeling the shame that she often felt when she put her our aspirations ahead of duty. *Teaching is for spinsters. Then there's nursing but men don't want their wives tending other men—even sick ones—in bed.*

"Maybe later when the kids are older," Will conceded. "Maybe we could work it out. Why worry about that now? We've got plenty of time. Just think, though. You'll be in a nice city house with steam heat and streetcars and no cows to milk," Will smiled and held Mariah's hands. For now it would be their lives together that mattered. Ladies who lived in steam heat had more choices of what to do with their time, she just knew.

Will looked into Mariah's eyes, his dark brows moving subtly, his green eyes actively taking her in. Although her skin was fair, her dark eyes and hair gave her an exotic look, something of the Mediterranean, he thought. She studied his face, the dark shadow of beard under the smooth skin. Mariah's lips parted as she lifted herself to him for a kiss, and then remembered herself. There were other eyes watching. She put two fingers to Will's lips and demurred.

"Will, do you realize that the farthest I've traveled is Dover?" She slumped back in her seat, pursing her lips at the thought of the narrow confines of her fifteen years, an admission she would not make to anyone but Will. Mariah's vicarious experience, through her books, rescued her from the utter ignorance of the outside world. She picked up a *Harper's Weekly* left on the empty seat across the aisle, and began perusing it as the train's rhythmic clatter reached a fast cruising tempo.

"Will, here's an interesting article about the huge increase in America of people suffering nervous diseases."

"I guess a lot of people can't take the pressure, but I think competition brings out the best in people."

"Maybe so, but listen to this. 'One cause of the increase of nervous diseases is that the conventionalities of society require the emotions to be repressed, while the activity of our civilization gives an unprecedented freedom and opportunity for the expression of the intellect— the more we feel, the more we must restrain our feelings.'"

Will laughed and answered with a mocking tone. "Do I act like I'm repressing my feelings? I know for sure *you're* not." He reached over and wiggled her chin.

"Will, I'm serious. I think this is happening to lots of people. If people want to be considered ladies and gentlemen of respectable society, you can't express yourself freely. Now isn't that true?"

"Of course. So I guess it would be healthier for me to just punch the next guy who annoys me." Will twisted his mouth to the side and raised an eyebrow to punctuate his point.

"You're being silly. Now listen. It says that 'being civilized' is becoming a very unnatural way of living, and I agree. Don't say anything. Just listen," said Mariah in utter seriousness. "Nature, however, will not be robbed; constant inhibition, restraining normal feelings, keeping back, covering, holding in check atomic forces of the mind and body is an exhausting process; and to this process all civilization is constantly subjected."

" 'Atomic forces.' Whatever they are," chuckled Will. "People I know aren't restrained like that, at least not all the time. Really, I think he's exaggerating. Wait till you spend some time out in society. You'll see. People aren't nearly as repressed and inhibited as the good doctor claims. You've never been to Puddle Dock. Now there's an education in natural expression," said Will with a laugh. He took the magazine and tossed it back into the empty seat across the aisle.

"Are you talking about Portsmouth?" asked Mariah.

"Yup. Closer to nature than a zoo down near the docks." Will smirked. Looking out the window, he thought of gaslight and smoke, loud pianos, drunken singing, sawdust floors, stale beer. And women. Women spread in dim doorways in gaudy dress, women purring like kittens along the raucous docks of Portsmouth near warehouses, women earning more money from sailors and bargemen in a night than an honest mill girl earned at her looms in a week.

The train started up a slight grade, and a cloud of steam enshrouded the left side of the car and curled over its roof, disappearing quickly into the clear, dry September air. Will watched in thought as the steam moved in the air like lace. *A man's gotta let off steam sometimes, too. A little beer, a game of cards, fast music. A woman. Diversions. It doesn't mean anything as long as you don't live just for that. Not me. I've got a future and now I've got a wife.*

"Are you going to take me to Portsmouth sometime?"

"Ladies don't belong down near the docks. Your parents would be shocked."

"Mother's shocked that I bathed naked in the river," whispered Mariah. Then she resumed her normal voice. "She's even shocked that we're going to the fair. 'Stay away from freak shows and burlesque, for heaven's sake,' she said. Well, I guess I'll know when I'm ready for a shock, and I think I'm ready to see Portsmouth, shocking or not."

Will nodded without comment. The train slowed as it approached Farmington station. As the steam and smoke blew away, he could see the passengers waiting to board. Slowly he slid down in the seat again and covered his face with his hat.

"What are you doing?"

"I just want to rest a little."

"Oh, Will, I don't know about you. You're missing some interesting characters—like cage cars on a circus train. A rotund woman with matted gray hair carried a rooster in a wicker cage. A scabby-headed

43

boy scratched his stubble following with a second bird that was clearly much better groomed than the mother and son. Mariah leaned heavily on Will to avoid contact with the local fauna.

"Don't be afraid of him, Sweetie. We got his beak tied so he don't peck nor crow, but ain't he a handsome sight with that plumage?" she laughed through crenellated teeth.

Will peeked from under his hat. "Nice, fat broilers."

The woman's smile disappeared as she exhaled a noxious, exasperated sigh. "I'll have you know them's prize birds, not broilers. Nobody's pluckin' them for dinner, boy. Them's breedin' stock."

" I guess I can't recognize breeding when I see it," said Will as he looked the woman up and down and disappeared under his hat once again. The lady and her son moved on, grumbling.

Next through the door were a flashy redhead and an older gentleman, well dressed with side-whiskers and top hat. The redhead was quietly singing a few bars of a song, seeking the man's opinion. This was a singer who was used to an audience wherever she was.

"Poor wandering one, if such poor love as mine, can't help you find, true peace of mind, why take it, take it, it's thine." The car grew quiet as people attended to the singer as though she were in limelight.

"Open your eyes and take a gander at this pair." Mariah whispered with urgency before they came within earshot. Before the singer la, la'ed into the chorus, Mariah pulled the derby off Will's face. He sat up, reaching for his hat to no avail. An elegant rustling of taffeta came to a stop before Will and Mariah.

"Well, if it isn't Will Dunfield," said the redhead with an attitude that expected a gentleman to rise and take her hand. Will complied, his flaming face nearly matching her hair. "And as handsome as ever." He kissed her hand and forced a smile. He motioned for Mariah to stand and be introduced.

"Alice Townsend, this is Mariah, my wife. We just got married today."

The redhead rested one hand on her hip and looked incredulously back and forth between the two of them.

Will cleared his throat. "Well, Alice, did I hear you singing a few bars from 'Pirates of Penzance'?"

"Yes, and I could always use another dashing pirate," said the redhead. "Actually I've just selected some arias from Gilbert and Sullivan to sing this week at the Rochester Opera House. Big crowds during fair week, don't you know?"

Alice Townsend descended into a moment of silence as she surveyed Mariah again from head to toe. Smiling in condescension, she said, "Robbing the cradle, aren't you, Will?" She gave no further acknowledgement to the bride.

Before Will could speak, Alice let out a pained screech, moving with unchoreographed steps, gracelessly into the protection of the tophatted gentleman's arms.

"I'm sorry," said Mariah in cold tones and a fixed gaze. "I'm afraid I stepped on your foot."

"Indeed," said the redhead, refusing to acknowledge the pain any longer, but anxious to bring this unrehearsed scene to a quick conclusion. "Just an accident, of course."

"Of course," repeated Mariah.

"Congratulations, Will. Here's a girl who can probably push cattle through a gate with the best of them."

"Ya, I've moved a few uppity cows, that's for sure," said Mariah, putting a special emphasis on "cow."

"Ladies and gentlemen, please be seated. The train is ready to depart the station!" called the conductor, and the whistle soon sounded.

Passengers in the aisle moved down, leaving Mariah with the last word. The train moved forward with a lurch.

"Who is that woman?" snapped Mariah.

"A singer, that's all. One of the theater people I know." Will moved her into her seat like a pan moved off a hot burner. "You know, you shouldn't have done that," said Will in an agitated state. His face showed uncertainty. Should he take the upper hand with Mariah or try to pacify her? Other passengers were watching with eager interest.

"Will, I'm not a child."

"Sit down, sit down," he pleaded. Will tried to take her hand, but it was withdrawn. "Forget her. Please," Will said in a forced whisper "She doesn't mean a thing. She's an entertainer, that's all." Mariah's eyes met his. "You're my wife," he said, begging with his eyes. Will held his derby over their faces and kissed her so passionately that it nearly took her breath away. "You're more of a woman than she ever thought of being," he whispered as the train whistled its way through another crossing. Will replaced his derby at a jaunty angle. He ran his finger over Mariah's lips. "And look at what she has to do for those fine clothes? Getting up in front of crowds gawking at her. That's no life for a lady. My wife is a lady," said Will whose eyes traveled over Mariah's face.

"Will, this scares me."

"Scared of her? Why she's…"

"No. That's not what I mean."

"Mariah, what do you mean?"

*Don't ask. It could spoil everything. Whatever there was between them, it doesn't matter. He gave her up for me. That's all that matters. I've got to trust him.*

"I don't know," she said softly, "I don't know."

Will held her and didn't ask more.

# CHAPTER 6

## The Lion and the Lamb

wind had come up in the night. Sarah struggled to go to sleep thinking of Mariah in Will's arms at a hotel. She had raised her daughter in the nurture and admonition of the Lord, just as she had pledged before God and the congregation nearly fifteen years ago. The Great Commission was a lien on her soul, despite her best teaching. "Go ye, therefore, and teach all nations…" *I've tried good Lord; you know I've tried…* "baptizing them in the name of the Father, and the Son, and of the Holy Ghost…" *Oh, Lord, I have failed on that count. We Baptists don't sprinkle babies, so what more can I do?*

Violent sounds woke Sarah again in the small hours. The rattle of windows, the creak of gate hinges, and the bamming of the barn door, wobbly in its rusty tracks, brought Sarah upright and staring into the dark. Amos remained asleep, maddeningly still and contented. How could Amos sleep contentedly knowing that Will Dunfield was working his arts on their daughter in a hotel room near a honky tonk carnival?

Amos always slept well. "Sure I sleep good. You purge the devil out of men every day," he joked to Sarah. Dreams were written across his face, his eyes rolling under their lids, his lips moving. He was jovial by day; even by night a smile lightened his dark features. Sarah envied the peace that passeth all understanding that Amos enjoyed. Sometimes his optimism absolutely exasperated Sarah, but at other times, it saved her from the depths. The death of their daughter Laura three years earlier in the agonies of lockjaw tested them as nothing else. They cried copiously together, and together, his hand taking hers, they moved on. "Finally, brethren, whatsoever things are true, whatsoever things are honest, whatsoever things are just, whatsoever things are pure, whatever things are lovely, if there be any virtue, and if there be any praise, think on these things." And Amos did think on the positives. He didn't care if you couldn't make a silk purse out of a sow's ear. There was virtue in a sow's ear, just as there was in every other part, even the oink that brought laughter.

"Amos, are you dead or just deaf?" She gave him a poke, no, a jab.

"Half the apple crop'll be on the ground by mornin'," he said. "More cider fermentin' for the winter, that's all." He rolled over and closed his eyes. Sarah jabbed him again.

Finally she could see one eye open in the moonlight. "Getting' up and worryin' all night won't stop the wind, you know," Amos mumbled in exasperation.

"No, Amos. There's a sound out there. It's not just the wind." Sarah didn't always trust Amos' judgment, but she never doubted his heart. He would do what he could if there was any point to the effort. Despite the devilish glint in his eyes, she knew that he was as innocent as he looked in his sleep. From the first awkward, but gentle attempts at lovemaking on their wedding night twenty years ago, Sarah knew that Amos had never made love to another woman, and she trusted that he never had since.

Another strong gust, and the barn door banged again. Amos' eyes remained closed until an explosive sound of breaking glass tore the curtain of his sleep. The cluck-flapping, ewe-bleating alarms portended a mauling marauder.

Amos went from recumbent to armed for battle within seconds. Sarah could not remember a time when she had seen her husband move with such dispatch. He had his pants pulled over his nightshirt, his boots on, and his shotgun in hand before Sarah could light a second lantern.

Frederick came into the room armed with an oak club they kept behind the front door as a special welcome for intruders. He was determined to be strong despite a consumptive cough that had come and gone over the course of his twelfth year. Sarah took a lantern and gave a second to her son to light their way.

Sarah pulled Frederick to her side, stroking his hair. He resisted. "Ma. I'm not afraid," he said with a touch of reproof in his voice for a woman who doubted a man. Frederick lifted the oak staff from the floor with the resolve of a knight.

"I know, Dear. I'm the one who's afraid." She was afraid she would not see her elder son reach manhood, afraid that his breaths would shorten and stop no matter what his parents and the doctor did to intervene.

Florence and little Moze entered the kitchen wide-eyed. When they realized that they were going to be left by the cook stove in safety, they clamored for a part in the action. "We want to go!"

"You're staying here!" ordered Sarah. Their eyes began to fill. Their daddy intervened. "You and Florence get two big pot lids and a coupl'a wooden spoons. You're goin' ta raise a ruckus and scare whatever's in the barn away if it gets out alive. Now we're dependin' on you. If you see an animal come outa that barn, you bang those lids and shout till you drive it a week from Sunday. Understand? Remember the stories of Dr. Livingstone in darkest Africa? This is a big game hunt and you're the beaters." Florence and Moze smiled and went to the window, armed and ready.

Frederick stood by the small door on the right side of the barn waiting for a signal from his father to lift the latch. Amos slid open the main door just wide enough to get in, Sarah following with the lantern. He pulled the door closed.

They couldn't see to the back of the barn or into the hayloft. Moonlight streamed through the high windows on the left side. The sweet smell of new-mown hay filled their nostrils as they breathed slowly and silently. The oinking and blaying in the right stalls subsided with the comfort of light and human presence. On the left side, the frenzy was only slightly abated. Sarah looked to the left and pointed. A window, weathered to weakness, was knocked out, pieces of sash hanging inward. An explosion of animal power had burst through. No fox. A climber.

"Look." Amos nodded to the sheep pen. Blood. He counted. A missing lamb. Sarah scanned the area. On top of the farm wagon, still loaded with the last gleanings of hay, were two large green eyes glowing back at her. A bloodied mouth dripped onto the kill laid out on the hay like an offering on an altar. "Catamount," she whispered in fear.

Amos leveled his shotgun and let out a blast. At the flash, the side door flung open and Frederick rushed in. The mountain lion howled in agony and retreated into the darkness, poised for another attack. "Freddy, no!" called his mother. "It's still alive. Get out now."

Frederick didn't move. Amos had just enough time to insert a new shell when he heard heavy movement. He raised and aimed into the growling darkness; the gun discharged and was knocked from his hands. He fell backwards. Sarah screamed as the huge cat took wobbly steps and readied to pounce on Amos. Frederick ran into the small circle of light and clobbered the catamount with three whacks to the head. A frantic goat broke from its pen and dashed out the open door. The percussion came on cue from the kitchen. Even from inside the house, the spoons and pot lids separated the goat from the sheep by a half a mile before it stopped running from the wrath of hell.

"Sai, go tell the kids it's all right before every critter in here breaks out," shouted Amos, just rising from the floor.

The cat was nearly five feet long with claws like sickles. Frederick stood over the dead catamount, caressing the end of the oak club. Amos clutched Frederick's hand and patted his back. "Well done, Freddy. I woulda been in big trouble without you." Sarah held her son firmly, choking back tears. "Today I'll write to your Aunt Bertha and tell her what a brave young man you were."

The sun pierced the thin clouds hanging over the Ossipee Mountains to the east. Florence worked with her mother at making a pot of oatmeal. Little Amos set the table. Outside fair-haired Frederick worked with their father, stopped from time to time by fitful coughs, digging a grave fit for a lion and a lamb.

# CHAPTER 7

## In Sickness and In Health

*A*unt Bertha was a presence at the Brandon table even though she lived a half continent away. The children had heard her story in many tellings, simple at first, then embellished, for all of their years since the sound of words had taken on meaning. Aunt Bertha was the prime example of proverbs of darkness and parables of light. Praise to the woman who worked as hard to be a good wife as dutiful Bertha Parker; mercy for the girl who learned from her mistakes; but woe to the woman whose marriage was folly, the folly Aunt Bertha in her youth. The children heard the lessons until they could recite them: Only by God's grace had Bertha gotten a second chance. She had left long ago in shame and purgation, born anew, she shone like a beacon of light that reached all the way back to the mountains of New Hampshire.

As the story goes, the year was 1856. Bertha made a final visit to say goodbye to her first husband who for the past year had rested in unfamiliar peace behind the Free Baptist Church in North Sandwich. She planted a hardy perennial on Charles' grave and retreated to the wagon. It was in a long line of more than two dozen Conestoga wagons loaded with provisions for the long trek to the West. Her nine-year-old daughter Jane lay still on a blanket near the front door of the house, her seizure having passed, the foam wiped from her lips by her stepfather Jim Parker who knelt beside her. Her black-haired little brother George sat nearby on a stone watching his two new step-brothers playing tag along the banks of Cold River. The boys had not witnessed Jane's thrashing fall, but they had seen it before and it no longer frightened them. Bertha's six-year-old son George studied his new father whom he had finally taken to calling "Pa." Jim Parker was a happy man come rain or shine, nothing like little George's dark and somber father.

A year seemed so very long ago when George, his mother, Jane and several Taylors in finest black threw handfuls of soil on Papa's coffin. "Papa" was George Charles Taylor whom everybody called Charlie. He was one of the few Taylor's to blight the family tree as the weak limb of failure.

Charlie Taylor's shortcomings were understandable to a community where failure marked the landscape in weathered, swaybacked barns, in fields taken over by saplings, and houses abandoned to acquisitive Mother Nature. Twenty-five notch residents—all familiar with failures of various kinds—had formed a company in the fall of 1855, and pooled their cash to buy a tract of good western land. They sold farms, livestock and non-essential furnishings and invested in huge Conestoga wagons drawn by six horses. They met in the congregational church to vote on where they should settle. Some, with evangelical fervor, voted for the Kansas Territory to keep it from the hands of Southern slavers.

Kansas land was up for grabs thanks to the decision of the Pierce administration to let the territory go to whichever side could muster a majority when Kansas applied for statehood. Yankee idealists yearned to set up a shining abolitionist city on a hill, if a hill could be found in the smoke of the North-South battle for Kansas. The Kansas vs. Iowa debate was heated and close. Marston and Fellows argued for Kansas, bleeding or not. Then Jim Parker, the cheerful widower from Wonalancet, got up and argued the case for Iowa.

He painted a rosy picture of the Hawkeye State that had joined the Union ten years before as a Free State. Iowa had rich topsoil two feet deep and black as a moonless night. And the wagon train master had scouted out Iowa's landscape well and found a little piece of New England in the northeast corner of the new state. An oasis, richly watered by a river called the Wapsipinicon, Linn County was hilly in places and thickly timbered here and there like Sandwich Notch. Yes, this corner of Iowa would suit New Hampshire Yankees well, a hub of spiky timber rising high on hills over Midwestern flat grasslands a suitable place to erect a Yankee beacon of freedom. How could Bloody Kansas compare to the peaceful green, forested hills of Linn County?

"What do you say, folks?" Jim called out to the men who would cast their votes for their families. " The Kansas land may be cheaper, but how much is your life worth to ya? Are we gonna risk our wives and kids to save a few dollars?" Jim sat down and let reality sink in.

Jim Parker was no admirer of Franklin Pierce, the Democrat from New Hampshire, and he wanted no part of Pierce's Bleeding Kansas strategy to keep Southern Democrats in the party. Parker's enthusiasm was contagious, but the crowd was still not ready to commit to changing their plans and turning toward Iowa. They had already mapped out Kansas parcels, and they wondered how they would come up with the extra money it would take to close a deal for the Iowa tract.

Jim Parker was the best man to present the case for Iowa. He was popular all in all. A man who could pull up stakes and marry a poor widow with a little son and an epileptic daughter had to be under a special blessing or an undeserved curse. The hall broke into murmurs of doubt until a crafty pro-Iowa farmer from the Intervale Road asked Jim to sing a hymn before they prayed.

Jim Parker had a wonderful baritone voice. He sang in church in Wonalancet, but he had no idea his voice could move a vexatious crowd through song. "Jim, pick a hymn and Elmer here'll play the piano for you, then we'll pray before the vote." In shirtsleeves rolled to the elbow and his shirt comfortably open at the neck, the barrel-chested Parker stood beside the pulpit and waited for the piano player to give him the introduction to "Guide Me, O Thou Great Jehovah." His eyes focused not on the divided fellow travelers to who knows where, but on a beam of light coming through a tiny circular window over the balcony. Jim Parker stood in the light.

> Guide me, O Thou great Jehovah,
> Pilgrim through this barren land;

We are weak, but Thou art mighty,
Hold us with Thy powerful hand;
Bread of Heaven, Bread of Heaven,
Feed me till we want no more.
Feed me till we want no more.

Almost everyone knew the hymn, and they knew that Jim had changed it from the singular "I" to the plural "We," and when he got to the final verse, he asked the group to join in, the men on the ground floor and the women seated behind or in the balcony. He called out each line before leading them, editing the lyrics to sway the group to choose Iowa for their new home. The Jordan became the Mississippi; Canaan became Iowa.

When we tread the mighty Mississippi,
Bid my anxious fears subside;
Bear us through the swelling current;
Land us safe on the *Iowa* side:
Songs of praises, songs of praises,
We will ever give to Thee,
We will ever give to Thee.

Then there was silence. The pastor rose and prayed for God's guidance in hushed tones. When the men voted, Iowa won the day with little dissension.

There was even less dissension in the newly expanded Parker family. Jim Parker was a good man, and he soon took his stepson under his arm. Little George showed little emotion except for confusion about what "Father" meant. He had hardly gotten to know his father Charles during his short spans of good health and even shorter spans of successful work.

Charles Taylor was the fourth of nine children of James Hazzard Taylor and Dolly Smith Taylor. Two other sons of James and Dolly died in infancy, three daughters had no children, and the youngest son, named after a deceased infant older brother, never married. Other Taylors in the valley had flocks of bright, robust children, successful and learned, for the most part. The name Taylor was a proud name before

Charles came into the world, and it would be after him, a family tree as mighty as the flowering, fruitful chestnut. Charles was one of the few inconspic-uous dying limbs obscured by the shade of those reaching boldly for the sun.

When Bertha met the young Charles, he looked like a Taylor, walked like a Taylor, and talked like a Taylor. Everyone in Sandwich understood how she could have been deceived, for after all, the Taylors were one of the proprietary families that established the town in the 1760s, and they had made a name for themselves—scholars at Dart-mouth, the University of Pennsylvania and Amherst, ministers, writers and teachers. And those who worked with their hands as well as their minds—chair makers and farmers—honored the family name.

It was Bertha Brandon's misfortune to have been grafted to an anemic branch of the Taylor family tree. Charlie Taylor was a failure physically, financially, and philosophically. Although he never read a word of Kant or Marx, he was a determinist convinced of a certain inevitability that relieved him of responsibility for failure. His currents easily turned awry, and he was forever losing the name of action. His inactivity was not due to deep pondering, however; Charles was nei-ther a man of thought nor a man of action. His rudderless boat moved with the current or spun around in life's eddies. He scratched survival out of the granite-strewn soil for a time, and then laid down spade, pitchfork and body. Ever faithful Bertha lifted the first two for Charlie as much as she could, but she could not raise the third with ministra-tions, balms or prayers, and he slipped ever so slowly away leaving little to remember him by except for the weakened seed, his daughter Jane. Bertha thanked God little George Washington Taylor was healthy and strong.

Not even a year after Charlie died, Bertha had to sell the family farm to raise enough money to join a wagon train. She was forced to live with her parents who had little space to store Bertha's worldly goods. On moving day she held an auction with embarrassingly little to offer townsfolk of real value. Abandoned furniture sat in the middle of the yard. The few neighbors and relations who came offered pota-toes, seed or cider, but little cash. They had done what they could do for yet another farming family who could not coax a cash crop out of the Granite State's soil. Bertha was fortunate that at least the house and land had some value. Many Notch families got no offers for houses or land and had to leave their property for the elements to reclaim.

Mariah heard time and again how—thank God—Bertha listened to her family the second time about the kind of man she should marry. The family approved of Jim Parker, a robust, hard-working man with a positive attitude. A combination of utility and attraction brought Jim and Bertha together just a few weeks before the wagon train was to set off. Bertha and Jim combined their families, their assets and their hopes for the future with vows at the altar.

Bertha's story of folly and redemption was repeated many times as Mariah and her siblings grew. They could narrate how Mr. Beede, the captain of the wagon train, stood up to tell the families of Sandwich Notch what to expect when the giant Conestoga wagons thundered down the Ossipee road. Beede was responsible for getting the wagon train safely to the east bank of the Mississippi. His word would be law; he was sheriff, business agent, judge and military commander. There were no bridges across the mighty "Father of Waters," so the crossing would depend on how long it took to get there. If the wagon train moved with unusual dispatch, they would arrive in late fall and would be ferried over by great flat-bottomed barges, a few wagons at a time. If the river had iced over, they would be best advised to wait in Rock Island, Illinois until spring. They would need money and provisions for the wintering over whether they crossed to the other side or not.

The children could picture the scene as though they had been there to watch the wagon train with their own eyes. On the day of departure, so the story went, a subdued, sometimes teary crowd of townspeople gathered to wave goodbye, townspeople who knew that they were unlikely ever to see the departing families again. A long prayer by the young Baptist Pastor Bean invoked God's protection; embraces followed. Womenfolk helped Bertha get her daughter Jane settled on a pile of mattresses in the larger of the two Parker wagons.

Some family members seeing off their kin handed them handkerchiefs with the cash they could spare. The most generous of the relations were those with the least themselves.

Mariah's father, then a young lad of seventeen, gave up his savings of three dollars to the sister he never expected to see again. Little brother was uncharacteristically quiet. Usually the ever-talkative one, Amos could work a crowd like a carnival barker if the spirit moved him. He admitted to his children that he avoided the eyes of the neighbors, all of whom he knew from childhood. They pitied Bertha and felt sorry that she had to go far away to find a new life. Amos vowed that he would never be the object of such pity; Sarah always added that she hoped that such a fate as had befallen Bertha would never befall her children.

Amos felt special pity for his six-year-old nephew George who sat on the high seat of the Conestoga wagon acting like his mother's protector. George was tall for his age, and dark. He took his mother's right hand, her left hand given to the youngest Parker boy. Jim Parker took his place on the left wheel horse to drive the mighty wagon with rear wheels as tall as his new wife.

The Brandon's received their first letter from western Pennsylvania a few weeks later. Jane had died. Mr. Beede could not hold up the wagon train more than a few hours for Jim and Bertha to give what rites and tears they could to Jane. She had insisted on walking with her mother on a day when the wagon train had to ford a racing river recently swollen by heavy rains. As they each struggled with their footing, she fell into a fit and slipped on wet rocks into a whirling eddy. Separated from her mother and sinking in deep water, she was overcome with a seizure and drowned before her family could rescue her. They laid her in a grave in shaley ground near Pittsburgh, a nondescript spot along a rutted road that they would never see again.

The second letter was posted from a bustling general store in Rock Island, Illinois where migrating hordes normally stopped for provisions and to schedule barge crossings. Across a white expanse of frozen river they could see some signs of what they were told was the town of Davenport, Iowa, settled largely by New Hampshire Yankees who had braved the crossing before. Their new home, Central City, lay another sixty miles to the west. They could not trust the wagon and team to the ice, but Jim and Bertha decided not to wait weeks more with the wagon train. They had no recourse but to store the wagon and what little furnishings they had, and strap essential tools and provisions to their horses.

With each child assigned a horse and the parents each taking two, they spread yards apart over the creaking ice, the children terrified by the groaning, blinded by the wind-driven snow, and knowing that a collapse of the ice beneath them would mean almost certain death.

They trekked following Jim's voice singing joyful hymns and ballads, inserting each of their names into the songs so ancient and legendary lore became their own hallelujahs. In Davenport they were able to borrow a wagon from some church people, much smaller than the Conestoga, but ample for what few possessions they managed to transport across the ice, and they pressed on.

The Parkers arrived at Central City and found that the stories about the area were true— rolling hills and a grove of trees along the banks of the Wapsipinicon River to provide lumber for their homes. There they built a log home, unusual in those parts, and in the spring they started breaking through the tangled sods and planting the good seed they had brought from the Granite State.

Throughout the passage of twenty-seven years, Bertha and Sarah formed a bridge of letters half way across the continent, the only bridge to keep the families as one. Bertha shared Amos and Sarah's joys and sorrows, and Sarah felt the hail and smelled the rich, black earth through the stimulus of a thousand words. The torrent of Sarah's black ink that showered down from Mariah's wedding brought back chilling memory of Bertha's dark first marriage. Bertha answered with a letter of hope.

Shortly before Mariah's wedding day, Sarah received a joyous letter from Iowa. Bertha was optimistic no matter what doubts Sarah might have. Bertha told her sister-in-law to concentrate her thoughts on what is good and pure and lovely, just as the Apostle's letter to the Philippians said. Spilling from the envelope were dried rose pedals to bless the wedding couple. Bertha wrote a fervent prayer in a firm hand, a prayer that Sarah's premonitions about the bridegroom would prove to be wrong.

# CHAPTER 8

## Fair Ladies

*B*right posters on a high board fence displayed tempting scenes from the fair at Rochester's Cold Spring Park. A buxom beauty soared high in the tent rigging on a trapeze, a lion tamer cracked his whip at the indomitable king of the jungle, and a giant hot air balloon pushed through clouds over a vast city. The fair promised titillating, death-defying dangers to crowds of farmers and factory workers who gave little thought to the fact that they faced greater risks to life and limb in their daily work than they would ever see for the price of admission. Once in a while the crowds would get more than they bargained for.

Will and Mariah admired the posters from the tufted seat of a hired hack that drove them from the Hanson Street railroad station around downtown Rochester and then back to the square. As they crossed the bridge near the Cocheco dam, Will pointed to the left. "Frenchtown," he said. "How's your French? At Wallace's, the foremen have to parlez vous 'cause half of the workers don't know English. There's four hundred and eighty shoe workers working five and a half days a week. That's a lot of shoes to sell," Will smiled and winked.

Mariah slid her hand between Will's bicep and chest. "I bet none of them have stayed in a hotel."

"Dodge's is no standard of luxury, Sweetie," said Will with a laugh, "but it's the best you can find up here on the fringes of civilization."

"The city scares me a little," admitted Mariah as they clattered over paving stones.

"I don't know if I'd called fourteen hundred people a city."

"It's big to me, and you only hear English half the time."

"The town fathers are talking about a city charter. They can't lay brick on brick fast enough. North of the river's mostly foreigners now. They say a third of the population's immigrants."

Mariah surveyed the downtown hubbub. "Nothing like a farming town, is it?" she said.

"Nope. This is just a glimpse of the future, sweetie," said Will with pride at being part of the industrial boom. Rochester had plenty of what it took to attract industry: water. Three rivers, the Isinglass, the Salmon Falls and the Cocheco, were dammed to serve the growing industry. The biggest, the Cocheco, ran through the heart of the town, turning the spindles of the Norway Plains Woolen Mill and powering the stitching machines of the Wallace Shoe Company. Lesser factories hugged the banks of the Salmon Falls and Isinglass. The Isinglass was famous for its big sheets of mica used for windows in stoves and in folding bonnets of buggies. The potent engine of industry also powered a construction boom, and the selectmen had ordered plans to be drawn up to pipe water to all homes and businesses in the downtown. If the voters approved, the water mains would be in the ground by the opening ceremonies of the fair in 1885.

Mariah leaned forward trying to catch a glimpse of all the goods on display in shop windows, shiny kitchen gadgets for coring and peeling apples, chopping onions and squeezing fruits for juices, brightly labeled medicine bottles and cans of preserved foods, and fabric for clothes–an amazing array of patterns and colors in the windows of dressmakers.

"Oh, Will, I've got to get in there," exclaimed Mariah, bursting with excitement after the driver slowed in front of Feineman's Department Store with a façade of white glazed brick four stories high. Huge plate glass windows showcased wondrous window displays like the sets for stage plays.

"Tomorrow I'll take you shopping," he whispered into her ear giving her a gentle kiss on the cheek. "Right now we only have time to make a quick tour and look at the downtown all lighted up street." It was dusk and nearly closing time for stores.

"They installed them six years ago."

"The gaslight is so bright you could even read the price tags in the windows," Mariah said.

"We could," said Will as she captured her eyes, "if we didn't have anything *better* to be doing tonight."

"Shush," whispered Mariah playfully. "The driver."

Will gave Mariah another discreet peck on the cheek. "We'll get out here," Will called out to the driver who seemed oblivious to their conversation. "Deliver our bags to Dodge's, will you? Tell 'em we'll be there in a few minutes." He handed the driver a few coins and the man smiled and doffed his hat. "You want a quick look inside before they close?" Will gestured toward the white-fronted Feineman's lit brightly all the way to the fourth floor. He held Mariah's hand as she descended, proud that she turned eyes in her powder blue dress with navy trim.

"This is the first department store in the county. Two floors to explore, then offices above, but maybe I shouldn't tell you that or we'll never get out of here. You haven't ridden an elevator before, have you?" Will asked rhetorically. "Well, this will be your first Fair ride, and it's free."

After walking the aisles, they entered the elevator that whisked them upwards, Mariah clutched Will's arm with alarm followed by amazed excitement. "Honey, wait 'til you ride the Ferris wheel," said Will as the elevator operator opened the gate. On the fourth floor doors with frosted glass invited patrons with names and office hours. "The offices on the left have great views of the river and the fair grounds." They walked past Dr. Alexander's office that displayed a large molar under his name. "Painless Dentistry," he promised. Next was Louis Braum's hairdressing salon.

Will approached the last door and started in. "But, Will, you can't just walk into an office for the view."

"Don't worry. I know Nellie. She won't mind." The black and gold lettering on the next door read, "Nellie Parker Piano Instruction. Lessons according to the New England Conservatory Method. By appointment." Mariah followed him warily into the waiting room. A mother was quietly waiting while her daughter ascended arpeggios haltingly in the next room. The door to the instruction room was slightly ajar. A sweet, young voice guided a child's fingers through scales as Will and Mariah took in the view of the fair grounds with the new gleaming white exhibition building in the center, a pennant flying in the breeze proclaiming the eighth Rochester fair at Cold Spring Park. Mariah had never seen so many people as were milling around the fifty or more acres of Cold Spring Park in the distance.

As Mariah gazed across the landscape, Will left her side and went into the instruction room. The door closed and the piano scales stopped. A moment later, Will emerged, leaving the door as he found it. "Well, Sugar, it's time for dinner," he whispered. "She's busy so I won't introduce you."

"How do you know her? You aren't taking piano lessons, are you?" she asked, ready to believe that he would surprise her with a hidden talent.

"Lessons? No, not me. I'm too busy. You get to know a lot of people when you're in business. You'll meet Nellie some other time."

"Will, maybe I should take piano lessons—you know—if I have time," Mariah said with some tension in her voice.

Will stopped and held her arms. He looked straight into her eyes. "If you want, but you don't need to do that for me. You're really smart. You've got your own talents. Who knows? You'll probably have a shop with your name…"

"Our name," Mariah said.

"Our name up in gold letters. Dunfield's Fine Fashions. How does that sound? That's what you'd like, isn't it?"

"Yes," said Mariah proudly. "That and a family," she added.

"Both, of course," Will replied. It would really be something if you could do both. We'll just have to see," replied Will.

"It wouldn't be easy, but I know I could do it," Mariah replied with a touch of defensiveness in her voice.

"If anyone could, you could," Will said with a smile. "It's nice to think about anyway." He took Mariah's hand and led her down the hall. "Well, what do you think? Time for dinner?"

Momentary pensiveness fled and Mariah managed a smile. "Let

me push the button," she said. Mariah watched the elevator's workings as the cable pulled the car up through the cage. "Wouldn't Freddy love to see this?"

They walked hand in hand across the square to the door of Dodge's Hotel.

A doorman in a black uniform with gold piping opened the varnished door for them. "Someone to open the door, someone else to carry our bags, and a maid to make the bed," said Mariah, imitating the airs of the rich. "But you know what I love the most?" Mariah whispered before they got to the desk. "You." Will squeezed her hand.

Dodge's Hotel was tidy, but Spartan. The best room in the house had double windows on the square, but the same iron bed, dresser, and small round table with two straight-backed chairs as all the other rooms. Dodge's only claim to elegance was the wallpaper with giant pink roses set off against the dark oak woodwork. The hotel would be home for a few days as workers finished with paint and varnish on an apartment on Hanson Street. That would be the Dunfield's first home, a world away from the farm by Cold River. Except for Will's bachelor second hand furnishings, they would be starting fresh with some new things, and would add more luxuries as Will brought in more income. A kitchen, a parlor, a bedroom, and the spare room—the spare room that Mariah fancied as a nursery.

Mariah would select linens and blankets for their bedroom. The thought of sharing a bed with Will, a bed decked out in brand new linens from Feineman's quickened her blood. She remembered reading Omar Khayyam and Swinburne, the silken, perfumed pages that described the pleasures of the flesh so richly that you felt it and smelled it as you read. These books she kept from her mother. Suddenly she remembered the poem she had memorized but never recited to anyone but herself. Coleridge's "Kubla Khan." In Xanadu did Kubla Khan a stately pleasure dome decree…

A savage place! as holy and enchanted
As e'er beneath a waning moon was haunted
By woman wailing for her demon-lover !

Mariah thought about a magazine article she had gotten from a friend a few weeks before that made it seem that all of the potential pleasures of intimacy were the husband's; the wife's only joy was in giving. She just knew that Will wouldn't be like most husbands who took pleasure, but seldom gave it. Her husband—husband, a word she kept repeating to herself—seemed to be a cornucopia of pleasure, and their first night together was only hours away.

The article, "Being a Good Wife," in *Godey's Ladies Magazine* hardly began to answer her questions about men. "Being a good wife means understanding your husband's need for intimate moments, a duty for the pleasure and comfort of her husband." Was there something wrong with her that she longed for pleasure in her *duty*? She had read that there would be a brief moment of pain, and some blood the first time. There was no mention of pleasure for the wife except in having pleased her husband. *Godey's* urged brides not to fear.

It was not fear that consumed her thoughts about the coming night. Mariah and Will dined at a window seat, and with the clink of glasses and the warmth of linen napkins in silver rings. The fiery sunset gave way to the glow of lamplight as two men leaned their ladders against the crossbar and touched the gas mantels with a flaming wick. Circles of brilliant light ran together to form a path of golden warmth. Carriage traffic stilled and pedestrians moved from window to window like performers in limelight. A constable in a domed helmet and a nightstick hanging at his side checked doors and looked down alleys, nodding to passersby as he did his rounds.

In eight hours the good citizens of the fair city would rise from their beds by the light of the sun and the clanging of bells. The mysteries of stars and lovers' whispers would drown in the deluge of light and mechanical noise of day. Mariah thought about the ladies and gentlemen, starched, perfumed and well-mannered closing their doors and tossing stiff formal clothes aside, freeing the flesh from the day's restraints.

A couple not much older than thirty talked softly at a nearby table, touching linen to their lips with grace. The husband brushed his trim moustache. His hair, as black as his moustache, was dressed with macassar oil and shone in the light. His wife twirled a cascading lock around her finger as she looked into his eyes. They moved with grace and deportment, but Mariah imagined them an hour later, closing the door on the watching world, transformed by the freedom of the night, free to let passion reign. A few hours later, when the sun peered through the windows, they would once again answer civilization's reveille in stiff starched shirts and crisp worsted frock coats, crinolines and bustles, click-healed marching in unison with echoed pleasantries, tipped hats, and gloved handshakes, inhibited by society's rules.

Mariah saw through the disguises of civilized middle class propriety as never before. It was fascinating, but at the same time sad to see nocturnal creatures looking through masks.

Will and Mariah enjoyed an intimate table by the window with fine china, sterling and crystal. It was the first time Mariah had been presented with a printed menu and the first time she had ever been addressed as ma'am. Her dark eyes glistened with excitement.

"What are you thinking?" asked Will with his glass of port warming in his hand.

"The world at night. People can let themselves go."

"A lot of the swells never do. That's what amazes me about what they call 'polite society.' There's a time when you have to run with your instincts, but some people always hold back. Like my boss. I think he must wear a collar and tie to bed, for God's sake," said Will with a contemptuous laugh. "He and his wife go to the Methodist Church every Sunday, and I bet he's praying, daubing sweat with an embroidered handkerchief, sitting in the pew with his eyes closed confessing thoughts and feelings, confessing everything he ever ached to do and never dared. He's one of those people who are afraid of the night," said Will, sipping his port and looking over his glass into Mariah's eyes. "You and I aren't afraid of the night, are we?"

"No. I might be afraid if I was your boss's wife. I'd be afraid of being bored to death." They both laughed. Mariah thought of the boys swimming in wild seclusion in Cold River, and her brief plunge into the freedom of water swirling around her body, liberated from the gravity of a burdened world. She thought of Will's powerful body, of his hardness and her softness. And then she remembered the comments of two of her married friends who made her promise never to repeat their stories of their inept husbands' wedding nights, struggling in the dark, stumbling like newborn foals, ashamed of their nakedness, and collapsing in stifled groans with the release of their pent up desires. The disappointed brides could not talk about the experience or guide their husbands into a tender nurturing of desire. The husbands treated sex as weakness of the flesh; animal behavior of the sinful nature brought on by forces of darkness and cured by the light of day.

The bellhop set their bags down in front of room 206 and inserted the key into the shiny brass lock. The honeymoon suite was no pleasure dome of luxury, but the velvet draperies and silken rope tiebacks fed Mariah's imagination of the bedroom she would one day have. Will locked the door and turned the gas light down to a golden glow. He kept his eyes fixed on Mariah as he removed his tie, color and cuffs, then unbuttoned his shirt. Sitting on the bed beside her, he took her hand and pressed it over his heart and kissed her. Mariah invited his eager hands to her buttons. "I'm never going to forget this night," she whispered as his lips caressed her neck.

Will's warm hands moved with a slow feather touch over her body from neck to breasts. He slipped her clothes off effortlessly, and stood to let Mariah unbutton his pants. As his hands moved with fluid ease over her body, he paused with deep kisses that aroused them both. He slowed their passion, exploring Mariah with hands that knew every intimate spot of pleasure. In the dim light they enjoyed the sight of their nakedness, and then Will rose over her. They could not keep the explosion of their passion quiet. Tantalizing pauses, and the arousal built again. After they rested in the warmth of each other's embrace, Mariah whispered, "Let the night go on and on."

The light of day broke through the draperies in slender beams. Mariah lifted Will's heavy arm from across her chest and slid out of bed. She studied her sleeping husband in the dim light, thinking of what she would dare say about the pleasure he brought her, wanting to believe that his amazing knowledge of just what to do was instinct freed from the stranglehold of "polite society's" oppression.

*Oh, Will, I'd like to tell everyone how wonderful you make me feel. I've been raised to do my duty, but last night was no duty. It scares me, though. It's like liquor or opium, I suppose. There's got to be danger 'cause they warn about it. But you're my husband. I just don't under-stand where the danger could be.*

Mariah brushed his warm back ever so lightly. *I just want to be the only one. It's just natural that you're so good at it, isn't that it? I can't let myself think about those other women…that redhead…with you.* Mariah tried to stifle the tears.

Will rolled over, squinting in the shaft of sunlight. "Why are you crying? Did I…"

"No. You did everything just right. At least I think so. I'm not speaking from experience, of course…" Mariah began to laugh self-consciously. *Experience.* The redhead. Other women. And then she broke into tears again. Will sat up and held her, soothing her with caresses and murmurs until passion overcame her other emotions.

The light of day did not drive passion into shadowy corners or erase the memory of the night. She ran her hand gently down his back. He reached for the sash holding her silk robe closed and pulled it slowly until the robe fell open. They made love again, this time in the warm morning sun. Her thoughts could take her to dangerous places, places in her heart that could rob her of the joy she was feeling in the moment, dangerous places contemplating Will's natural gifts as a lover, or his skill that came with experience.

Mariah asked Will to walk rather than ride to Cold Spring Park. Arm in arm they window-shopped. Mariah pointed out fabrics and furnishings, lamps and kitchen gadgets saying, "Don't let me forget," or "Which do you like better?" The day before other people fascinated her; on this day she behaved as though Will and she were the only people on the sidewalk.

At the fairgrounds, the agricultural exhibits were immediately ahead. "Please, let's not watch oxen pulls, and forget about the poultry exhibit," said Mariah.

"The only chicken we'll see will be on our plates," said Will as they stood at a sign pointing the way to attractions. They both agreed they had seen enough of pigs and cows, and decided to move on to machinery and manufactures. Then came games of skill and chance where Will demonstrated his strength with the hammer and bell and his marksmanship with darts and archery.

A steam calliope bellowed out cheery music while crowds gawked at freaks of nature from a two-headed goat to acrobatic dwarves and giants. After two hours of walking and weaving around people, Will and Mariah were ready to sit and rest. A barker on a high platform announced upcoming events. "Watch a hot air balloon ascend hundreds of feet in the air! Watch Professor Allen of Providence, Rhode Island and his beautiful companion fly into the clouds!" Mariah and Will headed for the field beyond the great exhibition hall.

For ten cents apiece, a crowd gathered in the shade of the grandstand as a kerosene burner blasted hot air into a huge red sack trimmed in gold, tasseled rope, lying flaccid on the ground. A brass band in silver and black uniforms thundered from the grandstand as attendants held the balloon on long poles over a kerosene burner. Slowly the giant red bag began to rise. The band fell silent with a wave from the professor. Through a megaphone he explained the science of the atmosphere—currents, downdrafts, thinning oxygen—and he predicted that some day people would travel from city to city through the air.

"Isn't that amazing, Will? Do you suppose we'll ever ride in a balloon?"

"If you want to, Sugar, but I don't think you can make the thing go where you want."

To the fanfare of a small group of musicians Professor Allen walked around the cordoned circle waving his hat to the crowd and escorted his beautiful red-haired companion.

"Well, look who it is!" said Mariah to Will with disgust. It was the tophatted gentleman and the flamboyant singer from the train. Mariah crossed her arms and scowled.

"Mariah, don't get so upset. You taught her a lesson, but don't hold a grudge. Please. Just forget about her and enjoy the spectacle." Will circled her waist with his arm and pulled her to his side.

In a few minutes the balloon rose hesitantly over the large wicker basket weighted and tethered to the ground. "And now I'm going to ask the beautiful Alice Townsend—yes, the same lovely lady you heard sing on opening day—I'm going to ask Miss Townsend to accompany me into the gondola. Won't she grace the skies, ladies and gentlemen?" The crowd murmured with delight and broke into applause. Although few in the crowd would have accepted the invitation to soar into the sky, the diverse faces glowed with anticipation with no signs of fear. If few could imagine soaring into the sky, even fewer could imagine falling from it.

Alice Townsend was escorted in front of the crowd, waving a gloved hand with the grace of an elegant lady used to condescending to the masses. Just before she reached the open door of the gondola, she caught Will's eye and winked. Mariah snarled.

"She's a performer. She knows how to work the crowd."

"You're not the crowd. You're my husband."

"Sweetie, can we just enjoy the performance?"

A small band played martial music as the aeronauts were secured in their places. Attendants jettisoned restraining ropes and allowed the hot air balloon to take its human occupants into the realm of birds and angels.

The balloon rose higher and higher. The professor untied the tether and let it drop. Soon the crowd could hardly make out the two occupants of the gondola. Bags of sand dropped from the sky stirring clouds of dust on the ground like artillery shells. The huge red bag drifted against the cloud-dotted sky in serene silence, a wonder of human ingenuity defying the rules of nature.

As the balloon cooled, it began its slow descent. As big as an elephant, as light as a bubble. The crowd watched in awe. Then suddenly, something terrible began to happen. The balloon began to plunge downward. The remaining sandbags fell and smashed violently to the ground. As the great red sphere came closer to the ground, some sharp-eyed spectators shouted and pointed. The bag began to flutter and collapse. A rip had opened in the side of the great red balloon. The professor could not slow the descent. The balloon changed from a great floating bubble to a crimson ribbon snaking to the ground. As the occupants of the gondola came close enough for people to make out their faces, their terror was evident. Some in the crowd turned their faces away. Others stared in disbelief.

Attendants and a constable rushed across the field while a barker called for stretchers and a doctor. Most of the crowd was standing, murmuring, comforting one another.

Mariah sat, stunned and confused. Will took her hand, pulling her through the crowd, refusing to look back. When they were clear of the chaotic scene, Will stopped. A look of anguish swept over him; his breathing was labored.

Mariah took his hands. "I'm sorry. I really am." He nodded slowly and they embraced.

"I'm so confused," Mariah mumbled as she looked into Will's strained face.

Will looked back with anguish in his eyes, too numb to speak.

"I'm confused about her."

They were soon engulfed in a tide of bodies, some moving toward the disaster, some fleeing the site. Will pulled Mariah through the crowd fighting vainly to leave the confusion behind.

As they left the fairgrounds, they averted their eyes as they passed the vivid posters of "fair ladies" and "wonders of modern science." She firmly gripped Will's cold hand as people surged by murmuring, hysterical, weeping, wondering, and shouting. "What happened?…Did you see it?… La pauvre femme, morte, je pense… It fell the last two hundred feet like a rock …I heard one of 'em died…sacre bleu, c'est terrible… I can't imagine goin' up in the sky in a thing like that…Did you see it fall? What a sight!…Mama, why do we have to leave?"

"Listen to them," Will said, anger forcing sorrow aside. "They don't really care. It's just an exciting moment in their humdrum lives. I knew it was too dangerous," he said. Tears began to well in his eyes.

"Please, Will, let's get out of here!" Mariah cried out in anguish. "I don't understand, I really don't understand," she wailed as Will held her against him as they walked away.

"We can't let this spoil everything," implored Will as he gripped Mariah's shoulders.

Mariah looked back and forth at his eyes, even more confused by a tone of anger mixed with regret.

"We've got to leave this all behind. All I want you to think about is how much I love you."

Mariah squeezed Will's hand. They crossed the just as a horse-drawn ambulance scattered the crowd left and right with the frantic ringing of its alarm bells.

# CHAPTER 9

## Sewing and Reaping

The corner room had in recent months become the busiest space in the cozy apartment. Two bureaus swelled with fabric of every description, and bolts of bright summer prints and shiny black crinoline were stacked on shelves. Mariah had dedicated everything in the room to her thriving sewing business. Even a beautiful walnut cradle was filled with bolts of cloth. As the morning sun glinted off Mariah's money-making Singer, she emptied the cradle with hope she had not felt in months.

Humming nursery rhymes, she stuffed remnants into cotton bags. *I'll have Will put these in the attic. He'll be so glad to see the place uncluttered.* At last three knee-high bags sat in the hallway. Mariah's eyes darted back and forth between her two most prized objects: A Singer sewing machine, a purchase that set them back as much as a buggy, and an walnut cradle with wrought iron fittings that suspended the box from its sturdy waist high base.

The room was hardly big enough for more than a chest of drawers, a changing table and a cradle, and over the past eighteen months the room had served double duty—to the present as a sewing room, and to the future as a nursery. The two purposes vied for space, but when six months turned to a year with no sign of family on the way, Mariah and Will began calling the space the sewing room. On this day of hope Mariah emptied the cradle of bolts of fabric and bundles of Butterick patterns and made it up with a quilt her mother had made.

Mariah sighed, content with the transformation. A dress form—expanded to the ample proportions of an elderly society matron—stood in the dark inner corner like a headless godmother: Sentinel over the empty cradle and the shiny black Singer, a figure of divided loyalty. "It looks like things might be about to change," Mariah said to her mute companion in the corner. She closed her eyes in a silent prayer. Mariah would not break the news to anyone—not even to Will—until she was more sure.

Gathering up a crinoline mourning dress that was still held together with pins, she dropped it into the cradle to cover the quilt. Will would be very suspicious if he saw the cradle emptied of all of Mariah's sewing projects. _Oh, I want to tell him, I want to, I want to, but I can't disappoint him again. If I miss my monthly twice for sure, I'll know._

As Will left for work in the morning, he promised a special surprise on this, their second anniversary. "Be dressed for the weather. I'll be getting the horse and buggy from the stable for a ride up Wakefield Street." Wakefield Street, the most fashionable address in town, especially lovely in the slanting sunlight of late afternoon with falling leaves.

The rich light struck the black and gold Singer first, then spilled beyond to the walnut spindles of the cradle. She admired one, then the other, as she thought about how angry it made her that the world expected her to choose one or the other. Mariah was sure that she would be able to keep both treadle and cradle rocking.

The bell in the clock tower of the Methodist Church rang the fifth hour. Within a few minutes the sidewalks along South Main Street filled with mill girls, their hair and clothes whitened by lint from the looms. They babbled in French or complained in thick brogues about little mouths to feed, mice in near empty cupboards and drunken husbands to shove out of bed.

"I'm home!" Will shouted. He placed his hat on a shelf over the hissing radiator and lifted Mariah off the floor with a robust hug. "So, are you all ready to go?"

"I guess so, but what about dinner?" asked Mariah who suspected that Will's surprise was probably a dinner out.

"Cook on your anniversary? I should say not. How does Dodge's sound?"

Mariah put her hand on Will's cheek and looked into his face as though she had just noticed something new.

"Don't tell me I've been going all day with a shaving nick," said Will who ran his hand over his face.

"No, you silly man. I'm just thinking how you've become even more handsome."

"I don't know about that, but every man that sees *you* takes a second look unless he sees *me* make a fist." Mariah and Will's laughter faded into a prolonged gaze that warmed into a sustained kiss.

"And I really like it when you have that extra flush in your cheeks." Will looked around to see if Mariah had selected a wrap against the chill fall air. He pulled his gold Waltham pocket watch out of his vest pocket and popped open the cover. "Oh, we'd better hurry."

Mariah took a fur-trimmed cape from the hall coat stand and donned a matching bonnet in burgundy. "So why do we need a buggy to go up to Dodge's? We could walk there in fifteen minutes."

"We're going up Wakefield Street first." He put a finger to his lips when Mariah started to ask more questions. "Remember, I'm surprising *you* tonight."

"You surprise me lots of nights," said Mariah with an impish grin, her eyes cast downward.

"Why Mrs. Dunfield, you're shocking your husband," said Will, making a face feigning prudery. After two years of marriage, this was the first time that Mariah had ever alluded to their lovemaking outside of the bedroom. Will had moved Mariah by small degrees out of the darkness of routinized Victorian sexual customs of the middle class. Girls were taught, if taught anything at all, that sex was meant first for procreation, and second, to relieve a man's needs. It was a wife's responsibility to please her husband, but not to fan flames of sexual fantasy. Will taught by demonstration that lovemaking could be, should be, mutual exploration of passion and sensual pleasure that heightened and extended desire. Will and Mariah's sex life would have been utterly blissful if only it had resulted in the fruit that marriage was supposed to bear.

"This could be a whole night of surprises," said Will before he kissed Mariah one more time.

The lamplighter was starting his rounds on Rochester Square and shopkeepers were pulling down their shades. The buggy's tires clittered and the horse's shoes clattered as Will drove past the old parson's statue and onto the broad sweep of Wakefield Street lined with arching elms.

The owner of Norway Plains Woolens, the president of the First National Bank, the chief civil engineer of the Boston and Maine Railroad, all had homes graced by those stately elms.

"Now you've really got my curiosity going. Are we really going to a party?"

"No, we're not going to a party, but I hope we'll be giving one before too long," Will replied.

"If inviting over one or two couples is a party, then we…"

"We'll be going to a party soon, but not tonight," said Will who wanted to leak his news is small amounts.

"Who's inviting us?"

"Why none other than Mr. Charles Wallace himself, that's who."

"Why would Mr. Wallace invite us to a party? I didn't think he had anything to do with people who couldn't afford at least a ten-room house."

"That's right, but we've been invited to his home for a Christmas party."

Mariah dropped back against the tufted horsehair seat. "Now, Will, you've just got to tell me what's going on," said Mariah whose face reflected anxiety mixed with anticipation.

"I've been promoted. I'm now director of sales for the southern region. I'll be making twice as much money within a few months."

Mariah hugged and tugged at Will so much that the horse veered off to the left and frightened an oncoming farmer who reined in his team and shouted, "Hey, there, keep to your side!" Will doffed his hat in apology as the farmer directed his horse back across the streetcar tracks.

"Yes, we'll be in the money, and that's why we're driving up Wakefield Street," Will added. "Don't ask any more questions. We're almost there."

"Where?"

"No more questions." Will turned right into a driveway of stone dust leading up to a canopy on the north side of a house with bare windows. It was a two-story house with a fashionable mansard roof adorned with scalloped slate roof tiles in three shades. An old man in a top hat and gray, bushy side-whiskers met them at the door.

"Whose house is this?" asked Mariah as Will helped her from buggy step to the curb. "It's vacant, isn't it?"

"Not for long. It'll be ours in a few days if you like it."

"How is that possible?" asked Mariah who gasped in astonishment, but Will shushed her as he led her to the gleaming front door with polished brass, shiny oak and a huge oval of frosted, patterned glass.

"Ah, Mr. Dunfield," said the rheumy old gentleman who fumbled for a key from his vest stretched over an alderman's paunch. "And Mrs. Dunfield," he managed after a series of coughs. "It's a pleasure. I'm Cecil Harvey and I represent the builder. Not a big house by Wakefield Street standards, but such workmanship!" exclaimed Harvey with flashing brows as thick as an overgrown hedge. "You only see this in the finest homes. Just wait till you see the floriated cornice in the parlor..." coughing chopped Harvey's booming baritone into short phrases—"and the marquetry in the dining room." Harvey managed his top hat and gold-headed cane in one hand and the key in the other. "Extraordinary, really, for this price." The old man's voice echoed through the empty rooms of the ground floor. Will's eyes rolled as the old man uttered more errant sounds than a leaky boiler, hissing, rumbling and swelling with dangerous pressure.

Mariah stopped at the staircase and took off her glove to feel the finish of the oak newel post and banister. She beckoned Will as the old man rambled on about the features of the house. "You'll love being the mistress of this place, little lady, and just wait till you fill it," he added with an appreciative glance at Mariah's expansive bodice and tiny waist. She ignored him and gave her attention to the marble mantel around the parlor fireplace and the dining room chandelier with four frosted glass globes hand-painted with mountain scenes.

"The Alps, little lady," said Harvey. "Made in Bavaria."

Mariah nodded and smiled briefly.

"Can we afford this place?" Mariah whispered to Will.

"Yes, but it may take a couple of years to furnish all the rooms," he admitted. "Don't worry. I've talked to the bank," he added quietly, pointing at the old man to warn Mariah not to let him overhear them and make him nervous about their ability to raise the money.

Harvey was breathing heavily just from the combined stress of walking around the ground floor and talking non-stop about wainscoting, pilasters, and the herringbone brick pathway to the door. "Could you show yourselves round…" he coughed and gasped until Will finally helped him settle on a lower step of the staircase. "Could you do… the upstairs… on your own?" Harvey wheezed.

"Of course," replied Will who took Mariah's hand. On the landing suitable for a grandfather clock, they looked back at the old man sitting on the step coughing and wheezing. Mariah watched him for a moment, perplexed at what drove aged, infirm people to more and more wealth when they had so little time left on the earth to enjoy it.

"Thank goodness," said Mariah when they were finally alone on the second floor. I just want us to look and talk about this ourselves. The place is impressive enough without all those twenty-five-cent words."

"I hope you noticed….arrrgh, arrrgh… the balusters," Cecil yelled upstairs with as much air as he could capture and expel. "Three different turnings. Place is no doggery, that's for sure!" he shouted, laughing at himself.

"It's a banister. Why doesn't he just call it that? Why is he shouting?" Mariah asked after uncovering her ears.

"He's as deaf as the newel post until you mention dollars. Balustrades cost a lot more than banisters, you know," quipped Will with a chuckle.

"Wainscoting, cornices, balloon framing, I don't know half of what he's talking about," said Mariah with a wide-eyed shake of her head.

Will leaned in close to Mariah's face and whispered. "And he doesn't know the other half, so it's all gibberish coming through that natural megaphone of his. You'd think from his description that this was one of the grand houses of the elite."

They found the master bedroom and were delighted with its large closet, a rarity in any but the newest homes. The home smelled of rich wood and varnish, and the brass hinges and key plates reflected the prismatic light from the glass doorknobs.

"A guest room, this other bedroom…" Mariah did not call it a nursery. They stood silently admiring its two windows. *If only I was sure. I want to tell him.* "Will…" *I've got to wait a week. I just don't know for sure.* "Will, this room is just perfect."

"Have you picked out the nursery yet, folks?" shouted Cecil Harvey.

Will stepped into the hall and cupped his hands to his mouth. "Yes, Mr. Harvey, very nice. The veins in Will's neck bulged over his stiff collar. He stepped back into the room, flustered by the constant anticipation of bellows from below.

He managed a half smile as he watched Mariah survey the room. "We'll have to wait to decide on colors." He took Mariah's hand and led her from the room. Neither he nor Mariah called the room a nursery and neither mentioned preparing the space for a baby.

The next room was smaller with only one window. For a family with three children, a fine room for the child of the opposite sex. "This can be my sewing room," exclaimed Mariah whose excitement filled the silent void. At last I can have plenty of space to do my work."

"And just think. You won't have to do work for anyone else. Just for us."

Mariah's eyes widened. She turned to Will who was startled by her expression. "What do you mean?" said Mariah sharply. " I can't give up my business."

"Look, Mariah, you've been pushing yourself hard, working long hours on top of keeping up our place and looking after me. Don't you think maybe…?"

"No. That's not the reason. I'm not overtired. I haven't had a sick day in months."

Will moved closer to her and held out his hand. "None of the ladies on Wakefield Street takes in sewing," he said with a dismissive air.

"Then maybe we don't belong on Wakefield Street," Mariah responded with a hurt expression.

"I'm sorry, Mariah. I didn't mean it as an insult."

"Pretty soon I'll be making enough to open a shop and hire a helper."

Will looked skeptical.

"I have no intentions of being a 'kept wife'," she barked. Will stared. "Where are you getting such ideas?" he said.

"I do a lot of reading, you know," Mariah said. "There are some women writers these days that say it's time women had more voice in…"

"I just want my wife to take her place in society, the place she deserves." Will's soft words served only to add fuel to Mariah's fire.

"My place. Yes, I've heard about my place in society enough before," sputtered Mariah.

"It'll be *our* place I'm thinking about, Mariah," and this is it," said Will with more hurt than anger at his wife's reaction to the surprise that was turning sour. "I never thought I was taking you into confinement."

"Oh, God, Will, I'm sorry. Of course, it's a wonderful house, I know, but it isn't going to be my whole life."

Mariah turned to the darkening window where she could see the pained reflection of Will's face. "So do you think of my business as a social embarrassment?" She didn't wait for an answer, and changed her tone. "I'm making good money," she said with a coy smile and a hand pressed to his chest.

Will answered softly, fearing another storm. "But that would take you out of the house and then who'd…"

"No, I don't need a shop, not when the children are little. I know it seems too much to imagine, but I can manage the house and manage my business. And just think; all of the matrons of Rochester will get to see our new house." Mariah turned back to Will and he took her hands. Mariah smiled with hope, trying to convince herself with her enthusiasm and energy directed at her confused husband. Will saw signs that her mental wheels were spinning again.

*Should I tell Will now?*

Will had gotten used to seeing signs in Mariah's eyes—a turning inward, a darting, searching movement—that her mind was churning with new fodder comparing life as it was to life as it should be. There it was again—the inward eye.

"I'm sorry. I didn't realize how much it meant to you," Will said.

"It?" critiqued Mariah with brows pulling together.

"The business thing, bringing in money on your own."

"It's not the money itself. Even if I were rich, I'd want to know I could do something the world really valued, something that not every woman—or man—could do. Laundry and dishes, scrubbing floors, hanging drapes—anyone can do those things."

"Some do 'em a lot better than others," Will added.

"True. Here's an epitaph for you," said Mariah as she moved her hands over the face of an imaginary slab of marble. 'Here lies Eve, wife of Adam. Good at cooking, spinning and dusting.'"

Will laughed. "All right, all right. I get your point, but I know the pride you put into those everyday things no matter what you say."

Mariah's face softened. Her eyes turned downward, gazing at their hands intertwined.

"You want a nice home and kids, now admit it. Sure, woman's work can be menial. So is men's. But your work can be an art. And don't tell me you don't feel that way. Ladies pay well for your fine stitching."

Mariah could not stop a subtle smile of pride from lightening her face.

"Eventually, you'll have lots more business when these rooms fill up." Will struggled to believe his own hopeful words that things would change, that a baby, or two or more, would eventually come. Even the excitement of a new house could not offset the tension building in their relationship around the empty cradle. Colleagues at work, friends and acquaintances of their age were all celebrating one child after another. Middle class couples boasted families of six or more children, and wives were supervisors of servants and tradesmen as well as cooks, decorators, moral educators, spiritual guides and mistresses of good taste in polite society. It was accepted by proper Victorians that women were in charge of the home, a business in itself. In the absence of family, Mariah could not allow her hands to be idle even if polite society could not conceive of another role for respectable women but that of wife and mother.

Mariah could not hold her secret a moment longer. "Will, I promise I won't work too hard. I'll have to be especially careful not to be lifting heavy things." Her eyes gave away the implication of her words.

Will's eyes lighted up as he saw Mariah's smile and her eyes shine with moisture. "Are you sure?"

Mariah looked down. "No, not absolutely, but I missed my period last month and I'm two weeks overdue now."

"Thank God," he said. He paced in the master bedroom, breathing deeply, saying "wow" quietly to himself. Will's eyes glistened as he embraced Mariah. "I'm so happy."

"Two more weeks and I'll be sure," she added with a cautionary note.

"Well, are you happy with what you see?" shouted the stout old realtor as he reached the landing on his slow ascent to the second floor. "Can't you imagine a blissful life within these walls?" added Cecil Harvey.

Mariah and Will broke from their tight embrace. He handed Mariah his handkerchief as his own eyes shone wet in the gaslight of the hall. "No need coming up, Mr. Harvey. "We'll be right down," Will called.

"And as to the house…" called Cecil Harvey.

Will stalled and looked to Mariah who nodded and smiled as she daubed her eyes. "The house is just fine. We'll give you a deposit tomorrow."

As Will and Mariah rode slowly down Wakefield Street from one circle of lamplight to the next, they allowed themselves to speculate about the baby and the nursery. They tested the sound of names as hope quickly grew into certainty.

The night of happy dreams followed lovemaking so uninhibited and carefree that it fired the passionate pride of potency in them both. Mariah lay back and watched moonlight and shadows dance on the ceiling as her mind raced through verses that gave voice to her deepest emotions.

All through the night, your glorious eyes
Were gazing down in mine,
And with a full heart's thankful sighs
I blessed that watch divine!
*A son or a daughter, I wish I knew, but what does it matter? Chestnut*

*hair and green eyes or dark features like me—the baby's forming right now like a pearl in a dark shell. I hope we see each other in that little face.*

Mariah forgot about the clash between business and family, between her independent goals and her duty as wife and mother. Somehow that would be resolved. It had to be resolved for after all, a woman was meant to be a mother, and that duty, that bond, that love was the meaning of her life. But surely a woman's life was meant to be enriched by so much else. Didn't love overcome barriers of space and time itself like gold to airy thinness beat? And didn't love mean that husbands and wives helped one another to grow to be the best that God intended? There had to be a way to reconcile the demands of motherhood and a woman's aspirations.

Will woke to find the curtains still drawn and the other side of the bed empty. He could hear the purr of the Singer treadle. Mariah was already sewing. He came up behind her and stroked her neck. The treadle stopped and the room grew silent.

"I was hoping you might come back to bed for a little while," whispered Will with a kiss to her neck. Mariah turned and put her hand on his.

"You've been crying. What's the matter?"

Mariah let Will take her into his arms. "My period started this morning."

Will held her and let her cry. After she grew still, he said softly, "Maybe it's time for you to see a doctor."

Mariah felt accused. Had her desire for a role other than wife and mother brought on this punishment? Was that what Will was implying? She broke free of Will's embrace in sudden agitation. "Maybe it's not me. Did you ever think of that? Maybe it's you." Mariah had never seen a look of such pain and horror on Will's face, and she immediately felt shame and remorse. She went to him and wrapped her arms around him. "Oh, Will, I shouldn't have said such a thing. Please forgive me."

"You might be right," said Will coldly.

"No, no. We know there's nothing wrong. How could there be? I'm just feeling such disappointment, I just don't know…"

"We were so happy last night. We can't let this ruin it. You're not even twenty," said Will who seemed to be trying to convince himself as well as Mariah that her barren years would soon end. "There's plenty of time." Will said the right words, but there was a distance in his eyes, a withdrawal that alarmed Mariah. She had wounded him deeply and it would take time for him to heal.

Sun reached into the corner of the dining room as Mariah cleared breakfast dishes. There was a new house to furnish and decorate, a hope for new beginnings. Mariah walked Will to the door and handed him his overnight bag. "I'll start planning draperies for the house," she said with a wan smile. Will nodded and leaned down for a kiss.

"That house will be a happy place, I just know," Will added with a smile as unconvincing as his words.

Mariah thought of her parents and remembered the constant drone of the river in the fall, a voice reminding them of life slowing down, of close quarters and hours around the woodstove. How much she missed the noise of children. She thought of her brother Frederick starting into a growth spurt, and her little sister Florence at her mother's elbow learning to cook, and her little brother Amos—anxious to help his dad—struggling to lift a pail of milk. Mariah remembered the voices of Cold River, of seasons and rhythms of nature and of the fulfillment of essential work. Had she turned from her intended role and violated something sacred in the scheme of things? Was God denying her a child because of her rebellious spirit? Mariah was haunted by Will's crestfallen face and by words of poets that spoke of the happiness of submission to what is meant to be.

> Come to me, O ye children
> And whisper in my ear
> What the birds and the winds are singing
> In your sunny atmosphere.
> For what are all our contrivings,
> And the wisdom of our books,
> When compared with a child's caresses
> And the gladness of his looks?

"Will, I'm so sorry," she said as she embraced him and sent him off to another day of work. The door closed and the house grew grimly silent. Mariah filled the lifeless air with the hum and whir of her sewing machine.

# CHAPTER 10

## *Peace Like a River*

"Come home as soon as you can. Frederick is weakening." The regular letter from Mariah's mother dropped through the slot a day earlier than usual, and for the first time in months she did not ask if there was "news." *Please stop asking me if there is news. When the day comes, I will be bursting to tell the whole world.* There were still no signs— nearly two more barren years had passed—and Mariah and Will were frustrated that their lovemaking hadn't produced fruit. But Mariah couldn't think about that right now. Frederick was asking for his sister, and it threw Mariah into a panic to think that his illness had taken a turn for the worst. Will was traveling south of Boston seeking to extend Wallace's market to Hartford, so Mariah would have to take the train to West Ossipee alone.

Will and she had nearly finished furnishing the house on Wakefield Street, and although it hurt Will's pride, Mariah's sewing business paid for much of the finery. The house was rich with color and appointed with taste, but one upstairs room remained dark with the door closed. That dark place took some of the joy and adventure out of their lovemaking; they talked of work and acquisitions and travel, the life they had sought and the life they had achieved.

The letter from home came at an especially bad time. It was postmarked January 5, 1887, two days earlier. Mariah was under the weather—a stomachache and cramps, and a canker sore in her mouth, to add to her discomfort. There was hope in her discomfort, though; she had missed her monthly again. Her doctor could find no reason why she could not conceive and had urged patience and avoidance of undue stress. Patience, unlike stress, was in short supply. Neither she nor Will had any further discussion about any possible male medical problem. Mariah assured him that she never had any such thoughts. *There can't be a problem, not that kind of problem, with a man made like him. I know Will is all right. I feel it, and I see it in his eyes when we finish making love. Please God, let it happen this time. What's wrong with me?*

On Main Street mill workers picketed against the 48-hour workweek despite the biting wind. Mariah walked, head down, face shrouded in a fur-trimmed cape, a neighborhood boy following with her bags. Her traveling attire, a rich taffeta in a subdued red and blue plaid, drew the attention of working women. "Remember us, missus, that makes your finery!" one wind-tussled lass shouted at her.

"I make my own finery," replied Mariah curtly. She stopped long enough to stare down one of the tarts that dared to suggest that she lived off the suffering of others. Handmade signs flapped in the gusty December winds. "A living wage, the eight-hour day. More holidays. No laborers under fifteen." Mariah looked at the pickets and snarled.

"There are plenty of days I work more than eight hours," she said to another unkempt young woman with missing teeth and foul breath. *These hands know what work is, and I don't complain. You're lucky to have jobs and children. Yes, God knows I can handle work better than most of you gutter snipes, so why do you deserve to be mothers and I don't?* Mariah pulled her hood closer to shield her face from envious eyes and stinging sleet.

Laboring men congregated farther down the street, closer to the gates of the Norway Plains Woolen Factory. Irish stood with Irish, French Canadians with French Canadians. Nearby Protestants tried handing them tracts aimed at converting them from their papist apostasy, but they were spurned or threatened. The Women's Christian Temperance Union also appealed to the ragtag workers to warn them that "demon rum" was their real enemy.

Police were out in force with nightsticks at the ready. The Republican town fathers feared the anger and power of the idle working class as discontent and liquor moved them to violence. They also feared the lines at the ballot box as workers reached out for the dollar they received from precinct captains who delivered guaranteed blocks of votes.

Unions across the nation were growing; some of their leaders were gaining national reputations. But even the president of the American Federation of Labor admitted that overworked laborers often turned to alcohol. "The general reduction of the hours of labor to eight per day would reach further than any other reformatory measure…The man who works longest is the first to be thrown out on the sidewalk because his recreation is generally drink."

Capitalists and the management classes could depend on the fear of civil unrest, drunkenness and the vices of growing urban life to attract the votes of the Yankee majority—upper class or poor farmers—to check the power of labor as they sought to organize.

Mariah did not hear the word "strike" from any of the picketers. Anyone who stirred the laboring hordes to walk away from their machines would find it hard to get a job in textiles, shoes, or any other mill. The owners were in bitter competition, but they joined forces to fight unionism, socialism, and other political plagues brought to America's shores from foreign places. An article in the local paper quoting the U.S. labor commissioner, Carroll Wright, stirred much anger among the union leadership.

"Better morals, better sanitary conditions, better health, better wages, these are the practical results of the factory system…The factory brings progress and intelligence…the lyceum, the concert, and even literary institutions. Industry and poverty are not handmaidens, and as poverty is lessened, good morals thrive." Mariah had always been taught that hard work built moral fiber. While others trusted in collective action, social justice, or a merciful God, Mariah relied on sheer individual determination.

"Out of my way!" Mariah shouted at a rowdy group of picketers whose broken line blocked the sidewalk on Hanson Street.

"Oh, make way, girls, for a lady of leisure!" laughed one gap-toothed girl.

Mariah surprised herself in not blistering the girl with a sharp retort. She had to admit to herself that their work was vital while hers was trivial. No one, not even Will, really depended on Mariah's work for survival. Her labors merely embellished society ladies and their homes and provided luxuries for Will and her. The mill workers were coarse and dirty, but their labor mattered, and Mariah envied them in a way they could never understand. They had mouths to feed; yes, Mariah had a house on Wakefield Street and a husband making good money, but an empty cradle stood motionless in a darkened room.

After a silent face down, the line of picketers parted and Mariah moved on toward the station. Mariah kept a middle ground between haranguers as she made her way down Hanson Street followed by the nervous porter who lugged her bags. Her insides recoiled with what she hoped was morning sickness as the train pulled out of the station, sad to be separated from Will at such a time, but happy to be going home—home—where she was needed.

Mariah held Frederick's hand as he opened his eyes. The hair on his cheeks had thickened, and when he spoke her name, it was a full register lower than his boyhood voice. His breath wheezed in and out. His eyes were sunken, but glittered with brightness. "Hello, Mariah," he whispered.

"Frederick, and why are you in bed at this time of the morning?" she joked. "You know how much needs to be done out in the barn. I know it's bitter cold; snow's coming on, but you're a man now. Sixteen, and look at the hair on your face."

Golden down, thick at sideburns and the upper lip, golden as corn silk, and eyes, ice blue like angels from the realms of glory. God, don't take him from us now. Not now, dear God, he's only just becoming a man.

"You know, Frederick, I hope you didn't think I came all the way here from Rochester on the train just to see you lying down on the job. There's a lot's gotta be done around here. If you'd get up out of that warm bed, you'd see. Daddy needs another man to help out, don't you know?" Frederick managed a weak smile. Mariah embraced him and smothered the sadness within that threatened to break into tears.

"I'm going to get a basin of warm water and a razor because you need a shave. Yes, you do. Just feel your face. Why, your hand hardly came off the blanket. Let me help you. There, now. See. You need a shave."

Frederick's skin looked waxen, almost transparent, after weeks of spasms, shortness of breath and little food. All of the remedies for consumption had been tried except escape to the south of France, the favored treatment for the rich and famous like the poet Elizabeth Barrett Browning.

*Oh, God, Frederick, don't let your eyes close. Talk to me. I want you to live to know what it's like to love and be loved. Yes, you devil. I know how curious you've been about girls and such. There are girls that would love to give you kisses, if only you were well. It would embarrass you to say it, but it's true. You're handsome like Daddy, but fair like Mother.*

"Tired? Yes, I know, but I'm not going to let you sleep. Frederick, listen to me. Don't let your eyes close. Fight to stay awake." Mariah stroked his head and face and looked into his eyes, smiling. *I want you to know what life's all about. You're going to be a man. It's happening right now. Don't let this sickness take it away from you. You're going to have a taste of the world. I just won't let it be otherwise.* "Yes, Mr. Frederick Brandon, you've got a beard started. By tomorrow night you'll rub your face and you'll feel some stubble."

"I'm drying your face and neck, Freddy, and I'll button up your nightshirt. You don't have to be embarrassed. I'm your sister, and I've seen a man before. Yes, Will has hair on his chest. It's black. Chestnut hair on his head, but his body hair is black. You're all golden haired, but I can see that it's coming in thicker now."

"What do you want to do when you're all grown up? I can't hear you, Frederick. Frederick, speak up. Don't close your eyes."

The wind rattled the windows, and Frederick's hands felt like ice although his head felt warm with a fever. Mariah asked her father to use a knife to push rags into the cracks to silence the rattling and keep out the drafts. She would sleep at Frederick's side to get him through the night in peace.

Sarah brought a bowl of broth that cooled quickly after a few spoonfuls. Florence and little Moze began to whimper when they saw their brother's feeble attempt to eat. "I know you're a big boy and a big girl," said Mariah in a gentle voice, "but Frederick and I have to talk about some adult things now, so you can see your brother in the morning." Amos ushered the little ones out of the room.

Mariah looked into her mother's face. Neither spoke. Neither needed to. *Don't look at your son that way. It scares me.* "Mother, you've got to eat more, too. You're thin as a reed," Mariah said. "Can you leave me alone with Frederick?" said Mariah to her parents. "I haven't had a chance to talk to him in quite a while." Mother and daughter communicated with their eyes. *Mother, you look so frightened. Hold it together for his sake.*

Her mother had given up, and maybe now, even her father. Mariah couldn't let her brother go without a fight. Rising from the side of the bed, she motioned her parents out of the room and closed the door. "Tomorrow Freddy's going to take his breakfast at the table with the family."

Sarah looked at her daughter in disbelief. "Oh, Mariah, I don't…"

Mariah stared her mother down with hope. *Yes, by God, I mean it, Mother. Your son is going to be up and dressed tomorrow. I don't want to see fear and doubt in your eyes. You're the one who's always telling me I need to put my trust in the Lord. We must accept the Lord's will? Surely it's not God's will to take Freddy from us now.*

"Mother, why don't you go rest for a while?" Sarah nodded and carried Frederick's dishes downstairs. Amos beckoned Mariah down the hall and into the slanting light of the west window.

"Freddy was much stronger this summer," said Amos. "Now your mama thinks the Good Lord wants him home." Amos held Mariah's hands; he was almost overcome and could not look his determined daughter in the eye. "We've heard all the theories and we've tried all the cures—except for sending Freddy to Saranac Lake. There's a sanitarium there. A Doctor Trudeau. But they can only help when you still have some fightin' strength."

Mariah had read about the Brehmer-Dettweiler method. It advocated lots of exercise to stimulate breathing and blood flow, cool air, and lots of time outdoors. She had not heard whether or not the method was achieving success. "I don't think your mother could bring herself to send Freddy away," said Amos, slowly shaking his head. "And they only want patients that's just startin' the cough, not when they're spittin' up blood and thin as Freddy is."

"Is it expensive?" Mariah asked.

"No. They take patients for next to nothin', but they gotta have plenty of strength. If they got plenty a strength, they'll prob'ly get over consumption on their own," Amos answered. "Mariah, we put Freddy through everything the doctors suggested, and look where we are. "At the first of it, the doctor tapped on Freddy's chest to check his lungs. He gave him that antimony tartrate. That just made him sick to his stomach."

Amos went on to tell Mariah the whole series of treatments the doctor had inflicted on the frail boy. His voice quivered with the pain it brought him to be reminded of the litany of failed medicines. "We've given him cod liver oil every day, and for a while, it seemed to make him stronger. You were here when we gave him digitalis. You remember how that agitated him, and then he fell into a worse weakness."

Amos looked into vacant space as though he were trying to conjure up an angel of mercy as an answer to their fervent prayers. "We put the boy through so much. He didn't want to be sent off to a sanitarium." He closed his eyes and hung his head. Mariah wrapped her arms around him.

In the evening, after Frederick fell off to sleep, Mariah and Amos joined Sarah in the parlor. Sarah sat on the sofa, her eyes closed and her head bowed. She hummed a family refrain.

"There'll be no dark valley when Jesus comes, there'll be no dark valley when Jesus comes, there'll be no dark valley when Jesus comes to gather His loved ones home."

Sarah opened her eyes slowly and looked down into her open palms, her fingers interlaced. Amos watched her in silence, breathing shallowly, unable to move. His wife's prayers had always been the impetus to action, a confirmation of her empowerment to grapple with just about anything she needed to accomplish. But in the last few days, Sarah's prayers stilled her hope more than steeled her resolve. For Mariah, her mother's stillness was unsettling. "Mama, isn't faith all about not giving up?" she said with a soft touch and a gentle voice.

"I'm not giving up," replied Sarah with a trembling sharpness in her voice. "Faith isn't about what I can do. If the Lord called me to spill my blood for Freddy—or for any one of you—you know I'd do it," she cried. "The Lord's calling me to accept. Don't make it even harder for me, please." The edge in her voice did not invite discussion.

Through the night, with a lamp burning dimly, Mariah slept fitfully in a chair bundled in blankets with a pillow against the wall. Frederick lay still, his nearly imperceptible breaths accompanied by occasional shudders. Except during those spasms, his face was serene.

Wind buffeted the house, searching for crannies to penetrate. Frederick's temperature spiked in the evening, falling gradually as the temperature in the room dropped; Mariah put her brother's cold hands under the blankets. His knuckles were swollen like an arthritic old man's, a sign that consumption was in its advanced stages. She tiptoed in stocking feet downstairs to the smoldering stove. Opening the draft and turning the damper upright, she lifted the lid in stealthy slow motion to avoid waking people with iron clattering. She deposited oak logs on pine kindling until the glow illuminated the kitchen, crackling robustly. Mariah stared into the fire, comforted by its power to banish cold, darkness and the nocturnal vapors of contagion. Mariah had learned to love the night, but this night she was wide-eyed with anger, and the specter of the Grim Reaper that lurked in the corners beyond the dim moonlight. What had Frederick ever done that he deserved this?

*The Lord shall smite thee with consumption and with a fever, and with an inflammation… and they shall pursue thee until thou perish.* Where was the Lord who mourned the fall of a sparrow?

Mariah watched the shadows dance on the ceiling and studied the flames imagining them to be signs from God; answers to her own pained queries about benevolent design or heartless randomness. Was suffering punishment for sin, like the demon-possessed man whose dark spirits Jesus sent into a herd of pigs, or did disaster befall us like victims of stray bullets? Jesus said, "The rain falls on the just and the unjust." If we fight back, are we defying the will of God? Mariah returned the lid to its place, and the shadows vanished. She lighted her way back to the cold upper room with a candle.

The sun rose with the promise of a golden day. Penetrating the cold air and the wavy glass panes, the morning rays warmed the foot of the bed. Frederick pulled himself up by gripping the quilt tucked firmly under the foot of the mattress. For the first time since his big sister arrived, he agreed to go downstairs. Mariah rose up from her chair in the corner with a start, the blankets falling in an avalanche at her feet. She went to the door and called to her father with a voice filled with joy and determination. "Daddy, can you help Frederick dress? He's going to join us at the table." Her parents, still in nightcaps, bolted up the stairs and into the room like Martha and Mary into Lazarus' tomb.

Frederick had slept fitfully if at all for the last several weeks, and the pain in his intestines had wrung him to the point of exhaustion. Months before, raised red sores covered his legs. A night of painless sleep, and a smile in the morning, no matter that it was a weak smile, was a miracle. The hope Sarah had nearly abandoned to night specters flooded back. She embraced Frederick regardless of the danger of contagion.

For three days bright sun warmed the house, and the winds stilled. The new-fallen snow sparkled in blue-white purity on hanging limbs. Mariah tried to ignore the rash, her canker, and the tender sore inside her. She had never talked to anyone about intimate matters except Will. Her symptoms, she wanted to believe, were harbingers of new life stirring within her. She had read that women have many different symptoms when they're first with child, but Mariah had no experience with pregnancy, and her four barren years made her reluctant to ask.

Mariah felt miserable, but today was a day to celebrate. Frederick's improvement, even though he could not walk unaided to the table, was enough encouragement to dispel any concerns for herself. Her parents noticed her wan complexion, pained movements and poor appetite, but it seemed only natural after several days and nights as a stalwart guardian of her brother's revival.

The family was gathered around the table once again in the warmth of the kitchen. They held hands and transmitted hope and love in an unbroken circle. The children talked about school and sledding, Amos regaled the family with the story of his struggles with a pregnant and irritable cow, and Sarah responded with laughter and smiles that the family had not heard or seen in weeks.

In the course of an hour the sun rose beyond the window and the direct light reached only Frederick's hands that lay on the warmth of the table. Amos lifted his shuddering body and carried him back to his bed. Before they turned to go up the stairs, Frederick faced Mariah, and with a faint smile said, "Thank you."

After he was tucked away, Amos went to the woodshed. Mariah followed. "You've given him a few good days," said Amos. "But look what it's taken out of you. Go back in the house and leave this to me," he insisted.

"I need the fresh air. I think I'll take a little walk," said Mariah.

"The water pouring over the rocks has formed domes of ice," responded Amos. "Why don't you go down and take a look?"

Mariah walked through the snow to the edge of the river to see the formation of ice that grew thick and tall in the depths of winter. The flowing water sounded through the hollows as it cascaded over rocks and splashed behind dams of translucent ice. Except for an occasional whispering of wind through the pines, the sound of the ice-bound water was the only voice of nature in the cold and barren scene. As it had so many times in the past, Cold River told her that life and movement and energy thrived even when death itself seemed to reign over the world.

Plodding through the snow along the riverbank, she got to the pothole where Cold River built the tallest blue-green organ pipes of ice. The waters broke devilishly from under the confines of pure, frozen white, mocking the stillness that ruled the land with water music. The sounds from icy pipes recalled childhood laughter, excited screams, and violent splashing of summer when voices of Paisleys, Weeds, Brandons and Taylors echoed from the walls of the pothole. Behind closed lids Mariah could see Frederick standing on the ledge for his first leap at age eight, a chorus of older children treading water in a circle, forming a bull's eye and calling "Jump! Jump!" with voices ranging from soprano to baritone. Frederick's feet pierced the water like an arrow, the water closing over him in a tiny circle.

Mariah opened her eyes, squinting as she surveyed the glittering landscape. Suddenly a distant sound turned Mariah's thoughts from the river. She heard sleigh bells in the distance and hoped that it was Will coming from the train station in a rented rig. Mariah smiled at the thought of Will's playfulness, exciting, childlike tickling and romping that heated to a passion in tantalizing rounds. Would that sleigh ever come, or was it some neighbor headed home from Sandwich?

Mariah saw the sleigh making the great sweep on the Tamworth Road as it flattened from the slope of Juneau Hill. It was Will indeed, and he knew it was Mariah high on the rocky perch near the river. He stood up and waved, calling, "Mariah! Mariah!" His strong baritone voice carried a quarter mile over the sparkling white fields.

With what little energy that remained in her, Mariah ran and walked and ran to the point where the Tamworth Road passed Brandon Loop.

"Will!" she yelled, but she was so weary that she could only find a stump to settle on and wait for him to come the rest of the way.

Will jumped from the sleigh. "Mariah, are you ill?" he asked when he saw her poor color and exhausted eyes.

"I'm just worn out."

"Caring for Freddy—and how is he?"

"He sat with us at the table for breakfast," she said with the look of determined hope Will had seen in her eyes so many times before. She hugged Will and held on. "A little better the last few days." They rode slowly to the house as Mariah told him of her week.

"Is he afraid?"

"No. He's beyond fear, and I know that's good, but it seemed that everyone is giving up. I got him talking about the future, his dreams, and his wishes. In his stronger moments, he was even talking about being a lawyer. Can you imagine Freddy as a lawyer? I never realized he had that interest."

Will smiled weakly in response. He started to speak, but instead offered his hand to help Mariah into the sleigh.

"All right. I know what consumption is like. But he sat with us for breakfast. Can you imagine?" She saw in Will's face that her determination could not dispel his doubt. They glided over the pristine field of snow with no sound by the jingling of bells.

As they walked to the front door, Will took a deep breath and blew it out again. He stopped Mariah before she opened the door. "You're coming home today and you're going to see a doctor right away. I'm really worried about you. It won't do any good for Freddy to have you in a sickbed, too."

Mariah looked down and nodded in acquiescence.

Just outside the front door the wind lifted the powder-fine snow into drifts that trailed wispy veils over the white mantle. Mariah glanced at the tiny rabbit tracks as they filled and vanished, the ghostly landscape quickly erased signs of life. Nothing living makes its mark on the world for very long. She pushed the thought out of her mind like an unwelcome guest. The wind was from the west; the day would be cold but fair.

Will opened the door. No one was in the kitchen. The house was silent. "Mama? Papa?" Mariah called. A moment later they heard a door open upstairs. Her father descended a few steps until his eyes met Mariah's. Amos bowed his head and shook it slowly from side to side.

Mariah broke into tears on Will's shoulder.

# CHAPTER 11

## *Distant Cousins*

It was March and the merciful sun shone on longer days. 1887 had begun in grief; the Brandon family longed for hope and new life that comes with spring. Mariah had written with the long awaited news. She was sure she had to be pregnant. Yes, yes, she would go to the doctor again. She had missed another monthly and after another ten days, she felt at last that there could be no other explanation for her symptoms. The gloom of January was behind them. Surely the signs this time signaled that a baby was on the way. This time it just had to be.

"Mariah's saying it's morning sickness, but I've heard that before. And to think that I expected that son-in-law of ours to give us a coach load of grandchildren." Sarah vented her frustration on paper to her sister-in-law Bertha in far off Iowa.

"Sarah, think how they are feeling," chided Bertha through the scratchings of her steel pen point. Bertha had a soft spot for her niece's handsome husband, a young man she had never seen except in studio photographs. "You've never liked him and you've never trusted him. Somehow you're blaming him for not having children. I hope to God the visit to the doctor next week changes all of that."

It was true that Sarah blamed Will; she had to admit that. There were no specific signs to point to that Will was not the upstanding gentleman and devoted husband. Still, there was something wrong, something missing. Mariah was still very much in love with him, but she wasn't the happy young woman who left Sandwich Notch a few years before. Maybe it was all about the empty cradle. Maybe the doctor's visit would bring an end to all of the tension.

Although Sarah and Bertha had not laid eyes on one another for decades, and they were not blood relations, their monthly letters cemented a bond that linked not only two women, but also two families. Each month they nurtured a vicarious love between Iowa and New Hampshire cousins as they read letters at dinner and sometimes had the pleasure of passing photographs, and, oh, didn't both families long to feel the fine threads of hair from little babies too far away to ever hold.

For years their letters carried their "two cents' worth" over rutted roads, down shimmering rails, and onto mail cars armed with marshals against armed robbers and flaming arrows of whooping Indians. The letters wound westward through the Adirondacks, past the hellish Bessemer steel furnaces and blackened skies of the industrial East, and across the Midwest's flat fields of corn. For the first twenty years answering mail came eastward from a steel hook on a trackside pole where a canvas bag stenciled with "Central City" was snatched by a passing train that scarcely slowed, never mind stopped for that little town west of nowhere with not enough people for a platform.

"Dear Sarah, as soon as you hear, you let me know and I'll start knitting a white blanket as warm as an August afternoon."

The letters started as private exchanges between the two women, but as their children grew, interest developed in letters, so as they read aloud at the table, Sarah and Bertha edited spontaneously with eyes flashing and brows hovering over candid comments not meant for others' eyes or ears. Bertha and Sarah found themselves becoming inhibited in what they could share.

Finally Bertha found a way for the "Sisters in Spirit" to share their private thoughts. One month Bertha included a separate sheet of paper containing the most candid thoughts that could be removed from the envelope before dinner. The secret correspondence began late in

96

1887 when Bertha decided that she and Jim needed separate bedrooms. Bertha's days of childbearing had come to an end years ago, yet Jim's desire continued unabated. She told Sarah that she had decided on separate bedrooms because God made sex for procreation, and that duty was over, so Jim and she needed to "show their tenderness differently." Sarah allowed that couples might differ on what God intended in his design of man and woman. Amos and she still shared the same bed, and that wasn't going to change. Bertha and Sarah resolved their different views of intimacy in the Xed pages, and secreted them into the fire.

One of the coded pages was blunt about Bertha's suspicions about George's wife Miriam. "She's a better field hand than a wife. There's something odd about her. She's a cold one. I've paid close attention, and I'm telling you, I don't think much is going on after dark that ought to be with young folks like them."

"Oh, my," sighed Sarah as she opened the stove lid and consigned the Xed page to the flames.

Sarah remembered George as a pitiful little six-year-old sitting up on the high seat of a Conestoga wagon trying to act brave as Bertha and her new husband headed to the West. He had grown into a lanky, wiry man with abundant opportunity for work, but little opportunity for female companionship. His mother told him that Iowa dirt didn't yield diamonds, and he better accept what the Good Lord provided him. Miriam, a neighbor's only daughter, was a blessing in furrows and barn, but no comfort when the sun finally sank into Nebraska and the time came for a little tenderness. Bertha kept hoping for the day when she could write happy news that the Taylor legendary fecundity had evidenced itself in the next generation, but that day had not come in fifteen years of marriage for her eldest son.

"You've been waiting for five years. I've been waiting for fifteen," Bertha wrote to Sarah. "I'll confess to being a little envious if the Good Lord blesses you with a grandchild before me." Bertha marked the page with an X. "I can hardly wait for your next letter."

Bertha had never laid eyes on Mariah, and didn't expect to, nor did she ever expect to meet her new husband, but Sarah and Amos had sent photographs of the wedding couple, and Bertha liked what she saw. The page was coded. "She's a beauty, and he's a real looker," she wrote to Sarah, "and just because he has a way with women, I wouldn't assume the worst. We all like to dream of a handsome prince, so no one should be surprised to find out that a prince knows how to dance."

"Dance?" wrote Sarah under the circled X when she read Bertha's words. "You can call it dancing if you want, but it's not dancing that I'm worried about it and you know it."

"Why were you shocked to see him with his shirt off helping Amos load hay?" Bertha wrote the summer after the wedding. "What is it for a man to work bare-chested when it's hot? It's easier to wash a body than to wash a shirt." *And besides, if I was there, I would a took a good look myself.* "Thank your stars that the man comes to help and that he has such a good job to boot. You'll never have to worry about your daughter with a man like that to comfort her." But Sarah spent a good deal of time worrying about her daughter. No one heard her complaints except Amos in bed and Bertha in the Xed pages.

The monthly letters were a lifeline in both directions. News of plantings, blights, storms and harvests; news of milk cows, timber lots, cash crops and new rail lines; but no news from the East or from the West that first cousin seed had sprouted. The latest letter about the upcoming doctor's appointment set off more excitement around the Central City dinner table than any news in several years.

Cousin George was more subdued in his well wishing. Bertha could see it in his face. He envied his beautiful raven-haired cousin for her expected blessing, and he coveted her as an unreachable goal. "You're first cousins far removed," his mother told George with a sigh, wishing that Mariah was closer by land and further by blood.

George was frustrated and lonely, but he didn't know what to do. It wasn't Miriam's fault if she just didn't feel that way toward him. She was a good wife in other ways, but their lovemaking was rare and mechanical. Working under the hot sun, there were many days he thought he would cry or burst, so he worked harder and longer and let his body recover from the pain in undisturbed sleep.

There were times he thought of getting on the train for Des Moines or even Chicago where you could at least buy some love-making and tenderness for a night, but he could never bring himself to do something so shameful. At times he wondered what life would have been like for him if he had stayed in Sandwich, New Hampshire, but the only certain satisfaction he had ever found in life was the rich soil of Iowa that blessed his labors tenfold. And so, he rose before dawn, worked the land elbow to elbow with wife and family, and only occasionally let his imagination dive into the beckoning eyes of beautiful women like his distant first cousin.

The week passed slowly with rains holding up planting. George had errands in town and came home in the midst of a snow burst. Bertha met him at the front gate where a gust of wind laden with gritty, skin-stinging snow nearly tore the letter from her hand. Bertha left George waiting impatiently at the kitchen table. "Here, you look through the Sears Roebuck catalog. I'll be out in a minute." In what had become an unquestioned ritual with the Aunt Sarah letters, Bertha disappeared into the parlor like the chief rabbi entering the Holy of Holies.

Bertha closed the parlor door, her breath visible in the unheated room. She tore the letter open. Gusting snow pelted the wavy windowpanes like sand. The lace curtains rustled. A Currier and Ives print of storm clouds over the White Mountains of New Hampshire hung over the mantel. A clock shaped like the rounded New England foothills counted the seconds that added up to thirty-five years, thirty-five years since the clock was wrapped in a blanket and stowed in the mighty Conestoga wagon, its chimes clanging out the bone-rattling hours and weeks that brought Bertha and Jim to Ford Road, Central City, Iowa. Thirty-five years measured in windrows, bushel baskets, and board feet, in labor and births, sicknesses and celebrations, acres of corn, and inches of rain, and the tick-tocking, chiming, relentless passage of time.

The great parlor stove with its nickel trim still shiny from little use stood cold in the room as musty as a crypt. A small daguerreotype of herself, her first husband, her son George and daughter Jane reminded her of the torments of her young adulthood.

When she finished the Xed page, she felt faint and descended into a tufted chair. A wave of pity swept over her for her poor niece, Mariah. So Sarah had been right about Will all along. "My Lord, what will become of her?" she whispered to herself. She was only to tell the family part of the story. It would be Mariah's decision when to reveal the full and horrible truth.

# CHAPTER 12

## Mourning Sickness

Mariah picked at her dinner, too nauseous to show the excitement she felt. Will bubbled over with enough enthusiasm for both of them. "Just imagine this. When I get back from Boston in a couple of days, I get off the streetcar as usual, drop my bags inside the door, and instead of me asking you what's for dinner, I wait and you say…Come on, now. You say…"

"I'm going to have a baby," said Mariah with a weak smile.

"And then we dance around the parlor—not too fast because you'll have to take it easy. We talk about names and we go upstairs and open up that nursery. Now how does that sound?"

Mariah nodded slowly with her eyes closed.

"And after you greet me with the happy news, we go right over to Dodge's for a fine meal and celebrate!" Will lifted Mariah from her chair gently, holding her tight until she relaxed in his warmth.

"Let's hope that's the way it will be. I can put up with this sickness morning, noon and night if it 's the price I have to pay for a baby."

"I'm so sorry, Hon. If the world was fair, we'd both be paying the price," said Will with a gentle kiss.

Dr. Burt Andrews had his office over Willey's Laundry. Mariah saw him occasionally when she went to pick up Will's shirts, and once when she thought she was pregnant and had a miscarriage. Dr. Andrews was only a few years older than Will, a pleasant looking, thin fellow, as correct as a grammarian. His hair was precisely parted and slicked with a pomade to guard against ruffling in the wind. He always tipped his hat to the ladies with a gloved hand when he came down the stairs with his black leather bag for his afternoon house calls. His smile didn't show teeth, and his eyes didn't engage. Objective and professional, that was the role, but he still observed all the formal courtesies that made his patients feel comfortable.

Will had gone to him once for a scratched cornea when a coal cinder blew into his eye on the train platform. A patch and some soothing drops and two days' rest solved the problem. Will made a second visit a few months later and never told Mariah.

"Hysteria in women is one of the major causes of barrenness. That's been confirmed. Does she do a lot of reading other than of light novels?"

"She does like poetry, but she likes factual books even more than literature. You don't know my wife. If you did, you'd never say she was hysterical. A temper at times, yes, but she is the last woman I can imagine who'd lose control of herself. Nope, doctor, that couldn't be the problem."

"Well," continued the doctor scratching his chin, "make sure she isn't overworked or having too much to worry about."

"Her brother's death still gnaws at her. She was almost ruined her health trying to save him. We thought if he got through the winter, he would make it another year."

"Sorry to hear that. What was the cause?"

"Consumption."

"Did the family know about Saranac Lake?"

"The sanatorium?"

"Yes."

"Too late." They both shook their heads and sighed.

"My recommendation is this. Make sure she has quiet diversions. Projects around the house to distract her. Have her join a ladies' circle. Literature, church work, those kinds of things." The doctor paused and reddened. He avoided Will's eyes. "And don't force yourself on her—you know what I mean—when she says it's not a good time."

"Doc, I never have to force myself on her."

"I see. Well," said Doctor Andrews who visibly blushed. "If she isn't in a family way within the next three months, have her come in, and please accompany her, and I'll make sure to have a nurse here to assist me in the examination. There are things we can do nowadays."

Will left the office with a bit more hope. The doctor never asked him any questions about himself. There was no examination.

Over the three months after Will's secret visit to the doctor, their lovemaking was regular and ardent, but on a few occasions of late, he seemed to cause her some pain. Will prided himself on regularly giving pleasure and the sense of her pain disturbed him. More gaps of silence came between them; Will was even reluctant to go into the sewing room and having to confront the cradle buried in sewing projects.

When Mariah entered Dr. Andrews' office, she looked drawn with dark circles under her eyes. The doctor and his nurse worked to disguise their concern that such a lovely young woman of refinement seemed so wan, melancholic and fragile.

After examining Mariah, he left the room in silence. "He's probably consulting his book, Mrs. Dunfield," said the nurse. "He'll be back in a few minutes. Now don't you be anxious," she said unconvincingly.

*If I'm pregnant, why doesn't he just say so?* As Mariah completed dressing, she knocked on the connecting door where she could hear the doctor vigorously washing his hands. He came in drying his hands nervously; the news was not going to be good.

"Mrs. Dunfield, I'm sorry to say that you're not with child." Although Mariah tried to control herself, she could not stop the tears. Doctor Andrews only made matters worse with his clinical objectivity. "Please don't lose hope," he added quickly. "You might be able to have a child some day, but…"

"Might? Is that supposed to be good news, Doctor?" Mariah blurted out through her sobs.

"I'm very sorry, Mrs. Dunfield; this is not going to be easy for you."

"I should have my husband here with me," cried Mariah.

"Actually, I don't think that would help. In fact, it is probably a blessing for you that he is away at the moment."

The shock of the doctor's words brought a cessation of tears. Mariah stared into Dr. Andrews' face, wondering just how deep his descent into bad news was taking her.

"Did I have another miscarriage? It doesn't seem the same this time."

"No. It's not the same."

"Mrs. Dunfield, I can tell you're a very nice young lady, but I need to ask you some questions. I'm sorry. Some of them will have to be very personal."

"Yes?" Mariah's eyes darted back and forth between the doctor and the nurse. It was rare for Mariah to be afraid, but the doctor's words were a smoking fuse snaking its way around a dark corner. She felt so terribly alone. *Will, I need you with me.* The nurse studied Mariah's face, then reached and took her hand, somewhat to the consternation of the doctor who was afraid the personal touch might bring on a torrent of emotion.

"Now remember. I'm asking you this as your doctor. I need to know the answers to some questions so that I can do my best to make you well again."

Am I really sick? I've been a little uncomfortable, but what are you telling me? What have I got?

"Have you known any man other than your husband in an intimate way?"

Mariah was shocked and afraid. Her voice rose in a crescendo of indignation. "No. Never. I was a virgin on my wedding day. I've never even taken a second look at another man. I love my husband; I respect him. How could you …"

"I'm so sorry, Mrs. Dunfield. Then there is only one explanation."

"Explanation for what? For why I can't carry a child?" Tears welled in Mariah's eyes.

"No, not just that. The explanation for how your symptoms came about." The doctor finally broke the news. She was gravely ill, but the symptoms were minor in the first phase, but without treatment, they could be ruinous to her health in time. What was it? Why was Dr. Andrews being so indirect? Mariah felt herself descending into a well. She couldn't hear anything except a ringing in her head. The doctor's mouth was moving, but she could hardly hear a word. Then her chest felt the weight of a great stone pressing down.

When she recovered, her eyes smarted from the fumes of smelling salts, and the nurse was drying the perspiration on her face. Dr. Andrews was vigorously patting her wrist.

First come the chancres, usually on the genitals. Sometimes women don't notice them. Sometimes the sores appear on the lips like a cold sore. Then comes a rash, often on the soles of the feet and palms of the hands. It is all very contagious, but the early symptoms disappear after a short time and may never appear again.

But for some people the disease reappears. The old adage, "Blind lust blinds" expresses a medical fact. The disease can form corneal ulcers and destroy a person's sight. Lesions on the face can be terrible. Many of the victims end up with their noses completely destroyed. Often the disease ends in a terrible madness.

"Mrs. Dunfield, are you listening to me? I know this is a frightful shock, but we can help you, we really can. I'm supposed to report all cases to the county health officer. He could quarantine you, and your husband, too. Yes, your husband certainly has the disease, too. And there is no doubt how you caught this disease. But you're a woman of good repute. No need to quarantine you."

"So I got this disease from my husband," Mariah stated with anger breaking through the tears.

"Undoubtedly. I'm so sorry."

"And he got it…"

"Mrs. Dunfield, I'd rather not speculate…"

The immediate shock had passed, and Mariah sat erect with her head held high, a look of complete resolution on her face.

"I'll need to see him right away, Mrs. Dunfield. The disease is passed on by physical contact when there are these open sores."

Will's women. It was true. Mariah's mother had been right all along. Faces flashed before Mariah's inward eye. The actress on the train, the piano teacher. How many others had Will known? His romantic ways. So this is what it really was. His expert lovemaking—the result of much experience. *But he loves me. I know he does. How could he do this to me?*

"I won't be passing this on to anyone else, that is for sure."

"Of course not, Mrs. Dunfield. You're a respectable lady. This is not your fault."

"You said you could help me. What can be done?"

"In more than half the cases, people seem to recover on their own strengths, but that is taking a terrible gamble, and frankly, Mrs. Dunfield, it seems that your health is a bit run down, probably since the time you were nursing your brother."

"How did you know about that?"

Dr. Andrews was suddenly embarrassed. "Oh, dear. I'm so sorry. That is really a breach of confidentiality, but considering the circumstances, I will tell you. Your husband came to me a couple of weeks ago concerned about your inability to conceive and he expressed great concern over your well-being after the experience you endured with your brother."

Mariah could not stop the tears. *Yes, he does love me, but how could he have other women? How could he betray me? My God, what am I to do?*

"There, there. I am going to prescribe Van Swieten's liquor of mercury. It is too late to cauterize the chancre. Potassium iodide is somewhat efficacious, but we get the best results of all the treatments we currently have at our disposal with the mercury. But Mrs. Dunfield, you need to know that this is very hard on the body until the regimen is completed, and there's something else I need to warn you of."

"Yes?" Mariah tears had stopped, and her iron will began to appear again.

"It often results in sterility."

"At the moment, doctor, I can hardly imagine having anyone's child, least of all Will's."

In a rare break from his objectivity, Dr. Andrews took Mariah's hand and said, "Now, Mrs. Dunfield, I don't think you really mean that."

Mariah's eyes welled again.

At the beautiful bow-fronted drug store on the square where Mariah often came with Will to buy powders and perfumes, she handed the druggist the prescription unaware that "liquor of mercury" was associated with only one disease. The druggist was unused to taking such a prescription from a delicate gloved hand of a demure lady of fashion. His eyes widened. "Yes, Mrs. Dunfield."

After she left with the bottle, the druggist's wife turned the sign from open to closed and drew the shades. "So what's the doctor treating the lovely lady for?" she asked her white coated husband.

"Syphilis."

The shade flew up from her hand, flapping violently against the sash.

# CHAPTER 13

## Ill Repute

*E*xcept for the hissing sound of a single gaslight in the hall, the house on Wakefield Street was silent. Mariah took her first dose of Van Swieten's liquor of mercury and followed the thick, foul-tasting concoction with a peppermint candy. She took her place in a red velvet tufted rocker that she turned facing the bay window that looked onto the street. It was a new chair Will had recently bought her for nursing their first child, the child he expected to celebrate when he came through the door. Beside Mariah's special new chair rested two carpet-bags with essentials for travel. Her closets and bureaus were empty. Tucked in her purse was her one-way train ticket home, home to the place she had spurned in her pride.

It was a raw day. Yellow leaves spiraled downwards to the cobblestone street except when gusts gave them a short burst of vibrancy. Their color, a reminder of her golden wedding day, was soon lost in the brown and soggy mat of foliage that settled against the curbstones. Across the street, two of the neighbors' boys were rolling hoops still dressed in their school knickers and hose. Mariah checked her pendant watch. Ten more minutes. Her heart raced. Her stomach felt queasy.

The familiar clatter of hooves and the high tinkling sound of the bell announced that the streetcar had stopped to let off passengers. Will was home; he was expecting dramatic news. His joyful humming stopped when Mariah didn't meet him at the door.

"Sweetie, where are you?" Will called in surprise. Mariah rose from her chair, and as Will caught sight of her in the dim parlor, he saw her standing rigid and grim with bags at her feet. "What's this? What's happened?" he said in bewilderment. He walked quickly to her and reached out his arms.

Slap. Will recoiled like a small boy whose loving mother had suddenly turned on him in fury. He stepped back shaking his head slowly. "No, no, no," he cried out as though his whole world had come apart. Without Mariah spelling it out, Will knew. He knew that his sordid life on the road had caught up with him.

"So you understand that you haven't given me a *baby*, don't you?"

Will stared at Mariah, open-mouthed and rigid.

"Have you no idea what you *have* given me?" Mariah said with cold wrath.

Tears ran down his face. "No, no, no," he repeated as though his denial could erase the truth of his profligacy.

"So I don't have to tell you, do I?" she said with trembling fury. "So you just need to know *which* vile disease you've passed on to me from your ladies of the night."

"Oh, God, no." Will dropped to his knees before Mariah; his big shoulders rose and fell in a paroxysm of shame. He hung his head in the most abject sorrow Mariah had ever seen. His cries wrenched her and her own tears resumed, but she could not bring herself to touch him.

*Why do I feel sorry for you? Why do I still love you? You've bedded down with whores and now I'm pained by* your *suffering?*

The agony of Will's betrayal was as deep and final as the grave. Mariah felt alone, without comfort. Her parents would take her in, indeed, show compassion, but her mother had been right about Will. What would be worse? The disease or the shame? Or the loss of the great love dying in front of her.

After his cries subsided, Will looked up, begging for forgiveness he knew he did not deserve. He shook his head, apparently mystified at what drove him to a life in the shadows, revolted at the man he was on the road, the man he had successfully left behind time after time when he boarded the train for home—for home and the arms of a loving wife.

"Why? Why?" said Mariah even though no answer could satisfy her.

"I don't want anyone but you. The others, it's just a weakness. When I'm away I'm in another world. I just let myself get mired in it. I just couldn't stand it, you know, that you, that we… after years of waiting for something to happen, I mean. I know it's no excuse. I never touched another woman from the time we got married, not until…"

"Until what?" Mariah shouted.

"I thought there was something wrong; my fault maybe, I just…" He looked up and realized there was nothing he could say to excuse what he had done, not now, not in front of his afflicted wife. He had sated his animal appetites on poisoned flesh; even if an antidote could restore their infected bodies, nothing could undue the damage to Mariah's shattered heart.

"God, what have I done? I don't love those women. You're the one I love."

"Love? You satisfy your needs and you love the feeling; you go back for it more and more. That's what you love, isn't it?"

"That's not love. It's just a need. I've let it take control of me, I know. You're nothing like them, you're…"

"No, I can't keep you happy so you turn to whores?" Mariah slapped Will again.

"When I gave up hope of having a baby, only then. I, I…" Will's words trailed off.

"Is this self-pity? Are you turning this back on me?" The fire of Mariah's indignation rekindled and consumed the sympathy she began to feel for Will in his agony. "Because we haven't had children, you feel like a lesser man? Well maybe that is so. The great lover who turns ladies' heads with flashing green eyes. And that precious member of yours. Maybe that man of men you see in the mirror isn't such a potent specimen of virility after all!"

Will rose from his knees, his eyes narrowing, the muscles in his jaws tightening. "I know that I've done wrong, and I promise to you I'll stop, but don't…"

"Don't attack your masculinity? Is that so sacred? Am I to take the blame because I'm the wife and it is my duty to make you happy? I've been fed enough on duty. If I'm to blame, it's because I trusted you— even though my mother warned me."

The doorbell rang, then a second time with a furious spin. "That's the boy who's carrying my bags to the station. The train won't wait. I've made an appointment for you with Dr. Andrews." Mariah's voice was suddenly calm, almost tender. "You'll need to start treatment right away. You may have to tell your mother because I won't be around to take care of you if you get sick." Suddenly tears came again. *He'll be alone in this house, sick and alone.* Despite all of her efforts to be in control, to be hard on the man who had disgraced her and had even placed her life in danger, she could not stop herself from thinking about him suffering without her comfort. The doorbell rang again like an alarm.

Will swung the door open with a glare. "She'll be out in a moment," he shouted and slammed the door in the boy's face.

"I've sent all of my other things ahead—except the sewing machine. I won't be needing it for a while."

"Are you coming back? Can I come see you?"

"I don't know. I've got to get well first, if that is possible. I can't think straight right now."

Will approached her with arms outstretched and she fell into his embrace. They held one another in silence.

The door opened slowly. "Ma'am, I'm sorry to intrude, but you'll miss the train."

Will reached for his wallet. "You'll need some money."

"No. I emptied my savings account. I've earned quite a bit, you know. All for the baby," she said, her voice starting to tremble. "Now you go to the doctor. Ten o'clock tomorrow. Write and tell me what he says, but don't expect an answer. I don't know when I'll write." She passed by Will without touching him again, looking back briefly after descending the steps. "Goodbye, Will," she said softly. "I hope we both recover. That's about all I can hope for right now."

Will stood in the darkening doorway and watched until Mariah and her porter turned the corner at Hanson Street. He stood looking out at the darkening sky until he heard the shrill whistle of the five o'clock train.

# CHAPTER 14

## Idylls of Spring

*A* wet and dismal spring suddenly turned to a balmy June. In the months Mariah had been home on the banks of Cold River once again, her anger had dissolved into a profound sorrow, and sorrow devolved to shame.

The first few weeks into her secret treatments, she was greeted at the Free Baptist Church with warmth and compassion. It seemed only logical to people that a young wife would come home to her parents to convalesce from "women's problems," as it was explained. Mariah had had at least one miscarriage and problems conceiving. Neighbors thought her illness might be the hysteria doctors commonly found in women. She was apparently home for the rest cure—purges, bleedings, emetics as a precaution to cleanse her system—and rest, including protection of her mind from excess intellectual activity that was known to be harmful to the weaker sex.

The kinder folk made excuses for her and rejected the salacious gossip of the lowborn. Her husband wasn't with her—"Surely he has come to visit; has anyone seen him in town?"—because he had to earn a living, and when he was away, there would be no one at home to care for her.

The delicacy of the Notch's better class was a fragile dike against the surging current of vicious gossip. It hadn't taken long for Sandwich Notch to echo with gossip about "The City Lady," as some envious farm wives had taken to calling Mariah. *Oh, she left Sandwich as a common country girl, and returns a city lady, but where's her dashing, fast-talking husband? She's sick, but with what? There's things you pick up in the city you don't get out here in the country, isn't that right, girls?* Some of the Notch girls had begun to laugh at Mariah's humiliation, especially when suspicions were confirmed by the growing stream of gossip that came from Rochester. *Can you believe it? Yes, it's one of them social diseases, that's the word. Now how do you s'pose that happened?* Then the cruel laughter.

Why should farm wives give the benefit of the doubt to a young woman too good to mingle with her former peers? Word trickled, then poured into town, the warmth and compassion she had received in church and on the street became nods with quick, close-lipped smiles; many turned a cold shoulder. Society accepted that men had little control over their conjugal needs, and a wife who failed to satisfy her husband brought great woe into the marriage. This was established fact in manuals of advice to women from the best men of science in this age that looked to the dawn of the twentieth century with confidence in Victorian enlightenment.

The longer Mariah stayed in town secluded and secretive, the more imaginative the analysis of her circumstances became by feathered creatures that circled outside of church and store and train station.

"She's always been strong-willed, you know. Why her mother told me time and again how she ignored her advice."

"No one's gonna tell that girl what to do, even a husband, mind you. Yes, well we all knew that it would take quite a woman to keep a man like Will Dunfield content, if you know what I mean."

He's very ambitious, you know. Has a fine job. And don't you know that a man who's building a career that pays more than a thousand a year, he also wants to be building a family. And she's given him nothing but a string of barren years. A seed should o' sprouted by now." "Well, it all goes to show, you gotta know your place in God's scheme o'things, and if you don't, you're gonna pay the price."

"True, but she don't look none too contrite to me."

"Nor to me. What's she gonna do now? No one seems to know, but she's got to be right with God 'afore anythin' else."

Even Miss Locke, Mariah's former teacher, added a touch of high-brow legitimacy to the gossip. The school marm said what Mariah's mother had said before and was surely thinking again. Mariah's prideful waxen wings had taken her too close to the sun, and from those heights, our raven Icarus had taken a great fall into the notch over which she once soared. Poor thing indeed.

Mariah chose this late spring day to walk the banks of Cold River. There would be no children pointing and whispering; school was still in session. She would have the pothole and even the upstream rapids to herself.

It was the time for lady's slippers. This delicate pink orchid hides in the shadows of pines with a bulbous, pink, sensuous blossom, deeply creased, like lips for the kissing. Mariah ventured along the path, her first outing alone since the pristine snows had turned dirty then melted into mud. Life was struggling out of the mire, and Mariah was determined to share in the rejuvenation.

Will's letters told her that he had undergone treatment and the symptoms had gone away; she was thankful for that. Her father had written a few brief notes back to tell of Mariah's progress, but Will received not a touch nor a glance, not even a word for many long months of loneliness and confusion.

Mariah continued on the path slowly, looking at each flower like a child discovering life in its many forms for the first time. Mariah remembered there was a place along the path where a cluster of lady's slippers grew. It seemed that even rambunctious boys left them alone, knowing that their delicacy, once abused, stopped the flowering. Mariah searched for the spot she remembered, occasionally stooping to move obstructing brush and brambles from her line of sight. Stooping made her dizzy when she stood again. She held the trunk of a sapling to steady herself and to fight off nausea.

In the bright sun along the roadway, Orange Hawkweed was in profusion. She remembered its popular name, the Devil's Paintbrush, and touched its small-headed, furry, fiery blossom of yellow moving to orange.

114

Spotting the hayfields beyond were pink Canadian thistle, yellow tick weed, and white, sun-eyed daisies, innumerable, common, but uncommonly beautiful. A few purple harebells stood as high as the tasseled timothy. There was only a little time to enjoy the wild outburst of spring before haying struck down blossoms with hay and tossed them green, yet dying, into the loft for winter feed.

Mariah looked into the canopy of translucent foliage of maples, birches, ashes and hickories. Newly unfurled, the delicate new leaves cast a yellow-green light on the forest floor. Juncos and gold finches darted busily, building nests.

In a boggy, low area, invaded by the stream, she noticed a tall plant at the water's edge with leaves like arrowheads. On its sturdy stalk it bore a yellow, rod-like, fleshy cone that reminded her of an ear of corn. It was a half a foot in length and partially sheathed in a curled, green cover. She was surprised to encounter a plant—the arrow arum—that she could not name, and found so mysterious.

There they were. The lady's slippers. They hadn't gone by; in fact, they had multiplied over the years since Mariah last walked the path to bathe in the crystal purity of Cold River. Saplings had grown thicker along the path, and the forest seemed to shade the river more than she remembered.

But nothing could bring Mariah greater joy and hope than the delicate, pink bulb-like blossoms, as fine as blown glass, but soft. They held such promise. Despite fallen limbs of winter, despite a thick carpet of brown, musky dead leaves and pine needles, the lady's slippers had pushed their way into the filtered light to claim their spot among powerful giants, and now where there were six or eight blossoms, there were a dozen, and another cluster had sprung up a few feet away under the fan-like branch of a fragrant hemlock. She knelt to touch the delicate pink blossoms.

She reached the jumping rock over the pothole. It was a cool, dry day, not warm enough to invite swimming, so she was assured of being alone. She spread her blanket in the sun and watched as grosbeaks and chickadees, tree swallows and gold finches flew into the open sky, and then back under cover, their beaks often carrying raw materials for their labors.

Thoughts of family and home intruded, even into this wild place with no signs of civilization in view. Her mother had gotten a long letter from Aunt Bertha. Something was brewing between them, but she heard nothing direct in the letters read at the table. They had been in correspon-dence even more frequently since Mariah's sad home-coming. Mariah loved this aunt she had never met, and felt more comforted by her compassion than by her mother's. She realized that her mother had to contend with the gossip of Sandwich Notch while nursing a grown child back to health and also tending to the needs of two younger children, but understanding didn't relieve the pain of her isolation. Sarah was most angered that Florence and Moze had to bear taunts from some of the other school children about a sister who had "caught a social disease." Mariah knew she had become a burden, even an embarrassment.

Lately her mother had spoken of a "resolution." What could that be? Go home to Will—she could not imagine that— and yet she missed him and worried about him. What other resolution was there for a married woman that would not plunge her into deeper disgrace?

For Mariah the most painful thing was the gradual withdrawal of her father's counsel. He had been her anchor when she first arrived home. "Now you just get better, and we hope the same for Will. Never mind about these gnats buzzin' about. They'll die out in the sun," he said about town gossips with a sweep of his hand.

But after months of buzzing, there was a difference in her father. Amos avoided Mariah's eyes. He was tense as he often was when he faced something unpleasant. Before she left on her walk this bright June morning she had felt his tension. She saw it in his eyes even as he opened the front door and helped her down the granite steps. "You take your walk, and later on your mother and I want to sit down and talk."

*Your mother and I want to sit down and talk.* Mariah knew what that meant. Her father had acquiesced to her mother's strong will and that they had agreed on some kind of resolution for her future.

As she walked toward the river, Mariah had looked back and saw her parents standing in the parlor window watching her. Mariah had offered to write to Will for money, but her parents refused. When Mariah's money ran out, the burden of support would rest on her parents'

116

weary shoulders.  She saw in their eyes, it was more than money that worried them about the future.

The sun felt good on Mariah's face.  The river was like an oasis in a desert of unhappiness, and she dispelled thoughts of the world encircling her.  The air was still, yet she could hear a rustling in the distance, a coon or porcupine, perhaps.  She closed her eyes and imagined herself in the water below, as it had been so many times before, liberating and sensual, a feeling she longed to experience again.  She was still weak and thin, but the darkness around her eyes had diminished.

She thought of Will's recent letters.  He had experienced little from the disease except for the nauseous effects of the liquor of mercury.  He begged to see her.

"I love only you…I'm so ashamed…Please, please let me come to see you.  I know your mother wonders if I go to an empty bed, but I do, I promise I do.  Oh, God, Mariah, if you could only believe me that I haven't been with another woman since…I'm tired, very tired.  Every day seems gray and gloomy no matter what the sky tells me.  When can I come to see you?  Or when will you come home?  I've learned my lesson.  I love you.  Please believe me."

When Mariah finally wrote, her letter was filled with anger and hurt.  "I thought you loved me…Do you know how much you have shamed me, and what you have done to my family?  We can hardly bear to go to church or even see the neighbors."  A few tender lines let Will know that she was relieved that he was also getting better.

Will tucked Mariah's letter in his pocket and walked along North Main Street to the bridge overlooking the falls at the woolen mill.  The roaring of the turbid waters over the splashboards and the thundering of the great mill wheels and the machinery inside sent a vibration that he could feel through his fine stitched shoes.  There were few on the street on a misty, cool evening, but as he saw a young woman approaching, he turned his tormented face away from the gas light street lamp that hissed into its glowing mantle.

"I'm still not strong.  I can't see you in my parents' home.  My mother couldn't bear that.  I think of you alone and it grieves me, but…have you told your mother the truth? …Did she have to learn through gossip? I just don't know what the future holds for us."

Will tore up the letter and threw it into the roiling river, the pieces spreading like contagion until they were swept into the foaming white water dashing onto the rocks below the dam.

"Will, is that you?" said the young woman on the sidewalk. He wiped his eyes with his handkerchief and turned his face into the light. It was Nellie Parker who had a late lesson and found herself alone on the street after dark.

"What are you doing out here in the dark?" Before she let him answer, she blurted out more questions. "What's wrong? You look terrible. I've never seen you like this."

"My wife's been sick. She's home with her parents. I just read a letter from her."

"Oh, I'm so sorry, but I'm glad that, well… It must be very hard on you to be alone. How long has she been away?"

"All winter and spring."

"It's no good for a husband to have to visit his wife in her parents' home. No privacy. I'm sure it isn't easy to get back on a train with all the traveling you do for your job."

Will said nothing. He didn't want to admit that there were no visits and he was unwelcome and unwanted.

Nellie put her warm hands on his. "Will, I want you to come with me." She took his hand and walked him across the bridge and down Washington Street until she reached her house. "I'm going to give you a good, hot meal, and we can talk."

"What about the neighbors?"

"They don't pay much attention. With all of my piano lessons, singing groups and all, they are used to a steady stream of visitors coming here."

She fed him a hardy soup and a slab of sharp cheese and homemade bread, and he relaxed, smiling for the first time in weeks. Nellie had a bottle of wine made by a French family whose child seemed to be a prodigy at the keyboard. "Let's see if we can open this. I've had it for a few months. I keep it hidden because you know how much most people—well, we Yankees—frown on drinking."

"Don't I know. I don't have much at home even though Mariah never says anything. I don't want to get a temperance lecture."

They drank a glass and talked. Will feared that the wine and the company might loosen his tongue about the real reason Mariah had left, and the fact that he had not seen her, never mind touched her—or any woman— since she left him.

Nellie laid her beautiful, tapered octave-reaching fingers on Will's thigh. She was known for her rare touch, from pianissimo to fortissimo, her hands flying effortlessly at the command of her passion.

"No, Nellie. I can't. I've done enough harm. Besides, I'm sick, too."

"Why, Will, what's wrong?" She saw in Will's face that he couldn't tell her more, and that was all Nellie needed to reach the obvious conclusion. "So that's why she's gone, isn't it? I'm sorry for you, Will, dreadfully sorry." She showed him to her door with a quick peck on his cheek. "I hope the medicine works," she said with a look of sadness mingled with disgust.

Mariah heard rustling again and opened her eyes. A man was emerging from the shadows in silhouette, a young man, broad of build, with his jacket thrown over his shoulder. When he came into the light, she could barely get her breath.

"Will, what are you doing here? I told you not to come."

"How could I not come? I love you, and I want you to forgive me."

"Do you think that is going to be easy?"

"What more can I do, just tell me."

"The last time I was here I swam, and it made me feel so free."

"Just like us boys. You told me."

"I told you, but I never told anyone else." She could not resist a half smile at the thought of her slipping into the water with all of her clothes piled neatly on a dry rock.

"All of us boys swam naked, upstream where it's hard to reach. They're no beaten paths along the banks."

"I know what you boys did. I went up there once."

"You did? You mean you spied on the boys?"

"Yes, I did."

A silence fell between them, broken at last when Will sat beside her and tried to take her hand. "Don't do that. I don't want that."

"I have always loved you. I've never loved anyone else." Will's words echoed Mariah's, and she felt it.

"When we said our vows, we promised before God to be faithful to each other…"

"In sickness and in health," said Will. "It's all been a sickness with me, but I know I'm going to conquer it. You just wait and see. I've been alone all these months thinking of no one but you."

"What you're describing is not a sickness; it's a sin against me and against God."

"I'm sorry, I wish you could understand how sorry I am. Haven't these terrible months helped you forgive me, even a little?"

Suddenly her resolve and her anger seemed to fall away.

They embraced and kissed, and in words coming fast, and with eyes looking deep into eyes, they could not resist telling each other how much they loved and wanted to be loved. Will caressed her neck. Mariah felt the warmth of his breath as he repeated, "I'm sorry, I'm so sorry. I love you so much. If I didn't love you, would I come back and face you? If I didn't love you, how could I knock on your parents' door and face them? You can't believe how hard that was."

Mariah broke into sobs and held him and told him that she had never stopped loving him even when she hated him and could not look at his picture.

"Please forgive me," he whispered tearfully. Mariah held his face in her hands and kissed him, and he responded with hands that brushed her breasts, and a deep, penetrating kiss that fired Mariah's passion. They moved to the seclusion of tall grass. He kneeled before her and gently pulled her dress open; she unbuttoned his shirt and felt the warmth of his body. At that moment the past weeks of pain and alienation evaporated, and she was overcome by the hunger for him. Mariah felt in that moment all of the pent up tension of self-loathing leave him as he moved on her and in her in the warmth of the sun.

"Let me drive you in the buggy back to the house."

Mariah looked down in silence and took his hand. "You know you can't do that."

"But when can we be together again?"

"I don't know if we can. I just don't know. Yes, I love you; I can't deny that. But please, Will. You need to go." Her firm words were softened by a gentle touch. Then she withdrew her eyes, avoiding his plaintive glances.

"But what about what just happened?" asked Will in disbelief.

"I think it was a dream. I fear it isn't real."

"Of course it's real and it always has been."

"The infection eating at us is real, too, isn't it? Will, you need to go. We'll talk again later." She blocked his advance with her hand against his chest. "I mean it. I don't know what is going to happen, but I have become an embarrassment. I don't know where to go where people don't avoid me up close and stare at me from afar."

"But you love me. Can't we go somewhere and have a fresh start?"

"I feel like Guinevere even though I'm the innocent one. Men always get off easier, it seems. The shamed Guinevere grovels across the stones to Clifford's feet. Lancelot rides off to France, a sadder man, but his life goes on for him. Guinevere goes to a convent and does penance for the rest of her life. That's what it feels like for me now. That's how I'm being treated, and it's all because of you. I can't forget that. I have to live with that even if I forgive you. " She struggled to hold back tears and the desire for his comforting embrace.

"But you do forgive me?"

"I can't deny what I said, but you have to go."

"Can you kiss me again?"

Mariah put her fingers to Will's lips arresting the kiss, but she walked with him hand in hand, as much as the wooded trail allowed, until they got within sight of the buggy and the road. She dropped his hand and stopped in her tracks. "We'll say goodbye here." Will leaned to kiss her, and she turned away. "Goodbye, Will. I'll write to you. I just don't know what more to say."

Will nodded with a weak smile and boarded the buggy. In a moment he was gone.

Mariah opened the door as quietly as possible, but her mother was waiting. "Did you see Will?"

"Yes. He walked up to the pothole. I was there resting in the sun." When Amos heard Mariah's voice, he came in from the parlor, removing his reading spectacles. He stood at her side facing Sarah as though he wished to soften the exchange.

"I told him to go," said Mariah quietly, her head down.

"Mariah, could you come sit at the table just for a moment? Your father and I went to Preston Samuels…"

"The lawyer?"

"Yes."

"We asked him for advice about what would be best for your future."

"And?"

Sarah took an envelope off the shelf between the two kitchen windows and set it before her daughter. Her father stood behind her and placed his hand gently on her shoulder. Mariah looked back at him before opening the envelope.

The title in bold letters said, "A petition for divorcement."

Mariah stared at it in silence, and slowly rose from the chair. She returned the document to its envelope and carried it to the stairs. She took each step slowly and silently, hardly able to breathe.

# CHAPTER 15

## The Ring

*W*ill took a deep breath and knocked on the Brandon's front door. Months had passed since the agonizing divorce proceedings. Will had confessed to adultery, and had agreed to a division of assets. The house was sold. Will moved into a walk-up apartment close to the shoe factory, considerably better accommodations than laborers, but nothing like the handsome house on Wakefield Street. His marriage was over, his career in doubt. Mr. Wallace knew everything. He found his former star salesman to be a social liability.

Although Will had told himself time and again that he had only himself to blame for his fall to the base degrees from which he had ascended, he could not accept that the punishment fairly fit the crime. He couldn't accept that his marriage was really over.

Why had Mariah given in to her parents and the taunts of cruel townspeople? He had to see her again. Would she be able to tell him to his face—now that she had so much time to reflect—that she no longer loved him?

Florence and Moze stood in the shadow of their parents. Sarah's expression was icy; Amos', pitying. The children were dispatched with a single word from their mother—"Upstairs." The Brandons stood in the doorway like sentinels barring an intruder.

"What do you want?" said Sarah.

"I just want to see Mariah, just once, just for a few minutes."

"She won't see you," said Sarah, still gripping the doorknob.

"Mariah went to Center Sandwich. She's leaving for…"

"Amos!" Sarah uttered through clenched teeth.

"I'm sorry it turned out this way, Will." There was compassion in Amos' tone and in his expression. He could not withhold his pity for a man who had lost the love of his life, and had lost the respect of everyone he knew.

Will turned on his heels and whipped the horse into a trot.

"Amos, why did you tell him where she was? She would have been safely on the two o'clock train."

"They're divorced, but she still has feelings for him. We both know that," said Amos.

"Still has feelings? After what he's put her through? Oh, Amos, the damage that man has done to her, to us, and you still feel sorry for him? I'm surprised you didn't offer him your hand."

"Might a lost it if I had. You would a slammed that door so hard it would a taken it off 'fore Will could a grasped it." Amos wrapped his left arm around her waist. "At least I'm left-handed."

Sarah didn't laugh, but she softened, as she generally did, in Amos' loving embrace.

"Sai, everybody knows what he done, and he deserves all the pain he's feelin'. But when does it stop? If God can forgive seven fold sin, who are we to heap on more punishment?"

Sarah's voice quivered. "But she shouldn't see him. It would make it all the harder for her to go to her aunt's. That's what she has to do, and you know it. She can't regain her dignity if she stays here."

Amos' voice took on a harder edge. "Her dignity, or ours?"

Sarah pulled away and folded her arms. "I know she's not responsible for what happened, but she married him. We warned her."

"This is what comes of not knowing your place, isn't that right?" grumbled Amos as he left Sarah standing at the kitchen door. He rarely expressed any anger toward his wife, but his greatest anger he directed toward himself for giving in and sending his own daughter away from the one place on earth she should be able to call her own.

Amos walked down the path toward the road. He could barely see a small plume of dust from Will's buggy where the road curved to the right. "I doubt he'll find her," he said to himself with pain and sadness. "It's already noon," he thought. "Mariah has to be in West Ossipee for the two o'clock train." Amos continued to watch the black speck until it disappeared. In his heart he wished Will God speed.

Mariah had walked the Ring many times before, never with such emotion. "The Ring" was what the good citizens of Sandwich called the three converging roads that formed the town common. Stopping to find a little comfort in the steady breeze, Mariah looked over the familiar center of town life she feared she might never see again.

Except for the stone-faced library, every building around the Ring was white. Columns and pilasters and pediments graced the proud edifices, many built during the Greek Revival period. The pristine architecture was fit for the "pillars of society" that could afford the gracious homes that intermingled with large public buildings that closed The Ring to all but the best families. Two churches, the library, a bank. Chestnuts and elms arched over the streets. Leaves rustled in the westerly wind. The Ring was tidy in its whiteness. "A place for everything and everything in its place." There was security—social and eternal—when everything and everyone was its place.

As Mariah passed the door of the Free Baptist Church, the Reverend James Bean was coming out the door, adjusting his top hat. He immediately removed it again, pulled off his glove, and offered Mariah his hand. "Please step in, Mrs. Dunfield."

Mariah had been frozen out of communion with the saints of the North Sandwich Free Baptist Society, but for a brief time she had found more accepting souls in the church on the Ring. It was a ride of several miles, and it was not her parents' church, so she had only attended a few times. Stories followed her from place and place, but the reverend had been kind.

"Mrs. Dunfield, I'm glad the Lord has given us this opportunity." The pastor, a man approaching sixty, was a short, portly man whose jolly nature seemed at odds with his black frock coat, black tie, black top hat, and black cane. His pink cheeks and bushy white side whiskers drew the eye to the light of his countenance and offered a counterpoise to the expected demeanor of a strict Baptist. "Now I know about the divorce. Let me assure you, my dear, that although scripture weighs heavy on those who would put a sacred union asunder, our Lord Jesus did cite adultery as a justification, and there can be no doubt…"

"Reverend Bean, I've been the target of glares and snubs as hard as stones since I came home."

"Why people blame the wife when the husband wanders I can't understand. It isn't from the heart of Jesus."

"I might as well be wearing a scarlet letter the way people avoid me." Mariah held her head high in indignation.

"Give it time, my dear, give it time."

"I've given it time, Pastor. Now I'm going to give it distance. I'm leaving Sandwich today."

"Oh?" said the pastor, his bushy eyebrows rising over the rim of his glasses.

"I'm going to Iowa."

"Iowa?" Bean blurted out in astonishment.

"I'm starting a new life out there," she said with a brief, defiant resolve, but she could not hold the eyes of the minister without acknowledging the truth. Iowa was more of a banishment than a fresh start.

"Yes, Iowa," she said sadly, "Whether I want to or not." She looked at her left hand where there was no longer a glitter of gold.

"So this isn't really your idea, now is it?" the pastor added with a sympathetic expression. "But the die is cast, as they say. Many have gone west before you, and they've generally prospered, so go with God's blessing. My dear, try to forgive those who've judged you."

Pastor Bean escorted her to the door and tipped his hat to her. It was the first polite acknowl-edgment she had experienced in weeks.

At the bank Mariah withdrew the cash she had remaining from the divorce decree as her seed money for her new life in Iowa. The teller, a young man named Samuel Weed whom she had beaten in a spelling bee in eighth grade, nodded with a blank face, but did not speak. She walked down Main Street emerging from the shade of a giant elm when she saw Lydia Ludlow, the soloist at her wedding, coming in her direction accompanied by a grandson carrying a canvas bag with his grandmother's purchases. Lydia shaded her eyes from the sun, and when she could make out who was approaching, she grabbed her grandson's hand and steered him across the common toward the town hall as though her taxes were overdue. Mariah could hear her warbled soprano voice intoning, "Never mind, never mind!" as she tugged the child in an unexpected direction.

After a visit to the apothecary's, Mariah made her way up the front steps of the Sandwich House, the inn where she would await the coach. Within seconds of one another, the bells of the Methodist, Baptist and Congregational churches rang the hour. It was one o'clock, and the coach to the West Ossipee station clattered into view as it made its way around the Ring. Mariah took one last look at the pristine whiteness of the town's heart and all that it had meant to her. Parades, fairs, tent meeting evangelists, political campaigners and summer band concerts colored her memories against the background of unrelenting white. Although Mariah always wanted more than the narrow, bounded valley could offer, it was her benchmark, a place she always intended to return to as a measure of the new and a balance against destructive change. As much as she wanted adventure in the world beyond, she also wanted the community, nestled behind the protective mountains, to welcome her back to its unchanged bosom.

Only a few years before she was sure that the town would be talking about her and her husband. It had come to pass that indeed they were. The Ring was the heart of the community, and as a girl of fifteen, she had expected to win its heart. Instead she had become an embarrassment; now she was to be exiled. She realized that the pride she had struggled so hard to maintain was the very thing the town expected her to sacrifice on the white altar of Yankee propriety. The ring was no longer hers.

The coachman loaded her two trunks on the roof and helped her up the step into the brightly painted Concord coach, its leather strap suspension protecting the passengers from the thumps and crashes of uncertain roads. The man smiled with a look of admiration as he helped Mariah gather her silk skirts and train before he shut the door. He was not from Sandwich and knew neither her name nor her story. Once she was settled in the coach, Mariah looked at Will's picture and placed it in her purse. With startling commands and a crack of the whip, the coach bolted forward. Mariah, like Lot's wife, could not help herself from looking back.

"Has Mariah Dunfield been here recently?" Will asked the apothecary.

"Yes, but she's not using that name any more. She's going by Brandon again," said Christopher Fellows, standing before rows of glass stoppered bottles of powders and elixirs. "And you are?"

Looking down, the handsome man said, "Will Dunfield."

"Oh. I see," replied the apothecary, his eyes moving nervously from side to side. "Well, she got medicines and left a while ago. I think she was headed for Heard's."

Will was out the door before Fellows could utter another word. *Mariah Brandon. How could she drop my name? I know she still loves me. She's still my wife. I don't give a damn what the court said. Mariah, Mariah, don't do this to me. God knows I'm sorry, and so do you. Don't listen to your mother. Listen to your heart. Please, give me another chance.*

A hay wagon passed him mounded ten feet high smelling sweet and fresh. Two lads drove the team of four slowly, worried that a sudden dip in a hole might topple the load on Main Street before they could get to the livery stable. The boys driving the wagon were fifteen or sixteen and were feeling their oats. "Let's pitch this into the loft as fast as we can, then let's go to the pothole," said one to the other. Will wished with all of his heart that he could join them in both work and play—once again to be young and free and innocent.

Sure enough, Mariah had been to Heard's, but that was a half hour before. Everyone seemed to be pretending that they had no idea who this Mariah was. "Where was she headed when she left the store?" No one seemed to know.

Will let the door slam behind him and leaned against the pilaster, surveying the green. "Where else could she be?" Suddenly Ben Paisley, an old rival from his youth came up behind him.

"Well, if it isn't Will Dunfield."

"Yes, it is." Will answered without a smile and without a hand.

"I understand you've been under the weather."

"No. I'm feeling fine," said Will deflecting the innuendo about his vile disease.

"Not from what I've heard."

Will didn't want to fall into the trap. "Whatever you've heard doesn't count when I'm telling you I'm fine."

"Well, if fifty girls from here to Hartford's got the syph from you, how's it that you're fine?"

Fists flew, and Ben went down with blood pouring from his nose and a gash opened above his brow. No one was in sight, and if Ben had not begged him to stop, Will might have killed him. Ben got to his feet and staggered to a horse trough where he dipped a handkerchief in the water and cleaned his bloody face.

"Where's Mariah? Have you seen her?" Will held him against the wall of the store, around the corner out of sight of passersby.

"One o'clock coach." Will dropped him like a potato sack and ran to his buggy. *If I can just talk to her alone... The Boston train... where's she going alone? It's been months. I tried. I really tried. I've gone back to an empty bed for weeks. My letters keep coming back. I can't stand it any longer... She's got to talk to me*

Will whipped the horse into a gallop, risking a turnover at the corners and over arched bridges. He flew over the south branch bridge and up Guinea Hill with pebbles hitting the dashboard from the shoes of his terrified horse. He arrived just after two, dusty, frantic.

The 2 o'clock train of the Dover and Winnepesoogie Railroad was rolling away from the platform with the whistle blasting a pillar of steam into the calm air, and the skirts of the train white and curly with steady blasts from the steam boxes. He stopped and watched the train disappear down the tracks. He wondered where it was taking Mariah, and his heart ached at the thought that he might never see her again.

# CHAPTER 16

## *Mail Order Bride*

Mariah waited on the Union Station platform for the next leg of her trip west, a trip that was feeling more and more like punishment. "So they call this the Hub of the Universe," Mariah thought, "then why do I feel all alone?" Whatever resolve and hope she had mustered in trying to accept her future had collapsed without a hand to clasp or a shoulder to cry on. The man she had loved, the man she still loved, was the very cause of her misery, and the parents who had nursed her back to health were exiling her across half a continent.

Boston's Union Station was quieter than it had been in weeks. The Panic of 1893 had reduced commerce, and reduced commerce cut into passenger traffic as well. One bright spot was Chicago that was humming with the Columbian World Exposition, a world's fair that intended to outdo the Philadelphia Centennial and the Paris World's Fair. Chicago, "The place to be in '93."

Mariah wouldn't be seeing the fair. She'd merely be passing through, along for the ride, but not part of the excitement. She wondered when there would be any excitement for her again.

She tried to lose herself in the distraction of other people's busyness. Travelers enjoyed the May warmth of outdoor benches or just leaned against the granite exterior walls soaking in the sun and watching people pass. Fair-bound passengers were easy to spot: Well dressed, excited, talkative, and almost always in groups.

Not far down the platform were clusters of disheveled and dusty little people, quiet and submissive. The railroad workers called them "Zulus" because they seemed as bizarre in language and dress as the tribes from the Dark Continent. The universal accessory among the mostly Eastern European immigrants was the woman's headscarf, folded in a triangle and tied under the chin. The eyes of men and women alike darted back and forth, fearing every encounter with the English language and American ways. Whenever a conductor called out a destination or a whistled sounded, the Zulus huddled around a "chief" who buzzed like a queen bee directing her swarm. Whether young or old, the immigrants gripped their tickets like life rings. Their meager belongings bulged out of battered bags and boxes that often doubled for seats when station benches or train seats were scarce.

Another easily recognizable group gathered on the platform was a bevy of mail order brides. When railroad workers or regular travelers saw a group of young women, or those pretending to be young, with one male escort, it was a sure sign that these women were going West to give themselves to a man who was likely to be smaller, homelier and poorer than advertised. The husbands-to-be were often disappointments, but they provided passage out, and a roof and the promise of a future to a woman who had found matrimony in the forlorn New England countryside to be close to impossible. At least they were sent *for*, not sent *away*, thought Mariah as she looked at the women preening.

Mariah watched two young men who stood near the leading drive wheel of the locomotive of the New York Central's Empire State Express. They admired the mighty machine that had just set the land speed record. Engine 999 raced at one hundred twelve and a half miles per hour in its twenty-five hour station-to-station run to Chicago on May 10. This was the mighty machine that would take her to her Iowa purgatory showering her pathway with fire and brimstone.

One of the men, an Irish lad in a brown suit with a tan vest and a brown derby, chatted with a fellow of comparable age, height and build. The second fellow was dressed in the greasy overalls of a "master maniac" as railroad workers like to call master mechanics.

"It's a ballast scorcher, that's for sure," said the mechanic as he oiled the slides and joints from the steam box to the check valve and along the three connected drive wheels. "Fastest in the world. They rapped the sack on this 'un. Lucky with the throttle wide open they didn't melt the fire box."

The Irishman gave the mechanic a quizzical glance in response to railroad slang, but he didn't ask for a translation. "Yup, if you ever want to see a hog fly, just watch this 'un in open country. I wager the dining car sold more liquor than coffee on that trip. An' I bet you was afraid expresses would cut into your imports," said the mechanic, knowing that his friend imported Irish and Scotch whiskey. "On slow trains they drink 'cause they're bored. Expresses they drink 'cause they get terrors of a cornfield meet at over two hundred miles an hour."

The Irish lad finally had to ask the master mechanic to explain himself. "Cornfield meet?" Mariah listened while trying not to appear to notice the two young men.

"Why a head-on 'tween two expresses out in the open, both goin' full tilt." The mechanic went back to his oiling, climbing up to the connector joint that had ended up on the top of the wheel when the 999 rolled to a stop, its firebox starting to glow red just a few miles before it reached Boston and went to the turntable to be pointed back to the West.

"An' I'll tell yer, iffen every movin' part don't get the attention it needs after every run, this thing could blow worse 'n a Bolshevik's bomb."

"Aye, now tell me, what does a master maniac know about Bolsheviks anyway?" retorted the Irish lad who laid on his brogue with a trowel.

"I seen more Russies comin' through New York than Micks," he said with a sardonic smile, "for two or three years, 'specially after the Reds blew up the czar. New czar blamed the Jews, I guess, 'cause the old czar drove the Jews out like locusts 'fore a fire. The new czar weren't azackly right. Only half o' the Jews was Reds."

The Irish lad laughed heartily. Mariah couldn't resist looking up. *He laughs just like Will.* Mariah studied him for a moment. *I can't stand it. I wish he'd go away. God, is this Irish devil mocking me?*

"Now the Reds are fannin' up the unions," said the lad from the

Old Sod. "Soon as pickets appear 'gainst the railroads or the steel companies, the coppers seem to know which'uns in the crowd to clobber with nightsticks," he said with a sneer. His memories of English constables in Ireland did not endear the son of County Killarney to the police. "We're getting' more Irish in the Boston police every day," he said with a cocky, sideward tilt of the head, "and when they know you're one o'their own, and if you got an extry dime in your pocket, you get along fair."

Suddenly a metal shoot swung into place over the tender, and coal poured into the bin with such a clatter that it made conversation on the platform impossible. Coal was fast replacing wood as the fuel for America's locomotives as the forests of the East were disappearing except on steeper elevations. Next, a pipe lowered into place to fill the other part of the tender with enough water to get the Empire State to Albany.

After the racket ended and the mechanic had finished his lubrication and inspection of 999, the two young men turned their attention back to the passengers gathering on the platform. The Irishman scanned the platform as the mechanic checked his watch. A half hour before boarding.

"Well take a look at her!" said the Irish dandy to his overhauls-clad friend. If she ain't one to make the blood quicken the heart." Mariah pretended that she couldn't hear.

"The heart, you say. I'm feelin' it quicken somewhere else," said the mechanic, elbowing his friend as he studied Mariah, dressed in pale yellow silk, sitting on a bench reading. Her raven hair was pinned up in clustered ringlets cascading down her neck under a small hat decorated with white ostrich plumes. She had a rather melancholy look they both attributed to the story she was reading. With some difficulty Mariah kept her eyes on the book.

"I bet you she's Irish."

"With that black hair?"

"There's some of us," said the Irishman, without taking his eyes off the lassie in yellow, "descended from Armada Spaniards. The Catholics of Ireland welcomed them. They married and stayed, and we ended up with a breed of Irish with black hair, but fair of skin and blue of eye. We call 'em 'Black Irish.'"

"She's lookin' down. I can't see her eyes."

"You don't suppose she could be a mail order bride? If so, that's a surprise package I'd sure like to open," said the mechanic with a leer.

"Well, lad, there's only one way to unlock these mysteries," said the Irishman, adjusting his tie and cocking his derby slightly to the side.

Mariah saw the cocky lad strutting her way, but did not raise her eyes as he neared. When he cast a shadow on her book, she looked up briefly, in annoyance, and went on reading. She had noticed that the young Irishman was good looking and well dressed; she had also noticed that no one admired him more than himself.

He eclipsed the sun, but Mariah steadfastly refused to look up. Placing a foot on the end of the bench and holding his derby in his hand, the lad excused himself with a cough. "Miss, are you traveling alone?"

Mariah looked up from her book. "I see you're not Irish, miss, but you're a rare beauty, wherever you're from."

"I beg your pardon?" she said without a smile and after a moment's hesitation.

"I'll be askin' the pretty lassie, if she was traveling alone."

"No. As a matter of fact I understand that I'll be traveling with a whole car full of people, most of them well-bred, I'm sure, but a few may be unduly forward. Those I will avoid." She focused her eyes on the book once again.

"Are you off to the Exposition?" asked the Irish lad, brushing off the rebuff.

"No, I don't care for flashy exhibitions." Mariah held his gaze to guide her dart to the bull's eye.

"If you're a mail order bride, you'll fetch top dollar," he whispered in a vulgar attempt at flattery and humor.

"No, I am no mail order bride, but I have business in the West, and unless there is a strange coincidence, *my* business is not *your* business." She looked down at his foot that was nearly touching her dress. She looked into his blue eyes when the foot did not move. "I'm sure you *have* business, since you're so well dressed for it, and I certainly don't want to keep you from your business."

She stared once again at his finely stitched shoe, still resting on the corner of the bench. Her heart sank at the thought of another handsome young man who wore elegant shoes. The young man removed his foot from the bench and stepped back, his smile fading. He excused himself and resumed his conversation with the mechanic, admiring the locomotive without another glance in her direction.

Mariah closed her book and checked her watch pendant. At the opposite end of the bench sat a young couple that was clearly expecting a child within a few months. The husband, attired in fine but conservative clothes, carried a case for a musical instrument. The couple seemed especially uncomfortable during Mariah's exchange with the young man in brown.

"Miss, I don't wish to intrude, but I wanted to assure you that I was prepared to say something if that young man had pressed you any further," said the gentleman.

"Thank you, but I've learned how to handle his kind." Mariah sat ramrod straight, pursing her lips like a stern school marm in a test of will with a rebellious student. She was not going to allow fear and loneliness to sap the strength she knew she had to have to take back control of her life.

"We're sorry you have to travel without your husband," said the young wife with a severe countenance. She noticed the wedding ring that Mariah had decided to wear for the trip, an attempt to avoid just the kind of encounters she had just had with the cocky Irish lad. "Bertrand, you really should have said something to that young man."

"No, not at all. Women can't always rely on their husbands," said Mariah, looking straight ahead. "Sometimes they have to stick up for themselves." Bertrand and his wife looked at each other and kept their silence as porters rolled carts of trunks and boxes to the baggage cars and food to the dining car.

When there was a let up in the clatter, Mariah broke the silence. "And what takes you to Chicago?" she asked politely, but not warmly. Mariah learned that the young man was the lead cornet player of a band from Salem, Massachusetts. Bertrand Keyes and his unsmiling, pregnant wife Amelia were to spend two weeks at the World Exposition with almost daily engagements at the fair and in the city. They hoped to be back home for the baby's arrival a month hence.

It was Mariah's turn to introduce herself. "My husband's business keeps him away much of the time…My aunt in Iowa needs my help…I've always wanted to go west…My first trip alone…I'll miss my husband, yes, indeed I will…but trains are so fast nowadays…No. No children. Not yet…Yes, too bad I can't see the Exposition… maybe on my return…When? I haven't decided."

*Never? Maybe never. What am I going to? Cornfields. Back to a farm, a farm in the middle of nowhere. I'll hang my water colored photograph of Mount Chocorua in my room. Will I ever see the real thing again?*

"This is a picture of my husband and me. I hate being away from him, so I carry this in my bag. It may be a while before I see him." *I may never see him again. Please let this conversation end.*

The musician's pregnant wife saw strong emotion rise into Mariah's face. She patted Mariah's hand. "He's such a handsome man. Parting is so difficult. I couldn't bear to have Bertie away, especially now," she said demurely casting her eyes downward. The young couple was clearly mystified as to how a husband could let his wife travel to the West alone, but they knew better than to ask.

Mariah was left alone to her thoughts. She had lost control of the chain of events leading up to and following the divorce, and it left a bitter taste in her mouth. Mariah now felt that her aunt was a co-conspirator in her mother's plot to direct her life as she felt best, regardless of Mariah's wishes. She was a child again.

A new life, but back on a farm once again. Mariah imagined the Fates shouting in victory as they circled over her head, "You're nothing but a farm girl, a farm girl, a farm girl." The opening of a poem she had read on the train ride to Boston haunted her.

O let the solid ground
Not fail beneath my feet
Before my life has found
What some have found so sweet…

The train whistle blew and the conductor shouted "All aboard!" Mariah looked at the harbor and watched seagulls soar. She smelled the sea air as she took the steps onto the Empire State Express. At first the train rolled slowly and quietly; within a few miles, when the train reached open country outside of Boston, the engine roared to life and they were off to Chicago with frightening speed.

A few days later, and all was silent but the Iowa wind; no clatter-ing of wagons and carriages, no hustle bustle of freight and rail, no foreign tongues or tall buildings, or clouds of smoke from engines of industry. Mariah discovered that Central City was neither central nor a city, unless the middle of nowhere qualified as "central" and a "city" could count livestock into its popu-lation. Streetcars and electric lights were novelties that required a day trip by rail to Cedar Rapids or even farther.

Aunt Bertha had done up a nice room for Mariah at the end of the hall. Auntie told her she would have a "view of the waves" when the summer's west wind gusted over the wheat field. Mid-June was hot and humid; the air sat oppressively on her chest as she rested from the morning chores. She did not want to open her eyes and confront the truth that she was once again a farm girl.

Her time to rest was brief, and at noontime Mariah and her Aunt Bertha laid out a hearty meal for the field hands at one table and the family at another—Mariah's Uncle Jim, round and jolly, and her lanky cousin George, newly divorced and confused at age forty-three. His wife and field partner, Miriam, had gone to live in Cedar Rapids with another woman. When Mariah rested the final steaming bowl down, she looked for an empty chair. Bertha had set a place for her beside Cousin George. Her new family joined hands around the table for the blessing. Silently Mariah prayed to God that He would one day show her the way back home.

# CHAPTER 17

# *Blessed Assurance*

B ertha primed the kitchen pump with a cup of water and worked the handle until the soapstone sink filled with water. She was proud of her new kitchen in the biggest framed house along Ford Street. She sang as she poured hot water from a pail into the dishwater, her hands moving busily, gathering dishes, pots and silverware. "This is my story, this is my song, praising my savior all the day long. Blessed assurance, Jesus is mine; oh, for a foretaste of glory divine. Heir of salvation, purchase of God, born of his spirit, washed in his blood."

"Starting the day with a song, Auntie?" said Mariah as she entered the kitchen. "If I tried that, I might make the whole day start off flat or sharp." Mariah made an effort to be friendly and gracious although in her heart she was feeling empty.

"Oh, good to see you up and looking fresh, Honey. I'll wash, you dry?" Bertha reached up to get Mariah a towel from the rack fanning out its bony fingers over the cook stove. The towel was an old flour sack turned to a new use as everything was for country folks. Bertha was plump and white as her niece was slim and dark. Smiling with her daily dose of optimism, she continued singing softly as she plunged her hands into the dishwater. "Perfection submission, perfect delight! Visions of rapture now burst on my sight; angels descending bring from above, echoes of mercy, whispers of love. This is my story, this is my song, praising my savior all the day long."

Mariah responded to her aunt's outpouring of joyous faith with an outpouring of work. She dried faster than Bertha could wash. She tidied every shelf and sill in her unspoken, dizzying doctrine of purgative labor, thinking she was climbing Jacob's ladder steadily, rung by rung, by doing her duty to a God and a society she had apparently offended.

Yet Mariah's duty did not obviate her doubt in the justice of society and of God. *Perfect submission? The only thing you get from submission is abuse. Will had his way with whores. They submitted every time for a few dollars. Now, there is a record of perfect submission.*

When she couldn't stand it any more, she asked as gently as she could manage: "Aunt Bertha, why do you think submission brings a person happiness?"

"Why, Honey, even Jesus prayed to the Father in Gethsemane, 'Not *my* will, but *Thy* will be done.' In the flesh he couldn't understand why he had to face death. Didn't seem fair. Well, fair or not, he had to be nailed to the cross. He did what none of us could. Trustin' when you don't understand. Faith in his father." Bertha stretched to put a serving dish up on a high shelf. "Bring that stool over here, would ya, Honey? You gotta believe that the Lord's got a plan."

"Too bad they won't let women be preachers," said Mariah with a wan smile.

"Maybe some day they will," replied Bertha with good cheer. "I get up to the pulpit pretty regular as it is. I throw in a little sermon into my missionary society reports now and then," Bertha added with a chuckle. "Can't never give Baptists too much sermonizing, now can ya?" Another chuckle. Central City Baptist Church had grown to one hundred fifty members, but it seemed to Mariah that God had not provided a single eligible young man with appeal among the whole praying lot of them.

Bertha got down from the stool and plunged a crusted baking pan into the dishwater. The suds had gone flat and the water was murky. "So I'm an unordained preacher, am I?" Bertha said with a laugh. "Well, even though the Lord gives us gifts, we're all just jars o' clay, now ain't we?" Bertha asked without waiting for an answer. We're all guilty of pride. We want to take matters into our own hands, now don't we?" Again, she didn't expect a reply.

Mariah's right eyebrow rose in response and her lips pursed, but she said nothing.

" 'Pride goeth before destruction, and a haughty spirit before the fall.' You know your proverbs, Sweetie?"

Mariah nodded and murmured in the affirmative. *Do I know my proverbs? I heard them enough times from Mother to memorize the whole book.*

We all just need to know the Word and open our eyes to see the truth," said Bertha. She applied her lessons to everyone, but her words hit home and irked Mariah nonetheless. Mariah was sure that the Good Lord was whispering some verses in Bertha's ear just to get her stubborn niece's goat.

Mariah remained stiffly silent, as impervious to her aunt's godly seeds as the rocky path in the old parable. Bertha took the dishtowel from her niece and held her hands. "My dear, I 'preciate your help, but there are some things in life more important than hard work. You've been laboring like a slave since you came here. You don't owe us anything. You've been paying your expenses, and you've done more work than any two women I know. But I can tell you're always thinkin' about what went wrong back East. Let the past go." Bertha smiled like a nurse over a patient who needed a strong dose of hope.

Mariah nodded and went back to work at a deliberately slower pace. Suddenly two simultaneous blasts shook the kitchen windows. Bertha dropped a slippery dish and they both rushed to the window. There stood Jim and George pointing shotguns into the air. George's significant height advantage gave his shot a head start, and a hawk dropped from the sky releasing a writhing chicken from its talons as it fell.

George was a haunting scarecrow one moment and a tender minister the next. Silhouetted in the early morning sun, he kneeled beside the tormented chicken, picked it up and stroked it. Mariah had never seen anyone feel sympathy for a chicken, but George's compassion didn't surprise her. She had watched his bronzed and calloused hands work gently with lambing ewes and lame horses, talking them through their distress with a deep, soft whisper, a gift of animal tongues and their interpretation that seemed miraculous. In his hands God's creatures found comfort and God's seed received multifold blessing. This man was born to bring forth the fruit and fauna of the land. George had been kind and thoughtful to her in his reticent, unpresuming way. He displayed tenderness for the weak and had an amazing touch in transforming the runt of the litter into a blue ribbon winner. Nothing in modern technology could take the place of that intuitive, life-nurturing gift. George was one of those people more comfortable in nature than in society.

George, eighteen years Mariah's senior, was tall and straight. Iowa's constant west wind had not bent or broken him although his face was starting to line and permanently darken like bark. When he faced sadness or disappointment, he went to the barn and talked to the animals or scooped up the rich earth to smell the reassurance it gave for a prodigious spring.

Jim Parker had adopted George as his own, and the harsh journey thirty-seven years earlier, a harsh trek delayed by storm, flood, cold and death, had cemented a bond as thick as blood. Jim was in his seventies, and the only reason he had confidence in facing the labors of each sunrise was the helping hands of his stepson.

"Your cousin's a good man," said Bertha as she pumped a pail of water to heat on the back of the stove. Mariah smirked at Bertha's reference to George as a cousin rather than a son, providing enough distance for objectivity in her assessment of him.

"Yes, he is, a born farmer," Mariah replied. Her voice could barely disguise her unhappiness at resuming life on a farm. A life sentence to farming was one of several reasons that Mariah kept George at arm's length. "I don't know what you'd do without him, especially with Madison married and gone to Cedar Rapids."

Only weeks after Mariah's arrival, Jim's son by his first marriage had kicked the manure from his heels for the last time and decided to farm only by extension; he left for the city to sell the wondrous machines of McCormack and Deere. Let other men do the dirty work from now on. Madison was more than willing to provide the newest technology.

"Hired help is nothing like family," Bertha whispered and patted

Mariah's hand. She began humming a hymn Mariah had heard every year in the Sandwich church during harvest time. "We plow the fields and scatter the good seed on the land, but it is fed and watered by God's almighty hand."

Bertha's effusive hope drove Mariah in the opposite direction to look at the dark underside of the world and the mysterious workings of the divine hand. *Sometimes He waters it, sometimes He shrivels it, and sometimes He sends a blight.*

"He sends the snow in winter, the warmth to swell the grain, the breezes and the sunshine, and soft refreshing rain. ..."

Mariah cynically invented her own verses. "*Sometimes He sends the torrents that wash the seed away, or dries the land to parchment and leaves us in dismay.*"

*If I have to be wed to the land, let it be my own land, my mountains, and trees. Lord God, to see our stand of tall timber once again would be such a blessing.* As days turned to weeks, Mariah surveyed the interminable Iowa fields and wondered whatever kept her relatives there. And she thought of her place, the rise and the fall in society's pyramid, and the place she had spurned and how that place now spurned her in return. Was she condemned, as was her aunt, never to see her place—her home—again?

When Jim and Bertha arrived in Central City in February of 1856, a small congregation of New Englanders who had come a few years before took them in. They pledged to help the Parkers with the understanding that when they prospered, they would give to the Lord and to the church to help others after them. Jim and Bertha lived in the shelter of others' kindness for a few months, riding out to their parcel on Ford Road, felling trees in the low land near the pond to build a log cabin, and clearing the land for planting.

For the first three years, the isolation was nearly unbearable. Central City wasn't big enough for a post office until 1859. Farmers took turns driving the fifteen miles to the county seat at Marion to pick up mail once a week. The same year that a little post office came and Central City got its charter, John Peet built a gristmill at a new dam on the Wapsipinicon, and life got a bit easier for local farmers. Jim had taken nine-year-old George with him to help neighbors build the first bridge across the Wapsie only to see it washed away in the spring flood a few months before the post office opened. One step forward, two steps back. Life in Central City according to the letters that made their ways home to New Hampshire.

With glass and millwork more than thirty miles away and with the family savings having to go for seed, tools and basic furniture, the Parkers could only afford windows of thick oiled paper to let in light. The family didn't see the outside world through glass for two years--eight seasons and two dreadful winters of melancholy that flattened even Bertha's effervescence.

Jim and Bertha were into their seventies when the railroad finally came to Central City in 1887. Porter & Clark soon opened a farm machinery business, a bank opened, and by 1889 there were eighteen businesses clustered at the end of Ford Road only a couple of miles away from the Parker homestead.

Xavier and Permelia Sawyer's new 12-room Italianate home graced the square beside their prosperous store. Painted a slate gray and adorned with ornate jigsaw trimmings in white, the house was topped with a smaller third story giving it that wedding cake appearance. In the Sawyers' big stone store on Main and Fourth, a few of the appurtenances of civilization were available.

George had taken the cabin as his home after marrying Miriam, and when she left him, he continued to live there alone, sharing the work on his land and that of his parents who comforted him in his loss. The cabin, even with glass windows and a new cast iron stove from a Pennsylvania foundry, was no longer a home but just an outbuilding where he went to sleep.

On a recent night when the day's heat had settled into the house, Mariah went out on the back porch to gaze at the stars. *The rest of my world is gone; at least the stars are still mine,* she thought. But then it struck Mariah that even the firmament had changed. The polar star had moved from its rightful place over Mount Chocorua, and the familiar constellations now hovered over verdant rolling hills stretching out to the vanishing point without boundaries or benchmarks to fix your place in space and time. *I'm alone in a lifeboat on a green sea, and even the stars don't tell me where I'm headed.* One of the few blessings of the night was silence.

###

The next day was the usual—breezy and bright outside, hot and steamy inside; and as usual, Mariah spent much of her day in the kitchen with her perpetually vocal aunt. "How many songs do you know?" Mariah asked in a mixture of admiration and annoyance as she and her aunt prepared dinner. "It seems that every day you're singing a different one." Mariah didn't wait for an answer to her first question before asking a second. "Don't you know any sad ones?"

"I know dozens of songs, and yes, I know some sad ones, but Honey, you can't see the path to the future through tears, now can you? We don't need songs to make us sad. Life can do that for us. A good song is like a spring tonic, don't you think?"

"I guess you could say that," replied Mariah tepidly. *And sometimes just as hard to swallow.*

"Come on, Honey. Cheer up. Don't make me work so hard at it," said Bertha with a little squeeze on Mariah's arm.

George and Jim came into the house just long enough to put away their shotguns and say good morning to Mariah. She handed each of them a warm muffin to tide them over till noon. George held his hat in his hand. Pushing his brown hair back, he revealed a broad white forehead above his thick, dark brows. He nodded as he thanked his cousin whom he still treated like a special guest in his parents' house.

In a few minutes the women could hear the clinking of harness rings and buckles, stomping, and loud imperatives as Jim and George tied a team of horses to a new McCormack seeding machine, a proud new addition to the farm's technology that would spare them back-breaking hours of punching seed into the furrows stretching to the vanishing point in a north-south direction.

The Good Book said, "To everything there is a season, and a time to every purpose under heaven." It was time to plant, and Bertha was sure it was also the time to heal—the time had come for Mariah to heal and move on. The time to rend had given way to the time to sew.

As they set the table for dinner, Bertha told Mariah that two letters

144

had come, one for her and one for Mariah. Both were from Mariah's mother. "Dearie, could we wait until after dinner?"

"Why? Is there bad news? If so, I'd rather know it now than worry over it."

"No, no bad news. I'd feel better if we could wait, that's all."

"Very well," Mariah responded reluctantly. She was quite sure that whatever her mother said to her was also in Aunt Bertha's letter. It had been many months since anything in her life had been truly private.

When Jim and George came to the table, washed and smiling as they entered praising the aromas of fresh bread and a roast of pork, Bertha spoke the blessing with a special emphasis on thankfulness for the bonds of family.

As soon as the usual comments about work and weather were past, Bertha startled the family with a rhetorical question. "It's time George moved back into this house, don't you think?" Everyone had expected that he would tire of his daily treks back to the empty cabin, but Jim, George and Mariah wondered about the timing of Bertha's announcement.

"A half-mile across the fields every day. That ain't easy in any season when you work long hours. It's a waste of wood heating that old cabin," Bertha said, pointing with her fork for special emphasis. You eat just about every meal here, don't you George?"

Mariah looked at George with the hope that he would interrupt his mother and express his own wishes, but Bertha went on like a telegraph key.

"With Miriam gone, there's no reason for him to be all by himself, now ain't that right?" Bertha passed the bread with a big smile.

"Yup," said Jim who couldn't manage more with his mouth full. He looked up and nodded before continuing his ascent to the top of potato mountain erupting with brown gravy.

Mariah finally broke the ice. "This is your house and George is your son. I think you need to do what you think best."

Bertha waited only as long as a chairman holds a gavel over an un-contested motion. "I think the God Lord is telling me that it's time for George to come home."

"Home, yes, of course, he belongs home," said Mariah dutifully but without enthusiasm. But her words were all that was needed to elicit elation from her aunt and uncle. Jim smiled and nodded and looked back and forth between George and Mariah. Mariah smiled briefly, but went back to her meal with a degree of tension in her face that indicated a fear that more was being decided than just George's housing circumstances.

George's face revealed a certain disappointment in how Mariah received the news. Jim took out his pipe, signaling that it was time for Mariah and her aunt to withdraw to the kitchen.

"Could I see that letter now?" asked Mariah who was not quite prepared to discuss what had just gone on around the table.

"Of course, Dear." Bertha withdrew two letters from her apron pocket, one already opened addressed to her, and a second addressed to Mariah. Will had taken up with another woman. They weren't married, but they had been seen together more than a few times. "Apparently he has come to accept the divorce as final," she wrote.

"So now you know," Bertha said in a low voice to her niece. Mariah tried to conceal how stunned she was. Will had accepted that their relationship was truly at an end, a closure more painful than court papers or legal pronouncements.

"I see that it is," said Mariah without expression. She turned her face away and left the kitchen abruptly, fighting to control the pain rising from her stricken heart.

# CHAPTER 18

## *The Season for Silk*

To everything there is a season. The seed of spring received rain and sun of summer and grew according to the time and purpose that heaven ordained for the earth below. God had put all of the elements in place in Iowa for cornucopian bounty. All that man and woman had to do was respond with heart and hand, and seedtime, in the divine scheme of things, would turn to bounty.

As George and Mariah lumbered down Ford Road in the farm wagon, they saw the signs around them that it was the season for silk. With corn silk came the ripening of the kernels, the fulfillment of the promise of seed into swelling fecundity. The best tasting sweet corn was picked about three weeks after the silk appeared, and all along the road the corn stood seven feet tall with big, plump ears topped with sun-singed tufts of silk.

"I bet this harvest'll even top last year's," said George with a contented smile. "Remember the year you came? Good harvest, but the bottom fell out of the market."

"Then '94 was the worst harvest ever. Yes, I know," said Mariah with a joking tone of voice. Hey," she shouted as she gave George's shoulder a push, "are you trying to tell me I've been a curse on the land?"

George smiled and looked embarrassed. "I guess it sounded that way, huh. Well, if so, you're making up for it this year. Just look at those tassels."

"And with a good economy again, you should rake in the dough."

"What do you mean, 'you'?" said George who suddenly looked serious. "Shouldn't it be 'we'? After all, you're part of the family now."

"Being first cousins, I guess we were born family, but thank you for saying that, George. Yes, you've all tried hard to make me feel welcome."

George and Mariah looked at each other in a moment of seriousness. George broke the silence with a slap of the reins and a "getup" that set the horses into a brisk trot.

"So, George, why did you ask me to come to town with you? Your mother could have used my help this morning."

"I just thought it would be good if we had a little break in the routine."

"A little break, huh?" thought Mariah skeptically. George avoided her eyes.

He pulled on the reins to slow the horses as they approached the narrow passage under the new railroad trestle. Although the trestle was nine years old, the timbers still reeked of the thick creosote that rose out of the wood in the scorching summer sun. Mariah squinted and shook her head to clear her eyes of the acrid fumes.

"We'll take our time and enjoy the beautiful day. No need rushin' right back home after we do our shoppin'," said George. "While I go into Mills' for the bolts and brackets I need for the reaper, you can do the shopping at Sawyer's, then we'll drop off the cream at the creamery, and…"

"Yes, and then what?" asked Mariah in evident good cheer.

"Just look under the seat. See that blanket? Pull it off."

Mariah leaned down and folded back the blanket and found a covered basket. When she opened it, she found bread and cheese, cold roasted chicken and some sugar cookies. George smiled.

"So did anyone I know help you put this little picnic together?" asked Mariah with the inquisitor's stare.

"Nope. I put it all together myself."

"Really?"

"Hey, don't you think I know how to do things up nice?" said George with slightly wounded pride.

"Just asking," replied Mariah. "Well, a picnic, huh?" Mariah decided not to ask more and let George take the lead.

Throughout the summer there had been few of the ill-disguised nudges and hints from Auntie that Mariah and George should be more than cousins, more than friends. After the news about Will and another woman, Bertha backed off, and let reality sink in. By midsummer Mariah seemed to be coming out of the doldrums.

"I thought we could get a couple of bottles of root beer…"

"Or Coca-Cola, if you're lucky," Mariah replied.

George pulled back on the reins as they came around the bend and had a full view of the square. "Look at this crowd."

"Wooo. Maybe we'll have to settle for sarsaparilla. Sawyer's will be out of Coca-Cola by now; unless Adelia has a few sodas saved."

"I don't know if it's worth a dime a bottle," challenged Mariah. "I understand it's a nickel in most parts of the country."

"After we leave off the cream, I'll have some spare dimes, and I don't mind spendin' a couple of dimes for a special occasion. There's another special occasion comin' up next Saturday night."

"The dance," said Mariah with a hint of skepticism. "I didn't know you danced."

"Well, I might be a little rusty, but…" George replied. "I just thought…" Suddenly he felt uncomfortable. Mariah jumped right in.

"I suppose we really should hear Gisella tickle those ivories. She can pound out quite a tune on that upright."

Gisella, the wife of George's half brother Madison, was the musical jewel of the community. She passed on her gifts to her children who played instruments or sang to the delight of a spread out farming community desperate for amusement.

"Square dancing?"

"Sure, but they do waltzes and fox trots now, too."

"My. Central City is a daring social scene," quipped Mariah.

"Oh, you'll be impressed."

"And will I have to worry about my feet?"

"As a matter of fact, no. Your feet will be perfectly safe. Believe it or not, I can do the two-step and the waltz better than most."

"My, my. Who would have imagined?" said Mariah as she sank back into the seat with a wry smile.

"Yes, who would have imagined?" echoed George. He glanced at her with the hope that she was thinking the same thing he was. Yes, who would have imagined that in just a couple of months Mariah would have made such progress in putting the past behind her, and who would have imagined that she would have begun to warm up to him? Only a few months before, Mariah had told George that he was "like a guardian older brother."

"Older brother, hrummph," he had murmured under his breath. George had given Mariah time and kept his distance. He had never even held her hand except to help her down from the wagon. Furtive glances, catching her eye during lulls in the conversation at the dinner table, flirtatious teasing, nothing more serious. It had taken time for her to trust a man again after what she had been through, and trust was not something you could ask someone to give.

As they came into town, there was hardly room on Main Street to get the wagon through the mass of farm vehicles that lined the streets for market day.

"Looks to me like the madding crowd has finally reached Iowa," Mariah quipped.

"Madding crowd?" asked George who knew that there was always a big room behind any door he opened into Mariah's mind.

"Thomas Hardy."

"I guess I heard of him," said George sheepishly.

"Remember when I asked if any Iowan ever wrote anything more than a post card and you said Emerson Hough.

Of course. *Field and Stream.*

"But that's not all he wrote," Mariah whined in mock disgust. "I guess you could say he's the cheery version of Hardy. All of that nonsense about how wonderful it is to live out in the middle of nowhere. I'm afraid I'm about excited about rural life as Eustasia Vye."

George looked at Mariah as though she were speaking Latin. "I'll stick *to Field and Stream*," he said, hoping she would leave her books out of their conversation.

"Yup. All these folks moved from anywhere to nowhere thinking they were making progress," said Mariah whose sunny disposition suddenly turned cloudy.

George could read Mariah's face. *What progress have I made coming to nowhere? Land stretched out for miles, miles populated with corn, Indians, wildlife and a few pioneers.* Mariah looked beyond the buzzing of the swarm of farmers to the silent fields encircling the town and mumbled: "Here it is. Thoreau's life of quiet desperation."

George didn't let the comment pass. "I'm not sure your books give you much comfort."

She looked him in the eye and said, "I'm not going to live in any part of nowhere for the rest of my life, I'm sure of that."

George's face fell. He looked awkwardly down at his sunburned hands that had worked the deep soil in his rich and verdant nowhere for forty years. If he asked Mariah to marry him—and if she accepted—the day would come when he might have to leave everything he had known from the time he crossed the frozen Mississippi forty years before.

The silence between them was relieved by the cacophony of the marketplace where three out of four of Central City's two hundred citizens gathered once a week during fair weather to buy, to sell, to gossip, and sometimes to court.

Mariah's mouth turned up in a mild, polite smile as P.G. Henderson, Central City's version of a magnate, crossed in front of them with his gold watch chain glimmering against his new gabardine suit. He was jawing at Augustus Hatch about stepping up brick production for a warehouse near the new railroad station. They waved and touched their hat brims to Mariah, but never let up a moment in their negotiations.

Just down Fourth Street behind Sawyer's Store, Willard Butters clanged on an anvil just outside the open doors of his blacksmith shop, trying to escape the heat of the forge in the breeze and the shade of an ash tree.

"Well isn't that the classic picture?" said Mariah with a tone somewhere between wit and sarcasm. "The village smithy."

"Naw, his arms aren't anywhere near as strong as iron bands," retorted George with a smirk. "And it's supposed to be a chestnut tree, not an ash," Mariah added, and they both laughed.

George sought Mariah's eyes. She was smiling again. She turned and looked into his hazel eyes with a softened expression. She studied his thin, angular face momentarily and relaxed in the comfort of his ingenuousness. Although he was no intellectual, his face was animated with active eyes that revealed a mind equally so. It also didn't hurt that his hair was still mostly brown and just starting to thin at the crown. He was always clean-shaven and as tidy as farm life would allow.

"Townsfolk are forever asking him to jury rig a tool or farm machine to get one more season out of it," said George who waved at Butters when the smithy rested his hammer for a moment and looked down Fourth Street to see who had just driven up for market day.

George found a hitching post right in front of Sawyer's with space enough to tie up the wagon. "Just smell that coffee," he said after inhaling the wafting aroma from the whirling grinder near the open door of the store.

As George climbed down on the left, Mariah gathered her skirt to step down on the right. George came around to her side quickly. "Now wait just a minute and I'll help you."

"Are you sure you want other men in town seeing you doing this? It could set a standard just like railroad time," said Mariah.

"It wouldn't hurt any of 'em to offer a gentlemanly hand," George said as he helped her to the ground. Then he winked.

Mariah showed a flash of pain and turned her eyes away. George recoiled at his faux pas. For some reason, the wink had disturbed her and it unsettled him. "I'll go ahead to Mills'," he said, and made a quick, uncomfortable exit.

Mariah thought, "What have I done to him? It was a harmless wink."

A wink. The gentle and tender and ever so sensual gesture. The wink had been Mariah's downfall, the trap the Fates had laid for her as punishment for defying the stars and the order of things. George had inadvertently mocked her in his first attempt at intimacy. It was just a wink. George had worked so hard to help Mariah accept the new flow of her life, to coax her into the current and to move with it, not against it, to swim again without looking back, to move on, to leave

Will in her past for that was the only reasonable thing she could do. She had warmed up to George; he had gained her trust. Mariah would not—could not—hold the wink against him. The wink forced her to confront the truth that everything had changed with Will and was about to change with George.

"Mariah!" called Adelia Sawyer as she came out of the door of their stately home onto her porch. "Don't go to the store just yet," she said. Adelia sat in a rocker in her rose-colored shirtwaist and patted the empty rocker next to her. She dressed fashionably, but she still had the direct, unpolished manner of a farm girl. "Come sit a minute."

Mariah tried to clear her mind of confused emotions as she stepped onto the shaded porch and sat down beside one of the few women in town who did not have to risk her fair skin in the unrelenting elements.

"So I see you and George came in by yourselves today." Adelia pursed her lips and raised an eyebrow with the confidence of a gypsy decoding a message in the bottom of a teacup.

Mariah nodded without comment and looked out at the hubbub of traffic.

"How are you doing?" Adelia probed.

Although Mariah knew that Adelia meant the plural "you," she decided to keep it to the singular.

"Oh, I'm fine. I've just got to pick up coffee and sugar, and I thought I'd take a look at what you've got for yard goods. I haven't had a new dress in a long time."

"And there's a dance coming up in a week. Can you find time to put a dress together in a week?" asked Adelia. Mariah didn't take her eyes off the ebb and flow of Main Street.

"I probably could find the time, if I had a mind to," said Mariah.

"Well, don't you think it would be nice?"

Mariah turned her gaze on Adelia that warned her not to stick her nose into someone else's business.

*Is this whole town in league with Aunt Bertha? I wish they'd let us run our own lives. Adelia, I won't be trifled with.*

"Now look, Mariah. We've become good friends…"

"I really need to get to the store before George gets done at Mills'.

I wondered if I might be able to get a couple of Coca-Colas from you. Store's likely out," interrupted Mariah.

"Sure, I'll get them."

When Adelia returned with the bottles, she resumed her rocking. "We all think a lot of George here in Central City. Never could understand what got into Miriam. Wasn't his fault they broke up. We all know that."

"I think a lot of George, too." Mariah nodded, looking straight ahead. Adelia's move.

"I'm glad to hear it." The chairs rocked opposite one another until Adelia abruptly stopped and synchronized her rocking with Mariah's. "You know, Jim's gettin' along in years and…"

Check. Countermove. Mariah stopped rocking and turned to her friend. "Adelia. When Jim dies, that farm isn't going to George. And you can't make a go of it with less than forty acres. George's half brother and sisters will have to settle for it being divided up. George is only Jim's stepson."

"Yes, but he's the one who stayed…"

Mariah shook her head. "Stay or not, the farm isn't going to be his. When the time comes, George is going to have to make it on the little nest egg he's been able to put together, and that isn't much."

"But he's a hard worker, and what a good, good person he is." Adelia put her hand on Mariah's.

Mariah resumed rocking and looked straight ahead again. "Don't you worry about George and me. We understand each other. And we watch out for each other."

"Is that all?" asked Adelia.

Mariah gave Adelia a sideward glance that served as a warning that she was moving in too close.

"I'm not a kid anymore."

"Oh, Mariah. Love's not only kids…"

"And George is old enough to be my father."

"Barely. But who cares? There's still a twinkle in his eye," said Adelia.

"Oh, stop," said Mariah with a smirk that helped ease the tension. Mariah rose from the rocker. "It'll be a lot cooler down by the river."

Adelia's eyebrows rose and fell with intense curiosity. "Oh?"

"George and I are going to have a little picnic down by the mill," she added.

"Under that big elm?"

"I suppose. We're wary of the sun; we've both been burned before if you know what I mean," said Mariah, her eyes locking on Adelia's and a brow raised.

"I s'pose," replied Adelia, standing with arms akimbo, "but nothing flourishes without the sun either." Adelia shook her head with a smirk, having grown used to Mariah's metaphors and allusions that often baffled others.

As she reached the sidewalk, Mariah turned to face her friend once again. "Well, will you be at the dance?" she asked.

""Of course. We'll see you there?" The "you" bore the clear implication of the plural once again.

"I guess so," replied Mariah, teasing Adelia with her deliberate evasiveness.

Mariah was spared any further friendly inquisition by the noisy arrival of Adelia's twelve-year-old son Jay who came running down the sidewalk behind a rolling iron hoop. The boy—tall, lanky and sandy-haired—brought back the memory of Frederick before consumption sapped him of his vigor and joy. Mariah caught the hoop before it struck her. He stopped and pulled off his cap and tucked his disheveled shirt back into his knickers. "Sorry, Miss Mariah. The hoop got away from me."

A pained expression swept over Mariah's face that unsettled and confused the boy who had uncommonly good manners. Young Jay looked back and forth between his exasperated mother and Mariah and began stammering. "I didn't mean…well, I guess I was foolish to… .I'm awful sorry, really I am."

Mariah handed the hoop back to him with a slight smile. "If you go that way," said Mariah pointing to the east away from the busy square, "you'll be able to drive that hoop at full throttle without running into anybody."

After the boy rolled onward, Mariah turned to Adelia for her last salvo. "That boy's got a lot of his mother in him. A good looker like his mother, too," she added with a pert smile.

Mariah waved to Adelia and walked briskly to the busy steps of the store where the front doors were propped open with blocks of local limestone to accommodate the oscillating tide of commerce on market day.

Shaded kerosene lamps hung over glass counters. Shelves lined the walls all the way to the tin ceiling with a ladder running along iron rails to allow clerks to fetch goods from on high. A special favorite of young families in recent months were the new breakfast cereals from Kellogg's, and kids often pooled their penny candy money to buy a pack of Wrigley's new Juicy Fruit gum for a nickel. What new commercial wonders had come out of the Chicago fair.

Spices from distant lands, coffee, tea, chocolate and hard candies scented the air. A balance scale with a suspended metal pan pointed its black finger at pounds and ounces, and an ornate brass National cash register clanged prosperously as the flags rose and fell in the glass window to announce the total sale.

Mariah took out her shopping list and gathered items she or Aunt Bertha had put on the list. They went into a washed flour sack that she used as her shopping bag. Then the special treat: The back room where bolts of fabric stood on end in racks around the outside with a cutting table and a display of Butterick's patterns at the clerk's counter.

Muslin for aprons and work shirts; calico and gingham prints for daily wear; wool for winter warmth. Sawyer's carried dyes, needles, buttons and trims, but mostly the basics that farming families could afford. There at the end of dress fabrics stood a bolt of shiny, rose-colored material as out of place among cottons and wools as a rose among daisies. Mariah ran her hand over it. Silk. She closed her eyes.

Once again she was in her sewing room on Wakefield Street with her dress form standing in the corner. Her Singer whirred with the oscillating treadle as another elegant evening dress came together one dart, tuck or ruffle after another. She could hear the clang of the streetcar bells as it came to a stop in front of the house. And then the sound of Will's footsteps coming up the broad oak steps to the second floor, the gentle calling of her name, the strength in his embrace, the feel of his stubble, the scent of the man who still made her heart flutter with passion—and the feel of silk when his hand caressed her.

"Excuse me. Are you all right?" said the clerk.

Mariah opened her eyes and took her hand off the bolt of rose-colored cloth. "Oh, yes, yes. Just imagining. It doesn't cost anything to imagine."

"You know," said the tiny, gray-haired woman with ramrod posture, "this silk isn't expensive at all." Then, with furtive eyes and a whisper she added, "this bolt is a second, but we'll look it over real good. The dye ain't even. They call it 'Gossamer Rose.' More like 'Wilted Rose' if you ask me." The clerk chuckled under her breath. I'll throw in a couple of extra yards if we find some with bad streaks."

"Let me show you the newest Paris styles," said the clerk after she finished folding up the rose colored silk and some dark pink grosgrain ribbon for trim. "I've got some that aren't too complicated."

Mariah rolled her eyes. "I'm used to complications," she said with an ironic expression as she flipped through the Butterick's patterns for the fall of 1896. "The Viennese Waltz." A daring neckline for Central City, but a gauzy lace panel could provide for modesty. A myriad of tiny opalescent buttons would offer a challenge to an experienced seamstress. "I'll take this one," said Mariah.

"Are you sure?"

"I'm sure." A light seemed to illuminate Mariah's face. "Yes, I'm sure, and after I've worn the dress, would you like to display it?"

"Display it?"

"Yes, and you could give my name if anyone's interested…"

"You're going to sell the dress?"

"No, no. My services. Someone might want a special dress. Beyond their abilities," said Mariah looking the clerk in the eye like a traveling salesman with a tempting new product from the East.

"We've never done that before, but I could ask Mrs. Sawyer.

Mariah laughed confidently. "Oh, she'll be happy to show it. She's as partial to complications as I am."

"Well, I hope this works out for you," said the clerk as she wrapped the rose silk in brown paper."

Mariah touched the package with a pensive gaze. "It's a second, but I'll see what I can do with it," said Mariah as she drew open her purse strings. An expression of determination, even defiance, passed over Mariah's face as she left with her silk.

George left the smithy behind and started down Fourth Street. He carried a piece of hardware from the hay baler that had been repaired. When George looked up and saw that Mariah was looking his way, he broke out in a smile that conveyed a truth he could no longer disguise—he had fallen in love with her.

And Will had fallen into the embrace of another woman. No wife's scented memories could change that fact. It was the year of our Lord 1896, the corn squeaked as it grew toward a bumper crop, and anything that could grow had all the right conditions to flourish. George arrived at the wagon in a buoyant mood.

"You ready for a picnic?" he said as he helped her up onto the seat of the wagon. "Yes, I certainly am. I've got two cold bottles of Coca-Cola in the bag for us." Mariah smiled, but she was not relaxed. She clearly knew that something was up. No doubt she had grown very fond of George. She had complimented him as a hard worker, cautious with money, multi-talented. She made hopeful comments that he was tiring of field and furrow and was ready to do what his stepbrother Madison had done. Move on to something new. A desk job in the city, the state department of agriculture, the railroad, sales of farm machines. Something other than dirt and manure. Maybe a fresh start back East.

The undershot water wheel of the gristmill near the Methodist Church splashed and dashed. The ground around the mill usually rumbled with the spinning of the millstones as bags of raw grain arrived by wagonloads and left as cracked corn, feed or flour. Midsummer, however, was the season of low water. The Wapsipinicon moved slowly and silently around rocks and trees fallen from the banks into the stream. The water fell over the log dam like a veil rather than a torrent. The harvest was more than two months away. Things needed time to grow in the summer heat.

A blanket in the summer sun, the sound of lazy water, wildflowers and the darting flight of dragonflies—all familiar; lovely and sad. Hundreds of miles away children dove from a high perch into a swirling pothole of cold, mountain water that magnified sparkles as the granite walls magnified children's laughter. The blanket. A special meal. The hope for a brighter future.

"You know, I've been doing a lot of thinking," said George after he had laid out the food and handed Mariah a linen napkin.

"Oh?" responded Mariah with a down under glance as she put some cold fried chicken on George's plate. "About the harvest? I know you've been thinking a lot about winter wheat and alfalfa."

George started to laugh. "Right. Winter wheat and alfalfa. That and corn silk and steer prices in Chicago. I must bore you worse than a worm in sweet corn. I sometimes think of other things, you know. I read the entire "Cross of Gold" speech in the paper, I'll have you know."

"So you're against the gold standard and you're going to vote for William Jennings Bryan," said Mariah, once again toying with George about his deeper thoughts.

"Maybe I will vote Democrat. But I haven't been thinking about that, at least not today. Now, come on. You're not making this easier."

"Not making what easier? Am I supposed to be reading your deeper thoughts?" Mariah said with a flirtatious grin as she sipped her root beer.

"You and I are getting along real well, don't you think?"

"Can't remember a cross word since you spilled your coffee on me at the church social."

"If you'd been wearing that yellow dress of yours, I don't think I'd be forgiven to this day," said George with a chuckle.

"Other than that," said Mariah, "I think we're getting along about as well as any two people could expect to get along."

"Sounds like Sears and Roebuck. A working partnership," said George shaking his head. He held her gaze for a moment, a serious expression on his face. "I guess I'm not the most romantic guy in the world."

"George, look at this picnic lunch and this beautiful spot. I'd say you might be one of the most romantic men in Linn County."

"I guess I'll take that as a high compliment, considering the stiff competition in the world of romance in Linn County." George and Mariah laughed.

George took Mariah's hand. He let silence and the contact of eyes that had both known love and loss to lead her where he wanted to go. "Mariah, I'd like to go to that dance next Saturday night with a new understanding between us. We're cousins, we've both been married before. I want us to forget about all that. Are you willing to put all that behind us?"

"George, there's a lot from the past that I want very much to forget," replied Mariah who looked down at her ringless hand.

"I just want a fresh start. I can't ask more than that."

Mariah nodded.

"You must know I love you," said George. He looked down. It was too hard to look her in the eyes and say those words.

"I'm not the only one who knows," replied Mariah, chiding him ever so gently.

"Land sakes. I haven't told anyone else. Not even Mother."

"I guess it's obvious without saying it. You know, the way you act around me. People in town know."

"But now I need to know something. Do you love me, can you love me, are you feeling anything for me, I mean, more than just good friends?" The words came fast and he found the courage to look into her eyes for an honest reaction.

"Certainly more than cousins," Mariah said with a blink and then her expression changed quickly to introspection. She took a few breaths. "George, you're asking a lot of things. I think the answer to them all is…well, favorable," she said with a blush. "Let's go to the dance with a new understanding—we're more than just friends. How could any woman who's been treated so well by a man like you not be in love with him?"

George might have hoped for more, but he was more patient by nature than the moment indicated. He took Mariah in his arms and kissed her, not a passionate kiss, but sustained and eager.

They relaxed and laughed and ate in the pleasure of one another's company. A courtship had begun. George had understood, rightly, that it was too soon for a proposal, but he helped Mariah into the wagon with the confidence that a proposal could come in its season as naturally as all things ripen and grow in their season.

They took the road along the riverbank then back to Ford Road. Black-eyed Susans swayed in the welcome breeze, and dust swirled in eddies where the gravel road broadened on the west side of the trestle. George pulled the team to a stop on the curve that rose as Ford Road leaves the downtown behind. A freight train was leaving the station with slanted smoke and steam blasting into the breeze and bending to its will. George and Mariah looked to the left and saw the sun gleaming off the brass headlamp. The slatted cattle cars were a cacophony of mooing and moaning as the train gained speed, and the bright caboose shone with a new coat of red paint. The whistle sounded with such force that the steam defied the wind and rose straight as a Fourth of July rocket.

George and Mariah watched contemplatively as the iron horse moved with absolute determination. Mariah imagined her life moving on invisible rails down winding routes with junctions that flipped open and closed according to a mysterious plan directed from far away. If the steaming locomotive jumped the rails, it brought disaster on itself and those that were coupled to it. But then, even train wrecks were part of the plan. The mystery of free will on the paths of destiny troubled her. If she hadn't found her place in the world, possibly this day was a new beginning to getting there.

After the train clanged over the trestle, George clicked the horses into a trot. He took Mariah's hand and smiled. He looked down below the seat and saw the package wrapped in brown paper. "So, what did you buy?"

"Oh, just some material for a dress," Mariah responded nonchalantly. "You got me thinking about silk."

George nodded and smiled and didn't ask more.

# CHAPTER 19

## *Kissin' Cousins*

Dear Sarah,

*I have exciting news. George asked Mariah to marry him, and she accepted. They will be married in October after the harvest. For now they will live in the log house until they can affourd to build a fraim house. If only you could be here.*

*I think they will learn to love one another. They are both hard workers, and they are good company for one another. We don't expect any children with both of them married before and no children either one, thank the good Lord now that I think of it. George turned forty-six on the twentiuth of July. The eighteen years diffrance between them might matter if they was marrying under the usual sircomstances, but they have to except thier lot in life.*

Here we are aunt and uncle to Mariah, and now her in-laws, and you, too, with George. To think it's been forty years since we've laid eyes on each other. Can you imagine? George was only six when we said goodbye.

Bertha's latest letter dated September 5, 1896 closed with news of Bertha and Jim's son Madison and the birth of his son Glenn. Madison bought forty acres a few miles south on Sawyer Road and built himself a fine house with a corner tower room with a conical spire.

He made good money on Red Poll cattle. Madison, Gisella and the baby had just come back from Cedar Rapids where they rode in an electric streetcar and took an elevator to the top of a building six stories high. Bertha was thrilled. A son returning home, another getting married. "The Lord is piling blessing on blessing," Bertha wrote.

Sarah folded the letter and put it back in the envelope. This was the first letter in a long time that didn't have a page marked with an X.

"Are you gonna announce Mariah's wedding in church?" asked Moze who had grown an inch taller than Amos. His hair was as black as his father's before the gray invaded.

"Moze, you have to promise me that you won't tell anybody about this. Do you understand? No one," said Sarah sternly. Amos junior's eyes widened, recoiling at the strength of his mother's words.

"Now, Sai, you know we can't keep this a secret for long. Mariah has a few friends that still write to her now and then, and she's bound to tell them."

"That may be, but *we* aren't announcing any second wedding or it'll be over my dead body."

"Moze, I guess we're not gonna announce it in church," said Amos, brushing his beard and taking on a very dramatic look, "because that would be an act of murder."

"Oh, stop now," said Sarah. "I'm serious. We've gone through enough embarrassment and attention. We don't need any more. If people find out by word of mouth…"

"Gossip, you mean."

"If they find out somehow, we'll live with it, but we aren't about to stand up in church and announce that our divorced daughter is going to marry her divorced first cousin."

"I thought people would be happy for her," said Moze with downcast eyes, pained by the shame that continued to be attached to his beautiful older sister's name.

"Honestly, Moze, you look so grown up, but sometimes you seem so naïve," added Florence who looked at him with her head cocked sideways, her fair hair piled on her head accentuating her graceful neck. Moze stared down coldly at her from nearly a foot above.

"Now, now. Let's not squabble," said Sarah. "It's only natural that you want to stick up for your sister, Moze, but society has its rules."

"Some of the rules aren't very Christian." Moze grumbled, then smoothed his shiny, black moustache.

"Well, Mother," Florence interjected with a tactical glance at her brother, "it *is* very Christian that you aren't supposed to divorce, and if you do, you aren't supposed to marry again."    "Will was the adulterer!" shouted Moze, crossing his arms to keep his hands from flying in anger.

"That may be," said Sarah modeling a soft voice, "but she was warned. As to first cousins, I doubt if anyone in Central City, Iowa knows or cares, but around here, people are going to talk."

Amos looked from one face to the next as though he was about to offer them the bread and wine of communion. "Family comes first, so let's not be worryin' about what others think right now. Your sister has suffered enough, and we don't want to add to it. We're gonna pray for her. We'll deal with the gossip when it reaches us."

For three years the family had prayed for Mariah to accept the end of her marriage to Will, and for two years, Will's letters worked at cross-purposes with their prayers.

*Do you still love me? Yes, but how could I trust you?…Remember, I didn't want the divorce …I promised you there wouldn't be other women, and a few days later, I get a bill of divorcement… What do you expect of me? I'm flesh and blood. I've waited and waited until I thought I'd die of loneliness.* In the spring of 1896 the letters stopped.

In the late summer heat Mariah spent all of her spare time in her room with the door closed. The hum of her Singer sent vibrations through the house, a very pleasing sound in the ears of Aunt Bertha and Uncle Jim, and most of all to George because they knew Mariah was making a very special dress. The Page family attended the Baptist church on Fifth Street, a tithing family who served the church with a heart for God.

Then the word came down from the pastor.   Mariah and George could not be married there.  Divorced people at the altar for a second blessing? Unheard of. What God has joined together, let no man put asunder. George and Mariah, with the immediate family, passed the closed doors of the church, the wedding cake house, and the homes of respectable Central City neighbors and rode all morning to the county seat at Marion to be married by Mr. Treat, the justice of the peace. The town understood how George and Mariah felt. They even wished them well. But there were certain standards that could not be relaxed.

George Washington Taylor and Sarah Mariah Brandon were now husband and wife, cousins, niece and nephew, son-in-law and daughter-in-law in a tight-knit family. "George and Mariah took a few days to go to Cedar Rapids," wrote Bertha. "There's some nice shops there now since the last time we was there. Mariah's picking up some bolts of cloth for dreses she's been asked to make for some ladys in town. Mariah got the Singer all oiled and polished. She vowing to save every dime she makes. Says she wants to make a visit home. It's a dream we've had, too."

"Amos, she can't leave the two of them," said Sarah as she set the letter down. "Bertha's all crippled with rheumatism, and she says Jim can hardly get his breath just climbing the stairs."

"No, she won't be visiting," said Amos as he stood at the window watching a thunderstorm pour sheets over Cold River. He turned and looked Sarah in the eyes. "If I know my elder daughter, she'll be coming home for good when her duty is done out there."

"What about George?"

"Mariah's the one who'll decide," said Amos as he watched a flash of lighting in the distance.

Sarah looked at Amos in astonishment.

# CHAPTER 20

## The Deere Reaper

*J*im sat in his easy chair with the newspaper dropped on his lap. His voice, once so powerful, failed him as he wheezed and coughed. A few years had passed since he had last sung a solo in church, and the sparkle of joy in his eyes had dimmed. He took some comfort in his stepson's happy marriage. For the past two years George and Mariah had lifted the load from Bertha and him. At eighty the one thing that Linn County's oldest resident could hope for was that his wife would not be left helpless when he was gone.

Bertha dried his forehead and poured several of Humphrey's pills into his hand. "Here's some water, Dear. And I don't care what you say, I'm gonna call for the doctor."

"Oh, no you're not…" His coughing choked off his words, and his face reddened. His ankles were thick, and he had no strength to get himself out of the chair without help. Bertha dispatched the hired man to town to fetch the doctor.

"Them thing's ain't worth…" Jim scoffed at Humphrey's, but swallowed them down nonetheless. He was no believer in modern medicine, and especially skeptical of homeopathic medicine in particular. "Might's well take a spoonful of sugar. Tastes a lot better and prob'ly

166

does more good. And don't waste our money…" Coughing racked his body again. "Don't waste our money on the doc."

Bertha and George got Jim to his bed, and his coughing eased. George started to pull down the green shades when Jim called out, "No shades, George. No shades. I want to see my land."

The crop of wheat ringing the Parker house glistened in the morning dew.

Within two hours the doctor came and went. "It's his heart more than his lungs, Mrs. Parker. I'm afraid there's nothing more we can do. It's called congestive heart failure. The old pump just isn't working efficiently anymore." Bertha sat in a chair at his side reading. When her husband nodded off, she prayed silently.

Mariah and George sat at the kitchen table composing a letter to the folks in Sandwich, New Hampshire. Sarah's last letter celebrated the end of the fighting in Cuba because her handsome, black-haired son would be coming home miraculously spared the wounds of war or the pestilence of yellow fever. The Spanish-American War that had begun a few months after the battleship *Maine* exploded in Havana ended before Christmas of 1898. The whole family—Iowa and New Hampshire—feared that the war against an old European empire might drag on for years. Instead, the war lasted only months. American technology had stunned the world with a new kind of efficiency of destruction and conquest.

"Tell Moze he looks wonderful in that uniform except for that flat-brimmed hat," wrote Mariah with Moze's studio portrait propped up against her teacup. "I'm glad he learned to duck better than Daddy," Mariah added. When she read her letter back to George and his parents, they all laughed with the relief that the Brandon's only living son was safe and coming home.

"Anything you want me to add?" asked Mariah as Bertha started up the stairs with pills and water for Jim.

"Maybe we shouldn't mention Jim right now," said Mariah. Bertha shook her head, her face grim. "We don't want to put a damper on their happiness right now."

The medicine that the doctor left allowed Jim to sleep peacefully through the night, and Bertha trusted that a couple of days' rest would bring back some of his strength. With fair skies the harvest had to begin, but not with Jim directing it.

Early in the morning, as soon as the dew evaporated from the fields, George climbed into the spring seat of the new John Deere threshing machine, a big model whose six cutting blades did the work of twenty men. With a fistful of reins strung out to six horses, George guided the cutting wheel and conveyer belt, jutting out to the left into the wheat.

The clanging and shuffling of this great new American machine frightened the horses at first, but George's steady hand moved them smoothly forward. Irregular gusts bowed the top-heavy wheat east then north. The sea of grain fell in great swaths before the ingenious engine of American efficiency, stalks separated from heads, bushel upon bushel taken from the land, the stubble trampled under the hooves of draft horses driven forward and shielded from the frightening machine by blinders.

The morning view from Jim's window was a ring of gold around the Parker home. By sunset, the scene was barren and stark. The fields to the north were cleared; the harvest of wheat was finished. Men and machines fell still. George opened the kitchen door, and pulled off his hat. "Well, that's the end of it," he said. "Did Jim see us finish?" Bertha and Mariah rose from their chairs. Bertha's eyes were red; Mariah's expression was grim. "Oh, Ma, I'm so sorry." George wrapped his long arms around the women as they wept together.

# CHAPTER 21

## Blown East

A thunderhead grew in the afternoon heat and eventually turned into a gray anvil blocking out most of the sun. Far to the south, the tower spire of Madison Page's house reached defiantly into the sky daring lightning to strike it. The intense heat on the mid-July plains rushed upward toward the mound of boiling clouds.

Mariah fought to retrieve the day's wash from the clothesline before the wind turned the sheets into sails. A forked pole held the dipping line high above the ground, but it suddenly flipped like a compass point toward the east and fell to the ground, dropping the line into the dust.

Three years had passed since Jim's death, and with the dawn of a new century, and Aunt Bertha felt it was time to hold a family council. In June she had let her children know that upon her death the homestead would have to be sold so each one would receive an equal share.

"Ma," said George in despair. "I don't have enough to buy the others out."

Madison suggested a mortgage, but the sisters reminded him of the debt for all the farm machinery, and in another week, the insurance was due again. Equal shares meant the days of the Parker Farm on Ford Road were numbered.

"George, I guess I'm gonna have to stick around for a few more years," said Bertha with her perennial optimism being put to the test. "Bumper harvests and stable farm prices, that's what we need. And my old ticker's got to keep tickin'. You all gotta pray hard."

What was troubling news to George gave Mariah new hope. Although Mariah had grown to love her fervent, God-fearing aunt, she knew that when she was gone, there wouldn't be much to keep George in Central City. George would just have to consider pulling up stakes—maybe even moving back East. *God, please grant me my wish.*

Despite eight years in the isolation of Central City, Mariah had not grown used to the adversities of wind and weather, nor had she forgotten the pleasures of paved roads, steam heat, and running water that she had briefly enjoyed during the halcyon early years with Will. The Sears Roebuck catalog was one of the few links to the modern world, a world and a life that seemed as distant as her childhood days on the banks of Cold River.

Mariah worked hard at making Iowa her home, and she had worked at loving George Taylor, a good man, a loving man, a man who deserved to be loved. And in some kind of a way, she had come to love him. But there are many colors of love, some more vivid than others.

No mountains shielded Mariah from tempests, and no Iowa stream could offer her the hope of escape. George was only a boy of six when he left the notch, and for him the old home represented sadness and failure. Whatever the hardships of Iowa, it rewarded hard labor and yielded great bounty. For Mariah it was Iowa that was the symbol of failure of her dreams no matter how bountiful the harvest.

Mariah's discomfort amplified with the new century. She had not been home to see her brother and sister grow to maturity. She had missed her parents' prime years. Letters only deepened her yearning. In the weeks after the family council, Mariah's dream became a plan. By God, she would not be absent when her parents needed her the most. And although she hated to admit it to herself, the years of separation, a new life, and a new husband, had not healed the grieving for the loss of William Channing Dunfield and the life he once promised her. She felt terrible guilt, but she longed to see him again. Her yearning felt all the more sinful because she wasn't letting George know what else was disturbing her mood in recent weeks.

"Mariah, Mariah!" shouted George into the wind. "I'll get the animals in. I'll pick up the washtub and anything that'll blow." He leaned into the wind and walked up to his wife. "We haven't got much time before it hits."

"Where's your mother?"

"She went over to Madison's this morning. He'll watch out for her," replied George as he held his straw hat down.

The roiling clouds rose in fluffy curds high into the western sky, dark and menacing. The few trees that surrounded the farmhouse turned their leaves over to the silvery side. The trunks and branches pointed to the east as though they were ready to pull free of their earthbound roots and run to a safe haven.

George led Mariah to the kitchen and closed the door. The tormenting wind was muffled. "All's we can hope for is that it's just rain and not hail. The roots are well set, and the corn is ready to tassel, but a heavy hail could wipe us out."

"Yes, a half hour of hail could ruin everything. Why do we keep subjecting ourselves to it? If we lived anywhere near civilization, I'd be making good money as a dressmaker. We'd have our own house," she blurted out in frustration.

George took her hand and led her to a chair. "What's wrong? Is it all this stuff about Ma and the farm? You haven't been yourself for the last few weeks."

The wind caught a loose shutter and slammed it against the house, startling them both. "I'll go out and check the others." The door nearly knocked George down when he opened it. Rain in large drops struck him at a sharp angle. A minute later and the door burst open again. George rushed into the kitchen with a look of horror on his face. "Twister! Mariah, let's get to the shelter."

"Wait. We've got to take a few things." She ran up the stairs.

"Mariah, never mind. We only have a few minutes."

Taking a pillowcase from the bed, Mariah threw a picture album, a small box of jewelry, a tin box with their cash, and the deed for the property. Then she went to a bookcase and took the family Bible and an old book of Emerson essays that Mariah had prized since her youth. At the essay on "Self-Reliance" she had marked her place with a battered wedding picture with Will.

"We don't have much time!" George shouted. The rumbling reminded Mariah of the Empire State Express. They could feel the house begin to shake. The ferocious wind forced their clothes against them like a second skin. The distant sky, alive with debris, swirled like planets around an evil, dark void that sucked its children into its gravity and destroyed them. The tornado threw out its upper clouds like the skirt of a whirling dervish, and its long funnel waved back and forth, a cobra of cloud with a hooded head.

George ushered Mariah into the shelter, a bulkhead nearly flat on the ground over a set of steps leading down to a stone cellar hole. The kerosene lamp and matches, water jug and chamber pot he kept stored there were covered in dust. Mariah feared that the matches might have been ruined by moisture, but when George struck one, it lit immediately. He barred the door, wrapped himself and Mariah in a blanket. All they could do was listen and wait.

The hellish sound came closer. Splintering wood, flying metal, and squealing animals penetrated the ground. The bulkhead shook as though a barbaric marauder was trying to break in. Flashes of light invaded as the doors lifted and settled, lifted and settled, each time with a terrible bang that made Mariah think that the entire covering was about to rise like a blanket on a clothesline and leave them exposed.

After twenty minutes, the sound distanced. George opened the doors to find the roof of the barn scattered across several acres and only two walls standing erect. Despite some broken windows and missing roof shingles, the house had survived. They didn't even want to take a good look at the fields of corn and wheat. The first task was to gather up what animals had survived and get them into makeshift pens.

Strewn on the ground around them were carcasses of dead animals—some of them their own and others carried hundreds of feet from neighboring farms—and broken fragments of buildings, fences and trees. The tornado had etched a zigzag path across the landscape. Mariah surveyed the destruction wondering if it was a random, amoral force or divine judgment on a sinful world. George set to work with a wheelbarrow, but after he filled it and dumped it once, he turned to see Mariah sitting on an old keg staring motionless at the house.

He dropped the wheelbarrow and ran over to her. "What's wrong?"

"What's wrong?" Mariah repeated with pent up emotion. "I can't live here any longer."

"What do you mean? We can fix the house. It isn't really that bad," said George, down on one knee, holding her hand.

"It's not *your* house, and it never will be. Even if it were, I don't care. I can't live here in Central City or any place like it. I've tried. Both of us have worked hard, damned hard. I just can't live here any longer. I need to go home." Mariah remained silent, but tears began to roll down her cheeks.

"But this *is* home. We've got some time to work things out about the house. We'll have a good harvest. A big cash crop. We can have a good life here, you'll see."

"And when your mother dies?"

"We've got some time, and if we save..." pleaded George who held Mariah's arms.

"I've got family, too, and I'm going to see them, by God, before they die," responded Mariah with tearful anger. George felt that he was being sucked away from Mariah by forces he couldn't control. In her despair, she wanted her father, and for the first time George flared with anger for being pushed away.

"Do you know what you're saying? Don't you know what Ma and Jim and I, what we all went through to come here? We were nothing but poor relations back in New Hampshire, and now we own forty acres of rich topsoil."

"*We?* We don't own anything. It's your mother's place and it will be sold and the assets divided. As it is, we have to hire help just to keep up with it all."

George's face fell in the realization that what Mariah said was true.

Mariah's voice softened. She took George's hand and tried to undo the bitterness of her words. "Madison has a nice, big new house. He's offered to take your mother in. You might as well let her sell the house now. It'll comfort her to know things are settled before she dies."

George nodded reluctantly. Mariah could see that he was about to cry. "George, Dear," Mariah added with a tender touch of his hand, "in a few weeks I'm not going to be much good to you."

Looking at Mariah with a curious expression, George helped her to her feet. "Are you all right? Have you been keeping something from me?" He held her arms and looked into her eyes.

"George, I'm going to have a baby."

# CHAPTER 22

## *The First Lady of Sandwich*

eorge and Mariah Taylor stood on the platform of Boston's Union Station with four suitcases, an overstuffed carpetbag, a shotgun, a branding iron, and a baby. George and the pyramid of possessions hinted at some unpronounceable Slavic place, but if Mariah struck anyone on the platform as foreign, it was as an exiled princess holding her head high despite her sad displacement. In a few hours the prairie princess, now thirty-two, would return home from a nine-year banishment, matured and transformed, back home to a mountain hamlet that had cast her out in ignominy.

"We have more than two hours. I have some things I want here in Boston. It will be my last chance in the city. You can watch baby for that long, can't you, Dear?"

George's expression sank in dread.

"Dear, this is something I simply have to do. When I left Sandwich nine years ago, I found it hard to look anyone in the eye. Things have changed, and a lot of that is thanks to you," she said with a smile and a quick peck on the cheek. "And to you, my littlest darling," she said to the baby who flailed his arms in joy at his mother's caress. Mariah handed the baby to George loosely swaddled in a lacy blanket. "I need to look my best when I get off that train. You understand that, don't you?" Mariah waited for his reply.

George's mouth rose slightly at the corners and reluctantly, he nodded. After patting his arm appreciatively, Mariah disappeared into the crowd in the echoing marble of Union Station.

Little George Bradley Taylor was awake and looked at his father with an expression that signaled a likely outburst of wailing. Mariah had left him with a small tin of maple syrup that she found useful in pacifying baby's fussiness. George dipped in his finger, and offered it to the baby who sucked contentedly.

George thought of what lay behind him and before him. The past year, the first year of the new century, was as much of a whirl as the storm that changed George and Mariah's lives. George's mother moved in with Madison, and after the barn was repaired, the farm was sold. The siblings convinced their mother that George should get the largest share. The greatest test of family love and Christian compassion came when George and Mariah announced their intention to return to New Hampshire. Bertha knew that she would be saying goodbye to son and grandson forever.

Two cheery matrons, apparently twin sisters, took up the empty space on the bench, intruding on George's thoughts. "May we peek?"

"I guess peeking won't do any harm." George managed a faint smile. His face was as weathered as an Indian's, and his leathery hands fumbled awkwardly with the lace bonnet.

The ladies' bonnets were tied under their chins just like the baby's. The nearer of the two wore small, round glasses and like-size circles of rouge that Boston society forgave for ladies of a certain age. The sister with the glasses cooed, rustling her taffeta bonnet and jiggling her waddle. "Is Mama gonna be gone a long time?"

"Yes, his mother's gone on a few errands. You ladies know what that means. I might need to rent a room and come back here tomorrow." George raised his thick, graying brows, lightening his expression.

The ladies giggled and jiggled, patting George reassuringly on the arm. One wore a pendant watch pinned to her ample bosom. She checked it against the pedestal clock in the middle of the marble floor.

"We've got an hour before our train to Worcester, and who knows, it may be late again, so don't worry. We'll be here to help you."

George managed to express his tepid appreciation to the grandmotherly ladies.

"They call our train 'the Zephyr,' but we call it 'the Teddy Roosevelt.'" George looked at them blankly.

"The Rough Rider!" tittered the sister with the round glasses. They patted each other and George. George chuckled.

"So where are you people going?" asked the sister with less enthusiasm for rouge.

"To Sandwich, New Hampshire. Mariah's going home."

"So she's gone for something special for her husband?" George's expression sagged.

"For her *parents*. Her *husband* doesn't need anything else to carry." George cradled his son, giving him a gentle rocking. The ladies did not take the hint.

"So is her husband also New Hampshire born and bred?" asked the sister in glasses.

"Born but not bred," replied George, glancing at the clock whose hands moved arthritically.

"He must be New Hampshire bred. After all, he's a Sandwich man." The redder sister began to titter over the obvious pun she cleverly discovered. The twins laughed in unison, patted each other, patted George, and finally deflated like two bagpipes when the grandfatherly man with the baby failed to laugh.

George looked at them and realized that they were even jollier than his mother, insufferably jolly. He was not jolly at being a "Sandwich man," and he didn't want to be reminded of his age or the future he faced.

The baby's eyes were still open and he was beginning to fuss. Following Newton's laws, George's mood began to move in an equal and opposite reaction to the movements of the jolly twins.

"Smile for Grampy, smile for Grampy," said the sister with the watch.

Looking straight into their fleshy faces with no hint of a smile, George said, "I'm not his grampy; I'm his daddy."

The twins froze. "Of course you are," said the one with the glass-es.

The other sister lifted her lorgnettes and examined the baby's face. "Why yes. The baby looks just like his daddy." The twins were spared additional embarrassment when an announcer called through a mega-phone for passengers to board a train for Fitchburg.

"We're moving back to where her folks live. It's not my home."

"But it's pretty country up there. What are you going to do up there—for work—I mean?"

"I'm a farmer, been farming all of my life in Iowa."

"You're going in the wrong direction, aren't you for farming?" The painful truth of the lady's words cast a cloud over George's face. He had never had a felonious thought before, but if the ladies didn't leave for Worcester soon, he feared there might be two identical murders reported in the morning's *Transcript*.

"It's been a long trip," said George, "but when a man finally gets out, he's ready for some traveling." He was starting to fabricate a story with the object of the plot climax being the quick departure of the jolly, jiggly sisters. George wasn't a skilled fibber like Mariah or his Uncle Amos, and he wasn't sure he could keep a straight face to the end.

" 'Gets out'?" asked the twin with the round glasses.

George leaned toward the two moon faces and whispered. "Pris-on."

The twin moons eclipsed.

"How was I to know the old lady in the bank had a bad heart? I never touched a hair on her head. She just saw the gun and dropped dead." The twins excused themselves and with pursed lips dragged their own trains of taffeta across the station toward their gate, puffing at one another as they disappeared into the crowd.

When Mariah came across the station, George stared at her in shock and admiration. Her soft, wavy tresses were piled, pinned, and topped with a new close-brimmed white hat. Her deep blue skirt and light blue blouse completed the Gibson look that was all the fashion, a style they had seen in the fashion illustrations in newspapers on the train. "Well, don't you look like one of the swells," said George whose annoyance about her leaving him with the baby evaporated quickly. He didn't even care how much the dress or the salon cost.

Little Bradley was ready for a feeding. Mariah retired to a quiet corner and draped the white flannel over baby and breast. When she returned to her husband's side, she noticed that the train bound for West Ossipee had been moved into place, and at the end was a magnificently appointed car that the yard workers called a "private varnish," a privately owned railroad car with beautiful woodwork and richly upholstered furniture and all the other features of the parlor of a society home.

"I'm glad we're first in line," said Mariah.

"That car? Oh, Mariah, that isn't for regular passengers. That's a private car. I never saw one before, but…"

"It doesn't say 'private,' now does it?"

"Oh, Mariah, now what are you thinking?" George knew exactly what she was thinking. She could make a very grand appearance at home indeed if she rode in such a regal conveyance.

"It doesn't have to say 'private'. Everyone knows that car's not for folks like us."

"Folks like us? So you don't think so?" said Mariah who acted as though her fur had been rubbed the wrong way.

"I've got our tickets for this train right here in my purse, and that car is part of the train." Mariah rose and wrapped the baby more snugly. George could see that she was determined.

"Your folks aren't going to be there anyway, so what difference does it make what car we arrive in?" rebutted George who hoped to deflect her thinking and deflate her pretensions. "We're just renting a wagon at the livery and driving out. Besides, you *aren't* gonna be allowed on that car," George said with firmness.

"Well, we'll see." Mariah started for the shiny dark blue car with the varnished wooden trim. When she saw that George was not following, she turned to him imperiously. "Dear, go wire the folks. Tell them to meet us at the 4:00 train." Mariah's eyes were set on a plan.

"Mariah, what are you doing?" Before George could catch up to her, she was up the steps with the baby and into the car. He sputtered in exasperation. "Wire the folks, huh? To tell 'em 'Your daughter got herself arrested at the train station,' that's what I'll have to wire the folks," he muttered to himself.

A few minutes after George nervously took his place on the bench awaiting his wife's embarrassing expulsion, passengers started amassing on the platform, many admiring the last car. Emerging from the milling passengers were four uniformed guards, two taking positions at the polished oak and brass steps, and the other two entering the car. George recognized them as Pinkerton agents, a private security firm that protected the rich and famous. "Oh, God. Now what?" George stood up expecting to see his wife tossed onto the platform.

A party of richly dressed men and women came down a cordoned pathway. The center of the group was a very big man of sixty or more dressed in a black frock coat. The black was set off with spats, vest and shaggy moustache, all silver. George knew he had seen pictures of the man before, but couldn't immediately place him. The gentleman took the arm of a young woman, his daughter, George assumed, and helped her up the steps into the car.

George dispatched his and Mariah's belongings to the baggage car and continued to wait in agonized anticipation of the worst. Suddenly one of the security men dressed in immaculate dark blue with gold piping appeared on the upper steps. George just knew that this was the embar-rassing moment, the inevitable ejection while many passengers were still on the platform to witness Mariah's impending humiliation. The man descended the steps and headed straight for George. "Great Caesar's ghost, what's gonna happen?" he said to himself in smothered tones.

"You're Mr. Taylor, I understand," said the gentleman, removing his hat.

"Yes, and I'm very sorry…"

"Sir, there's nothing to be sorry about. It was an honest mistake. Suppressing a smile, the officer added, "Mr. Taylor, I'm afraid you're going to have to change your travel plans."

"I suppose so. Are we in some sort of trouble?"

"Oh, Mr. Taylor. I think you misunderstand me. You'll still be on this train, but you've been invited to join the party in this car for the trip."

George swallowed hard and found it difficult to speak for several seconds. "I'll need to wire my wife's folks."

"No need, Mr. Taylor. We can do that. Mrs. Taylor said you might have forgotten to do that. We'll take care of it."

As the Pinkerton agent escorted him to the sparkling blue car,

George walked like a death row inmate up the steps. Before he could get to his wife to find out how she had managed it all, the gentleman in silver and black approached with the young woman at his side.

"I see that you're rather perplexed, Mr. Taylor. Mrs. Taylor told us about your trip from Iowa. And the tornado. What you've been through. Well, well. I've invited you and Mrs. Taylor to ride with us to the West Ossipee station. After all, we're almost neighbors. You'll join our party for lunch on the way."

George's nodding silence prompted the gentleman to realize that his guest might still be unaware of his identity, or knowing it, was petrified by the realization. One way or another, George needed to be thawed.

"My apologies, Mr. Taylor. "I realize I have forgone introductions. This is my wife Frances Folsom and I'm Grover Cleveland." George went from a block of ice to a puddle almost immediately. He wasn't sure his legs would support him much longer.

"Mr. President…"

"Former president, and I dare say. I'm enjoying the ex more than the two terms. I'd trade a month in the White House for a day at Duncan Lake without hesitation."

Grover Cleveland was known for being as considerate in private as he was iron-fisted in public. Violent strikers had felt his heavy hand; he was not a man to be trifled with. Cleveland had rattled middle class morality with his admission that he had fathered a child out of wedlock, and later, in his mid-fifties, he surprised the nation when he married twenty-one-year old Frances Folsom in the White House. After two terms as president, the second ending in 1897, he was a curious mixture of the titled notable and a folksy glad-fellow-well-met. Cleveland loved the people he got to know near Duncan Lake where he had bought a summer home he called "The Oaks."

George and Mariah were offered bourbon or scotch.

"Oh, no thanks. We don't…" said George, attempting a polite refusal.

"We don't take hard liquor," Mariah interrupted, "but if you have sherry, I'd welcome a glass. And a glass of port for my husband, if you please." Mariah's firm gaze silenced George's temperance speech. "It would be good for his nerves."

The former president smiled without showing his teeth.

With stops in Dover and Rochester, the Taylors savored the comforts of the "private varnish" a little longer; they spoke of the day when they could tell their little son, the third in the line of Georges, that he rode in the private railroad car of the former president of the United States, and was cradled in the arms of the former First Lady.

The trees on the hillsides blazed with the fiery colors of October, a spectacle that George had not seen in such glory in forty-six years. Although he still felt a hollowness of heart when he thought of the farm and family he had left behind in Iowa, the beauty of the land, the beauty of his wife, and the auspicious blessing of their arrival gave him some hope that he would event-ually call New Hampshire home once more.

When the train expelled its final gust of steam in front of the West Ossipee station, curious bystanders moved down the platform to see the private car discharge its distinguished passengers. At the back of the crowd stood the Brandons who watched the other two passenger cars empty minus Mariah and George.

"I'll hold the baby. You'll want your hands free," said George. I'll get off after you've greeted your parents. There they are." He pointed to Sarah and Amos who were working their way through the crowd to the front. George was amazed that he still recognized them despite the passage of nearly a half-century. It was interesting to him, but sad, to see the marks of time and circumstance on people he remembered from his youth.

"No, no. I want to have our little sweetie with me," said Mariah as she circled the baby's eager mouth with a soft brush of her finger. "There's nothing more important than him, now is there?"

The Pinkerton agents were off the train first, then others in the retinue followed. The crowd murmured and some applauded when Mr. Cleveland appeared. The ex-president escorted his wife down the steps, and then took the hand of the next lovely lady, simply but elegantly dressed, and carrying a cooing baby. The proud mother hesitated on the final step until she caught her father's eye.

"Mariah!" called Amos in joy and amazement.

George remained on the car peeking out the window, making sure that his wife had the moment to herself that she had so artfully arranged. Sarah Mariah Taylor returned to the loving arms of her astonished parents from the hand of the former president of the United States.

# CHAPTER 23

## Consigned to the Flames

"So you have another fresh start," said Sarah as she took the last sticks of firewood from the box. Mariah stood silently beside her as Sarah lifted the cover and tossed the log on the glowing embers. "Now what's the matter?" said Sarah. "I know you were hoping to get George to try something new. Well, you know about old dogs and new tricks. George has been a farmer all his life. At fifty-two, do you think he's going to make a career in life insurance?" added Sarah, her patience with her daughter wearing thin. "Don't be so glum. He said he's going to find a second job in the off-season. He's plenty clever at a lot of things. And besides, you're enterprising. I bet you'll get something going before little Bradley is out of diapers."

"Maybe so," Mariah murmured. "It's just not the fresh start I hoped for. "I can never be satisfied with a life that's nothing but farming."

"I know you well enough," her mother added with a smile that deepened all of her lines. You'll come up with some idea, but George is meant to work the land."

"Yes, and he never met a pig he couldn't make into a friend." Mother and daughter laughed.

"Now, now. It's a gift. And what about you? Have you already got something up your sleeve? You're the only woman I know who can make a silk purse out of a sow's ear." Sarah smiled and patted her daughter's arm. "You've got to be patient. You already had one of your prayers answered, now haven't you?" Sarah nodded toward Bradley sleeping quietly in his cradle by the warmth of the kitchen stove. "So George is off looking at a couple of places."

"Yes. Two old farms on the fringes of nowhere. George has a special attachment to nowhere."

"You *are* in a sour mood, Dear. Now you put on the tea kettle and I'll fill up that wood box."

Mariah looked around the kitchen and thought of her childhood that now seemed so distant. The kitchen ceiling was cracked and stained, just as she remembered it. Everything in the house was much the same, yet crumbling and fading. Mariah's gloom was deepened by the perceptible change that a decade had made in her mother, but especially her father.

The joyous bounce had gone out of Amos' step. He talked about his joy in the Lord's eternal provision, not the joy at the break of a new day. The man she still called "Daddy" was ashen and hollow-cheeked. The loss of his fair-haired Frederick was the initial breach in his good-humored defenses against the world's powers of human erosion.

Amos depended on his bachelor son Moze for most of the heavy work. Moze's youthful vigor served to accentuate his father's decline. Amos spent this day, as he did many of his days, staring into the comfort of a fire.

Mariah also realized that soon the mirror would not look back on her kindly. Her happiness in finally having a child was dampened with fear that motherhood had come too late. The effort of caring for an infant was already taking its toll. Some days she felt self-pity at her thwarted dreams; on other days she felt the shame of just punishment for her greatest sin—her lingering love for Will Dunfield. Familiar surroundings brought his face, his voice, his body, his touch back into the forefront of her memory. If only that love had faded with time, distance, and the tenderness of a good man who had given up so much for her.

Although Mariah had not seen Will Dunfield in nearly a decade, she hoped that one day she would hear of him, that he would be well, and that God in his mercy might let their paths cross, just for a moment, just a glimpse of his face, a smile, and a few kind words spoken in passing. That's all there could ever be, but some kind of healing and reconciliation would allow her, just maybe, to forgive the hurt and forget the longing.

Her last words to Will had not been kind, but surely he knew, he had to know, that the depth of her pain was in the loss more than in the injury. Forces that he could not control had governed Will's life; she feared that he was destined for tragedy. She had spent several years as the victim of his fatal flaws, but she longed to shower him with the quality of mercy that would wash away all of his guilt.

The last Mariah knew was that Will was working the docks in Portsmouth. She wondered about his poor mother with her only son far away. There was nowhere in Sandwich Mariah could go that did not remind her of him, and Mariah knew that eventually she would have to encounter Mrs. Dunfield. For her own sake, and for George's, they had decided that they could not live in Sandwich no matter how much the town meant to her; she had no choice but to carry the burdens of the past into the future, but to live where her dreams grew and died would trap her in the past.

As Mariah put the last sticks of firewood in the stove, she pulled some old newspapers from the bottom of the wood box. Pouring boiling water into the teapot, she spread out the soiled old paper on the kitchen table. She thought she might catch a glimpse of what was left of the life she once knew in the notch.

The March 5, 1902 edition of the *Carroll County Gazeteer* was a month old.

A new carbonated cola called "Pepsi" is ready to challenge the popularity of Coca-Cola. A Concord restaurant offers a complete turkey dinner for twenty cents. The average salary in New Hampshire for a typical fifty-nine-hour workweek is twelve dollars and ninety-eight cents.

Mariah discovered a night watchman position offered for fifteen dollars a week: If she could only interest George in something like that. A small start, but a start. Just maybe they could eventually move into a town where she could set up her sewing business again.

International News: Buckingham Palace announces the June date for the coronation of the late Queen Victoria's son Edward. Teddy Roosevelt wields a big stick against trusts and the crowned heads of Europe and sending the Great White Fleet around the world. "In the Good Old Summertime" is the newest song in the music halls, and the shirtwaist is all the rage in women's fashions. Czar Nicholas II announces the birth of his fourth daughter, the Princess Anastasia. America prepares to send a team of athletes to the second summer Olympics, and Sherlock Holmes mysteries are still flying off the book-shelves in England and in America.

The silence was broken when Mariah's mother finally returned with an armload of wood.

"What took you so long?"

"Oh, I found the last of the maple syrup in a pail with a cloth over it. I guess your father forgot." Sarah turned to see that Mariah had retrieved the old newspaper from the wood box. She was visibly upset that Mariah had spread the dirty old paper out on the kitchen table.

"Don't worry. I shook off all the bark and dirt. I just thought I should get caught up with what's happening in the world. I haven't gotten to the local news yet."

"Oh, that's an old paper. Let me get rid of that. Must be a more recent one around somewhere. That's at least a month old."

Mariah saved the paper from her mother's grasp. "No, that's fine, Mother. Why are you so agitated? I'm catching up on the news. Here's you tea. Is it too much for you with us here, and with the baby?"

"No, no. Your father and I are delighted. It's just, well…there are some things I haven't gotten around to telling you." Sarah's eyes darted and her hands were suddenly busy tidying.

"What things?" asked Mariah.

"Oh, your Uncle Sumner died a few weeks ago, and…"

"You wrote to me about that just before we left. Don't you remem-ber?" Mariah was perplexed by her mother's discomfort."

"I just didn't want anything to spoil your homecoming."

"Mother, you're not making any sense. What's bothering you?" Suddenly they were both distracted by the sound of the wagon lumber-ing up to the barn door. George had returned with supplies and tools.

"I guess he must have been happy with one of the places. He's already got tools and bags of seed and whatnot," said Sarah as she stood at the window. "Why don't you go out and see what he bought?"

"Oh, I know what he bought. I don't really want to look at shovels and burlap bags. And honestly, I'm not all that excited to hear about the farm either. Believe me, we'll hear every detail soon enough. Mariah continued to flip through the pages of the paper. "I see the youngest of the Paisley boys got married."

"Yes. Yes he did. A girl from out of town. Mariah, get up from the table so I can clean it. Why don't you pour some tea for George and your father? I know I've got a more recent paper somewhere. That dirty old thing is messing up my table."

"For heaven's sake, Mother, you're as nervous as a gnat. You've hardly touched your tea." George opened the door and greeted his mother-in-law with a big smile and handed her a box. "This is for you and Uncle Amos. I know how much you love chocolate." Their nephew and son-in-law didn't bear much resemblance to his Brandon cousins. He was a lanky Taylor with long limbs and big hands and feet. Not handsome, but having a boyish, innocent manner, his sense of humor surely came straight from his Uncle Amos.

"Why thank you, George. You didn't have to do that. You should have saved your money."

"There's a Scotsman I once heard about who got to the square one hot summer day and sat down on the curb to take off his shoes. Along comes a couple of lads—must not a been Scots—but along comes these two and says, MacGregor…"

Mariah smiled wryly and shook her head. She had heard the story before.

"…what are you takin' your shoes and socks off for on such a hot day?"

"It's a long, rough road home, that's what fir."

"Well, MacGregor, there's no sense in that. If it's a long, rough road home, what possesses you to tread rough miles barefoot?"

""'Oh, you foolish lads,' MacGregor says. These are brand new shoes. Skin I can grow.'"

"Mother, you don't know what I have to put up with from this man." George leaned down and Mariah kissed him on the cheek. She folded up the old paper and made table space beside her. "Here, my dear. Come over and tell us about your day." She patted the empty chair beside her, and slid a teacup in front of him."

Sarah picked up the newspaper from the table and wiped the oil-cloth of bark and sawdust. She took the old paper to the stove and lifted the lid releasing tongues of flame.

"Mother, what are you doing? Don't burn that. I haven't finished reading it."

Sarah set the paper down and dropped the lid, subduing the flames.

"Mother, why don't you ask Daddy to come to the table? Don't you want to hear about George's day?" The pained look that spread over Sarah's lined and angular features startled Mariah. "Now, Mother, what is the matter? Something *is* bothering you. It's as plain as day."

"I didn't want to upset you just when you'd gotten home. I just wanted you to have a chance to get settled. I'm sorry. I should have told you." She sank into a chair at the table and buried her face in her hands.

"What is it? What could be so bad…?"

Amos heard the distressed conversation in the kitchen, and rose from his chair in the adjoining room. He came up behind his wife and put his hand gently on her shoulder. "I told you it was a mistake to keep it from her. George, will you come with me out to the barn? You can tell me about the places you visited. Go on, Sarah," Amos said with a loving touch. "

As the door closed, Mariah looked at her mother's anguished expression and felt sick. She didn't even know what the cause was, but the pain in the anticipation already gripped her.

"It's about Will. In there." She pointed to the old newspaper. "The next page."

"Just a month before you got home."

Mariah turned the page, and there under the headline, "Obituaries," was his formal name, so foreign to her that she felt safe in reading it. William Channing Dunfield. *That couldn't be my Will? No. Not in the obituaries. It must be someone else. Just a similar name. Will is barely forty. This can't be him.* "Mr. Dunfield passed away on March 2 of a thoracic aneurism…Mr. Dunfield was employed by….He is survived by his mother…" *Will didn't see the first budding of spring or see the robins return or smell the daffodils.  My God.  His heart burst, and I wasn't there to hold him when he died.*  Moments later, Amos and George heard Mariah's wail.

# CHAPTER 24

## The Anna

O n a shelf in Amos Brandon's woodshed above a window cloud-ed with grime and cobwebs sat an old sailboat, a single-masted schooner. Bradley stood on a rickety apple crate to reach it. He pulled it by the bowsprit over rotted pieces of harness and rusty tools until he could grasp it with both hands. The model boat was about three feet long and heavier than it appeared. In the light of the open door Bradley examined it. The sails were stained and mice had chewed off some of the rigging, but the boat was solid and sound from its lead keel to the crow's nest. The name *Anna* was painted in black on both bow and stern, and under the name just over the broken rudder was the date "1890." Brad just couldn't wait to ask Grandpa Brandon about the *Anna*. He shook the dust from its yellowed sails and marched into the house carrying his treasure. Being that it was 1905, Bradley thought the sailboat was as old as it looked.

Amos was wrapped in a woolen blanket, leaning back in his Morris chair, ashen and trembling despite a fire hissing in the Franklin stove. A cup of tea grew cold on the wooden arm of the chair. Mariah rubbed her father's hand, leathery with age and cold with the weakness of a failing heart. "Grandpa, whose boat is this?" asked Bradley, holding out the *Anna* with some cobwebs still hanging from lines and shrouds like the Ancient Mariner's ghost ship.

Amos raised his head, squinting to focus on the object his grandson held out to him. When he recognized it, his head fell back. He groaned and whimpered and made no answer.

"Now look what you've done!" admonished his mother who took the boat from her six-year-old son's hands. "Where did you find this?"

"In the shed," replied Bradley with a quivering lip.

"You're too young to be playing with a boat that big," said Mariah. George Bradley Taylor was tall for his age, long-legged, and long-armed like his father. An introverted, brooding seriousness often clouded his handsome features making him seem older than his years. He was slow to learn and preferred the company of animals or children younger than himself.

Mariah led her son into the kitchen out of earshot of his grandfather. Bradley's chin began to quake with the onset of tears brought on by his mother's admonition. Her irritations at the world and her circumstances sometimes spilled over onto her sensitive son. When she hurt him, she felt terrible surges of shame and regret. Mariah hugged him and murmured, "There, there," and at last managed to say, "I'm sorry, Dear."

Mariah could see in her son's perplexed brow that he was wondering what caused his grand-father so much sorrow about a toy boat. She remembered reciting "The Wreck of the Hesperus" to him months before and she recited a few lines from memory again to distract him. "Christ save us all from a death like this on the reef of Norman's Woe!"

"Was that story true? Was that Grampy's story?"

"I believe that story was true, but the *Anna* is another story." Mariah held up the boat she had last seen when it was in her brother's hands—Frederick's labor of love. "You never got to meet your Uncle Frederick."

Bradley's grandmother came into the kitchen carrying a pail of fresh milk and saw him standing in the middle of the floor with the *Anna*. Sarah stopped in her tracks when she noticed Bradley's sad and confused eyes. "Oh my, oh my," she sighed. "Did you show that to your grandfather? I had almost forgotten about that boat." She turned her face to Mariah. Your father hasn't given that a second look since, well, you know," she said as she patted her grandson on his head. "Mariah, would you try to get some oatmeal into your father? He doesn't have you nagging at him every day, so maybe you can get some food into him."

"Come here, Bradley, you sit down," said his grandmother who motioned to the table where she had rested the boat. "Would you like some cocoa?"

Brad's expression brightened. "Yes, Grammy."

Sarah had grown as thin as her husband, but unlike Amos, she stood erect and moved without pain or labor. Her thin hands and arms were heavily veined and speckled with what she called "liver spots," a term she never cared to explain to her grandson. Under her watery blue eyes were puffy bags that looked like they were made of crinkled tissue paper. To her children she merely looked tired; to her grandchildren she looked ancient. Despite her age, she still put on huge family dinners for a dozen people on most Sundays on top of daily chores.

"When you showed the *Anna* to Grampy, I imagine it upset him."

Brad nodded in shame at a wrong he still did not understand. She reached over and covered his hand with hers. "You didn't mean to upset him. Here. Drink some cocoa."

"Brad, let me tell you about the *Anna*." Has your mother told you about your uncle Frederick?" Sarah referred to her late son as Frederick, not Freddy. It made her feel that he had lived to manhood—a fuller measure of years than his brief sixteen.

"Yes. Mama showed me a picture."

"Frederick started carving this boat out of a single block of pine back when he was ten or eleven. He got too weak to do much work on it, so your grandfather helped him out by cutting a thin piece for the deck and making that beautiful carved railing at the stern." Sarah's thin hands cleaned the schooner with a damp cloth as she talked. She cut through years of dust and grime and revealed a varnished deck, mast and bowsprit atop a white hull and a dark green waterline. She took Brad's hand and ran it around the gentle curves of the beautiful piece of handiwork and remembered her son's hands sanding the sides to a warm, velvety touch.

Sarah gave her grandson the damp cloth and directed his hand to the black railing at the stern.

"Why'd he call it the *Anna*?"

Sarah paused, looked into space and sighed with a faint smile. "Anna was a girl in school that Frederick took a shine to. He would never have named the schooner for her. Too embarrassed. Grampy painted that name on her after Freddy died."

"Did Frederick play with it? In the river?"

"Oh, yes. One time when he got better for a while, but he was nearly grown by then. He said it was a beautiful sight under sail. Yup. Frederick sailed this with your Uncle Moze who was only your size at the time. One day not long after Frederick died, your grandfather put it away . It's been there in the shed all these years." Sarah watched Bradley's hands move carefully over the surface of the boat in silence.

"See. The rudder's broke."

"Brok*en*. Yes, I see," said Sarah as she covered Brad's hand tenderly as he held the boat by the keel.

"Gramma, do you think Grampa could fix it?"

Sarah rose from her chair and rested her hand on Bradley's shoulder. "I don't know."

By the fire in the parlor Mariah stroked her father's hand until he opened his eyes and smiled in recognition. "Mariah, I'm sorry. I must of scared the boy."

"Oh, Daddy, it's all right. Mama's telling him the story right now."

"Something else's botherin' you, now isn't it?"

"Nothing's the matter, Daddy."

"Now don't try to fool me. You never could, you know."

"Well, I'm worried about you."

"What's there to worry about? I'm seventy years old and wore out worse 'n an old boot. I'll be tradin' in this useless carcass 'fore long. The Good Lord's measurin' me for a new 'un right now."

"Don't talk like that. It gets me all upset." Mariah let her father's hand loose and went to warm herself in front of the fire.

"Look, Mariah, I know you're not happy, and I'm not gonna be around much longer to do anything about it."

"Daddy, what are you talking about?"

"You've been swimmin' upstream into the flood for years, and it's time to stop fightin' the current."

Mariah stopped rubbing her hands together and sat on a three-legged stool. She tossed a piece of wood into the stove, closed the door, and watched the fire through the isinglass window. The explosion of sparks reflected in her father's weary but steady eyes. "You're right, Father. You always are." As she turned to Amos, the light from the fire accentuated the lines that wind and sun had etched on her face; the random streaks of gray continued from her face to the careless twist of hair that told her father that she had given up on her looks. Mariah read the sad recognition in Amos' eyes. "Some things don't matter much anymore," she said as she looked into her weathered hands.

"Since Will died?"

Mariah looked down at her faded, patched housedress in the light of the roaring fire and shook her head with a sigh. "Not just that. I'm glad to have my little boy, but I'm losing my other dreams. Daddy, I feel like climbing to the top of Guinea Hill and lighting a signal fire, but there's no one to come rescue me."

"Oh, Mariah. Now don't you talk like that."

Mariah looked into the fire in silence. She thought of Eustacia Vye and her dreams of Paris and diamonds, and the men who failed her. Mariah wished she had never discovered the novels of Thomas Hardy, but she found herself drawn to them and to the cosmic tragedy that gave some kind of meaning to suffering. Other strong women striving and suffering against forces greater than all the strength she could muster.

As the fire died down, and the roar turned to tiny explosive sparks, Amos spoke softly. "There's a plan for us…"

"Oh, don't I know," replied Mariah with resentment rising in her throat. She didn't take her eyes off the flames. "Those plans, whatever they may be, have never matched the forces working inside of me, so what am I to think?"

Amos left Mariah's anger to the fire and silence. Mariah always understood that she was part of the notch, the mountains and Cold River as surely as Eustacia Vye was part of Egdon Heath, but just as surely, she too was a native in rebellion. In her heart she felt that it was unjust that God had given her hope and choice and then denied her the means to seek another world. And yet she had once believed that she had come back of her own enormous will to the place of her suffering. Her father believed that it was God's will, not Mariah's that had brought her home.

"I'm sorry, Daddy. I shouldn't have spoken to you that way. No matter what I've gone through, I don't want to hurt you and Mama."

"And George? He's been waiting for years for you to let Will go." And it was true. If there had been a high enough place in Iowa for Mariah to light a signal fire, she would have done so, even if by daylight she knew that Will and she could never be reunited. That George cherished her she could not deny; he would do all he could to make her happy, but it could never be enough.

"I know I've hurt George, but what could I do? Why can't he be anything but a farmer?"

Amos mustered the strength for some laughter. "You're askin' *me?*"

Mariah put her hand on the arm of her father's chair and he covered it with his.

"I shouldn't have said that, Father."

"No need apologizin'," Amos said.

"I hurt Will, too. I know he deserved to suffer, but not like he did."

She turned her anguished face to the fire. Amos left her to her thoughts. Will had tried so hard for reconciliation, and she had spurned him all the while wanting him to try harder. He had lost his job when the truth of his divorce reached Mr. Wallace's office, and his fall from grace broke him. He took up with a woman that the town called a "floozy" and even she abandoned him when second stage syphilis hit him hard. His halting steps marked him as a wastrel, and the only work he could find was in a crate factory. An artery burst as he lifted a heavy load, and he died on the box mill floor on a pile of swept up refuse.

Mariah turned to her father with pain in her eyes. "Daddy, what on earth can I do?"

"Honor George like Ruth did Boaz," said Amos with more command in his voice than Mariah had heard in twenty-five years. "When you stepped off that train, I thought you was a new creation. Do you know how happy that made us? You gotta love George in return."

He smiled that mischievous smile that made him suddenly seem hearty and healthy again. "And if you want to be settin' fires, I've got a lot of brush around here I'd like to get rid of. George wouldn't mind 't all if ya lit a fire for him, you know." Did her father know that she sometimes turned her back to her husband in bed when her thoughts turned to Will? Her father didn't have to read Mariah's books to read her. Amos gave his daughter that down under look paired with a grin that was his way of softening his admonition with love. "You know it's right in the scriptures about how to handle fires. "Hideth ye not thy light under a bushel, but warmeth thy marriage bed with coals of fire."

Mariah broke into a smile. "Now don't try to tell me that part about the bed's in the Bible."

"Sometimes you have to read between the lines to get the hidden meanin's, don't you know."

Amos' smile faded into an expression of concern. "I'm worried about you, and I'm worried about George, and I don't want to spend my precious few remainin' days worryin'."

"I do love him," Mariah protested.

"Like a brother, like a cousin. That's not enough."

"No, it isn't only like a brother. It just isn't the same as it was with Will. Can you make yourself feel what doesn't come naturally?"

"Mariah." Amos rested his head back against the chair, exhausted. It took a moment for him to collect the energy to go on. "Call it fate or call it God's plan, but you and George were brought together for a reason." He rested until his breathing slowed. "A man and wife can only be one flesh if they decide to love each other." Amos opened his eyes and mustered the strength to lean forward. He lifted his hand to Mariah's cheek as he so often had done when as a child she descended into sullenness. "The only thing we really choose is how we feel about what we're dealt."

"It's not the life I dreamed of." Mariah turned away.

"Light a signal fire, you said? I say you lit a fire and it was George that come. He brung you back where you belong. Even though it

almost killed him." Mariah was a silhouette against the dimming fireplace. "You do know that, don't you?" Amos urged.

"Yes, but I don't know if I can change my heart."

"Go to the river. It's always been good for you to walk along the
river. Take the boy. And take the *Anna*." Amos patted her hand to
urge her on. Mariah stood up. Her father smiled at her the way he
often did when he was going to lighten someone's mood. "Don't forget
to tie a string to that boat. If she gets away from ya, you'd look damned
foolish at your age divin' into the pothole in cold weather."

"All right, Daddy," Mariah said with a touch of humor in her voice,
"I'll keep it on a tether; that's what you've tried to do with me all these
years, but maybe you gave me too much slack."

Amos laughed weakly, ending in a prolonged cough. "I think
you're right," he said. "And now I'm too damned old to pull you back
to dry land."

Mariah started for the kitchen when her father suddenly called her
back. His voice was raspy and weak.

"Oh, Mariah. Send Bradley with an old shingle and a jackknife.
And I'll need the old rudder."

With his mother's help, Brad removed the rudder and carried it
and the boat to the parlor where his grandfather sat in front of the fire
wrapped in a shawl. "A rudder has to be able to take some hard blows,
now don't it?" Amos' hands worked slowly. From time to time a tremor
stopped him, and he let his hands rest in his lap with the small piece
of wood in one hand and a whittling knife in the other. "Now you get
your mama to put a little nail right here and then bend it over with a
pair of pliers. That nail goes into a tiny ring on the stern that lets the
rudder turn. But it'll fit tight so it can't turn far off a straight course.
I made it that way so the schooner won't just sail in circles. Can't get
anywhere sailin' in circles." Amos winked at Mariah and reached over
and patted his grandson on the head. "Now she's ready for the river."

Amos took a deep breath and rested his head against the high back
of the rocker and closed his eyes. Brad let his grandfather drift into a
peaceful rest with breathing so shallow as to be nearly imperceptible.
After a few minutes' help from his mother, the rudder was in place, and
Brad came back into the parlor and sat in a ladder back chair by the
window. He moved the new rudder with satisfaction, and hoisted the

mainsail to the top of the mast. The day had finally come when Uncle Frederick's prized boat would capture wind in its sails again and cut across the current of Cold River.

"Grampa," Brad whispered, "I'm gonna tie a long string to this rail." I'm afraid the wind will take her." He rose from his chair at the sunlit window and turned toward the darkness engulfing his grandfather. A few glowing embers was all that was left of the fire. All was stillness until the whittling knife fell from Amos' hand and clattered on the floor.

# CHAPTER 25

## Miscarriage of Justice

"Mariah, you're going to lose that child for sure the way you're working," Florence scolded as she tried to pull her sister away from the washboard. "For heaven's sake, I've come all the way out here from Wolfeboro to lend a hand, and what do I find you doing? Straining and pulling as though you were a fisherman hauling in a ton of cod."

Mariah was pregnant again. She was overjoyed with the miracle of her first child; she was happy that her second—five years later—was a girl. When her third pregnancy came at forty-one, she sank into despondency.

"You want this child, don't you? Every child is a blessing from God," Florence added, making her question clearly rhetorical. "You've got to take it easy. You could lose this child."

"Hard work never hurt anybody. Didn't hurt Bradley or Dorothy." Mariah stood and stretched her back and left a sheet half way through the wringer. She had grown thicker with each pregnancy, and the beauty of her youth lingered only in her eyes.

Florence stopped pinning the clothes to the line and stood with arms akimbo waiting for her sister to acknowledge her fixed gaze.

"So what are you staring at me for?" Mariah raised her sudsy hand to her face to catch wisps of gray that had fallen from her bun.

"I'm staring at you because I want you to think about what you're doing to that child. You have an obligation." Florence was a decade younger, and the years had been gentler. She had married Harry Blodgett whose family owned most of the shoreline of Lake Wentworth. Florence considered a full afternoon in the kitchen to be hard labor. She had hired girls for the laundry, the housework, and the guest rooms. She weeded her own flower garden for the pleasure of it.

Mariah stared right back. "An obligation? Are you telling me I haven't done my duty to my children?"

"The first two, I admit. Of course you have. But you've got to start taking care of that little boy before he's born or you'll regret it sorely later."

"He, she, whatever it is, will make it if it's meant to," retorted Mariah who resumed her aggressive wringer cranking.

"Yes, there are forces greater than ourselves. You should know that by now, after all of your fist-shaking in the face of God. That little boy—and yes, it'll be a boy—is part of the divine plan. You, dear sister, are an instrument of that plan, so take pride in that."

"Now don't you lecture me, Mrs. Blodgett. When was the last time you were down to your last nickel?"

Florence threw a wet pillow case back into the wicker basket and folded her arms, sniffling.

She and Harry had just bought a grand guesthouse with a wraparound porch for the rocking pleasure of her summertime guests. They had been married for five years and had everything they had longed for—except children. Florence served up meals that kept the guests coming back each season. She made a good home, and she mothered everyone under her roof. Mariah told her she was the best cook in Wolfeboro, and then backhanded the compliment by promising her that she'd never move into town and show her up.

Mariah walked over to the clothesbasket in silence. She picked up the pillowcase and pinned it to the line. Her anger had cooled. She understood the pain of her sister's childlessness. "Don't worry about me or yourself either. I waited eighteen years before I had a child. Be patient. " Mariah reached into the basket for another pillowcase.

"Here. You came to help, not to get us both worked up." Mariah patted Florence's hand before handing her the pillowcase. They resumed their work without conversation.

1908 had been a difficult year. In a farmhouse miles from electricity, Mariah was resuming the country existence that she had longed to escape from the time she was a schoolgirl. She and George sank their Iowa money into the farm on Ossipee's Brown's Ridge Road even though she pleaded in vain for an in-town house where George could find other employment. Mariah invested her ambitions in her children, and thanked God that at least her husband managed to keep the family fed, warm and clothed, though chronically short of cash.

The house was an eight-room colonial with four fireplaces three miles from the Center Ossipee courthouse that had granted Mariah her divorce fifteen years before. Built in 1732, the old colonial consumed ten cord of firewood a winter, and despite two woodstoves constantly ablaze and fireplaces to supplement during the coldest days, wash water in the upstairs bedrooms still iced over in the pitcher in mid-winter.

The harvest of 1908 was mediocre despite George's magic touch with soil and seed. He took pick and shovel work with the county road agent to make enough money to pay the taxes and buy staples they couldn't grow or barter for. George remembered the rich, deep soil of Iowa, and he swore that the Yankee stories of granite rocks growing in the soil like rutabagas were true.

After the third pregnancy was evident, Mariah sat George down for a talk. "Now, look, Dear. When this little one is born, you'll be fifty-nine. You'll be almost eighty before we get him grown and out into the world."

George looked down into his folded hands. A slight tremor had begun to trouble him, and he held one hand in the other to control the movements that put fear in his heart, and in Mariah's as well.

Mariah watched his hands. *Oh, what's in store for us? My dear George, something is taking control of you, little by little. Some day you're going to leave me alone with this farm and three children—three children to raise on my own.*

"This isn't going to happen again."

"Mariah, what are you trying to tell me?" George asked with an ominous air.

"I think we need separate bedrooms…"

George suddenly looked up with the pain of rejection washing over his face.

"Oh, George. Please don't look at me like that. Only till the change of life. Once I'm past the monthlies…"

George closed his eyes and hung his head. "You really mean that you want me out of your bed?"

"Only till I'm past child-bearing. It won't be that long."

"Longer than I have, maybe," he said with a depth of sadness that she had never heard in his voice before.

Although Will had died six years earlier, his specter roamed the house. George found the wedding picture in the Emerson book when he was moving sorting through their belongings for the move to the bedroom down the hall. The photograph was Mariah's icon of immutable youth and a veritable picture of Dorian Gray. George gripped it with an impulse to tear it to pieces as though the destruction of the picture could erase the memory the man and their youthful years together. Instead, he threw it down on the kitchen table in front of Mariah and stalked out. He went for a long walk, not returning until the sun was nearly set. He ate no supper that night and he spoke not a word.

The next day Mariah got George to sit down and talk again. "I want you to understand that I love you," said Mariah earnestly, compassionately.

"Not like you loved Will."

There was nothing she could say that could change the truth of what he said, or make it less painful to a man haunted by the ghost of another.

"I've gotta get back to work." George rose slowly from his chair. As he passed her, Mariah took his hand. "I never want to talk about him again. All that is past."

George leaned down and kissed her forehead. "I think in a way you really want that. Thank you for saying it anyway." He squeezed her hand. "No matter how hard we try, we can't leave the past behind." He let her hand go gently and returned to his chores.

"You're due in early April, isn't that right?" asked Florence as she pushed a pair of George's worn work pants into the grip of the rubber rollers, "so at least you won't have too much heavy work to do as you get close. You'll need plenty of help when he does come, that's for sure."

"I s'pose," murmured Mariah who never liked to admit that she needed anybody.

"It is good to have a newborn in good weather. It'll give him a good start," said Florence as she hung the last of George's shirts on the line with their sleeves hanging down like the arms of corpses pulled from the sea.

"Why do you keep calling it 'him'?" asked Mariah with annoyance in her voice.

"I just know it's another boy; the way you're carrying him. You don't have those dark circles under your eyes. And less morning sickness. I'm sure it's a boy."

"Maybe so, but…"

"But what?"

Mariah was going to say, "but how would you know?" Although she and Florence sparred constantly, Mariah did not want to inflict pain on her little sister, no matter how much she was irritated by her interference. "But I don't think it matters. I have one boy and one girl already."

"Little Bradley just loves working along with his papa."

"Yes, he does," responded Mariah, "and little Dotty wants to help with everything I do. They'll both grow up to be great helps."

"And each delivery gets easier, they say," added Florence.

Mariah stopped work and stared at her sister with her head tipped down and her lip curled. Her expression said, "Don't tell me about deliveries," and Florence got the message.

Bradley Taylor was a very difficult delivery by a young doctor who had never delivered a baby before. He had to use forceps, and the impression in the baby's forehead remained and marred his otherwise good looks. Whatever harm the forceps might have done inside, Brad's parents were only beginning to ponder.

Their first-born was black-haired like his mother, but with his father's face and body. He wasn't bright and talkative like his father.

Other than working with his father, he preferred being alone, and often talked to himself so that relatives who heard him in the next room thought that he had invented an imaginary brother or friend.

Dorothy came in early 1907. That fall, with all the weight and discomfort, Mariah was not much help in the fields while George turned a hayfield into high bush blueberries. Mariah had already made some good money from summer neighbors with her strawberry jam. It didn't take much persuading for George to see more money in preserves than in surplus hay.

In the winter of 1908 Mariah put her old Singer to work making frilly girl's clothes, imagining Dorothy living a life she had once dreamed for herself. There was no market for her seamstress services stuck out in a sparse rural setting.

After being cowed into a few minutes of silence, Florence started up again about the new baby. "What are you going to name him?" Florence hung the last of the clothes on the line that slumped with the weight. She lifted it at the midpoint with a pole with a forked end, wrinkling up her nose at the primitive solutions that were common among poorer country folk.

"*If* it's a boy," Mariah said with emphasis, "George wants him named after the two uncles."

"Elden Brandon, and…?

"Edwin Taylor."

"Oh, yes. So he'll be Edwin Elden Taylor. That's nice."

"And if it's a girl, he'd like to name her after his mother. Let's stop talking about babies, all right?" snapped Mariah. "I'll be forty-one when this one is born, and by the time it's twenty in 1929 I'll be sixty-one. I should be its grandmother, for the love of God!"

"I didn't come over here to help you because I think you're too old to have a baby. If God is giving you another child, he may be a special blessing in your old age."

Mariah scrubbed the underarms of George's sweat-stained shirt with vehemence "Just you wait," said Florence, smiling as she hung the last of the wash in the bright sun."

"If you don't kill him first, he's going to be a tough kid, this little Eddie, and I'm going to watch out for him.

"Oh, stop," said Mariah sarcastically. Florence's words struck hard.

She would watch out for him; protect him from his own mother? "I'm going in. I'll start peeling potatoes. And I don't need any help doing that, either." Mariah reached under the edge of the giant steel tub and lifted it with a sudden jerk. Grey soapy water flooded the yard and scattered cackling hens. As she stood, she felt a sharp pain in her side, painful enough to make her sit on her scrubbing stool and breathe shallowly.

"Now, what have you done?" gasped Florence who kneeled at her side. "Pray to God that no blood appears."

*Just another farm wife, that's all I'll ever be.* As the pain in her side went away, she felt the baby move.

"Are you all right?" asked Florence who held Mariah's hand.

"Me or the baby?" said Mariah with slow breaths.

"Right now they're one and the same."

"Then I guess I'm kicking myself," Mariah replied with a touch of sarcasm in her voice.

Florence smiled and sighed with relief. "Thank God he's all right."

"It's not his time." Mariah almost swallowed her words when she realized she had acknowledged that she, too, felt that she was carrying a boy.

"We're *both* waiting for our time, I guess." Florence's eyes began to fill.

Mariah wrapped her arms around her sister. Each wanted motherhood and an independent career, and each had only one. In God's time maybe each could have both.

# CHAPTER 26

## *Prince of the Paupers*

"*L*ook, Mama, auto!" shouted Dotty as she looked north down Brown's Ridge Road to see what was making the racket.

"Come back here, Honey," Mariah called to her daughter who had managed to unlock the screen door and make her way to the road to investigate the strange noise. Dotty was proving to be as precocious as her mother had been.

The day was hot, one of a string of late June days that made it difficult for Mariah to adjust her work to the baby's feeding schedule. She looked into the baby's face, pleased to see that he had fallen asleep and her nipple had fallen from his lips. Eddie was small for his age. He breathed in catches, stops and starts. Mariah and George feared that their second son, only two months old, might not survive the harsh winter. "Will he slip away from us with stalled breaths like Frederick?" Mariah wondered.

As soon as Mariah buttoned her blouse, Dotty was standing on the other side of the screen door shouting, "Lady, lady!"

"That must be Mrs. Landrigan, Dear," said her mother who rested her baby on the kitchen table long enough to gather fallen locks of hair into her bun and blot the sweat from her face with a handkerchief.

Dotty always asked her mother whom she was making the preserves for, and her mother often said, "For the lady" because Mrs. Landrigan was her best customer. Madeleine Landrigan, of the Beacon Hill Landrigans, summered on Lake Winnesquam in a twelve-room cottage with space for only two servants. Life on the lake reminded her of Thoreau.

Mrs. Landrigan had sampled Mariah's blue ribbon preserves at the Sandwich Fair in the fall, and had ordered several jars for when she returned the following summer. She had made some remarks to Mariah about the superb quality of her preserves and baked goods and had predicted that one day Mrs. Taylor's preserves might grace breakfast tables of those with discriminating tastes.

On that October day with Wedgewood skies and the smell of fallen leaves, Mrs. Landrigan also asked about the Taylor family's circumstances. Mariah had opened her heart to a woman who had flattered her. *How she struggled...worried about her husband's health...too old to have another child...might not live to see it grown.* Mrs. Landrigan was the soul of compassion--especially the baby still in Mariah's womb, the baby that Mariah apparently did not want. Mrs. Landrigan confessed her fear for the baby's future with older parents who were barely hanging on. Mariah lamented that the baby was not coming into the world at an opportune time or under favorable stars.

"I hate to think of this little one living like a pauper," Mariah said, and the thought of it touched Madeleine Landrigan's heart. Her order for twenty jars of strawberry jam came with a gift of five silver dollars to pay for jars and wax, enough jars for Mariah's entire strawberry harvest. Madeleine Landrigan had not forgotten and had followed up on her promise to visit in the spring.

Mrs. Landrigan stepped down from the right side of a bright yellow automobile with high wooden spoked wheels. The Firestone Columbus looked like a buggy with a leather folding top. A small hood covered the engine that chugged and hissed, and shook the whole automobile. Mr. Landrigan pulled his driving goggles off and reluctantly shut the engine down after his wife poked him, pointed to her ears, and shook her head. The engine whistled itself to stillness like a punctured balloon.

The Landrigans unbuttoned their ankle-length dusters and hung them from the brass lanterns on either side of the dash. "Well, Mrs. Taylor, we can make fifteen miles an hour on good stretches of the road. Can't help the dust. The town hasn't gotten around to oiling the road yet," said Mr. Landrigan who beamed with pride as he patted the engine hood with his gloved hand. He was a handsome, dark-haired man, tall and broad-shouldered.

Dotty held on to her mother's leg, peaking around her apron at the wondrous machine that had brought the Landrigan's all the way from Tamworth without a horse. Dotty had never seen a motorcar up close.

"Good afternoon, Mrs. Taylor," said Mrs. Landrigan who was dressed in a fashionable shirtwaist dress with gauzy sleeves. Her light green skirt complemented her strawberry blonde coiffure. She had a waist almost as tiny as Mariah's had been when she walked down Wakefield Street on Will Dunfield's arm. "And hello, Dorothy. I brought you some candy from Coursin's." She crouched down and handed the peppermint stick to the raven-haired two-year old who came out from behind her mother's skirt with a tentative smile, took the candy gingerly, then presented it to her mother to unwrap. Mrs. Landrigan offered to help. "Oh, your mama's got her hands full. Let me unwrap it for you."

"This is out of your way, though. I could have left the preserves with Mr. Coursin at the store."

"Oh, I simply had to come out to see the baby. A little boy, I hear. Mr. Coursin told me," she said as she reached down to touch the baby's soft cheek.

"Yes. This is Edwin Elden Taylor. He was born in early April."

"Well, congratulations," said the Boston society lady. "Mr. Landrigan and I have been married for five years," she said, "and we haven't been so fortunate." Her smile had faded and her eyes looked down in sadness.

"I was married quite a while before I had my first child, and now look," said Mariah with a quick touch of Madeleine Landrigan's arm. "I've got three. You met Bradley at the fair last fall. He's seven now. He'll be in the second grade this fall. It's amazing to me. For years I never thought I'd have a child, and now?"

"And now you have three and you must wonder how you'll provide for them," said Mr. Landrigan.

Suddenly Mariah remembered her emotional outpouring at the Sandwich Fair and blushed with embarrassment.

"Winthrop, you shouldn't say that," his wife said as she rested her gloved hand on his chest.

"I don't believe we ever met your husband," interjected Mr. Landrigan.

Mariah was glad that her husband wasn't nearby. She was also acutely aware of how old she must seem to have such small children, never mind that their father was soon to turn sixty.

"I don't know if I can find him," replied Mariah quickly. He might be…"

"In the barn," piped in Dorothy, leaving her mother with no choice but to send her little girl to get her husband. He came across the barnyard with the gait of the war-weary Abraham Lincoln. He was dusty and musty.

"George, this is Mr. and Mrs. Landrigan."

"Oh, you met Mariah at the Sandwich Fair," said George who wiped his hands before offering it to the elegant Landrigans. "We have your order ready. We're very grateful," he said with his usual warmth and brightness that countered the initial impression of a haggard and nondescript man of the country. "Let me get the box with your order," George added. He turned toward the kitchen door.

"Mr. Taylor, could you wait a minute?" added Mr. Landrigan with unexpected humility. There's something else we wanted to talk about first."

"Oh, let the poor man go," said Mrs. Landrigan who suddenly looked uncomfortable with having called George Taylor, "the poor man." "For the moment, let's just talk to Mrs. Taylor."

George was curious, but decided he could wait to hear the details. "Be back in a few minutes," he said and left to gather the Landrigans' order.

The Landrigans were nervous. Mariah wasn't sure why.

"We've got a proposal to make to you, Mrs. Taylor. But I want to warn you. This isn't going to be easy for any of us," said Winthrop Landrigan whose eyes, with the right words, might melt a woman's heart.

Mariah suddenly felt a terrible weight settling on her chest. The Landrigans' proposal wasn't just about preserves and gracing tables. There was something else they wanted, something that they were reluctant or even ashamed to bring up. *George, please hurry back.*

"You know how you told me that this third pregnancy was something you hadn't wanted," said Mrs. Landrigan with the tension of a long-tailed cat near a rocking chair.

"Well, yes, I guess I said that, but…"

"Well, what if there was a way to provide everything that a child would ever need for success in the world? Wouldn't that be in that child's best interest, especially if he wasn't really wanted?"

George came out of the house carrying a box with the jars of jam. He saw in the stances and on the faces of Mariah and the Landrigans that the conversation had turned to something very serious.

"Mr. Taylor, you can just put those in that little compartment in the rear. Thanks," said Mr. Landrigan.

"Mr. Taylor," said Mrs. Landrigan, "we're talking about what would be best for your baby's future."

"Eddie's future? Why are you concerned about Eddie's future?" asked George with a cutting edge to his words.

"Madeleine and I realized that you really didn't expect a third child, and you're worried about providing for him."

George folded his arms and looked Winthrop Landrigan squarely in the eyes. "Is that so? Is that what Mariah told you, that we didn't want another baby?"

Mariah's chin slumped toward her chest. With eyes closed she shook her head slightly from side to side. "I didn't really mean…"

"He's not going to live like a prince, but he's not going to go hungry, I can tell you that."

"I'm sure you'll make do, Mr. Taylor, but we are prepared to offer you enough money to fix up this house and fulfill your dream of starting a business based on your wife's wonderful preserves," said Mr. Landrigan who smiled as though he had turned a corner with Mariah and George and was close to closing a deal.

"Do you mean you want to invest in a business with us?" asked George skeptically. He looked back and forth between them with brows drawn together, trying to fathom what the Landrigans could possibly be proposing.

"Yes, I guess you could call this an investment in your business. If you accepted our proposal, there would be few strings attached," said Winthrop whose tone had become very businesslike.

"Why did you say it wasn't going to be easy for us?" added Mariah. George stood close beside her. Little dark-haired Dorothy wrapped herself around her mother's leg again. The family's smiles were gone.

"Mrs. Taylor, Mr. Taylor, just imagine how five thousand dollars would change your lives."

George's mouth dropped open. He looked at Mariah, wide-eyed.

"Just think of what you could do for Bradley and for little Dorothy," said Mrs. Landrigan as she knelt down close to the little girl who clung tightly to her mother.

"Five thousand dollars?" said Mariah with a gasp. "Why would you want to invest five thousand dollars in my preserves?"

"Madeleine, I think we've got to be direct with Mr. and Mrs. Taylor and get it all out." Mrs. Landrigan nodded to her husband and covered her mouth with her hand. She looked very anxious. "Mr. and Mrs. Taylor, we are offering to raise your infant son as our own."

"Raise our son? What are you talking about?" said George who looked at Mariah for assurance that this was not something she had suggested. He turned his dagger eyes toward the Landrigan's.

"Don't you see, we could provide everything that you could never provide, and you could visit him from time to time."

"You mean you want to take our son for five thousand dollars," said Mariah with acidic indignation. "Do you think I'd sell my child for any amount of money?"

"You're not selling your child," said Landrigan with a touch of moral indignation

"You're talking about adoption," shouted George.

"You'd always know he was your son, but just think of what that money could do for…"

"I want you to start up that fancy automobile of yours and go back to where you came from."

"Now, Mr. Taylor, I said this wouldn't be easy. I think you need some time to think about our proposal. We understand that the little boy isn't off to the best start. Just imagine the kind of care he'd get in Boston. You could come any time you wanted to see how he was doing."

"Mrs. Landrigan, you've twisted my words," said Mariah in anguish. "How could you think I would ever give up my child?" Fury mixed with anguish as Mariah stared at the young society woman.

"Would you deprive your child of a bright future when you can barely care for the two you already have? What hope is there?" said Winthrop Landrigan.

Mariah turned her fiery gaze on Madeleine Landrigan. "How could you come here to ask me such a thing?"

Madeleine looked down and began to sob. Her husband put his arm around her shoulder. "But I honestly thought that's what you wanted."

"At the fair? Was it what Mariah said at the fair?" asked George who looked back and forth at Mariah and Madeleine.

"Yes, when I talked to Mrs. Taylor…"

"You thought…?"

"That she didn't want that baby."

George looked at Mariah with anger and deep sadness in his eyes.

Mariah looked toward the Landrigans' bright yellow and black motorcar and thought of all they had and all they lacked. She looked down into the face of her infant son and felt ashamed that for months as he grew and moved inside of her that she had not wanted him, that she coveted the world of Madeleine Landrigan.

"Can you forgive me?" asked Madeleine as she put her hand on Mariah's arm cradling her little boy.

"Believe me, I know what you're feeling. I'm the one who…oh, maybe you'd better go," said Mariah who glanced at George and felt ashamed of the truth she hated to acknowledge.

Her face was contorted with guilt.

George took little Dorothy by the hand and walked toward the kitchen door. Mariah embraced Madeleine Landrigan with the baby between them. As Mariah walked her to the car and her husband cranked it until it churned to life, Madeleine noticed a field with new plantings beyond the stone wall running along the road.

"Blueberry bushes," said Mariah. "George planted them this spring."

"That's wonderful. So you're moving ahead with your plans," said Madeleine who was clearly relieved to be departing on a positive note. She opened her purse and took out a ten dollar bill. "Here, please take this as an advance payment on our next order. You really need to charge fifty cents per jar, you know."

"I think I'm lucky to get eighteen," said Mariah.

"We often undervalue what we have," replied Madeleine who touched Mariah's arm again. She started to extend her hand toward the baby, but pulled back.

Mr. Landrigan advanced the spark and turned the steering lever sharply to the right and the car turned around. A puff of smoke rose from the rear of the shiny yellow vehicle and it took off down Brown's Ridge Road like a specter, the occupants hidden under a canopy of black.

# CHAPTER 27

## *Holy Water*

"*Y*our father would turn over in his grave if he knew that his elder grandson had reached the age of fifteen unbaptized." Sarah Brandon's telephone voice sounded like a cheerleader using a tin megaphone. The background sound of a coffee grinder rumbling on the counter of Taylor's Store tested the limits of her volume. Although people living in the centers of bigger towns had had electricity and phones for over twenty years, the country folk in 1917 had no prospects that such modern conveniences would reach them strung to hundreds of costly utility poles. Sarah left her nickel on the counter and kept a careful eye on the clock.

"And God only knows, if this war goes on a long time, Bradley could be over there and dead before his sins are washed away." Mariah glanced around Coursin's Store to make sure no one was listening to her weekly call from her mother.

The Great War seemed as remote to Mariah as her youthful dreams. "Bradley won't even turn fifteen until August, so the Germans are going to have to wait," replied Mariah.

"Maybe so, but it's a mother's duty to protect her children, body *and soul*."

Mariah had gotten their *bodies* through the dangerous years of childhood diseases. Even Eddie, whose earlier sickliness confirmed his Aunt Florence's grim warnings, had recently exploded into devilish energy at age eight. As to the children's souls, Mariah had read them Bible stories and tucked them in with prayers, but her own doubts about the divine plan kept her from leading her children to the edge of God's cleansing waters. "You talk to them, George," she insisted, but his reply took it out of parental hands. "It's up to the Holy Ghost. When He's ready, it'll happen." And there they had left it for the past year, and with Eddie's health improving, they felt less urgency for the Holy Ghost to alight like tongues of fire on the children.

"Oh, for heaven's sake, Mother. Give them time. If it's God's will, it'll happen in a stroke. All these years you've been telling me to wait on the Lord, and that's what I'm doing."

"Well, if you've raised obedient children…"

"Obedience doesn't have anything to do with believing in God, so don't…"

" 'Children, obey your parents in all things'. That's right in the scriptures and don't tell me it's not," rebutted Sarah in her crackly elder's voice.

Mariah looked around at the customers whose eyes were on the shelves, but whose ears were on her call. "Mother, this isn't the time or the place," Mariah said in a forced whisper. I'll hope to see you tomorrow if it's all right with George." She hung up and blew out her breath in relief.

"Some day I might have a telephone of my own," said Mariah to Neal Coursin in exasperation.

"You know, Mrs. Taylor," whispered the bespeckled grocer, "if you'd baptized your children when they were babies, you wouldn't be going through this problem." He turned his mouth to the side and raised an eyebrow to emphasize his role as the community's wise counselor. He was a deacon of the church across the square, the church where Sons and Daughters of the American Revolution raised their sons and daughters in the subtle figurative language of God's mysterious ways.

"Neal, you know we were raised Baptists, so I don't get off so easy as you Congrega-tionalists." The baby-sprinkling Congregationalists placed their fragile infants under God's protection soon after birth, but the Baptists trusted in God's mercy until a child reached the "age of reason" and could make the free will choice to enter the narrow gate into Christ's protection. Baptists believed that baptism—literal immersion, not metaphorical dribbles—was a conscious choice to turn from the wide gate that led to worldliness and destruction. Congregational parents had more leeway. With the menace of childhood diseases ever looming, Baptist parents often pressured children—sometimes before they could read any Scripture themselves—to commit their lives to the Lord and submit their bodies to sacramental immersion despite all the rhetoric about rational choice.

Sarah had cajoled Mariah into the redemptive waters when her spirit was unwilling. Mariah remained ambivalent—vaguely comforted by the gift of God's grace while resentful of God's controlling hand.

Mariah put the canvas bag with her purchases in the back of the buggy and headed down Brown's Ridge Road surrounded by the sound of heat bugs sawing at the air. *Mother sure knows how to get to me. Just mentioning Daddy is all it takes.* When the horse stopped at the barn door, Mariah surveyed the fields and saw the three kids on the shady side of the barn pouring string beans into a bucket. There was no sign of George.

A hot spell hung over the mountains making midday field work a torment. The sun that grew the corn several inches a day wilted the farmer that tilled it. George worked out of the sun tending to light chores in the barn. He was sixty-seven, and much too slow even in cooler weather to keep up with the demands of field and barn, never mind the energy of his youngest child. Little Eddie, born blue and premature, was now an eight-year-old perpetual motion machine.

"George!" Mariah shouted into the barn.

Her husband came out flapping dust and hayseed off his clothes and mopping his brow with a checkered handkerchief, turning dust and sweat into muddy streaks. "I'm here," he announced.

"Mother wants us to come over tomorrow. She said the kids would enjoy a day of swimming. She's planning a special dinner."

The three kids ran into the yard from the shade of the barn with little Eddie jumping up and down, shouting hooray as though the decision had already been made to hitch up the wagon and head for the pothole on Cold River.

"Well, we'll see," he called back, setting off a trio pleas that added more heat than George could bear. "Now you three just shush! What's so special about the water at your grandma's anyways? You can cool off just as well in the brook."

"But Pa, you can't *dive* into the brook, and there's kids from everywhere at the pothole!" Eddie argued with the vehemence of a trial lawyer.

George scowled and guffawed only to tease the kids, but he was convincing enough so their faces fell. At last, after much tantalizing, George said, "Well, I guess you could all stand a good bath."

They burst into a chorus of cheers. When they subsided, he patted each child's head and said, "Just remember, I'll need you all out in the barn at sunup. I'm not doin' the morning chores alone."

Mariah crossed the yard and took her husband's arm. "You come in out of the hot sun. I've got a treat for you." She turned to the three children who could hardly stand the wait until morning. "You, too," said Mariah, and they all headed into the kitchen, curious to see what was in their mother's shopping bag. She pulled out a tall bottle, still cold from the tub of ice water at Coursin's Store. "Do you think you could drink a whole glass of Muriel Coursin's homemade fruit punch?" she asked. The children got down glasses, even remembering two for their parents, and held their own out like beggars.

"Almost as good as a plunge into the pothole," said George after a long, satisfied swig.

"Almost," said Eddie.

Four hours' ride on a stiff farm wagon on rocky, rutty roads was a lot to endure for the pleasures of Cold River. It was 9:30 and the day's full heat had not settled in. Sarah Brandon welcomed them and directed the kids to the soapstone sink and water pump in the kitchen to wash the dust of travel from their faces and hands before they sat down to a breakfast of steaming pancakes and her own maple syrup.

"Well, kids, this is going to be a special day," said Sarah with a slight quiver in her voice.

"You're so right," said Eddie with a big smile. He didn't show any of the reserve that his older siblings always displayed toward their grandmother. He aimed his fork toward the stack of pancakes, but his mother parried his thrust with a guttural warning from her throat.

Although Sarah's voice was a bit weaker, she had a triumphant pertness in the eyes and held her head erect. Somehow Mariah began to realize that the special day she was thinking about was something other than just a day of swimming at the pothole.

After an especially long grace with a blessing for every child, for the food to strengthen their bodies, and for the purifying waters of Cold River (Mariah peeked at her mother in astonishment: "The *purifying* waters of Cold River"?), they dug in.

George locked eyes with Mariah. His brows came together as he looked out of the corner of his eye, a look that asked her, "What is going on here?" Mariah rolled her eyes in bewilderment.

"You'll be having a special dinner tonight with a couple of guests," said Sarah as she surveyed her grandchildren's table manners. Before anyone could ask who was coming, Sarah launched into lessons of etiquette. "Now how did I tell you to hold you fork and knife when cutting? Bradley, straighten up. Just lean in a little with each bite. Don't hover over your plate as though you were expecting someone to try to steal your food. And Eddie, don't thrust your fork into your food like a dagger. Turn your fork over, that's right, finger on the base of the tines. That's right. And keep your elbows down."

"Now Mother, they know their company manners."

"Well," said Sarah as she addressed the grandchildren, "let's pretend Grandma's company for the sake of a little rehearsal."

"So who's coming to dinner?" Mariah inquired, fearing that little Eddie's next move with knife or spoon might reverse his grandmother's good mood.

"Oh, your Uncle Elden and the pastor from the church. It just seemed like a good opportunity for the children to make a decision about their future."

*A decision about their future? This is a trap, a water trap.*

Mariah almost dropped her fork. She gave her mother a look that reminded Sarah of the days of her daughter's youth when the two of them clashed regularly.

As soon as the children had cleaned their plates, Mariah announced:

"You kids go collect eggs and feed the chickens for your grandmother…"

"Aw, Ma," whined Eddie, "what about my future?"

"The future starts with eggs," said Mariah as she handed Eddie and his siblings wire baskets. "That's the answer to the eternal question."

"What eternal question?" asked Eddie.

"Which came first. I know the answer. Everything starts out small, so the egg was first. You know your mother's a smart woman, don't you, Eddie?"

"Sure," he responded dubiously.

"And then you'll clean Smokey's stall and put down bedding. When that's done, you can go to the pothole. So now you know your future."

"So we don't have to come back till supper?" Eddie had learned the value of a leading question.

"I'll come get you when it's time, and I won't want any argument," said Mariah with a commanding tone.

"Do we have to come home for lunch?" asked Dotty who loved her chance to visit with the girls of Sandwich, spending hours flipping the pages of fashion magazines and talking about boys.

"Here's your lunch," said Sarah with an expression that told them that their grandmother was a jump ahead of them. Her hands, spotted with age, bony and veined, held out a cloth bag with a small, fresh baked loaf of bread and three chunks of cheese cut in descending sizes to match the child.

"I'll go give 'em a hand," said George who seemed especially anxious to do more chores rather than get entangled in the mother-daughter debate that was about to go on stage.

"Very helpful, Dear," Mariah said sarcastically. "Running out on me, I'd call it."

"Just makin' it easier for you, Mother," he said with a smirk, and before Mariah could object further, he was gone.

"Thank God little Eddie's finally filling out. A miracle he didn't die in the first two years." Sarah turned from the door and headed toward her canister of flour. "Just imagine how we'd all have felt if we couldn't have gotten him breathing. Blue as death."

"All right, Mother. So what's this all about? You've made your point I don't know how many times that I nearly killed Eddie. Well, he's getting over his asthma and he's getting his size. If he gets any livelier, it'll be the death of his parents. I don't want any more reminding about him. So what's this about, inviting over Uncle Elden and the pastor? The special dinner. What's up your sleeve?"

Sarah bent down to a lower cupboard and lifted a great wooden bowl. She kept her eyes on her cooking, moving as she talked, her eyes on her business. "It's time for us to thank God for the life He's given to three healthy kids. And today God might give them another blessing. I just wish George's mother could have lived to hear of this day. Sure as there's a heaven, she'll be looking down."

"Mother, could you stay still for just a minute? What are you talking about?"

"Life eternal. All the three of them have to do is accept…"

Mariah dropped a wooden spoon on the counter and advanced on her mother. "So that's the 'future' you're talking about. The *eternal* future. Pretty crafty. We thought we were coming over here for a holiday, a nice dunk in Cold River, and suddenly I find out…"

"That's just what it is. A dunk in the river. There are two adults and two other children…"

"A baptism. Springing that on me like this," fumed Mariah.

"It's all up to the children. You said so yourself."

"Yes, I did. And it's going to be, too," said Mariah whose palm came down hard enough on the table to rattle her cup and saucer.

"Maybe, just maybe, after they see other children get baptized, maybe they'll decide to join them," said Sarah with a quiet, determined tone. She ignored the rattling china. "Three extra dunks in the river and that'll be three fewer things for me to worry about in my old age."

"The kids aren't prepared, at least not Eddie," said Mariah, her anger subsiding when she saw an anguished expression come over her mother's face, apparently afraid that her daughter might decide to gather up her children and head home in protest.

"If you've done your duty and taught them the four spiritual laws…"

"Don't tell me about my duty. All of my life I've heard about duty, and by God, I've done it. Is God angry with every woman who hopes for something more in her life than children? Did God give me a mind, and yes, a strong will, just to torment me?"

"Shaping the next generation is no small role on the world stage," said Sarah with her head held high.

"Of course," responded Mariah. The whetstone of her mother's strength took the edge off Mariah's voice.

"Mariah, a wife is to her husband like the moon is to the earth," replied Sarah who used all the powers of restraint in her.

"What, nice to look at, but useless?"

"The moon exerts tremendous influence on the Earth, and so does a wife on her husband and children. I guess I wouldn't turn the tide with my looks. And I resent the implication that my life is useless because I gave up teaching to be a wife and mother."

Mariah sank back in her chair seeing that she had wounded her mother. Her voice softened. "No, of course you didn't waste your life, but just think of all you gave up, and all the more your life could have been."

Sarah looked around the kitchen. Her eyes were wet as she gazed upon the same old stove she had fired up daily to feed her family, the same furniture, the same cracked and flaking ceiling that she had grown to accept as the limit of her upward vision. "Yes, there is much more I longed for, that's true."

"Well, I'm still longing for more, and I'm not giving up. I couldn't get George off the farm, for love nor money, and I've had three kids to raise, and so I'm doing my duty. If I have to say so myself, I'm doing a darn good job." Mother and daughter sat in silence for a moment, each taking sips from their cups. "So, when is this baptism service?"

"Well, the pastor and your uncle are coming over in a couple of hours."

"In a couple of hours? That's all the time I've got? And the whole neighborhood watching," said Mariah disgustedly.

"Gotta have witnesses to a baptism. You know that," said her mother.

"Their father has to be consulted about this, too."

"I asked him a few weeks ago if he didn't think it was about time for the kids to be baptized. He smiled and said he'd take all the help from Jesus he could get," said Sarah.

"And you took that to be his approval for getting them baptized?"

"Well, yes."

"Two hours." Mariah growled menacingly as she bolted out of the kitchen bent on a mission.

"Where're you going? I need help here!" shouted Sarah through the screen.

"I *am* helping!" responded Mariah through clenched teeth, stiff-armed, her hands in fists at her sides. "*You're* playing the Savior," she said in a sarcastic crescendo, "so *I'm* playing John the Baptist. I've only got an hour to prepare the way of the Lord."

George, the soft-hearted father, had taken over most of the chores and sent the kids on their way. Mariah ticked off the news to George like a telegraph key and told him to go in and change out of his work clothes and help her mother get to the pothole when the time came. "I've got to explain things to the kids," she said as she flung the barn door open and made her path straight to the banks of Cold River.

When she got close to the pothole, brambles and branches slowed her furious walk. She remembered her joys of youth and the freedom of the river. The waters of Cold River had always given her hope, but her life, like the river, was more often turbulent than calm. Mariah began to reconcile herself to the pothole sacrament. It would also be one more duty behind her.

*Daddy, what were you thinking by passing on before Mother? Do you know what she's doing to me? Damn it, I'm forty-nine years old, and I guess I don't need someone telling me how to raise my kids. Making a spectacle out of the whole family in front of the town. And never mentioning a word to them this morning. Them going off to the pothole for a swim. She could have said something. Bradley'll do this if his father even nods. Maybe Dotty too, but what about Eddie?*

The day was turning out to be hotter than the hinges of Hades, so at least her mother had picked a good day for baptisms. Mariah wasn't just preparing her children for company; she was leading them to the foot of the throne of grace to repent.

In the shade of a chestnut tree a short distance from the upper lip of the pothole, Mariah saw Dotty laughing and joking with one of the

Paisley girls and her two Weed cousins from Juneau Hill. "Oh, Ma, is it time to go already? We haven't even eaten our lunch."

"No, it's not time yet, but I've got something to tell the three of you, so you go get your brothers." Mariah's anxiety upset Dotty.

"Ma, is there something wrong?"

"Nothing's wrong, but your uncle and the pastor are coming over here soon."

"Here?" said Dotty with a twisted expression of complete incredulity.

"Yes, here. Here at the pothole."

"To swim?" asked Dotty, wide-eyed and grinning at the thought of her solemn old great uncle and the Baptist minister plunging from the jumping rock with all of the neighborhood kids.

"No, they're not coming to swim, but they're gonna be in the water. Now no more questions. Have you got a comb with you?"

"Yes, Ma."

"Well, start using it."

Mariah spun her daughter around checking to make sure that her swimming costume was covering everything from knee to neck. Now, shoo. Get Bradley and Eddie." Dotty left, flustered and confused, but knowing better than to ask more questions. In a moment she returned with her older brother.

"Where's Eddie?"

Brad, as he now insisted on being called, looked down, ashamed that he was not able to keep his kid brother under control although he stood nearly a foot taller. "He went up the river."

"Up the river? With the older boys? Why did you let him go?" she exploded. Eddie, was up the river, around the bend where his older brother didn't dare to go.

"You two stay here and dry off in the sun. Keep an eye out for Uncle Elden. Daddy and your grandmother are coming up here soon. There's going to be a baptism ceremony."

"Are we gonna be baptized?" asked George with confusion in his voice.

"If you decide to, yes."

"Me, too?" asked Dotty with an unexpected glee. She liked being the center of attention.

"Do you want to be?" asked Mariah.

"Sure. All the girls I was sitting with are baptized already. Just think. They'll see me do it," she said with a smile.

"That's not the best reason, but we'll talk about that when I find Eddie." Mariah turned and started up the rugged pathway toward the upper river.

"Ma," called Dotty, "you aren't going up *there*, are you?"

Her only answer was in the determined march through briars and branches like a mother bear in search of a lost cub. She thought about her first trip up the river thirty-five years before, curious about boys and determined to share in their secrets. She thought about Will, about freedom, and about the excitement of their lovemaking. As Mariah struggled through the overgrowth, she was going back in time when all of her feelings—joy, desire, shame and anger—were intense and indelible.

When she finally got around the bend, she heard robust voices of teenage boys, voices that reminded her that she was about to enter forbidden territory. She broke through the brambles when she heard the higher pitched voice of one smaller boy who had somehow intruded into the older boys' war game.

The United States had declared war on Imperial Germany in April of 1917 and American doughboys were marching across France in the summer heat, joining English and French soldiers in the trenches on the Western Front. Once the troops arrived in France, war news was in the papers every day, and Neal Coursin chalked up headlines on the blackboard on the front porch of his store—the place where news was discussed. The "news bureau" moved around the pot-bellied stove once it was too cold to sit on the porch benches.

"The world must be made safe for democracy...We desire no conquest, no dominion...We are but one of the champions of the rights of mankind...There are many months of fiery trial and sacrifice ahead of us..."

--President Wilson, April 2, 1917

For two years prior to America's declaration of war, German submarines—U-boats—had attacked ships of neutral countries and had sunk the ocean liner *Lusitania*, taking hundreds of American lives. Americans were alternately horrified and fascinated by the mechanized warfare that took the war under the oceans and into the skies. Mariah could hear the boys shouting as they took sides in the naval war.

"Watch out for the U-boats!" a boy called out as he cannonballed others who dove underwater and pulled the enemy into the depths. Boys rose coughing and gasping.

Mariah kept herself hidden in the thick brush, but came close enough to see her younger son standing on a high boulder, buck naked, smoking a cigar. "Battleship coming!" he shouted.

As one of the older boys on the German side broke through the surface to fill his lungs for the next undersea attack, he felt a warm stream pouring down on his head.

Little Eddie called out, "Piss on the Kaiser!" while he aimed his stream of urine with one hand and held the cigar with the other.

"I'll get you, you little bastard!" the U-boat bellowed as he swam toward the bank.

"Eddie!" screamed Mariah, "you get your bare arse over here right now!"

Suddenly every boy except Eddie plunged into the water.

"Mariah broke out of her cover just far enough so her son could see where the ominous voice was coming from. She had brought about an armistice quicker than the Expeditionary Force.

Eddie set down the cigar and sheepishly retrieved his clothes. "All right, Ma," he muttered. The older boys stood waist-deep in the water facing Mariah. "Eddie, you don't belong up here," she scolded, oblivious to the fact that her presence in the older boys' sanctuary was a much greater breach of community taboos. "And boys, don't you ever give my son tobacco again."

"Yes, Mrs. Taylor," the boys called in unison, hoping her eyesight wasn't too good.

"And boys," Mariah said as she pushed Eddie along, "that water is as clear as crystal."

Suddenly the boys' hands plunged into the water and crisscrossed in front of their privates.

On the journey downstream, Mariah filled in her perplexed eight-year-old on his grand-mother's divine designs. She went over the four spiritual laws again between gasps for air as she slipped and crawled through the vines and branches of the overgrown trail.

"The pastor asks if you have given your life to Christ, and what are you going to say?"

"I don't know. What does it mean?"

"I've explained it before, haven't I?"

"Yes, Ma, but I still don't understand it." He stopped in his tracks and looked his mother in the face with pain in his eyes. "Ma, I can't do it."

He was a smart little boy, and a bit of a hellian, but his eyes told her that he understood the magnitude of the sacrament.

Mariah had forced him to do so many things to bring him back from wayward paths, but she looked into his face and realized that she could not force him to believe. His eyes pleaded with her not to make him do what he was not ready for. She kneeled down in front of him. "It's all right Eddie. I'm not going to make you."

Eddie threw his arms around her neck and brushed away tears with the heels of his hands. "When I'm a little older, I think I'll understand," Eddie told his mother as he calmed down.

Mariah and Eddie met up with Bradley and Dotty just in time before Uncle Elden, the pastor and Grandma made their solemn processional up the path. Eddie would observe. One day, when he was older, he could decide to follow his brother and sister, but the decision would be his.

As the group came into view past the veil of forsythia, Mariah and the children could see that two of the men were dressed in long linen robes of white.

"Are they in the Klan?" whispered Eddie. "Where's their hoods?"

"No, it's not the Klan, Eddie. The minister and deacon wear those robes to do the baptism."

Every kid at the pothole circled around the worshipers. "Yup, you'd think it was a cross-burning." Mariah muttered as George came over to her to ask what the children had decided. She had only a few minutes to inform her mother of the children's decisions before the pastor called the two adults into the waist-deep water.

Eddie grew wide-eyed when his brother entered the waters, waters that had taken on a magical quality.

"George Bradley Taylor, do you acknowledge your sinfulness before God?" asked the pastor who stood only a couple of inches taller than Bradley.

Bradley's eyes darted back and forth and finally settled on his father's face. George smiled lightly and gave his elder son a slow and gentle nod of approval.

"Yes," he said softly.

"Do you acknowledge that Jesus' death on the cross was the price for your sins and the sins of the world?"

The second "Yes" was quicker and louder.

"And do you accept Jesus Christ as your savior and as your Lord?"

Bradley looked at the pastor and nodded as the reverend's big hands came at him. "If you accept Jesus, say yes."

"Yes," he said solemnly.

"Then I baptize you in the name of the Father, the Son and the Holy Ghost." Bradley's lanky frame descended into the vortex.

Dorothy followed with surprising gravity. She seemed mesmerized by the pastor's words and anxious to join the elect. After her immersion, she brushed the water from her eyes and looked at her friends who smiled and applauded. She blew a kiss to her delighted grandmother.

Eddie was wide-eyed with all of the talk of sinfulness and forgiveness. He had fought off German U-boats and urinated on boys twice his height, but he was not ready to take on the mantle of the Trinity. He stood by his mother who gave him a reassuring hug. He looked so small and innocent, as though he had already washed his sins away.

When the ceremony was over and the family started for home, Sarah took Eddie's hand. "Now you'll be ready the next time, won't you?" She squeezed him with reassurance.

"Gramma, why doesn't Jesus stop the war?" asked Eddie whose brow was furrowed with the weight of his question.

"Well, there's a lot of sin in the world." They walked hand in hand along the riverbank avoiding stepping on wildflowers.

"Why doesn't Jesus wash it away?" asked Eddie.

"It's up to us to ask for His forgiveness," Sarah replied. She gave Eddie's hand a gentle squeeze. "Soon it will be time for a nice dinner to celebrate." She turned toward her uncle and the pastor who stood next to their buggy in their wet clothes. "Now you're coming back this evening with the ladies, is that right?"

"Like the wedding at Cana. We wouldn't miss it for the world," said the pastor as the two men took their places on the tufted seat and waved goodbye to the family.

Sarah sent the children upstairs to dress for company. "Why, I can see the change in the children already. Even Eddie. He'll be ready before long, I just know it."

"Pastor," called Mariah whose expression had turned playful, "does this event qualify as a miracle?"

"I guess any baptism is a miracle," he said.

"Not just that," Mariah replied with a smile. "You turned Cold River into holy water." Mariah flapped the tablecloth into the air and it settled into place with a puff of cooling air. "I wouldn't mind at all if tonight you turned the water into wine," she added.

"Wine" was one biblical word that Baptists didn't take literally. "No wine will ever pass between these lips," he said solemnly.

"So why wasn't it a sin for Jesus to drink wine at the wedding?" Mariah asked with a checkmate glance at the man of the cloth.

"Well," he said, "that was different."

"Oh?" said Mariah who left the pastor cornered.


Sarah stood at the kitchen table kneading dough for dinner rolls. "Where are George and the kids?" she asked Mariah. The kitchen was hot, but a westerly breeze rustled the curtains.

"I gave George a list of things that needed fixing. The kids are helping. They've got plenty of time before they have to get washed and dressed for dinner."

"You didn't have to do that," she said with a relaxed smile.

"Oh, a nail here and a hinge there, what's that compared to a day of bliss for the kids—never mind a day—an eternity of bliss is in store for them!" joked Mariah.

"Well, we still have one little hell-raiser to contend with," added Sarah as they both laughed off the tensions of the day.

"Oh," said Mariah who stooped to take two jars of preserves out of her canvas bag. "I brought these for you. You were full of surprises today. I've got a surprise of my own."

Sarah held them up and admired the handmade labels with fancy lettering and color sketches of fruit.

"Yes, I made those myself and glued them on. When I start bringing in more money, I'll have labels printed over in Wolfeboro."

"That's a lot of trouble to go to, isn't it for...?"

"Ma, you don't understand. I'm making up preserves by the dozens now. I can get twelve cents or more for each jar, some of them, fifteen," announced Mariah proudly.

"Who'll pay that?" asked Sarah as she slid a sheet of rolls into the oven.

"I've got some summer people as customers now," retorted Mariah. "When the war's over, sugar won't be so high."

"Next year maybe all of us will be happier if we can get disentangled from all of those foreigners," said Sarah with a sarcastic laugh. "I'll have less to worry about, thanks to today, and now maybe my farm wife daughter will be a lady of business again."

"Just maybe," added Mariah as though a cloud of doubt had just drifted over her. "Life is full of surprises, not all of them welcome." Mariah saw George and the children crossing the yard from the barn. She took a pail of warm water from the back of the stove. "You weren't saving this water for something else, were you?" she asked her mother.

"No. There's nothing special about *that* water," Sarah said with a wry smile.

# CHAPTER 28

## The Spanish Lady

At Coursin's store Mariah tied her team to the hitching post between the judge's brand new Packard and a dented old Model T pickup from the Holt farm. Her wagon was loaded with pumpkins, squash, and potatoes that she planned to get on the eleven o'clock train for Rochester. Selling some surplus vegetables and a few preserves in the summer and fall was as close as Mariah had gotten to her long-deferred dream of starting a business once again. She needed capital. It takes money to make money, and farm crops yielded up little more than sustenance and barter. If Mariah were to market beyond the few customers she had cultivated by word of mouth, she needed more of the land under cultivation in fruit and berries.

Two things weighed heavily on Mariah's mind as she arrived at the square The best chance of raising the kind of money she needed was George's prize virgin timber, something that he valued like an arm or a leg. Once again Mariah found her ambitions frustrated. The other thing on her mind was a foreign pestilence invading the nation, a pestilence that was taking young people in huge numbers, a pestilence far more dreaded than the Kaiser's crack troops.

"Mrs. Taylor, you're damned lucky, you know," said the county clerk, Preston Meader, through a mask that everybody was wearing whenever they went to town.

"How's that, Mr. Meader?" asked Mariah who was curious to know what luck there was in a routine harvest shipment of food to Rochester and Dover.

"You'll just make it for the last train. Won't be no more shipments till this thing dies down. They say they've got the influenza less than forty miles down the tracks," said Meader who splashed some rubbing alcohol into his palm and rubbed his hands together. "Can't be too careful, you know."

"Here, you go," said Meader, offering Mariah a splash from the bottle. "Now don't touch anybody, and once you get through in the store, you wash up again. I'm leaving the bottle right here on the bench. "I swear, hand-washing and the masks are the best protection," he said authoritatively.

"I'm worried about my mother. You know she just turned eighty-one."

"I'd be a lot more worried about the kids. That's who it's hitting. Who'd a thought there'd ever be a health advantage to being old geezers like us," the tidy Meader said, straightening his tie in his stiff celluloid collar. He tipped his derby and started across the square to the court-house. "Quiet day," he called back. "We've continued most cases for a month. Don't want to turn little misdemeanors into death sentences," he said with a short laugh, and a shake of his head.

Mariah saw the headlines on the chalkboard on the porch of Coursin's Store that Camp Devens in Massachusetts was being quarantined, and some of the hard hit towns had barred roads to keep the flu from spreading. Mariah went inside where all was still except for the jangling of the bell announcing a customer. She would hate to have to admit it to her mother, but she suddenly felt relieved that her children had been baptized just eight months before the epidemic started.

She stood at the phone, but resisted picking it up, fearing contamination. "Neal, Neal!" she called out. Coursin came out of the storage room carrying a burlap bag of potatoes. "Yes, Mrs. Taylor." Coursin stretched out each word with resignation.

"Got anything to clean this phone with?" asked Mariah, her voice muffled by her mask.

Coursin rested a burlap bag of potatoes on the floor. "Everybody wants me to wash everything in the damned store. I don't know what more I can do," he sputtered.

"Well, Neal, you know you can't take chances with this flu. We've lost more people to it than soldiers in the war."

"That's true, but the closest it's come so far is Rochester." Coursin pulled a soft cotton cloth out of his apron pocket and a brown bottle off a shelf. He unscrewed the cap and doused the rag with its contents. "Here, Mrs. Taylor, give me that receiver." Coursin rubbed the earpiece and proceeded to wipe down the mouthpiece and the whole surface of the phone cabinet until Mariah and he were squinting and tearing up from the chlorine fumes. "I might be single-handedly driving the Spanish Lady out of the Ossipee Valley," said Coursin, dawbing his eyes with the skirt of his grocer's apron.

"Well, your Spanish lady will leave looking like a Seigfeld show-girl," said Mariah as she held a handkerchief over her running eyes.

"What?" said Neal who couldn't find anything funny since the war started.

"She'll be bleached!" Mariah blurted out, soured that there was no one in earshot to appreciate a joke. "Looks like I better stock up on bleach and alcohol. Course you know my mother. She'll have another theory about the flu, I'll bet you."

The pendulum clock on the bead board wall struck 10:00, the time that Sarah promised to be at the phone each Monday morning. It was Mariah's turn to call, so she placed a nickel on Coursin's counter close to the register. She made three rapid turns of the crank. "Gert, could you ring up Taylor's for me, please?"

As usual Mariah exchanged pleasantries over the phone with the owner of the North Sandwich store and found that there were no reported cases of the Spanish flu in the notch. Still, business had fallen off, and some of his fresh foods were spoiling before he could sell them. "Some folks are afraid to buy anythin' that's not in a tin or a box," he said. "Nothin' but superstition," he said disgustedly.

"Your mother's here, but I had to set her down by the stove. Dizzier 'an a top an' all agitated. No, no. Not the flu. No cough, no fever, but she's got me worried. She says she's plannin' on drivin' her buggy over to your place with a load of onions for some reason."

When Sarah got on the phone, she insisted that she had just driven too fast into town and was fearful and upset about the news she'd read in the *Concord Monitor* about the flu and how quickly it took people. "I read that four ladies were playing bridge in Boston one afternoon, and the next evening, three of them were dead."

"Mother, I wouldn't believe everything I hear. They say the Huns snuck spies into the country and spread the contagion in movie theaters in New York or some such thing. And they say that people's faces turn purple as an eggplant before they die. I think people are getting hysterical. I just read that the Surgeon General said these German spy stories were totally unfounded. Don't get yourself all upset over this. There've been no cases around here yet."

"Yet," Sarah emphasized.

"Then why are you thinking of coming over? Why risk it?"

"Some folks here offered to drive me over, but now that I bought old Tarnation from you, I could take a nap on the way and he'd take me down Brown's Ridge just as though we were on tracks."

"And to think that Florence has been trying to get you to buy a Model T Ford. I'll tell you something for sure. No car is going to find its way here by itself," laughed Mariah. "What are you getting at the store besides onions? We've got bags of 'em in the root cellar, so I don't know why we'd need more. I think we're well stocked with everything here. George and I are fixed with all we can think of."

"I bought some candy for the kids. Since school's been closed down and the harvest's in, they're going to be bored, so I bought a Parcheesi game so we can have a little fun to pass the time. And I'm bringing ten pounds of onions."

"That's like bringing coals to Newcastle. I told you we've got plenty of onions."

"You won't want to use up your year's supply to fight the flu."

"So onions are the secret weapon against the flu? I guess I'll dash a quick note off to President Wilson," snorted Mariah.

"Joke if you want, but I heard of a woman in Amesbury who used onions to save her whole family. Now you may be skeptical. You often are, but this is a time to listen to your mother. This lady made onion stew and fed it to her family each day. She tied strings of onions around the kids' necks at night, and she put bowls of chopped onions on windowsills. They say vapors kill bad humors that might come in by way of drafts." Sarah heard chuckling on the other end of the line. "Now, don't you laugh at me. In her neighborhood there wasn't a household that didn't face at least one death. Well, you know, the Grim Reaper passed them by because he couldn't stand the vapors. True story, dear, and if it worked for them, it can work for us."

"Are you sure it wasn't garlic? Did this lady circle the house regularly with a crucifix in hand?"

"Now don't you go having fun at my expense, now," said Sarah who finally admitted a little lightness into her voice.

"You talk about having fun; I think with all those onions we'll spend all of our time together crying," said Mariah.

Mariah heard her mother giving instructions to the grocer's son to put the sack of onions on the seat. She told the boy she'd be out directly. "Well, I'm setting out right away. I've got a trunk of clothes on the buggy and the neighbors will be looking after my chickens for the eggs. My arm's throbbing from holding this blasted earpiece for so long, so I'll let you go." Mariah heard in her mother's voice that her greatest fear was facing the epidemic alone.

The few customers at Coursin's stood yards apart as they exchanged stories about the flu. A lady from the Wolfeboro road told of a doctor who traveled the circuit around Rochester ladling tablespoons of whiskey into people, even little children. He told his patients that he didn't care if they were teetotalers or not; the spirits were for medicinal purposes, and he hadn't lost a patient yet who followed his instructions.

"Spicy soups," said Neal Coursin, thumbing over his shoulder at his shelf full of spices. "That's another good thing. Keeps all the passages open. This viscous pneumonia that sets in is what kills people. This flu closes people's throats with swelling. Poor things suffocate."

Coursin's stock boy just returned from the railroad station with a box of spirits of camphor, bottles of ammonia and boxes of boric acid. A run on these products had depleted Coursin's stocks. "I heard that the son of the owner of the Wallace Shoe Factory died yesterday. He took ill with the flu at Dartmouth," said the skinny lad of sixteen. "Football player. Big guy. Came home in a chauffeured limousine.

Dead in only two days." The ominous report silenced the customers, and they dispersed in fear. Mariah thought of Wallace's and of Will.

At the North Sandwich store, Sarah had already snapped her whip and got her horse into a trot in the direction of Ossipee, her anxiety unabated.

Only minutes after Mariah arrived home from Coursin's, Clyde Davis came by with the mail, masked and gloved and keeping his distance. "You know that Polish family farther down the ridge road. They think one's got it and they want me to send the doctor. Scares the heck out of me, that it does," said Clyde, shaking his head. "Mrs. Taylor, are you shakin' boric acid on your mail like I told ya?"

"Oh, yes, Clyde. I always do what you tell me to."

"Always?"

"Well, about the mail, that is," said Mariah with a smile that showed only in her eyes, the mask hiding the rest of her expression.

"If you'd followed my advice, you wouldn't be on this old fahm," said Clyde with his strong Yankee aversion to r's. "You could be a success in business—laundry, baking or any other thing you put your mind to—if you could just get the capital to get started on a bigger scale."

"Well, Clyde, just where do you think I could ever come up with that capital?" Davis gave a slow nod in the direction of the high timber on White Horse Ledge—George's pride and joy. They looked at each other from behind their masks. Mariah rolled her eyes and shook her head. "See you tomorrow," said Mariah.

"God willin'," said Clyde who climbed into his station wagon and puttered down the road.

Mariah called the family together around the table and told them about the Polish family. "The flu is probably only two miles away," she warned.

George wrapped his big, leathery hands around a cup of tea that rattled slightly on the table. At sixty-eight he could still do a full day's work in field or barn, but the tremor in his hands was worsening, and a twitch was beginning to develop in his head. Mariah bought him a Gillette safety razor for his birthday "to save you from cutting your own throat," she said when he opened the box.

"There'll be no more trips to the store and no visitin' neighbor kids till this thing passes," said George grimly. Your mother 'n me'll have to be the ones to go to town 'cause we ain't heard that old folks are catchin' it."

"How long is it gonna be?" asked Eddie, long-faced. "It's no fun sittin' around here."

"You don't have to sit around. There's always plenty to do," retorted his father.

"Ya, work," said Eddie whose chin dropped onto his palm. He began drumming the fingers of his other hand on the table.

"Look, Eddie, we're talking about death. This isn't just a runny nose." As she looked at each of her children, Mariah realized they had no fear, only curiosity. Death was not yet a reality to them.

Mariah looked at the places around the table and thought how many would be missing from the holiday celebrations. So many faces that once glowed in candlelight smiling across the table decked out in linen, and piled with steaming bowls of wafting fragrances--meat and gravy and bread warm out of the oven. She closed her eyes and recalled the faces of Frederick and her father. The sounds of voices echoed once again; the singing of Jim and Bertha carried over space and time. Then she remembered the gurgle of a wine bottle and Will's eyes shimmering with desire over crystal lifted in a toast to their future bliss. She felt her eyes welling up. The table had grown silent.

George covered her hands with his, still warm from the teacup. "Don't worry, dear. We'll survive. We've gotten through hard times before."

*Survive. Yes, I've survived. I used to dream about life's exciting possibilities. Now I thank God if He has given me a day without torment.* "Yes. Yes, many hard times." Mariah nodded and opened her eyes. Bradley, Dotty and Eddie were looking down, uncomfortable seeing tears in their mother's eyes. Mariah rose and kissed her husband's forehead and rested her hand on his shoulder. "Yes, we'll survive." She went to the kitchen window and looked up and down Brown's Ridge Road. "Well, kids, let's do some baking. And the first one who sees Tarnation coming down the road gets an extra cinnamon roll."

Nearly three hours passed before Eddie hollered that he saw the buggy in the distance crossing the bridge over the brook up beyond the Luddington place. The day had turned blustery, but he insisted on standing out at the edge of the road eating his cinnamon roll until Grandma Brandon clitter-clattered into the yard.

But as the buggy drew near, Eddie called out in alarm. "Ma, Pa, come out here!" The whole family left the warmth and the aromas of the kitchen and stood in the yard to see Tarnation walking slowly into the yard. The seat of the buggy was empty except for a bag of onions.

George set the bag on the ground and climbed into the driver's seat. He gathered up the reins that had fallen over the dashboard. "I'll head back to town," he said grimly. Dotty wrapped her arms around her mother's waist; the boys stood in the middle of the road staring toward Ossipee Center, wishing that they could hear a voice calling or any sign of hope.

Before George boarded Sarah's buggy, the family saw Clyde Davis's mail truck coming slowly toward them followed by a familiar black sedan. When they came to a stop, George and Mariah could see that Clyde's boxes of mail were piled in the back seat of Dr. Farrington's car. A figure wrapped in a blanket occupied the space usually taken up by the mail. "I found her on the side of the road just south of town," said Clyde who held his hat in his hand.

"Oh, God, no!" whimpered George, his tremor accentuated in the emotion of the moment.

"At least it wasn't the flu," said the doctor who patted George on the back. Signs are that Mrs. Brandon had a heart attack and fell out of the buggy. "It was quick. I'm sure she didn't suffer. At least you've got that to be thankful for."

Mariah stood rigid and pale by the station wagon looking in at her mother's serene face. The three children stood behind her holding hands. Dorothy was crying softly.

The men carried Sarah Sanborn Brandon into her daughter's house and placed her on the dining room table. "She's the last of her generation," said Mariah as George held his wife to his side. "She was still mothering me right up to her last day."

Eddie approached the table and touched his grandmother's hand. "Sorry about last summer," he murmured through sniffles.

Mariah took Eddie's hand. In the silence of the room she closed her eyes and remembered the sound of the river that always came to her when she needed its voice the most.

# CHAPTER 29

## *Loggerheads*

At the top of Kruge's Hill George reined in the horses and braked the wagon. Amidst the racket of hooves and iron wheel rims he thought he heard the echoing sound of chopping. The horses' ears turned and twisted. The sound was uncommonly deadly; the thwack-thwack that cut through two decades of rings in one blow, and in fifteen minutes laid low what it had taken a century to erect.

1923 had added the usual half-inch of girth to George's mighty stand of white pines. Timber was about the only bright spot in agricultural commodities. The "roaring economy" that pundits and politicians bragged about was Wall Street where stock was asset; "livestock" and virtually all agriculture in 1923 was liability. During more than four years of stagnation and lost opportunities, Mariah had not been able to make George budge about converting some of his pine stock into the assets they desperately needed. The Taylor pines continued to sway majestically in the wind, proud as money in the bank.

George's ears told him that the distant sound wasn't the thud of farmers' old pole axes chipping away at cordwood in erratic slow time. This was the sound of loggers who sent chips flying in a rhythm as accurate as a conductor's watch. Only he and the Holts had a stand of timber tall enough to interest loggers.

They couldn't be taking trees far from the road. Usually loggers waited until the ground was frozen and blanketed with snow so their teams could skid the logs to roadside or riverbank. It was mid-November and cold, but the ground was bare. Old Man Holt would have told him if he was selling off his timber. The sound of loggers could be coming from only one stand of timber.

Local mills had eyed his virgin pines for the last few years with a lust for forbidden fruit. "If not the whole stand, then the half on the east side of the road," bargained Mariah who pressed her case again when she emptied the cash box to pay property taxes. Even with their money depleted, no schemes, no shortages, no wants or needs swayed him to put the ax to his treasured stand of virgin pine.

"George, you can't go through another season like this one. Next July you'll turn seventy-four. Look at your hands shake. We need some help around here, and we've got three children who won't be around much longer to help. Bradley's already twenty."

George accepted that Dotty would marry and leave, and he knew that Eddie's eyes saw dollar signs in everything but farming. What George couldn't bear was the thought that his number one son would eventually set off on his own. George held on to the hope that Bradley would stay as long as his father lived. Bradley above all loved his father and he loved the land. George told Bradley that it was his hope that one day the land would be his.

But Bradley's devotion couldn't do anything about the leaking roof or the sagging barn sills. Everything was falling apart, and there was no cash to buy the materials to put things back in good order. Mariah declared that the calamity that called for the sale of the timber had finally arrived by painful degrees. First the place had to be fixed up; then Mariah could fund her fledgling business into a good income producer.

"At least half the stand. What else can we do?" Mariah had pleaded with her husband weeks before to listen to reason. "And now Dotty's got the promise of a job down in Malden, so I'll have no one to help me in the kitchen."

Mariah could not blame her daughter for having the same desire she always had—a better life than rural subsistence farming could provide. "She's about to turn sixteen, and who is she going to meet around here who doesn't smell of cow manure all the time? She wants a life, and I can't hold her back. God love her, she's not afraid to work." After Mariah pleaded her case following the last harvest, George left the table, speechless, shaking his head and looking downcast. He hadn't said yes, but God help him, he hadn't said no either.

The horses snorted and shook the reins, then fell silent again. Again, the rhythmic thwack-thwack rose from down the slope of Brown's Ridge. George knew the value of trees more than the typical New Hampshirite. Iowa had taught him that trees were worth so much more than a quick buck. The rock-pocked and pallid land of New Hampshire had little to boast about to farmers, but in centuries past it had raised trees like porcupine quills to defend against adversity of wind and warrior. Since George left with his mother for Iowa, the land was stripped as if by a holocaust. Nearly three quarters of the New Hampshire landscape was open land, much of it littered with the debris of discarded, rotting branches and bark and the occasional sawdust pile that looked like giant anthills.

George had been gone for a week working with the county road agent on repair of bridges and roads; it was the only work available to him that could bring him some of the cash they needed. At seventy-three, and with his shaking hands and head rendering him pitiful, George was sent home early. The county road agent handed him a pay envelope with a few extra dollars and a tender pat on the back telling him goodbye. The road agent wished he could do more. If they kept George on any longer, the job would turn into a charity case.

Hidden under a loose floorboard in their bedroom was a Schrafft's chocolate tin that served as their cash box. It still had the sweet smell of chocolate, but that was all. George did not look forward to admitting to Mariah that his last means of filling the box was now closed to him.

The truth of their poverty weighed heavily upon George Washington Taylor's bony shoulders. He had returned to New Hampshire only to become poor, and there was no likelihood of escape from poverty's grip for him or his wife. If there were escape for his children, then he and Mariah would face desperation alone. George agonized over the thought of ending up at the county farm, buried in a separate cemetery reserved for the poor wards of the government's largesse.

In the summers Mariah now had a little extra income from taking in laundry for the rich visitors who left cotton bags at Coursin's Store each Monday for him to pick up. By week's end, Mariah returned the linens and clothes, folded, mended and starched, wrapped in Brown paper and tied, just the way the "swells" expected them. Laundry was a new enterprise of Mariah's cottage industry. Even if they had bought a place in downtown Wolfeboro, Mariah could not have made money in dressmaking anymore. The bottom had dropped out of the business when department stores started selling ready-to-wear clothes in standard sizes. Preserves held out promise, but she couldn't meet demand. Mariah saw no other way out. She decided to take George's silence as consent to sell half of the virgin pines.

George looked down from Kruge's Hill and saw the top of a giant white pine quiver. He drove down the slope with a heavy heart, remembering that not long ago a timber cruiser with a thick wallet had come along Brown's Ridge Road and spied his stand of old growth pine climbing up White Horse Ledge. Much of the stand was on no more than a five per cent grade. He'd called them "the last virgins in the North Country," and made George blush. George was proud of his stand, and even enjoyed hearing how many board feet of prime lumber would come from their hearts. George swelled with pride to hear the appraisal and the offer. He said he and "the Mrs." would think about it. He meant no, but he hadn't said it either to the timber cruiser or to Mariah.

"So you're back early," said Rangeley the timber cruiser as he walked up to the wagon. The he saw tears in the old man's eyes. The lusty suitor of George's virgins stammered as though an angry father had caught him in the act with his precious daughter. Rangeley pulled off his sawdust-coated knit cap and scratched his bald head. "We're just takin' the ones on this side the road. You still got a mighty good stand up there against the ledge and we've got hahd ground and a shaht distance to the road."

George got down from the wagon without speaking. Rangeley followed him toward the front door, putting a hand on George's back in a misguided attempt at solace. "It's hahd, real hahd, George, but I'm payin' ya top dollah. You won't have to worry about cash for the next few yee-ahs."

Rangeley opened the door for him, and they were both met with the steaming scent of a beef roast with mashed potatoes and gravy that Mariah had fixed for the crew. "Mrs. Taylor's feedin' us 'bout the best we've et since I first put my hand to a two-man saw."

Mariah turned around and gasped at seeing George's face. She put down her gravy ladle and helped him off with his coat. "Oh, George, I wanted all of this done before you got home on Friday," she said softly, directing him close to the stove and away from the chatter and clatter of the lumberman's feed.

She sat him down at the small table in the corner she used for preserves. "You even turned the house over to 'em," he said, looking stricken.

"They're paying for this, too. Don't you worry about that," Mariah said with force in her voice that implied she had driven a hard bargain. He was not comforted.

"There won't be pines like these for more than a century," he mumbled, staring at his plate. "I won't even have a grandchild live to see trees like these. And half's not gonna be enough. They'll all have to go before long."

Mariah sat down and covered his trembling hands with hers. "They haven't got us licked yet," she said with defiance to a world that had knocked them down many times before. "You just wait and see! It takes money to make money," Mariah added with forced enthusiasm.

George got up in silence and went to the door. He surveyed the field of stumps and rubble that once was tall pine.

"George, I'm sorry," said Mariah softly. "I know this is a blow to you. But if that's what it takes…"

"It's gonna take everything I got," said George from the depths of his sadness.

# CHAPTER 30

## *Sour Raspberries*

M rs. Stevens' daughter, Ruth, sat on the porch of her mother's summer home watching Mariah pick raspberries. Ruth wore a short silk dress the color of pale peonies and a broad-brimmed sunhat of white straw with a bright pink ribbon. Her hair was bobbed in the newest fashion and she smoked a cigarette in a long holder. Mariah, in a cotton housedress and bibbed apron, reached through the barbs for the succulent, ripe berries that stained her fingers as she dropped them into her basket. Sweat ran onto her glasses and she stopped to wipe them.

"Oh, Mrs. Taylor, I say there, Mrs. Taylor," Ruth called in a falsetto. Mariah replaced her glasses and looked in the direction of the musical voice. The daughter, Ruth Luddington,  recently divorced, summoned her.

"Yes?" responded Mariah crisply, waiting only briefly for young Ruth to have her say. Ruth said nothing.  She waited then called out again with a touch of irritation in her voice. "Mrs. Taylor, please." She motioned Mariah to come.

*Now what does she want? She actually expects me to stop what I'm doing and walk through these brambles and across that lawn? Does she think she's calling a dog?* Mariah remembered her own fashionable days and the looks from the factory girls as she passed in her finery. She went back to picking pretending that she had merely been greeted rather than summoned. Mariah had orders to fill, but not for that silly strumpet, Ruth Luddington. The Taylor's new enterprise was bringing in a healthy profit with each successive crop of berries—strawberries in June, blueberries in July, and raspberries in August. The neighbors, the Stevenses, began to take notice of the Taylor's improving status when they hired a carpenter to reshingle the roof of the house.

When George and Mariah took possession of the old farm in the spring of 1903, Ruth Stevens was a girl of fourteen, a beautiful blonde, tall and fluid in movement. Her widowed mother wintered on the Chesapeake at an old plantation owned by her niece Josephine and her stockbroker husband. The transplanted Boston Brahmins loved the story that the plantation, named "Hard Bargain," was lost in the colonial days by a speculator in West Indies sugar who put the deed into the pot in a poker game. The Luddingtons loved to tell the Taylors about the plantation, sleeper cars and ocean liners.

The would-be socialite had just turned thirty-five, returning to her mother's home for the summer while her lawyer worked out the details of the divorce settlement with her novelist ex-husband. Ruth felt she had made a sure bet by attaching herself to her rich cousins whom she invited to join her for a couple of weeks of country air.

The graceful blonde pulled the stub of her cigarette out of the holder and crushed it with single twist of her white pumps. As she started down the granite steps, Mariah could see even from a distance that the poor thing was exasperated that the farmer's wife had not come when called.

*She thinks she's quite a lady. I oughta show her pictures of me at that age. Look at that useless gold digger strutting across that porch.*

Ruth's graceful hands never touched a cow's udder since the day she left Boston on a steamer for the "Grand Tour" with Richard Luddington, a second-rate novelist with inherited wealth that cushioned the shortfalls of mediocrity. At eighteen, but with the adopted elegance of title seekers, Ruth Stevens graced the salons and dining rooms of the *riche,* nouveau or vieux, as Mrs. Ruth Luddington. Ruth wore many lovely rings, some real, some paste, and one that passed as a wedding band. Richard did not marry her until they were steaming homeward. Ruth tearfully expressed her fear that she was pregnant, but soon after she returned, with a new ring and the Captain's blessing, she found that it was a false alarm.

Ruth's love for Luddington faded, but her memories of Europe did not. She had held the baby heir of Monaco in her arms and sat in the first ring at LaScala. These and other details of her European tour were kept vivid by frequent embellishment. She peppered her language with French, and her library was *de rigueur* with the works of everyone from Kipling to T.S. Eliot to D.H. Lawrence. Ruth had read a few of them and depended on the *New York Times* book reviews for the rest.

Mariah was well aware of the humble lineage from which fashionable Mrs. Luddington descended. The Stevenses had just been another subsistence farming family on the old farm that backed up to Whitehorse Ledge, but contact with urbane cousins—and a small inheritance from an uncle—gave them a taste for finer things. A spring-fed cistern provided water for a modern bathroom of marble with nickel fixtures. There was seldom a native who, as a first-time visitor, didn't ask to use the bathroom at "Brookside."

Otherwise the Stevens place remained essentially as it had been since it was built in 1743 with wide, wood paneled walls painted with brick dust and sour milk. The Stevenses ate jellied veal loaf and liver pate by the light of kerosene lamps and the warmth of the fireplace. They jokingly lifted their glasses of sherry "to the Amish!" at four in the afternoon to celebrate their immersion into bucolic simplicity. Prohibition was as irrelevant to them as to the Pennsylvania Dutch.

George looked after the place for a small sum when Mrs. Stevens closed the house for the winter. In the summer he and Mariah kept their flowerbeds and vegetable gardens for a little extra spending money, but they did not consider themselves hired hands. They were neighbors lending a helping hand. That had been the relationship since Ruth was a child.

"Oh, Mrs. Taylor. I'm sorry to interrupt your work, but I believe our property line runs across the raspberry patch about where that tree is, whatever kind it is, I never can remember."

*Of course you don't. You grew up right here in dirt and manure. Traipsing across Europe as a mistress wiped out your memory, I guess.*

"It's a hickory," replied Mariah coldly. She stood with a fist on her hip and a basket in her other hand. "And these are *my* raspberries." Ruth reddened as Mariah answered in simple, unadorned declaratives. The Taylors and the Stevenses had never determined the exact property line and assumed that it was the low stonewall that kept the raspberries out of the Stevens's lawn. Mrs. Stevens never had any interest in raspberries other than eating those given to her out of neighborliness. Daughter Ruth was very interested in clear boundaries.

"Now, really, Mrs. Taylor," responded Ruth, restrained in her gestures by the fear that the barbs might tear her silk sleeves. "I looked at the old deed. If you search the ground near that tree, you should find an iron pipe."

"I'll tell you what, I'm quite busy myself, Ruthie dear," replied Mariah, stretching deep into the brambles for a large, sweet berry, "why don't you go find the pipe, and when you do, I'll come take a look." Mariah saw the indignant, imperious expression on the blonde's seamless visage, but she went on picking.

Mariah looked up from her full basket and found that the lady in silk had left berry and barb behind and had waltzed herself across the lawn to the house. Mariah did not look up when the spring-powered screen door slammed shut. For a moment Mariah thought of herself pushing through the crowds of mill girls picketing in Rochester. She remembered herself decked out in yellow silk at Union Station. *Yes, I used to be a lady of fashion, but God help me, not a Ruth Luddington. I hope I was never that.*

More important things occupied Mariah's mind than Ruth Luddington. She was busy putting her family to work in a mass production operation to convert raw materials into fine processed foods, and to market them to everyone with high five-figure incomes in the growing resort communities. If she could only get her kids excited about her business plan and convince them to stay on—at least in the area— they could all realize a good living from a growing line of products, and eventually hire help for the most tedious parts of the work.

She knew that Dotty was a fair cook and liked seeing the family name on products in the store. Like her mother, she wasn't afraid of work, but at the same time, she longed for some glamour and excitement. Dotty spent some of her time watching Ruth, checking out her fashions, even imitating her walk. Dotty was saving up to buy a chemise with a hem right up to the knee.

George and Bradley loved growing the berries, fruits and vegetables that would go into Mariah's legendary recipes, and even Eddie at age fourteen would be able to use his network of older friends—friends with cars—to carry Taylor's Fine Foods from Wolfeboro to Meredith, and from Laconia to Center Harbor. Strangely enough, thought Mariah, Eddie was uncommonly motivated when it came to making deliveries and meeting customers.

"Mrs. Taylor's Fine Red Raspberry Preserves" would be the first product to hit the exclusive lakeside stores catering to what Mariah called, "First line clientele."

Mariah looked up from the raspberries when she heard the sound of a car starting at the Stevens place. A young man dressed in a pale summer suit was cranking the engine of a beige Chevrolet roadster with black fenders. In the driver's seat sat Ruth wearing a cloche hat that wouldn't blow off with the top down. She was laughing a trilly, operatic laugh, a regular Carmen of the rustic New Hampshire hills. Moments later the car stopped near the raspberry patch.

George was across the road picking string beans with his elder son. They stood up to admire the car. Dotty was in the kitchen cooking the first batch of raspberries, watching. Eddie, a lean and attractive young man who looked sixteen or more, was away carousing with some older bad boys from town and would miss the opportunity to see the beauty next door in her cousin's flashy car.

"Oh, Mrs. Taylor, Mrs. Taylor!" beckoned Ruth once again.

Here I am all sweat and bent over like a peasant. And doesn't she love casting her shadow over me.

Mariah pretended not to hear over the sound of the idling engine. "I say there!" When Mariah didn't stand to acknowledge them, the handsome, auburn-haired gentleman put his fingers to his lips and whistled a piercing signal.

Mariah stood, glaring. The young man pointed to Ruth. "Mrs. Taylor, my mother is preparing cheesecake for dessert tonight. She'd like raspberries to top it off."

"Well, Ruthie Dear, I'll see what's left when I'm done. Oh, and Dear— maybe your friend here could help you find that iron pipe."

"We don't have time for that. I've got to go to Wolfeboro to buy a new dress. We've been invited to the Oaks tomorrow."

Mariah didn't ask for details. The Oaks, ah, yes. The summer home of former President Grover Cleveland on the shores of Duncan Lake. The ex-president was long since dead, but his son had opened a summer theater and the Cleveland's remained significant in Lakes Region society. "Goodbye then," said Mariah coldly, adding a handful of berries to the basket that she had filled twice already.

Bradley, who was soon to celebrate his twenty-first birthday, crossed the road after the roadster had sped off down Brown's Ridge toward West Ossipee.

"What did she want, Ma?"

"She claims this raspberry patch is mostly on their land. Well, maybe so, but since we settled here in 1903 the Stevens's have never had a berry that I didn't pick for them." Mrs. Stevens told me long ago that if I didn't use 'em, the berries would go to the birds."

"I seen you take two big baskets into Dotty already. Why are you still pickin'?"

"We can use every berry I can find; why leave them for some fancy bird to swoop down and pick?" She winked at Bradley and nodded in the direction of the disappearing coupe.

"Do you remember where the line is? I could go look for you?"

"Never mind the line," Mariah said abruptly. "She's the one that crossed the line."

That night Mariah rested from her labors, her shoulders calling for one of Dorothy's soothing massages. Dozens of paraffin-topped jars of raspberry preserves sat on windowsills and shelves while the family pasted elegant labels for Taylor's first product in a line "for families with discerning tastes."

"Ma," asked Dotty who worked her mother's tense shoulders. "Why do you hate Ruth Luddington?"

"Oh, I don't hate her. She just rubs me the wrong way sometimes."

"I saw what was going on out there. She thinks we're dirt, doesn't she?"

"I don't care what she thinks," Mariah said with a bit too much acid on her tongue for her daughter to believe her.

"Look, Ma, you're building a business, and if it weren't for you, well, I just think…" Dotty's hands stopped massaging as she searched for words.

"Well?" said Mariah.  Dotty got back to work on her mother's neck.  "No, not that.  What do you think?  Ruth dresses well and she walks around like Gloria Swanson.  So what were you going to say?"

"Sure, I like her clothes, but the only things she's ever done is… well…she took that long trip with that writer…"

"And that's how she earned whatever she's got," added Mariah as she put her hand over Dotty's letting her know she could stop massaging.  "Bring me a note card and that roll of red ribbon."

Dotty watched as her mother wrote:  "My husband and I were once guests on your father's railroad car, a kindness we will never forget.  With our compliments.  George and Mariah Taylor."

"Ma, who's that for?"  asked Dotty.

"It's for the Cleveland family."

"The former president's family?  Why are you sending something over to them?"

"I just happened to think of them today.  Give me one of those little baskets with the calico lining. She wrote, "A Gift to the Cleveland's" on the envelope and placed two jars of preserves in the basket.  "There," she said with a triumphant smile. Dotty, bring this over to Mrs. Stevens.  Ask her if her daughter could take these with her tomorrow when she goes to the Oaks."

"All right, Ma, but why…?"

"I'll explain later.  Now go ahead over," said Mariah. "Oh, and tell her sorry about the cheesecake; we're all out of raspberries right at the moment."

"But Ma, we've got plenty…"

"Shush.  Now go ahead over."

"I'm not just another dirt poor farmer's wife," said Mariah as she glared in the direction of the Stevens place.

"No, Ma," replied Dotty weakly.

# CHAPTER 31

## *Evil Spirits*

*E*ddie arrived in his friend's car with the final rays of dusk; by the strict definition of the house rules, he was home before dark. If he didn't break the rules, he surely bent them. He was the only one of the three that got away with anything.

His father had turned in, but Mariah was still awake, reading. She never drifted off to sleep unless all of her chickens had come home to roost, especially her young rooster. After dinner Dotty had let the cat out of the bag about what Eddie and his friends were up to. The news did not come as a complete surprise.

Mariah's unbaptized prodigal had apparently found a new source of income while he and his friends were out distributing preserves, a source that could make him a lot of money, and get him into a lot of trouble.

"Sorry I'm a little late," he said with a sheepish grin. He kissed his mother with the smell of peppermint on his breath.

Mariah didn't return the kiss. Eddie got the message. He was in danger of crossing the line on her rules. "We'll need to talk about a few things," Mariah added with her eyes on her book.

"Mom, I won't be late next time. Promise." Eddie kissed Mariah's forehead. She couldn't help herself and allowed a brief and subtle smile to appear. He was a charmer, and he was safely home. His free spirit reminded her of herself. She was proud of his looks and his charm, if only he could channel it constructively. At the same time it was starting to show that his parents and the life she had made for herself wasn't good enough for him.

"Why don't you have your friends come in?"

"Well, Ma, they're in a hurry. You know how it is," said Eddie, his eyes avoiding hers.

"Are you ashamed of us? I know one of your buddies thought your dad was your grandfather." Mariah forced a chuckle.

"I don't care what they think," Eddie said with an uncomfortable insincerity. "So, Ma, what do you want to talk about?" he added, obviously itching to head upstairs.

"We'll talk in the morning," she said calmly. She decided she would not share what she knew with Ed's father, not until she had a chance to deal with it herself.


Eddie was at the breakfast table anxious to hear about plans for the next deliveries. His father was curious about his son's enthusiasm for the new family business.

"Well, Dad, you know I'm really good at selling. Besides I get to be on the road, see my friends. Help the business grow, too," he said with a smile as he picked up his forkful of homemade sausage. They all say business is what makes America great, you know."

"Who's *they?*" asked George with a little caustic emphasis on "they."

"Why all the bigwigs," replied Eddie with utter confidence. "It's in the magazines, on the radio. "Business is humming."

"Among the nations of the earth today America stands for one idea: Business…Through business, properly conceived, managed, and conducted, the human race is finally to be redeemed." --Edward E. Purinton, The Independent

"That's all well and good," said his father. George's head hung over the plate. He held Eddie's eyes with a stern but shaky gaze from under his raised brows. "But you and Brad's got crab apples to pick so's your Mother and sister can start boilin' 'em down for jelly."

The corner of Eddie's mouth curled down. He turned to his mother. "My friend Joe's s'posed to come by later this afternoon. Deliveries in Wolfeboro, isn't that right?"

"It's amazing how excited you and your friends are about delivering jelly. Quite interesting." Mariah gave Ed a squinting look.

Eddie froze.

Dotty's eyes met her mother's. George and Bradley dove into their breakfasts and didn't notice anything.

"You can pick crab apples this morning. We'll talk about deliveries after breakfast," said Mariah.

Conversation stopped with the clatter of utensils against plates and the slurps of coffee. When George and Bradley headed out for chores, Eddie stood up as well, but his mother tapped him back into his seat with an expression that warned him that something was coming.

Dotty seemed unusually anxious to stay in the kitchen to do the dishes, but her mother dispatched her to strip the bed linens for the Monday wash.

"Ma, I've got something for you upstairs. Can I go get it?"

*Oh, that boy is a clever one.* "All right," she relented, "then come sit down so we can talk."

Eddie sat at the table with a fancy store bag tied with a ribbon. Mariah opened it to find a beautiful Willowware milk pitcher that she had once admired at Feineman's Department Store on one of her rare trips to Rochester. Mariah lifted it up and examined it as though she expected to find a defect.

"Well, how do you like it?" asked the fourteen-year-old who could raise a mustache almost as well as he could raise hell. "This is an early birthday present," he added. His timing in present-ing it to his mother this morning was not lost on her.

"Now, Eddie, where did you get the money to buy such a beautiful present?" Mariah asked with a glimmer of admiration mixed with a hint of accusation.

Mariah and George's second son was tall and lean like his father and older brother, but with the flashy confidence of the city boys who summered at the lake resorts.

Eddie bristled at his diminutive nickname. "Ma, would you stop calling me Eddie?"

Mariah ignored him. He was her Eddie. There was great danger in accepting him as Ed. "You shouldn't have spent so much," said Mariah without taking her eyes off the pitcher.

"I'll have enough to buy you a whole set before long," said Eddie with pride.

"Just imagine what you could accomplish if you hadn't quit school." Mariah had a way of humbling her son's cockiness.

Eddie folded his arms in front of him and huffed until his perturbation collided with his mother's potent glare. Except for some crooked teeth, he had exotic good looks with his mother's black hair and his father's hazel eyes. It was not easy for Mariah to stay angry with him.

"I didn't *quit* school; I can't help it if they wouldn't let me finish."

"Oh, yes, you *finished* school the day that bullet hit the blackboard."

A sly smile turned up one corner of his thin moustache. "Nobody knows it was me."

"I do, and half the town suspects it was you. That's all people need to know. You got that .22 from Cowboy Nute, now didn't you?"

Eddie got testy. "Here I come in and give you a nice present, and you begin questioning me like the cops."

"I suppose you're used to being questioned by cops."

Eddie looked at his mother with a slight scowl.


He had taken some humiliating beatings from the Ossipee School's new teacher, Mr. Stanley Harding. Harding took over from a tiny young woman who affected a tough demeanor with the farm boys in the back row and ended up in a snow bank outside of a conveniently open window.

Harding, at six foot three, just waited for one of the cussin' crowd to cross him. Some of the farm boys were still in the eighth grade at sixteen after taking off planting season or harvest season, hunting season or rutting season. The learning season didn't come around very often.

When a farm boy sassed Mr. Harding or cheated on a test, he'd take the whole school outside. He'd carry out a chair and make the boy take a leap over it while he whacked the lad's rear end with a thick yardstick.

The younger kids laughed themselves silly at the sight of the scary big boys being cut down to size.

Eddie got the chair just after turning fourteen when he corrected Mr. Harding on some facts. Columbus didn't sail west to prove that the world was round. He sailed "for a new spice route," Eddie had said emphatically. "Anybody with an education back in Columbus' day knew the world was round."

"Is that right?" said Mr. Harding rhetorically. He took the measure of the Taylor boy with his three-foot piece of oak.

Eddie bided his time to punctuate his dispute with Mr. Harding. He was quiet in school for a couple weeks, but didn't show up for school one late May morning when all the other big boys were home for the spring planting. Eddie got to the school very early and got up into the attic through a trap door near the back of the classroom. He waited until Mr. Harding was doing penmanship lessons at the blackboard. Eddie opened the trapdoor so slowly it reminded him of Poe's "Tell-Tale Heart." He took aim. He decided he'd dot Mr. Harding's "i."

Everyone in the classroom spun around when the bullet shattered the corner of the black-board, assuming that the assailant had been standing at the open door on that especially hot day in late spring. Mr. Harding gave the children instructions to comb the area; kids scattered in every direction. Soon they were all hundreds of feet away from the school. Eddie got down, slipped out a back door, and made his way through the woods until he came out on Brown's Ridge Road. He ran like Mercury straight down the road toward home. His mother had gone to Coursin's with Dotty; George and Bradley were out of sight on the back forty oblivious to Eddie's antics. No one could prove anything except that he had skipped school.

"So did you get the pistol from Cowboy Nute?" Eddie stared at his mother, but didn't answer. Mariah raised her voice. "Don't you suppose Mr. Harding could figure out who shot at him?"

"I didn't give a shit if he did."

Mariah stood up and slapped Eddie across the face. "Don't you ever talk like that around me."

Her younger son's swagger melted into a puddle of shame. In an instant he changed from the confident early bloomer with sex appeal far beyond his years to her needy little boy. It looked like the first tears in many months might cascade down his cheeks. "I'm sorry, Mama, but I hated that man."

Mariah stroked Eddie's repentant face. "I'm sorry, too. I just wanted you to go to school. You're the smartest. You don't have to be a farmer."

"I won't be a farmer. I'll die first. But Ma, it costs to go to the academy."

"You're smart. It doesn't matter if we're not the academy kind of family or not."

"By next fall I'd be two years older than the rest of the freshman. They'd be laughing at me."

"Shave off that little moustache of yours."

"Oh, Ma. Don't be funny. I can't go to any academy. We're just starting to make good money. You can't afford to send me to school and hire somebody to do deliveries, too."

For the moment, Mariah didn't have an answer.

"Besides, we're gonna need a vehicle. The business has grown too big. I can't depend on my friends for much longer." Eddie sat beside his mother and rubbed her back while she thought. He wanted a car more than anything, and Mariah knew it would take him months more before he could buy one on his own.

"Eddie, you can't even drive yet."

"Oh, I can drive, Ma. I just can't get a license till the spring."

Eddie took out his wallet and showed his mother three tens and a five. "You see that? That's nothing compared to what I could be making if I had a car."

"If I get you a car, I'll probably never see you again."

"I promise I'll keep up with deliveries …"

"Whose deliveries?" asked Mariah, giving her son a knowing and disapproving look. "Mine or Cowboy Nute's? I know exactly what you're delivering, and it's not just preserves."

Eddie's eyes widened.

"I'm talking about an education and your future. What kind of a future do you suppose you're going to have with the likes of Cowboy Nute?"

Eddie stood still, his eyes aimed at the floor.

"You know, Eddie, I'm not the only one in town that knows what's going on." People in town were beginning to talk about the Taylors' enterprises. They complimented Mariah's "excellent preserves" to her face and gossiped about her son's "evil spirits" behind her back. The storeowner, Neal Coursin, told Mariah to "keep an eye on that younger son of yours." He blamed loose morals of the younger generation on cars and movies, the two things that Edwin Elden Taylor lived for.

North Country easy girls copied Clara Bow and Gloria Swanson. They bobbed their hair and painted their faces, and they didn't drive a hard bargain in the backseat of a young man's car. Eddie knew he would have no trouble disposing of his virginity as soon as he could borrow or buy a car.

"I've already saved about $50," Eddie announced.

"I see. Well. You know, you're not just putting yourself at risk. You could ruin my business if you get caught."

Mariah never mentioned liquor, but Eddie knew that she knew. Prohibition had been the law of the land since 1920 with the passage of the Volstead Act. The Eighteenth Amendment to the Constitution banned the manufacture and sale of all intoxicating liquors—hard spirits, wine and beer—throughout America. Some called it "The Noble Experiment." When Mariah read in the *Concord Monitor* the government's claim that Prohibition was working, she couldn't help but laugh.

*"In my judgment, the amazing thing about the progress ...of the Eighteenth Amendment is not that it is difficult to enforce...but that it has been as successfully enforced and as generally observed as it has been ... Prohibition is the greatest effort for human advancement and betterment ever attempted in history."*

--Roy A. Haynes, Prohibition Commissioner

"Don't worry, Ma. I know what I'm doing. You can just forget about school, though."

Mariah felt backed into a corner. She was going to lose her frustrated, ambitious second son to bad boys and bootleggers if she didn't come up with something fast. "Eddie, there's a way we can get a vehicle and send you to school, too. You and George would have to share the driving. I might even have to hire someone, I don't know, but there's a way."

"Ma, where are you gonna get that kind of money?"

"We've still got a good stand of timber."

"Ma, you can't do that," said Ed in shock at the idea that his mother would even consider taking down the last of his father's cherished old growth pines. Mariah faced a terrible rift if she went after the last stand. The family had been desperate then, there was no arguing with that. Now they were getting by, even accumulating some money for a rainy day. No emergency turned a desperate eye on the last stand of pines.

George had drawn a line in the sand after Mariah sold off the first half of the timber. "After I'm gone, and it won't be long, you can do what you please. We wouldn't have been in this fix if we'd stayed in Iowa. You weren't thinking of me, that's for sure." George had never come so close to outright denying that Mariah loved him.

Will Dunfield had been dead for over twenty years, but people who knew Mariah in her youth understood that Will still rode across Mariah's sky each day in a chariot, her Apollo carrying the sun that magically kept the past alive and perpetually verdant while Mariah's present moved inexorably toward death and decay. When Mariah came into town on her own, she always visited Will's grave while attending to those of her parents no more than a hundred feet away. If no one were looking, she would leave flowers at the base of his lonely, isolated stone.

"I keep bringing up the timber, and eventually your father will listen to reason."

Eddie shook his head with a grim expression in his eyes. "Ma, please don't do that."

Mariah studied her son's intense face, thinking of her attempts to kill him in the womb. She had nursed him and coddled him through his childhood, forgiving all, hoping to be forgiven, trying to forgive herself. Eddie had his mother's desire to run against the current, to snatch fire from the gods and to light his corner of the world with stolen light. He would never be happy fitting into the cycles and seasons that comforted his father and brother.

"Just you wait a minute, Eddie. You're the one I'm putting my hopes on; you know that."

"Ma, I won't let you down, but I don't want you to touch the timber."

The sound of a car horn startled Mariah. "A friend of yours, I 'spose. Tell him to come back this afternoon. Dotty and I'll have six or eight deliveries ready. You've got crab apples to pick."

"Ya, Ma, I know," replied Eddie. She smiled at him faintly and he knew. She could rail all she wanted against bootlegging, but in the end, she would let him go. Mariah was warning him of the danger, but not stopping him.

His mother followed him to the door. Joe got out of the car and took off his hat. "Mrs. Taylor, Mr. Coursin said your sister called. Wants you to come to lunch tomorrow. Something about Ed."

Mariah turned to Eddie. "Sometimes she thinks she's your mother."

As Eddie closed the door, Mariah's chronic guilt about her youngest child caused a tightening in her chest. Had she unleashed evil spirits? Like herself in her youth, Eddie was throwing caution to the wind.

# CHAPTER 32

## Cowboy Nute

C owboy Nute lived in a sawdust pile way out on the Moultonboro Road. He knew enough to keep his excavated sawdust cave ventilated with old discarded stovepipe from the dump. The fermenting sawdust produced methane gas as it turned the wood juices to alcohol, and the methane could kill you by asphyxiation or explosion if you didn't know what you were doing, but Cowboy Nute, guided by his own compass, knew what he was doing.

His sawdust home didn't need much more heat than fermentation could provide. He had a small, vented cook stove and that was sufficient for his two-room sawdust suite. He didn't have to pay rent or taxes, and upkeep only required a shovel. Nobody bothered him out there in the scrub woods that loggers had stripped a couple of years before. When Nute came to town, he was the center of attention.

"Cowboy," as the regulars called him, must have had a given name, but those who knew it didn't dare use it within range of the matched set of .45s strapped to his hips. Nute was approaching forty, not handsome of face, but with an athletic physique that intimidated other men even without the ubiquitous weaponry. He also wore a Stetson and boots down the boardwalk in Wolfeboro, a lakefront resort that did not advertise him as one of their many attractions, but an attraction he became nonetheless.

When the sheriff of Carroll County tried to relieve him of his Colts for unholstering them at unpredictable intervals, Cowboy made the sheriff dance until all but one bullet was left in each pistol. He and the sheriff reached an understanding that day that Cowboy could keep his Colts as long as he kept them holstered, except when clear and present danger threatened.

The week after the Fourth of July, Mariah had hired Clyde Davis to drive her to Wolfeboro. She was expected to pay a call at her sister's, something about Eddie's future. She also needed help in tracking down her husband. His seventy-fourth birthday was only about two weeks away, and it looked like he might not be home to celebrate it with the family. George had walked out the door in a huff two days before when Mariah let slip her designs on the remaining stand of pines. Mariah knew it wasn't just the pines. She had taken charge of everything. He was like one of the kids, told what to do and how. Mariah seemed to resent the fact that he couldn't bring in hard cash anymore. Her eye for his pines was just the last straw in the daily hurts that finally surfaced in uncharacteristic anger.

Old Man Holt found him walking toward Wolfeboro and gave him a ride. George asked to be left off near the logging road into Cowboy Nute's. Nute was always good for a stiff drink of the real stuff when a man needed it.

To Mariah it was as predictable as sunrise where George would go when he was madder than a hornet. Clyde had no clue where any place was that went beyond his mail route, but he was worried about George and was willing to help.

*He can't stay with Nute in a damned sawdust pile. What's wrong with him?*

The thought that George would watch his stand of pines cut down to provide schooling for his wayward son, the son that was seldom around to help when another set of hands was desperately needed, was too much for George to bear. The normally easy-going George who rarely had an unkind word for anyone, drew the line in front of his last stand of virgin pine. When Mariah kept harping, he left rather than saying some of the painful things he'd been thinking for a long time.

"Clyde, you just wait here a few minutes. I won't be long." Mariah didn't want to ask Clyde to drive in and risk facing Cowboy standing in the path of the car with both guns drawn. Davis found great comfort in the regularity of his route, and just driving out of Ossipee to Wolfeboro was enough of the exotic to unsettle him for a month never mind a confrontation with a wild man with two six shooters.

Once he had to drive all the way to Hanover to make a delivery for a nephew who was attending Dartmouth. Clyde had never seen a college before and expected it to be a building with a shingle hanging out for all to see like any other respectable business.

After driving in circles for half an hour, he stopped his Model T station wagon and hailed a pipe-smoking gentleman in tweed. "Nice town you have here, but where in hell's the college?"

"Well, it's all around you, sir. What part are you looking for?" said the gentleman with an exasperated puff.

Clyde finally made the delivery and made the tense trip back home, but he developed a strong aversion to long-distance travel that threatened to take him more than ten miles from the Carroll County Courthouse.

Mariah walked down the short path to the clearing where the sawdust pile stood. She called out, "Cowboy! Cowboy! Are you in there?" She started up the slab steps stuck at regular intervals into the gently pitched pile.

Cowboy lifted a slab door from the tunnel leading to his sleeping quarters, set it aside, and removed his hat. "Mrs. Taylor. Are you here about Ed?"

"That, too."

"All right, Ma'm, and what else do you have on your mind?" He spoke with his mouth hardly opening. He had learned to "talk Laramie" as a vaudevillian at the Lynn Auditorium where he developed his prowess with pistols, lariats and whips. For some performers, it was a well-rehearsed act; for Cowboy, it was his life. Cowboy had been preparing for a career in law when his fiancée was killed in a train wreck in front of his eyes. The young law student he was died with her, and after a few fitful weeks in an asylum he was reborn as Cowboy Nute.

"I'm looking for George."

"George?" he responded. He sounded as though he'd never heard of anyone by that name.

"You know who I'm looking for. I understand he got left off here by Old Man Holt on his way into Wolfeboro."

"Ma'm, he was here, but he didn't stay. He brought me a dozen eggs and some salt pork for a ride up to Mrs. White's." Mrs. White ran a guesthouse on the Governor Wentworth Road, a sympathetic woman, and a good listener. Mariah didn't like her one bit. George had never been so angry before that he actually left home, and he wasn't fit to be on his own. Mariah bristled at the thought that Mrs. White would be providing him shelter and comfort. She always wondered what was provided as part of the comfort.

"Is that all he got for my eggs and salt pork?" chided Mariah with her tight lips twisted to one side.

"Well, he needed a little refreshment when he got here."

"Lifted his spirits, I suppose," said Mariah with a sarcastic smirk. "Or should I say he lifted *your* spirits, whatever spirits you still got in stock after Eddie and his gutter snipe friends have supplied half of Carroll County with it."

"Now Mrs. Taylor, you know how hard it is to make a living in the North Country," said Nute with the soft answer that turns away wrath. Mariah did not look pacified. When Nute turned his eyes toward Mariah again, he was confrontational. "It's tempting to try to make a fast buck when you've got the opportunity, now isn't it, Mrs. Taylor?"

"All right, Cowboy. I suppose you got an earful from my husband. He's mad at me right now."

"The timber."

"Yes." Mariah stood up, brushing the sawdust from her dress.

"So what are you going to do?" asked Nute.

"I don't know. I feel like I'm gonna lose one way or the other." They stood in the absolute stillness with no sound but their breathing. "I guess I'll be going along." As she ducked and made her way out into the open, Mariah accepted Nute's hand as she negotiated the wobbly slab steps down to solid ground.

Mariah stopped when she had gone about ten feet and turned

abruptly to the cowboy. "You know you shouldn't have sold that gun to Eddie."

"I didn't sell it to him. He took it in trade."

"I see," Mariah said with a glare that let Cowboy know what he traded the gun for. She walked back to Davis's car without a good-bye.

Clyde Davis saw by her expression that Mariah was heavy of heart. He was always one to help people to see the bright side. "So George decided to stay with the Cowboy?"

Mariah got in and closed the door, looking straight ahead. "Nope. He's gone over to Mabel White's."

"Well, at least he's out of harm's way," said Clyde with good cheer.

"I think he'd be safer in the sawdust pile."

"Mabel's a good cook, but not so good as you, Mariah," said Clyde as he put his Ford into gear. A few minutes passed in silence. "I don't mean to stick my nose into anyone else's business."

"Go ahead, Clyde. There's not much left that you don't know already," said Mariah as she rolled up the window to silence the wind.

"Are you gonna sell the timber anyway?" asked Clyde.

"No. I can't do that. I went against him once. I won't do it again." Clyde looked relieved.

"So we're off to Florence's?" asked Clyde.

"Yes, Florence's." It was a hot day. Mariah closed her eyes and thought of the pothole, the glitter of golden flakes in the summer sun, the feel of the cool water running over her body.

"Florence wants to talk to me—about Ed."

# Chapter 33

## The Last Stand

Clyde stopped to let a Stanley Steamer and a buggy pass on their way down the hill by the tower of the town hall. He had made good time from Ossipee despite pokey vacationers leery of picking up the speed on uncertain country roads. Pulling up in front of the Blodgett's three-story guest house, Clyde ran around to open the door for Mariah as guests watched from their rockers on the porch. "Mrs. Taylor, I'll just leave you here, and I'll take a ride down to the lake. You know I like to watch the *Mount* dock."

"The way Florence goes on," Mariah whispered, "you might be able to take the cruise and come back in the morning."

Clyde glanced toward the kitchen door where he saw Mariah's sister standing patiently.

"No, M'am. I can enjoy that old side-wheeler just as much sitting on a bench enjoying a lemonade. Saves me a dollar. So, what time would you like me back?"

"One hour for lunch and another hour for the lecture," Mariah whispered. "If it was the off season, I'd stay overnight, you know, and take in the Valentino movie with her."

Clyde nodded. "I guess we can't chalk this up as a pleasure trip, now can we." Davis got back behind the wheel. He took out his pocket watch and popped the cover open. "Two hours it is," he said, and backed out of the driveway.

Florence wanted to talk about Ed again. Ed, not Eddie. "He's not a boy anymore," she had said during her last lecture, "and he might not be getting in with the wrong crowd if you didn't keep treating him like a kid." Mariah wasn't anxious to hear more about her son's shenanigans. She didn't know what it would take to straighten him out, but she was tired of being made to feel guilty about doing a poor job of mothering.

The news about Eddie was bad enough. She prayed that Florence hadn't caught wind of George's angry departure. Mariah had no intention of mentioning George's flight to the sanctuary of Mrs. White's. Florence had a very curious nature and a telephone to satisfy it.

Mariah watched Clyde chug past Huggins Hospital on the way back downtown. She wished she were going with him to watch the *Mount Washington* steam up to the dock, its magnificent red side wheels dashing forward, then reverse as a final sweep of coal smoke rose from its stack. It was hard for Mariah to imagine that there was so much hustle and bustle in the lakeside resort only a few miles from the bucolic stillness of Ossipee.

"Well, I suppose you need to wash the dust out of your eyes," said Florence as she gave her elder sister a hug at the kitchen door and handed her a hot washcloth.

"You treat me like one of your guests."

"You are," Florence replied graciously.

Mariah could smell roast chicken and watched steaming bowls of buttered peas and fluffy mashed potatoes being transported by the summer help to the dining room.

"Good day, ladies and gentlemen,' said Florence as she took her place at the end of the table and gestured for Mariah to stand at the place to her left. "My husband has gone to arrange for trail rides for those who asked, and for the rest of you less enamored of horses, he's buying tickets for tomorrow's cruise around Lake Winnepesaukee on the *Mount*. I'll pack lunches for all of you, of course."

Looking across an impressive array of silver, linen and crystal,

Mariah felt conscious of how underdressed she was for dinner at the Blodgett's.

"I want to introduce my sister, Mrs. Mariah Taylor. She's just motored over from Ossipee and I really don't want to ask her to take the time to change."

Really. As if I brought anything to change into. Mariah looked at her sister, trying not to glare. You know damned well I don't have a better dress than this. The guests all reassured Mariah that changing was unnecessary, and they moved quickly into grace sufficient for all levels and degrees.

Florence had begun to gray and thicken a decade behind her sister, but the refinements of her secure class showed in her handling of utensils, guests' questions, and the kitchen staff. In balanced measure there was delicacy, deference, and condescension.

After a variety of desserts, guests dispersed to horseback, porch rockers, downtown shops or robust activities with racquets or mallets that might promote some healthy perspiration. The house was still, save for the deep ticking of the grandfather clock on the landing of the oak stairs.

Mariah stiffened when she saw Ed drive in shortly after the Westminster chimes announced the hour of two. He was driving, that was the first shock, and in an unfamiliar car. This little discussion that now would include her son was a setup that threatened to take Mariah's control of her son out of her hands. She had been outfoxed.

"So tell me about the car," said Mariah as Eddie walked in, looking as surprised to see her as she was to see him.

"Ma, I didn't know you were going to be here. The car? I just borrowed it from one of the guys I know."

"One of the guys *you* know and *I* don't," sputtered Mariah.

"Oh, Ma," whined Eddie.

Florence looked back and forth between mother and son with a knowing expression.

"Mariah, I've been trying to get this son of yours to work for me here, but he doesn't seem to want to be tied down."

"It's not that, Aunt Florence," said Ed with his golfer's hat in his hand. Ma needs me to make deliveries. More and more every week."

"Oh, I know about the deliveries," Florence said. Ed glanced at his

268

mother, wondering if Aunt Florence meant anything other than preserves. "We certainly don't want to hurt your mother's little business." The word "little" annoyed Mariah, and she didn't hide her irritation.

"It's more important business I want to talk about." Florence said, adding insult to injury. She turned from Mariah to her nephew. "I want to talk about your future." She gestured to the parlor.

Ed looked from his mother to his aunt turning his hat around in his hands with his elbows resting on his knees. "So, what about my future? You're both looking at me like I don't have one."

"I'm sorry, Ed. It's just that we're both worried that you're not using your talents in the best ways." Florence looked at Mariah expecting a nod of agreement. Instead, Mariah pursed her lips and gave her a sideward glance that indicated she did not appreciate the interference. Despite her clear annoyance, Mariah said nothing. Florence ignored her sister's disapproving looks and kept the pressure of her intense eyes on Ed.

"I don't think I'm doing too bad," said Ed who made a sweeping gesture from head to toe pointing out his stylish clothes. Mariah looked down in embarrassment, knowing that her sister was thinking about the car and the kind of friends Eddie had made.

"You know, the automobile is changing this country, and not all of the change is for the good," replied his aunt. "I was very disturbed by what I read at the hairdresser's yesterday. Fellows are meeting girls in cars these days instead of in their parents' parlors, and you know what that leads to," Florence said with a down under glance at her nephew who suddenly took an inordinate interest in the carpet design.

"Well, anyway," said Florence in an attempt to ease the tension in the room, "it's nice to see both of you. You look very nice today, Ed. I suppose you really want a car, but I asked you here to talk about your future, not about next week or even next year. I'm talking about your whole life, a life you can be proud of."

Ed fiddled with the hat; his eyes darted from side to side.

"I haven't talked to your mother about this, but I know how much she's wanted to see you go to school." Mariah's eyes widened. So this was what she had in mind. She was going to take charge of Ed's future. Not in so many words, but Florence was saying loud and clear that Mariah had failed to provide an education for her son, and obviously she had failed as a mother in some other ways, too because why else would a smart fellow like Eddie be running around with bootleggers and other shady characters, all for flashy clothes and a car? Mariah began to stiffen with humiliation.

"Ed, I want to help you get an education," said Florence without giving Mariah a chance to erupt.

Ed sat up straight, astonished.

"Right here at Brewster Academy," said Florence with a smile. Florence went to the piano and picked up an application to the school and set it on the marble-topped table between her and Mariah. "Harry and I can afford it, and you could live right here with us during the school year. And if you want to, you could work here in the summers for spending money. Of course your folks would probably want you home to help with the business, but that would be up to you. Well," she conceded in afterthought, "you and your folks."

Florence made concessions to Mariah's "little business," and even promised to use her influence—and Uncle Harry's connections—to get Mariah's products into a couple nice stores in Wolfeboro, a town that catered to a better class of people. The Blodgetts were skilled at ranking society by class.

Uncle Harry knew business. He and Aunt Florence had done well for themselves. Harry was the kind of old Yankee who would not trust a man who had dipped into principal. He was an educated man, and he had his finger on the nation's pulse. He read the *Wall Street Journal* each day except Sunday when he paid his duties to God for his many blessings. Harry believed in the nation's formula for success—allowing the natural laws of business and America's lofty democratic values to work an economic miracle, but even more, a moral miracle. Harry agreed with Herbert Hoover that American industry and commerce were "pregnant with infinite possibilities of moral progress."

"So, what do you think?" Florence looked at Ed, bypassing his mother who could either endorse the idea or stand in the way of her son's decent, respectable, and promising future.

"Well, you know I wanted to go on with my education," said Ed, avoiding his mother's eyes. Yes, he liked the status of going on to school, and he liked the promise of a bright future, but if there was a faster and easier way to make a buck and have nice things and all

270

the girls he wanted, then school might prove to be a serious inconvenience.

"Yes, you can just ask Mr. Harding over at the Ossipee School how clever Eddie is," said his mother with ill-disguised sarcasm that Florence chose to ignore. If Florence knew about the bullet hole in the blackboard, she made sure not to reveal it to her sister.

"Why, Mariah, you've always bragged about how smart Ed is, and I know you want the best for him."

"Yes I do, and if he is serious about school, we have a stand of pine left that can pay the way." Suddenly she was promising away George's timber, the family's last hedge against calamity.

"No, Ma. You can't do that. Why don't you listen to Aunt Florence?" Ed jumped up from the ornate Victorian couch, startling his even-tempered aunt.

"Now, Ed, don't get upset. There's no need for your parents to sell that timber. We all know that it would kill your father to see those trees go," said Florence who rose from her chair and put her hand on Ed's arm to calm him down.

"I'm sure his father is willing to pay the price if he's serious about an education," said Mariah with a tone meant to close the door on Florence's plan.

"And what do you know about what an education costs?" spouted Eddie to his astonished mother. The disdain in his voice was a near-fatal blow to his mother's already battered ego.

Mariah got up, red-faced. Florence and Eddie had seen it before. An eruption had begun and anyone in its path would be consumed. The words came like an explosion from her mouth. "Ed is my son, and if he's going to have an education, we're going to be the ones to provide it." Mariah swept her eyes over the trappings of Blodgett money.

"You see these hands?" said Mariah, trembling with anger. "They have scrubbed and chopped and sewed and shoveled and I can't even begin to tell you what, and all to make a home for my family. I've given up a lot I hoped for out of duty to family. If they can build a business, by God, we can find a way to take care of our own kids."

Florence, shocked by her sister's anger, tried conciliation. "Mariah, you were the smartest of us all in school, and Ed has inherited your intelligence. Why not see what he can do with his *brains*?"

"It's taken a good brain to get through what I've been through, damn it, don't either of you think it hasn't." Tears were running down Mariah's face. Florence and Ed were frozen in agony at the pain each had inflicted on her.

Mariah took one step to the table and grabbed the application. Tearing it to pieces, she dropped the shreds of Ed's promised future on the floor. "Eddie is *my* son!"

"Ma, you know there's no other way except selling the timber. Why can't…" He looked at his mother's tearful fury and realized there was nothing either he or his aunt could say that would change her mind. Ed ran out the kitchen door, and in a moment, the squealing of tires broke the terrible silence between the sisters.

Florence started to reach her hand out toward her sister when the telephone rang. She was relieved that the house was empty. The call was from Mrs. White. George had come down with the measles and was terribly sick. He'd scratched places on his leg and he had a bad infection. Florence's face was contorted in pain when Clyde Davis arrived at the kitchen door.

Mariah quickly bottled up her tears and said, "Clyde, we're going over to Mrs. White's."

"I'm sorry, I'm sorry, Mariah for everything, I really am," said Florence, reaching out but not touching her sister.

Mariah let the door close between them. She walked on Clyde Davis's arm to his car carrying the weight of troubles besetting her in battalions.

# CHAPTER 34

## *Leeches and Witch Hazel*

*O*nce Bradley Taylor got an idea in his mind, he didn't let it go. He
was convinced that his mother was in league with mysterious and
invisible forces that could work good or work ill. Witches weren't all
bad, and Bradley had to give credit where credit was due. Mariah was
for all her crafty ways a good wife and mother, but in these dark days
of Papa's agony, the elder son was in terror of the waxing of her powers
and the waning of his father's. Bradley's father was everything to him.

His mother had brought Papa home in Clyde Davis's station wagon. When his father walked out the door only five days before, he was
healthy and strong, strong enough to walk all the way to Wolfeboro if
no one came along to give him a ride. He was sorry to leave Bradley
with the haying, but he had to get away, he said. "Your mother and
Eddie have got me riled up. I gotta think a few things through," he
told his loyal elder son. "Thank God I can always count on you,"
George told him with glistening eyes and trembling hands.

Bradley's suspicions of his mother's alliance with invisible forces
started with her uncanny ability to forecast the weather. With a stretch
of perfect, cloudless days, he planned on cutting the hay. His plans
were abruptly set aside when his mother admonished him to swap the

scythe and whetstone for the hoe. "It's going to rain tomorrow and probably the next day, so hold off on haying till next week. I 'spect your father will be back by then. Why don't you loosen the hard soil around the corn before the rain starts to let it get down to the roots? No rain had fallen in two weeks and a solitary cloud was last seen at sunrise passing over the crest of Whitehorse Ledge. The following day the rain came down in torrents.

Mariah didn't explain the signs that she read to predict the weather. They weren't, as Bradley suspected, tarot cards or tea leaves or one of those mysterious boards that worked with candles and incantations. Brad didn't know that she was watching the changing direction of smoke from the chimney or that she was feeling the coming rain in her arthritic joints. All he knew was that the clouds rolled over the ledge in the dark of the night, the wind announcing the changing air with whipping, snapping branches of the elm hovering over the end of the house. As long as Bradley believed his mother had magical powers, he was unlikely to challenge her word.

Now Papa's life depended on her powers. At least he was home—delirious, feverish—but home where his loving son could help watch over him. Bradley was horrified to see his father pelted with a florid rash that looked like he had been the victim of a shotgun attack. And even worse, one leg was festering and putrid. For all of this Bradley blamed his mother. She had driven poor Papa away by her manipulation—and her favoritism for brother Eddie.

As George lay in bed moaning, Mariah searched the kitchen for home remedies, some of which she made from bark and roots gathered in the woods or grown in the garden. In frustration she reached for a bottle of rubbing alcohol to cool her husband's fever and to clean the infected skin ruptures on his legs.

Bradley sobbed like a baby when he witnessed the immediate and terrible result. The writhing lasted only briefly, then his father slipped into unconsciousness that did not resemble the peace of sleep. Dorothy, who had been summoned from Malden, sat at her father's side soothing his brow with cold, wet hand towels, humming or whispering, hoping in vain for signs of a response.

Bradley's distrust in his mother grew with his terror of losing his father.

"Bradley, hitch up the buggy. You're going to town to get the doctor. If he's not home, get Elmer Wilkins. Here." She handed him a slip of paper with a list of things to get at Coursin's Store. "You've got to stop crying. It's just making matters worse," said Mariah, but George could not be comforted.

"Witch hazel, gauze, aspirin and leeches." The thought of transporting a bottle of leeches in the seat beside him was almost as bad as the thought of having to pick up Elmer Wilkins, a man that Bradley associated with the black arts. Could you really trust the health of his father to a man who grew up around voodoo?

Elmer Wilkins was one of a tiny number of black people in Carroll County. His parents had been servants to a wealthy Connecticut family that summered for years on Squam Lake. The Wilkinses "boy" shopped for the Sutherlands, and won the hearts of the town with his humor and his kindly manner. He didn't have to grovel with the country folk from Holderness to Ossipee as was expected back in Connecticut society. A black family was a novelty in the mountain passes and lake shores, and when the Wilkinses got a bequest from the grateful Sutherlands, they found no difficulty in buying a home not far from the county seat where Coursin's General Store, a garage and the post office served most of their daily needs.

Some of the village folk, most notably Brad Taylor, believed that the Wilkinses possessed the latest knowledge of the big city plus the intuitive and mystic arts of the Dark Continent. After all, Elmer was as familiar with Fifth Avenue as he was with faith healing and the ministering charms and amulets found in certain circles in Harlem. Anybody with common sense wanted to be on the good side of a person who had ridden an elevator to the sixtieth floor of the Woolworth Building and who set the course of each day by the compass of a ouija board.

Doctor Preston was on his way to Huggins Hospital and wouldn't be back until evening. Elmer Wilkins was dowsing with his forked willow branch just down the road at Lawyer Smart's new house. Bradley decided to pick up Elmer first, and the leeches second.

The willow branch trembled in Elmer's black hands. The tremors rose up his arms and shook his jowls until the magical forces of water witching pulled the willow down to the very spot where a spring waited to fill a well at ten gallons a minute. Brad stared at the branch in Elmer's hand, having spoken not a word to Wilkins or to Lawyer Smart.

"Here. You want to try it?"

"No. I don't want to touch the thing," said Bradley, recoiling as though Elmer had asked him to handle a leech.

"It's just an old willow stick," Elmer laughed, slapping Bradley on the back as few blacks ever had the freedom to do with white folk. "Let me take a look at you, Brad." Elmer looked into Bradley's eyes, felt his forehead, and pushed up his sleeve to examine his arms. He probed the glands on Brad's neck in a systematic examination that amused the lawyer who was used to searching for clues with different powers of observation.

"You been 'round some contagion, Brad, and it's comin' on." He asked Brad to puff out some breaths and he sniffed. "You's got only a few hours and you'll be flat on your back for a few days."

"My father's got the measles."

"Well, son, you got 'em, too, and you got 'em bad even if they ain't no spots yet."

Lawyer Smart said, "Drive a stake in the ground right there and send me the bill."

"This is your well," Wilkins announced with certainty.

Smart excused Wilkins and Bradley, unsettled by all the talk of contagion.

"Has your father got it bad?" asked Elmer.

"That's why I come. My mother needs you right away, and she's sent me to the store for witch hazel and leeches."

"Witch hazel and leeches?"

"She didn't have witch hazel, so she poured rubbin' alcohol all over Pa."

"God love the woman, she'd like to kill the man doin' a fool thing like that. Don't she know that drives the spots in? What happened?"

"He had a terrible spell, and now he's unconscious."

"Might as well thrown a rattlesnake under the sheets with him," shouted Elmer, shaking his head. "Iffen you'd came for me when it first struck, I coulda did somethin'." Elmer was nearly a foot shorter than Bradley, but he directed him with the same authority a rudder has over a ship. "And what about the leeches?" he asked as he took Bradley by the arm and hurried him toward the buggy.

"I don't know, but he's got a bad infection on one leg. Red lines runnin' up from it, and it smells bad."

"Blood poisonin'. No alcohol or witch hazel's gonna stop that. Might be too late for leeches. Well, let's get goin'." He'd have to share the buggy seat with a voodoo doctor and a bottle of leeches with a water witch stuck down behind them. Wilkins might as well have asked him to sit with a bag of rattlesnakes in his lap.

After picking up the supplies at Coursin's, they dropped the bonnet on the buggy to reduce the wind drag, and with Neal Coursin's blessing and some free penny candy for the family, they sped off with the crack of a whip. They moved so fast they even passed some slow-moving automobiles on the inclines.

The motion got Brad sick to his stomach, so Elmer took the reins. "You got some hard cider left?"

"Yes. I never drink that stuff," said Bradley, looking more green than red despite his rising fever.

"Well, you're gonna drink it today. When we get to the house, you het some of that up, not to boilin', but just as hot as you can stand to get it down."

"What for?"

"Well, boy, are you gonna do what I tell ya?" Brad was too sick to be thunderstruck at a black man calling a white man, "boy."

"That cider will bring them spots right out and break that fever. You'll have it all over with quick. After the cider, you pull down the shades and get into bed. You don't want no light till the fever's broke and you're startin' to feel better."

Elmer reined the lathered horse to a stop in front of the Taylor farm. He passed the reins through the iron ring in the granite post near the front door. Brad got down from the buggy holding the bag straight out as though it was sweating dynamite. "You forgot this." Bradley was anxious to rid himself of the leeches for fear that Elmer might decide to use them on him.

"Don't need any of it. Give it to your Mama." Elmer went in the front door and called up the stairs. Mariah beckoned him to George's room.

As Bradley drank the steaming cider, he heard voices as if they came from clouds. Huggins Hospital….gangrene….amputate. Dotty finally came to check on Bradley and told him that Pa was too weak to travel. They had to do what they could do at home. Bradley shuddered in fear at the thought of the hospital. The only people he knew that went to the hospital went straight from there to the graveyard.

Elmer Wilkins dispatched Bradley to his room after he forced the prescriptive treatment down Bradley's throat that burned with every swallow. Elmer drew the shades and left Bradley to drift into a fitful sleep in a silent house. Bradley was forced to entrust his dear father to the black arts.

The night air was heavy-laden and stagnant. Except for some light footfalls on the stairs, and the distant sound of murmuring, melancholy voices, the house was still. The usual late hour cacophony when Eddie often drove in with his raucous friends, laughing and swearing his way to bed, did not rattle the china on the shelves. Eddie had not been seen since he exploded from Aunt Florence's door. He would have to bear the guilt of his absence when everyone else in the family circled around the old man in his suffering.

In the morning, Bradley was less feverish. The spots were already appearing, but he actually felt better than the day before. He would tend to his father, come Hell or high water. No one loved Pa the way he did. No one shared the love of soil and seed like the father and his eldest son. Maybe he could help his father recover.

His mother's hands worked the farm hard and well, but without the love of the land that drove his father's every move. His siblings also showed no love for the farm.

No one showed more distain for the farm than the prodigal Edwin Elden Taylor. Bradley heard almost daily how much Eddie hated dirt and shit, flies and cows. Just as Ed got his full size and strength, he spurned the duties of field and barn to learn the sleight of hand of the fast buck. Bradley was glad that he was gone and glad that his mother was finally burning with anger against her precious boy. Now she would have to admit that it was Bradley the family could depend on; it was Bradley who rose from the sickbed to tend to chores, it was Bradley who was here when they needed help most.

The door opened, and his mother stood next to the bed silhouetted by the light from the door. Elmer Wilkins stood in the hallway, shaking his head. Mariah laid a gentle hand on her son's arm and asked how he was feeling. She said something about Dotty tending to Daddy, but she was holding something back. "What's happening? Is he better?" asked Bradley.

"You're really sick. Why don't you just rest for a while and we'll come get you when it's time?" said his mother with a softness in her voice that scared him.

His mother said she would be taking Elmer home. He had helped them as much as he could, and now he would go home, and Mother had things to attend to up town. They had done all they could. It was too late for the hospital. She would be coming back in a few hours with a man named Mr. Jenkins.

Brad began to sob. Mr. Jenkins, he knew who Mr. Jenkins was— the new undertaker on the road to Tamworth. "Ma, why didn't you come get me? He sank back into his pillow, dizzy and exhausted. The black arts had failed. He was kept from his father's deathbed for nothing. As the door closed, he murmured in agonized anger, "and where's your precious Eddie?"

# CHAPTER 35

## *Prince of Bermuda*

ariah was helping Bradley lift blue Hubbard squashes into a wheelbarrow on the south side of the barn when she saw Clyde Davis squeak to a stop. He boasted a U.S. Mail sign on the side of his new Studebaker. Bradley, who was rolled over in the garden like a fiddlehead fern, unrolled to his full six feet, surprised that Clyde hadn't slid the mail into the box and honked as he always did at ten forty-five, give or take five minutes. Bradley watched as Clyde got out of the car, apparently searching for them.

"Shout to him, Brad. He didn't see us out here," said Mariah. Bradley called Clyde's name, brushing his dirty hands on his overalls. He exhaled an exasperated blast. "You're not expecting anything special, are you?" he said to his mother.

"No, but go see anyway. If he stopped, it must be something important. Get moving, Brad. Don't keep the man waiting all day." Mariah bent over her work again. Bradley took long, slow strides over the furrows. Clyde, a fastidious man who always carried a whisk broom and rag in his car to clean his hands and feet, walked a few steps into the field where he could find fallen cornstalks and other detritus of the harvest to keep his shoes out of the dirt. He held only a few letters in his hand. Clyde was a slight man who wore his brown hair parted in the middle, slicked with bay rum. His round, metal-rimmed glasses sparkled in the morning sun. He always wore a bowtie, and only on the hottest days did he remove his suit coat.

Bradley offered his soiled hand; Clyde took it reluctantly. "Good morning, Bradley. Gonna get everything in before the frost, huh?"

"Ma says there won't be a frost tonight, frost don't affect squash anyways. So what ya got there?" asked Bradley curtly.

"It's a postcard from Ed."

"Well, jumped up Mike," said Bradley, raising his formidable brows in surprise, but with a tone of mild disgust in his voice. "Where in hell is he?" Before Brad gave Clyde a chance to answer, he shouted to his mother. "Hey, Ma. It's a postcard from Eddie." Mariah dropped a piglet sized Hubbard on the ground and it split in two. She almost ran over the soft, uneven soil.

Bradley and Clyde watched her coming. Clyde held on to the mail, much to Bradley's chagrin. "They say Coolidge will win in a landslide. Stock market's boomin'," said Clyde who had no intention of letting Bradley be the bearer of the news.

"To hell with Coolidge. Where's Eddie?"

"Why Bradley. You shouldn't talk like that about the president. I think we should wait so your mother can see her mail. After all, it's addressed to her." Clyde smiled with his chin held high. Bradley scowled and grumbled.

Mariah arrived near the edge of the road winded. She gave Clyde a perfunctory smile and a quick "Good morning." She had taken to wearing her hair in a bun near the top of her head. At fifty-six her hair was more white than gray, and her face with tanned and becoming deeply lined. She no longer bothered with a hat to shade her face unless it was uncomfortably hot, and despite her years of hard labor inside and out, she had thickened around the middle. Clyde handed her the mail with the picture side of the postcard facing her. Bradley looked over her shoulder. It was a scene of a white beach with aqua water, palm trees and a big, pink hotel. "Greetings from Bermuda."

"Where's Bermuda?" asked Bradley.

"Oh, it's an island, actually more than one, I guess. Bermuda's about six hundred miles off the east coast, straight out from North

Carolina, I think. It's a British colony," replied Clyde. After Mariah and Bradley had time to read the card, Clyde added, "He doesn't know yet, does he?"

"Not unless someone else in town knew where he was," answered Mariah curtly. She looked at Clyde without another word. She held the postcard against her apron as though Clyde had not already read it. Her expression was disapproving. A postcard may be open for public inspection, but her personal business wasn't.

"Well, I guess I better be on my way," said Clyde.

"You're five minutes behind schedule already," said Bradley as Clyde zigzagged across the furrows.

*Hello, Ma and Pa,*

I'm sorry it's taken so long, but I just wanted you to know that I've got a good job here at the Princess Hotel. I'm working my way up to being a chef. I'm sorry I left the way I did, but I just wanted to show you I could make it on my own, and not the way I used to. Hope you got the harvest all in. Say hello to Brad and Dotty. Love, Ed.

Mariah stopped to clean her glasses. Brad watched her trying to determine if it was tears or sweat that ran down her lenses. "Ed says hello," she finally said as though Bradley had not read the card.

"So when's he coming home?"

Mariah gave him a *how-in-hell-would –I-know* look. "He doesn't mention coming home, now does he?" She turned over the card and looked at the hotel again. Her scowl suddenly turned into a slight smile. *I just knew he'd surprise everyone, even if he didn't get an education.* "The Princess Hotel. He's going to be a chef. I'll have to tell your aunt."

"So he doesn't know about Pa," said Brad with a touch of acid in his voice.

Mariah gave Bradley a dismissive look. "Obviously not. Don't you worry, Bradley. He's going to hear about it with a piece of my mind besides. You get the rest of those squashes in; I'm going to write him a letter and it'll take me a little time."

Brad sighed and shook his head. Mariah knew what he was thinking. She would rant and rave for a little while, but sooner or later she would forgive Eddie for running off. She would even brag to town folk and Aunt Florence that her beloved bad boy was working in a ritzy resort hotel. Despite the fact that Eddie left her shorthanded, she would try to make it up to him for not providing him a high school education that neither Bradley nor his sister got. Mariah's look of satisfaction at Eddie's news added another brick in the wall between mother and first-born.

Bradley did as his mother commanded, as he always did when he was in sight of her. He mumbled, "Bet he's only a short order cook." Mariah ignored the barb.

The elder son gazed at the stand of pines, the greatest daily reminder of his father and the things they both loved. Papa had died defending his precious pines. And he died wanting his number one son to have the farm one day.

Mariah's return letter was not nearly as forgiving as Bradley imagined it would be, for the wound Ed had inflicted on his mother's pride in front of her younger sister could not be covered with a pink postcard.

"Your father died without your comfort…a painful death…Your brother was down with the measles, too…your sister and brother and I have gone through a very hard time…worried sick over you…wondering if you ran off with those hooligans…getting into trouble…relieved to find you have a job…not surprised you'll be a chef … you always lie about your age…liquor's legal there, I bet…Brad is making deliveries. We going to buy an old Hudson panel truck…We hire kids from town to help with the picking …I want to be proud of you…your father's pines are still standing, but we don't know for how long…when will you be home?"

Love, Mother.

Mariah sealed the letter, but she didn't want to wait another day to send it. Old Man Holt was going to sell a couple of heifers in Tamworth and would stop by in passing as he always did. She'd give him the letter and money for the postage. By the weight of her words, extra postage might be required, so she put two dimes in her apron pocket with the letter.

She met Bradley as he wheeled the last batch of squash to the root cellar. He was all in a dither. "Ma, I'm gonna hitch a ride with Holt to the train station. I gotta put a few things in a suitcase."

"What? Where are you going?" she said indignantly. Bradley never gave his mother advance notice when he was about to attempt an escape from her apron strings. "You never said anything about going anywhere."

"There's no deliveries for three days at least. I'm gonna go down to Plaistow for a couple of days."

"Plaistow? What business have you got in Plaistow?" Mariah thought about it for a moment, knowing that getting information out of Bradley was like pulling hen's teeth. Then she remembered. During the summer Bradley had met a woman at a Grange hall social. Mariah gathered that she was a middle-aged spinster that he had taken a shine to, especially when he heard her eighty-year-old father owned a successful dairy farm, but couldn't work it anymore. Edith Dayton was a skinny, plain woman, but pleasant, and very flattered to have the attentions of a man, especially a young one.

"It's that Dayton woman, isn't it?"

"And what if it is?"

"You have no business courting her. Why she's old enough to be your mother."

"She's nowhere near's old as you, for God's sake."

"Now don't you go swearing at me, Bradley Taylor," she shouted. Bradley cowered.

"I think she's only in her late thirties."

"She's at least forty, and you're twenty-two."

"She's a good woman. And who says I'm courting her? They could use a hired hand, that's all."

"And what's going to happen to me if you up and chase after Edith Dayton? With your father gone, and your brother in Bermuda, what's gonna happen to Taylor's Preserves?" said Mariah with a mixture of anger and fear in her voice.

"Get Dotty to quit her job in Malden and come home."

"Dotty comes up on weekends when she can. Look. She's got to find a husband and I'm not stopping her. She's got a beau down there. He's got a decent job. Don't be foolish."

"Well, Eddie can send you money. He's a chef in that big hotel, ain't he?"

"He's not a chef yet. I don't need money; I need help. I need somebody who knows what he's doing with plants and animals. Since your father…" Mariah looked up and saw a look of vengeful satisfaction crossing Bradley's face. His mother was admitting that she needed him just as she had needed his father even though she acted as though she had single-handedly built Taylor's Preserves into the profitable business it had become.

Brad gritted his teeth, thinking that he might let out a barrage of vindictive thoughts about his mother's domineering ways with him and her leniency toward his brother. He didn't quite dare. He turned on his heels and headed into the house to collect his things for the trip.

Mariah sat at the kitchen table, watching for Holt, adamant that she was not going to help Bradley get suitable clothes together for a few days of courting. "Edith Dayton. Now that's ridiculous," she muttered. "What does a woman like Edith Dayton see in a 22-year-old man? " she grumbled.

Maybe she was being unfair to Bradley, she thought, but he never seemed to have developed the thinking processes of a normal man, and without a firm hand to guide him, his life was chaos. He would wear the same clothes for weeks without ever washing them, and he'd eat like a pig at its trough if she didn't threaten him with a piece of cord wood to sit up and stop smacking his lips. Bradley never lifted his eyes from the plate during a meal no matter what the conversation at the table. He maneuvered the food on the plate like a cat that had cornered a mouse. Was it that forceps dent in his forehead or was it the seed of first cousins, or the effects of her loathsome disease that she had somehow passed on to her first-born?

Was God playing with her the way Brad played with his food? Had God willed her to desire what she could never have, and to pay a heavy price for missteps that she took, steps that were predestined by the divine hand? Where was the justice in the life she had been given?

Holt clanked up the hill carrying heifers in the slat-boarded truck. Whatever color the old Ford once bore had been consumed in a coat of rust and grime. Smoke belched from the upright pipe, and the truck backfired when it came to rest in front of her house. The clutch ground and clattered as he searched for first gear.

"Got any errands for me today?" shouted Holt with a briar pipe

285

clenched in his ill-fitting false teeth that dropped onto his tongue when he laughed hard.

Mariah walked up to the truck wary of its noises. "Would you mail this when you get to Tamworth? I missed getting it to Clyde in time. And here's two dimes. I don't think it can make it to a foreign country on one."

"Bermuda, heh?" said Holt, impressed.

"Yup. Ed has landed himself a good job. Be a chef soon. Can you imagine that at his age?"

"Ed always lies about his age."

"Well, he looks very mature."

"Looks can be deceiving," said Holt in his usual undiplomatic manner.

"Just the same, what kid his age around here has made anything of himself without going to the academy?" boasted Mariah.

Bradley came up behind her, disgusted by what he was hearing.

"The Prince of Bermuda," Brad mocked his mother under his breath. She ignored him.

"Bradley's going down to Plaistow for a couple of days." Mariah said dismissively "I'd just as soon *you* mailed this. He might forget. He's got his mind on other things."

"I'll get it mailed for you today," said Holt with a nod. "Lookin' for a job down in Plaistow?"

Before Bradley could answer, Mariah spoke up. "I suspect there might be some good money to be had down there," she said with a touch of sarcasm directed to her son. "So when will I see you?" Mariah asked in the most benign tone she could muster.

"Sunday night, unless they need me another day. I'll get a ride from the station."

"You'll be lookin' for a hired hand come spring, Missus," said Holt, shaking his head as he let the clutch up. The truck blasted and bucked its way onto the road flinging small stones. Mariah turned her face away and closed her eyes until the danger passed.

Bradley stared straight ahead. He didn't even wave goodbye. Yes, he loved the farm, but it was hers, not his. She knew how much that fact grated on her eldest child. He would eventually leave as the other two had. What else could she expect? As Mariah stood alone at the edge of Brown's Ridge Road, she feared she would soon be running Taylor's Preserves with no other Taylor to rely on.

# CHAPTER 36

## *Fine Ground*

*D*ot and Ed had already flown the coop. Brad was planning his escape. "Bradley" had finally become "Brad", a major concession for Mariah who was most reluctant to shed the diminutive second syllable even though "Dotty" had already become "Dot" and "Eddie" had finally become "Ed." Letting Bradley becoming Brad was one thing; letting him go out on his own was another, not just for Taylor's Preserves, but for the world that would have to contend with Brad off Mariah's short leash.

Mariah faced the prospect of depending entirely on hired help to keep her business going. To the younger generation growing up in the fast buck economy of the late twenties, "greener pastures" meant the city. If young people stayed around, they did exactly what Brad had been doing: they worked on the family farm.

Optimistic Wall Street capitalists touted 1928 as America's peak of prosperity, but in the North Country of New Hampshire there wasn't always one chicken in every pot, never mind two. Local folks were lucky if there was a horse in every barn, never mind a car in every garage.

The *Boston Globe* made fun of President Coolidge's one-line an-

nouncement regarding the upcoming election. "I will not run for president in 1928." The *Globe* declared, "The sap from Vermont chooses
not to run." It actually was a pretty good year for sap, the last sweet year
that the nation was going to see for quite some time, but for the folks
of the North Country, the swings of the economic pendulum between
plenty and want hardly moved beyond the small arc of bare survival.
Thankfully for Taylor's Preserves, more was going into the Schrafft's
box than coming out, but for how much longer, Mariah was unsure.

For a couple of years Mariah had managed to frustrate Brad's plans
to escape to Plaistow. It especially grated on Brad that his mother had
"Taylor's Preserves" painted on the doors of the Hudson panel truck
and wouldn't allow the business vehicle to go beyond the reach of her
delivery routes unless she was sitting in the passenger seat.

On Brad's twenty-sixth birthday, despite his mother's strong ob-
jections, he decided it was time to get married. He couldn't stand his
mother ordering him around. He missed his father sorely, and even the
pleasures of springtime and harvest, of lambing season and sapping off
were muted by his mother's carping, nagging control. If she had promised him the farm, he could have tolerated her heavy hand, but she
pledged to divide whatever she had equally among her three children.
Brad would suffer the same fate his father had before him.

Although Mariah paid Brad a steady salary, it wasn't much after
his room and board and local use of the truck were figured in. Brad
resented the freedom his siblings enjoyed while his mother treated him,
the first born, like a child. Dot was married and had her own life. Ed
had returned from his fancy Bermuda job, but he was no more help
than ever as far as Brad was concerned. When Ed found out that his
lack of education and formal culinary training blocked his ascendancy
at the classy Princess, he returned to what he knew. Ed, as ever, was
most attracted to whatever came easy.

Ed had his eye on a car. Henry Ford recaptured the interest of the
American public when he unveiled the new Model A. Ed lusted after
the roadster with the rumble seat. He'd even double date and let a
friend drive the thing, he told his mother excitedly, if he could just ride
with a pretty girl under the stars in that wonderful seat that folded out
of the trunk. When Ed found there were no good restaurant jobs in
driving distance, he got a steady job as an auto mechanic. But an eight

to five job week after week, saving his money and cutting out luxuries wasn't Ed's style. The temptation of the fast buck hooked him once again. Prohibition was still the law of the land, and Ed found plenty of people who appreciated his help in getting around the inconveni-ence of the alcohol laws.

Brad tried his hand at odd jobs in the off-season. Although he nev-er made the kind of money Ed did, he did better at holding on to his money. Ed and his floozies went through money faster than he went through a fifth of Canadian whiskey on New Year's. Maybe Mariah considered Ed the smart one, but he wasn't going to end up with land and respectability. Brad had his sights on both. Edith Dayton, as the heir to Old Man Dayton's farm, had both and Brad loved her for it.

After repeated trips to Plaistow, Brad finally turned friendship into courtship. Edith Dayton wasn't getting any younger.

The best time to make his escape from his mother's clutches would be after the hard frost. She'd be up to her neck in canning and making preserves for the summer market, but the outdoor work would drop off to a minimum. Edith had already said yes, and was anxious to tie the knot before change of life set in. Brad wasn't interested in becom-ing a father, but he certainly was interested in becoming the owner of a beautiful farm. The only thing that stood in the way was a feeble old man who couldn't last much longer.

Fred Dayton loved his daughter Edith dearly, and he had lived with her all alone in a big, rambling colonial house filled with antiques. He was widowed over twenty years before. Old Man Dayton wanted Edith to be happy, and if she married, he would welcome the groom into their house where he expected to live for the remainder of his days.

"You are going to marry that Dayton woman? Are you out of your mind?" said Mariah when Brad made his quiet announcement as she was blanching peas for canning.

"I know. 'She's old enough to be your mother'," he whined in a voice mocking his mother, a rare show of defiance.

"I know what you see in her," she said, peas spread over cotton cloths cooling. "Her daddy has some money."

*Oh, that witch.* Brad thought to himself.

"She's a good woman. I want to marry her and she wants to marry me."

"You're twenty-six years old, and you don't know a damn thing about women."

"You mean like Ed?"

"Never mind Ed," said Mariah sharply. She gestured to Brad with a big wooden spoon as though she was prepared to beat him into submission. "I don't approve of you marrying her, so let's make that clear right now." Actually she had made that clear four years earlier. Brad went to his room to sulk and to pack. His mind, despite its many deficiencies, was made up.

The next day at ten till eleven, Brad went out and flagged down Clyde Davis. Without a further word to his mother, he threw two suitcases into the back of the Studebaker wagon and headed to the railroad station as he had done several times before. Brad was gone, and for all she knew, he was never coming back. For two weeks Mariah heard nothing. It didn't take long for people in town to notice that the Taylor nest was finally empty.

"What ya gonna do for help, Mrs. Taylor?" asked Neal Coursin from behind the counter. He weighed five pounds of sugar on the scale, sprinkling on more as the needle inched to the mark. He was slightly younger than Mariah's sixty years. His slick brown hair was streaked around the face with gray. He wore bifocals and tipped his head back to read the dial. Neal had two white coats, one smeared red from the meat counter at the back of the store, and a pristine one hanging on a hook beside the front window bearing the store name in an arc. In good weather customers sat on benches on the porch reading the paper or talking sports and politics. When the Moxie thermometer nailed to the shady corner post dipped below the 60's, they retreated to a potbellied stove surrounded by Windsor chairs.

"Ed's around. He comes by when I need him," said Mariah defensively. "I'll hire help this spring," said Mariah with a curtness that did not invite further discussion of the subject. I'll take two pounds of coffee, and grind it a little finer this time."

"Can't grind it much finer for a percolator," he said with the tone of an expert. "It'll wash through the holes in the basket."

"As I said, Neal, I'll take it finer." Mariah didn't explain that she had taken to making her fine ground coffee tied up in remnants of old silk. She could stretch a pound for nearly double the coffee. She wasn't running the business to spend money foolishly. Mariah was tucking the money away, and not in any bank, that was for sure.

"Very well," sighed Neal, warning her with a shake of the head. He poured the dark beans in the hopper and spun the big double cast iron wheels of the grinder filling the air with the rich aroma. The bell on the door jangled, and two ladies stopped to inhale the pleasing scent.

As Mariah watched the grinding wheel spin, she thought about what Ed had told her about town gossip. Some people in town were referring to her as "poor Widow Taylor." *Poor? I have more cash than half those damned fools. I've got a farm with no mortgage, and I pay my bills… Ed says they feel sorry for me because I'm alone now. I suppose Neal's going to tell the whole town that I can't afford to make a decent pot of coffee.*

"Mrs. Taylor, I got a call yesterday from Mrs. Fuller, the lady you did summer laundry for last year."

"Oh, yes. The Duchess of Duncan Lake," Mariah responded. Mariah had accepted a few laundry jobs the previous summer. The laundry income paid Mariah's fire insurance. "Taylor's Preserves" provided for the rest of Mariah's expenses and more than half went into savings. With more fields planted in berries, Mariah planned to increase production of preserves for the 1929 season; she also planned to give up the demeaning laundry service to others willing to put up with the arrogance of rich dowagers.

"It seems that Mrs. Fuller is looking for someone else to do her laundry next summer," said Neal who kept his eyes on his work although he could not disguise his curiosity.

"You don't say?" said Mariah sarcastically. "If I had an enemy I wanted to torment, I'd recommend her to Mrs. Fuller. No, Neal, I have enough dirty linen of my own. I'm not taking in any more."

"Good for you," he said. "Too bad, though. Nobody gets blueberry stains like you." They both shared a good laugh.

Mariah hadn't heard from Mrs. Fuller since she returned her ten-foot long linen tablecloth in late August. Mariah had received the tablecloth in a typical weekly delivery at Coursin's Store. She had never had a complaint from a single customer before Mrs. Fuller. If perfect results were possible, then Mariah delivered perfect results. Some stains couldn't be totally eradicated in a single washing. Mrs. Fuller was one of those high holies who could not accept but perfect results.

It seems that a guest had spilled a considerable dollop of blueberry pie on Mrs. Fuller's tablecloth and it was allowed to dry and set. Mariah scrubbed. Mariah bleached. Mariah hung the tablecloth in the bright sun. Mariah scrubbed again. The stain was very faint, but it would take a stroke from the divine hand to make it lily white again.

Mrs. Fuller was not satisfied. The tablecloth returned the next week with a note pinned to the faint, but offending stain. The note said in an elegant script, "Rub!" The exclamation point aroused Mariah's attention, and she delivered an even more diligent acquiescence than Mrs. Fuller intended . After all, what would people like the Clevelands think if they saw a hint of imperfection at the Fuller table, thought Mariah, flaring with indignation? Tsk. Tsk, thought Mariah.

And so, Mariah rubbed. As long as there was a hint of blue, she rubbed. Eventually the stain disappeared as a hole began to widen. Eventually a hole the size of a half dollar successfully eradicated the blemish. Mariah starched and ironed, pressed and wrapped the tablecloth, having attached a note beside the former location of the stain. "I rubbed!" Exclamation point.

"Neal, do you know anyone down in Plaistow?" asked Mariah as she pulled her purse strings open.

"Oh, sure. I've got suppliers from down that way, and I've got a friend at the bank down there. He knows most folks in Plaistow, those with property, that is."

Neal didn't need to ask Mariah why she was asking. "I want to know about the Daytons."

"So you haven't heard from Brad yet?" asked Neal rhetorically. He suppressed his knowing smile as he took Mariah's money and started making change.

"I don't know much about the Daytons, but I can find out more for you. So Brad is working down there now? They say that farm is one of the finest pieces of ground in Plaistow, so I hear. Old Man Dayton is getting on in years and can't keep it up without help."

"Brad has asked Edith Dayton to marry him," said Mariah with tepid enthusiasm.

"Oh. I see. Well," said Neal with an effort to disguise his surprise.

Just as she reached for the door handle, Neal said, "I see Ed has a girlfriend." Mariah dropped her hand and looked at the men sitting at the potbelly stove. They were playing checkers, chattering and laughing. They didn't look up. Maybe they weren't paying attention. "That cute redhead that moved into the old Clayburn place," said Neal in a forced whisper.

"My ride's waiting," said Mariah as though she hadn't heard. "I'll see you next week. Let me know if you hear anything from Plaistow. I might need to arrange for Ed to take me down there."

As she descended the steps, a young lad she had hired as a farm hand for the business drove up in the Hudson, hopped out and opened the door for her. The checker players were at their seats buzzing about the Taylor offspring as the panel truck headed down Brown's Ridge Road. Coursin kept his distance. He hummed as he made a pyramid of Taylor's jelly jars at the end of the counter.

# CHAPTER 37

## This is What Lies Can Do

B rad was out of Mariah's control for the first time in his life. She had already lost his skills and labor for the business; now she feared that something might happen that would tarnish the family name emblazoned in red and gold on hundreds of jelly jars all over the North Country of New Hampshire.

When she had Brad under her watchful eye, he wouldn't defy her, and because he was afraid of his mother, he had become increasingly secretive and sneaky. His mind started following circuitous routes to his camouflaged goals. Fortunately for Mariah, he clumsily dropped clues along the path. When she confronted him with the evidence of his plans, Brad slipped into his shell like a hermit crab.

Brad married Edith Dayton and invited his family to see the Dayton farm. Mariah surveyed house, field and furnishings with her brain calculating sums faster than a Christmas cash register at Woolworth's. Edith mothered Brad while her aged father sat quietly under his throw by the fire. Holding Edith's hand, Brad addressed her as "my dear" and took great pleasure in looking after her and her father's farm. The only cloud over his sunny, new life was the frail and cranky old man.

"What are you worried about?" asked Ed as they drove away from the cheery yellow farm-house with the white picket fence. "He's sitting pretty. Who'd have guessed?" he said, lighting up a Chesterfield and blowing the smoke away from his mother. Mariah watched the Dayton farmhouse diminish in the side mirror.

"There's something strange going on there," she said, and nothing more. She hadn't heard much from Neal Coursin who promised to check with his banker friend. Plaistow had taken little notice of the quiet young man who now accompanied Edith Dayton to town in place of her father. Reports were that he seemed very proper, and he was always at work, a natural born farmer who cared for the prosperous dairy farm as if it were his own.

Many months passed before Mariah began hearing some early evidence that things were not so rosy at the Dayton place. Sightings of Old Man Dayton were becoming rare. Some said that the son-in-law was shy. Others said he was unfriendly. Small towns don't like change, especially change brought about by an outsider.

A clerk at the feed store gained Brad's confidence, a man who had dealt with the Daytons for years. Brad began to let down his guard. *The old man never leaves us alone…he's jealous of Edith and me…he always wants to hug her. I don't like it one bit.*

Concerned by Brad's animosity to the old man, and unable to counter it with gentle assurances about Mr. Dayton's good character, the clerk decided to pay a call when Brad ordered a delivery. He surprised Brad by leaving him with the truck and went to the door to pay his respects to the Dayton's. The old man, crippled with arthritis and suffering from a bad heart, seemed despondent. "It's not like it used to be around here," he said, his eyes tearing up. "It was better when it was just Edith 'un me." When the clerk left, he wondered even more about the state of mind of the old man. When he mentioned it the next time he saw Brad, he received a tart reply.

"Why don't you mind your own business?"

Word got around town in Plaistow that Bradley Taylor wasn't being nice to Old Man Dayton and that word made it back to Neal Coursin by way of a banker friend of his.

"Brad is normally a kind-hearted soul," said Mariah to Neal Coursin who nodded. "But he's pretty secretive."

"And thin skinned," added Coursin.

"You're right about that," said Mariah as she unloaded another delivery of preserves.

"Well, he's got a fine place there in Plaistow, I'd say," said Coursin.

"It's not his. You know that, Neal. Bothers Bradley. This farm and that one, both in the hands of ornery old fools," Mariah added with some humor in her voice.

"I think it's different with the preserves business," said Coursin as he read Mariah's list and reached up to the shelves with a long-handled grasper for a box of baking soda. "He knows he can't run that by himself. But down in Plaistow he's in his element. He doesn't need anyone to tell him how to milk a cow."

"Oh, he won't say much to the old man, but he sulks. He tries that on me just so long, then I give him what for."

"Old Man Dayton's not used to anybody around the house 'cept hired hands," said Coursin who stepped off a stool with a box of cocoa powder and put it in Mariah's basket. "Why don't you send Ed down to check on him?" he said with a quick laugh.

"Maybe I just might if I can pull him away from that little Irish vixen long enough."

Coursin laughed off the description. "Maybe you should worry about one son at a time. I think it would be an even better idea if you got down to Plaistow yourself."

A few days later Mariah penned a letter to Edith and Brad inviting Ed and herself—and very reluctantly, the vixen—for an overnight visit—making a point about the need for three bedrooms. If there were only two guest rooms, Mariah would have to share one with the girlfriend. She drove into town with Ed to post the letter. Neal was somber and tense, and asked if they could wait for him to catch up with other customers. He had something important to tell them and he didn't want others to overhear. Mariah and Ed sat outside on the bench wondering about Coursin's news and talking about Ed's job. They avoided the subject of Rita O'Brien whose perfume lingered in Ed's car.

The summer of 1929 had been difficult with Brad gone. Orders for preserves were brisk, but she didn't have Brad to manage the fields. Hired help came and went. Mariah's growing cash box didn't change the fact that when the sun went down, she was worn out trying to manage a business that had grown beyond her energies.

"Look on the bright side, Ma. You've got plenty of orders and you're fillin' 'em," said Ed.

"Brad married a woman with some money. You don't have to worry about him any more. Now you can concentrate on Dot and your first grandchild," he said with a smile and a pat on her knee. Ed had a nice roadster and a hot girl. He didn't lack for income. To him, the modern world was looking better every day.

Ed always jabbered on about exciting new developments in the world. Amazing things came over the radio every day. Stocks were soaring to unheard of heights; electric refrigeration and air cooling were reaching millions. Some day electric power would reach everybody, Ed was sure of that. "Ma, some day I'm gonna go up in an airplane," Ed said enthusiastically.

"Ya, well that's nice. Tell me one of these modern wonders I'll live to see right here."

"Hey, Ma. The town promised to tar Brown's Ridge Road this fall."

"Oh, ya?" she said with rather tepid enthusiasm.

"Well, if that doesn't excite you, maybe this will. They're wiring the Wolfeboro opera house for sound. Ya, talking movies at last."

"Good. I can see and hear an airplane ride without getting into one of the darned things."

Neal Coursin came out the door more agitated than Mariah had ever seen him. His expression cast a cloud over Ed's shining optimism. "I don't want anyone in the store to overhear," he said. "Mrs. Taylor, I had a call from my banker friend. Something terrible has happened. Yesterday Edith called the police, barely able to make herself understood."

"What's wrong with her?" asked Mariah. "I know Brad always treats her like a bone china cup."

"No, no. It's not her. It's Mr. Dayton. He's dead." Mariah and Ed felt a sudden sense of relief. It was bad news, but not unexpected for a man over eighty years of age. They looked at Coursin with confusion in their eyes. It was sad news, but why was it shocking?

"But Mrs. Taylor, " he added grimly, "they found him hanging from a lantern hook out in the woodshed." Mariah and Ed stared at Neal. Mariah's gloved hand covered her mouth as she shook her head in disbelief.

"He left behind a note. All it said was, 'This is what lies can do.'"

# CHAPTER 38

## *Change of Life*

Two years after old man Dayton died by his own hand, the grapevine had it that Edith didn't have much longer to live herself. Brad had started writing to his mother occasionally to keep her at bay. He said "the poor dear" was going through severe menopause, "womans trubbles" as Brad described it, and she "just needs to get thru it."

Edith wasn't one to complain, certainly not to her mother-in-law who, Edith knew, never approved of the marriage. Brad said it was throwing money away to go to doctors when it was best to leave Edith in his hands and God's. "If anyone can nerse her back to good helth, by God, it's me," wrote Brad spurning his mother's offer to come to Plaistow and stay for a while. Brad was cranky on the phone. "It's change of life. In due time, it'll be through. People gotta leave her be and let nature take its course."

Word was that a niece of Edith's visited one day when Brad was out on errands. She reported that her Aunt Edith was nauseous and losing weight. The niece was alarmed and when Brad arrived home, she insisted that he take her to a doctor.

All Mariah knew was that Brad called in a local doctor to examine Edith again, and the doctor came to the same conclusion. The neighbors down the road had a teenaged girl who came in for a dollar a day and nursed Edith. Neal Coursin passed on what he heard about the girl. Mira was a foundling foster child in the home of the Walters family, if a swaybacked, leaky ruin could be called a home. Poor as a result of their own idleness and ignorance, the Walters looked forward each month for the state check, but fed Mira begrudgingly.

Brad told his mother that the "little dear" was a great help. She also found a medicine that would calm Edith's cramps and let her sleep. There was a baby in the Walters household, and Mira witnessed the soothing effects of Paregoric when the baby was teething. A liberal dose of Paregoric let everybody in the house enjoy the silence of a cute sleeping baby. A little of this opium-laced painkiller rubbed on sore gums brought quick relief to an infant, so, Mira reasoned, a spoonful or two might settle an adult's stomach pains. Paregoric worked like a charm, and it wasn't hard to get more. Mira liked Bradley Taylor, she liked his house and his car and his full ice box. And of course she felt very sorry for his poor, sickly wife.

"Ma, we're doing everything we can for the poor dear," Brad wrote. "Doc says she just has to get thru it. I'd take her to the best doctors in Boston if anyone thought it would make a difference. She wants to be home," Brad's letter said, and Mariah had no doubt that was true. Brad didn't admit to his mother that he had money, but she knew he did. The Plaistow banker friend of Neal Coursin reported that Fred Dayton's probated will left the farm and over six thousand in cash to Edith.

"I hear the town's buzzing about Brad and his 'poor dear,' and 'little dear'," said Coursin. "I guess he takes Edith out for rides sometimes to give her a little fresh air and sunlight. That little waif's always in the back seat. Causing quite a stir down in Plaistow, 'specially after the old man's strange death," Coursin added with a sideways glance.

"They don't know him the way we do or they wouldn't make much of it," said Mariah. "As to that girl and what she's up to, that may be another matter," she added suspiciously.

"Mrs. Taylor, I know this is just rumor, but I think you need to know." Brad offered her a never-ending cause of headaches. "All right. Go ahead," said Mariah as Coursin bent over the counter to whisper in her ear.

"Some folks in Plaistow think Edith's being poisoned."

"Oh, God, help us," Mariah blurted.

Mira Landers was a scrawny kid, but she held out the promise of maturing into an attractive woman. Brad took a shine to the girl, that much was clear, but Mariah knew it was platonic just as it was with Edith. With any normal man this would raise sexual suspicions. Bradley was anything but normal.

"I know Brad thinks the world of Edith even if their relationship isn't exactly normal. As to this girl, maybe she's looking for a change of life of a different sort," said Mariah with a cynical snarl.

Life was indeed changing for everyone, and for most, the change was not welcome. It was 1931, a time when everyone tried to hold on to every dime, and a man with a job counted himself lucky even if the boss cut his pay or reduced his hours. For country folks it was back to barter-ing for many needs. A dozen eggs might get a gallon of gas from the general store, and a few pounds of nails might be the pay for turning a field of hay to dry in the sun. The boom of the '20s had changed to the bust of the '30s; for many, life in a house changed to life in a car, then life in a car changed to life under a bridge.

Brad needed Mira's help more and more. She got good meals at the Dayton farm, and Brad began giving her some extra money on the sly when he found out the Walters were taking her daily pay.

"You know, Neal, I think I'll have to make another trip down to Plaistow. I'm afraid Brad is about to get himself into a whole lot of trouble."

### 

Mariah sat in a ladder back chair next to the ethereal Edith and held her hand. Edith's eyes were sunken, her skin pallid. She looked like a woman of sixty-six instead of forty-six.

Mariah told Brad and the girl—whose name she promptly forgot—to leave the room. Brad stopped by the table to clear old dishes and left with Mira close behind him.

"Edith, have you been to the doctor lately?"

She managed a weak "no." Edith smiled slightly as one does when a comforting person takes charge and seems to know what needs to be done. "Bradley's taking good care of me," she added with a wan smile.

"Do you know what you're taking for medicine?"

Again, no.

Mariah examined a spoon with dried chalky medicine and a similar ring on the table beside it. She looked back and forth between Edith and the spoon with the eye of a detective and the sixth sense of a mystic. She sniffed. She tasted. Was there any chance that Edith was taking something more potent than Milk of Magnesia?

Ed and Rita, Brad and Mira sat around the kitchen table in silence, unable to find a suitable topic of polite conversation, and waiting for Mariah to emerge and dictate next steps. Within a few minutes, Mariah emerged looking suspicious."

"Bradley, call the doctor and get him over here right now," Mariah ordered.

"I'll have to go pick him up," replied Bradley with a whine in his voice. "He stopped drivin' a while back. Eyes not too good, I guess."

"For God's sake, Brad," Ed piped in. "Is that the best you can do for a doctor?"

"He's a good doctor. He just doesn't take a chance driving in the bright sun."

"So he's half blind, is that what you're telling us?" Mariah added acidly.

Brad made the call and grabbing his hat without question, he headed for the door with a scowl on his face. As he opened the door, Brad motioned with his head for Mira to follow. "No," said Mariah. "She's staying here." The door slammed shut and Brad was gone.

"I'll deal with him later," said Mariah to Ed. Rita eyes went back and forth between faces like a spectator at game point in tennis.

"Do you know what people in town are saying?" demanded Mariah of the wide-eyed "little dear." Mira was standing by the door where Brad left her. Her hopes for a quiet exit were dashed.

"Sit down. We've got to get a few things straightened out," said Mariah. Mira slumped into a chair at the kitchen table.

Ed shushed his mother. "Mom, Edith's gonna hear you." Rita poured Mira a cup of tea just for something to do to ease the tension.

"Now tell me, what have you been giving Edith?"

The girl was agitated and stumbled over her words. "Tea and toast, oatmeal. Whatever she can keep down."

"I don't mean food," Mariah barked. "I'm talking about medicine. You know what I'm talking about, so don't try that innocence game on me."

Mira's lips trembled. "Just some, oh I don't know what you call it, milk of something. Magnesium?"

"Magnesia? Milk of Magnesia?" corrected Mariah.

"Yes, that's it. But there's none left. Brad needs to get more."

"And what else?"

"Well, sometimes she has bad stomachaches. I tried some baby's medicine on her and it worked real good."

"The Paragoric," said Mariah. "Yes, I heard about that."

"Yes. It's for babies, so how could it do any harm?" Mira started to cry.

"Now never mind that. Do you realize some people in town suspect something bad is going on here?"

Mira looked up with alarm. "I'm not doin' anything wrong, and neither is Mr. Taylor," she added with teary indignation.

"That may be, but this whole situation smells pretty fishy to a lot of people," added Mariah in a far calmer voice than the way the interrogation began. "Why don't you go home?" said Mariah with confidence in Mira's immediate acquiescence. Mira closed the door slowly and quietly.

"So Ma," Ed piped in after the door closed, "do you think she could be poisoning Edith?"

"I doubt it. I checked Edith's fingernails to see if the half moons were blue. Didn't look so to me."

Ed and Rita looked puzzled.

"Arsenic. Every farmer's got it around. I'm sure some is out in the barn. Once you have a heavy dose of it building up in you, it shows up in the fingernails."

Rita went wide-eyed and reached for Ed's hand.

"Even if the doctor found a trace in her blood, it could just be in the water. It takes quite a bit to turn the base of your nails blue. But think about how this looks. Brad marries a woman twenty years older than himself and within a couple of years her father commits suicide and then she gets deathly ill. Add in a penniless little street urchin as a nurse, and you've got enough fuel to keep the rumor mill in full production for months."

The look on Rita's face as details of Brad's story unfolded worried Ed. "I know what you're thinking, but it's not like that. Brad's a little strange, but he's no murderer. If someone's suffering, he's always right there …"

"Yes, I don't think he'll ever get over not being able to help your father on his dying day," said Mariah, sitting ramrod straight and looking up at Ed from her tea.

Ed turned his eyes quickly back to Rita and away from his mother's reminder of his absence on the day of his father's death. Rita's anxious face registered the power Ed's mother had over him. She had not seen her bold lover cowed by anyone before.

"Brad almost seems to be drawn to people in need, isn't that right, Ed?"

"He was even that way with our dog," replied Ed who directed his words to Rita with a nervous laugh. "Never took much interest until the dog was crippled up and blind."

"What about the old man?" Rita asked, still not assuaged.

"Oh, Brad might have contributed to the old guy's problems, but I'll tell you, Brad was pretty shook up when it happened."

"I can imagine," added Rita. Nothing that Ed said inclined her to dismiss the case against Brad building in her mind.

"But what about this Mira? Don't you suppose…?"

"Aw, she's scared of her own shadow."

"I'm not so sure," Rita murmured and picked up her tea. She had a mind of her own; she would give Ed a run for his money.

"Well, it's none of your affair anyway," said Mariah as she stared Rita down. "We shouldn't have dragged you down here," she added with a quick, disapproving glance that told her son that she could put Rita in her place if he couldn't.

Mariah surmised that Rita was having second thoughts about getting involved with "black Protestants"—at least that was what she hoped. People in Ossipee already knew that Rita's mother was deathly against marriage to a Protestant, especially one who had no intentions of converting to Catholicism. And if Ed Taylor wouldn't sign a pledge to raise children of their union as Catholics, Rita would face excommunication. Catholic Mrs. O'Brien was now unknowingly joined in an ironic alliance with Protestant Mrs. Taylor to discourage a marriage between forces of light and forces of darkness, each mother convinced of her own shining righteousness.

In about half an hour Brad drove into the yard. Mariah watched him as he got out of the driver's seat and slowly walked around to the passenger side to help the aged doctor out. Brad's dark brow and deep-set eyes gave him a brooding, sinister look. One more reason for the good folks of Plaistow to suspect the worse, Mariah thought. She stood at the window watching Brad help the short, round doctor out of the car. "So that doddering old man is the best Brad can do for a doctor," Mariah said.

She studied Brad's scowling face for signs of his submerged feelings. There was no doubt that he was solicitous to his wife, and there was no doubt that Edith trusted him, and there was no doubt that Brad often shed tears over her deteriorating condition. But with Brad there were always lingering doubts about what else motivated his compassion for the weak. And did he feel anything for her but pity?

Months before, Ed had started to tell his mother that he knew for a fact that Brad and Edith had never consummated their marriage, but his mother waved him off. "Well, how would you know?"

"I asked him," Ed blurted out. "He told me that she wasn't that kind of a woman."

"You don't mean it?" replied Mariah in astonishment.

"'Not that kind of woman', huh? Well, what does that make me? I bet he just told you that. You know how secretive he is."

"No, Ma. I think he was telling me the truth." Ed shook his head and grinned.

"I knew I should have put a stop to this weird romance the first time he wanted to come down here," Mariah muttered. "You know, this makes me feel like a failure," she admitted to Ed.

"Oh, Ma, it's not your fault," replied Ed.

"No I failed. In fact I've failed by two counts. I failed to protect Brad from the world and I failed to protect the world from Brad."

Rita affirmed Mariah's verdict by gently clearing her throat.

Doctor Francis spent a few minutes with Edith, and emerged cleaning his glasses with a handkerchief. "She's got some poisons built up in her system."

"Poisons?" Mariah replied with alarm.

"Well, I…well, poisons from infection, poor digestion, that's all I meant. Happens all the time if you don't have a thorough purgative treatment every few months, especially a woman going through the change of life. I'll purge her with blue vervain, we'll give her a good enema, too. I think we'll see some improvement by tomorrow." Dr. Francis turned just before he opened the door to Edith's room. Where's the girl who's been helping out?"

"I sent her home," said Mariah emphatically, her gaze fixed on her elder son.

"Well, then, Mr. Taylor, I'll need someone in here with me."

Before Brad could open his mouth, Mariah spoke up. "Rita, you go in and sit in the corner. You don't need to do anything more than be there."

"Ma," Ed whined. "Can't you do it? Rita didn't come down here to help give an enema.

"I'm sure she doesn't mind making herself useful," retorted Mariah. "Brad and I need to talk."

Rita got up and followed the doctor without saying a word. The expression on her face said it all: "This woman and I aren't going to get along."

"I'm going out for a cigarette," said Ed who registered the women's belligerent coded messages and decided it was best to stay neutral for the moment.

"Now Bradley, you sit."

"Hrumph," he grumbled, but acquiesced.

"Now do you mind telling me what in hell is going on in this house?"

"We're doin' all we can, Ma, it's the God's truth," Brad blubbered as he often did when his mother gave him a dressing down.

"And who's the 'we'? You and Clara Barton from next door?"

"She's a… good little… girl," Brad muttered through sniffles and sobs.

"Now shut that damned faucet off and speak up."

"What about these poisons in her system? Are you watching everything that's going into Edith's mouth?" Mariah's eyes narrowed as she leaned across the table at Brad.

"I'd never let anybody hurt Edith," Brad replied indignantly.

"Well it doesn't look like she's getting any better. Maybe she needs to go to the hospital so they can find out what's wrong."

"Those knife happy fools. Most people come out of the hospital in a coffin. She wants to be home and that's where she's gonna be. Doc'll give her something stronger if her pain gets worse."

"Brad, do you know what some people in town are saying?"

He looked down at the table without answering.

"After what happened with the old man?"

"Edith knew he wasn't right in the head the last year. She didn't blame me. I admit I didn't like him, but honest to God…" Brad stopped abruptly, pulled out a handkerchief and daubed his eyes and blew his nose. "Honest to God, Ma, something was eatin' at him. It wasn't just me."

"Maybe so, but the old man left that note. Everybody in Plaistow's heard about it. Now Edith is sick and you've got that little bee buzzing around the honey pot. How do you suppose that looks?"

"I don't care. I ain't doin' nothin' wrong."

"Bradley, I'm telling you, you're gonna be in trouble if that woman dies at home without a competent doctor knowing why."

"Doc Francis is a good man."

"I'm sure he's a good man, and his experience probably goes back to the Civil War," Mariah sneered.

The doctor came out of the room carrying his black bag; Rita followed carrying a covered chamber pot. She looked like she was about to throw up. "Clear liquids for the rest of the day. You can make a good chicken broth, Mr. Taylor," said Doctor Francis with a confident smile. "Some oatmeal tomorrow morning. I'll be back in a couple of days to check her blood."

"Now, you see," said Brad to his mother, reflecting the doctor's confidence. Brad handed the doctor his hat and helped him out to the car as quickly as the old man could move.

"Very well," replied Mariah. "We'll leave it in your hands, you and this learned man of medicine." Her sarcasm was veiled behind a forced smile.

Doctor Francis nodded to Mariah, taking her description as a compliment.

"Well, we'll be going," Mariah said. "Just think about what I said." Brad's cold silence offered her little hope that her elder son would heed her advice when he was out of arm's length.

As Ed helped her into the front seat and Rita climbed into the back, Mariah shook her head in exasperation. "She's not long for this world, and when she dies, all hell is going to break loose."

"Oh, come on, Ma. Don't be so gloomy," Ed replied as he patted her knee and started up the engine.

Mariah put her hand over Ed's. "Promise me that when I'm gone you'll keep an eye on Brad."

Ed looked at his mother and nodded reluctantly. In the back seat, red-headed Rita sighed audibly.

# CHAPTER 39

## *Bread Line*

The winter of 1932 lay heavy on the land. An early January storm dropped such a load of wet snow that Mariah couldn't push the storm door open. She had to go out the cellar door that opened in. Her days were spent mostly indoors. Once she had the kitchen stove glowing and a hot cup of coffee to warm her hands, she opened the door to the connected woodshed and loaded the box for the day. She kept her sewing machine in the kitchen, and did most of her needlework and laundry within ten feet of the stove.

A pad of stationery sat blank on the kitchen table with Brad's latest letter open beside it. Nearly a year had passed since Edith's death. Brad offered to come home in time for spring planting. If that were all he had asked, Mariah would have welcomed him. Hired help didn't have the same devotion even though good jobs were hard to come by in the prolonged national depression. Cash was wafting from the Schrafft's box with the diminishing scent of chocolate. But George Bradley Taylor didn't just want to come home. He wanted to own the place, house, fields and business. He would be the new "Taylor's Preserves" and Mariah would have a place in town with all of the comforts she had given up when the Fates sent her into rustic Purgatory nearly forty years ago. The letter was blunt. "I'm offering to buy you out."

Edith died at home a few months after Mariah's visit. A couple of weeks later, the county sheriff took Mira away under suspicion of murder. Traces of arsenic, an open bag in the barn, plenty of motive, plus the rancor of Plaistow townsfolk fanned what started as gossip into a prima facie case not long after Edith was laid to rest.

Brad put on a clean white shirt and tie, and with five hundred dollars in his wallet set aside to defend his "poor little dear," he made an appointment with Wilson, Thorndike and Rabinowitz. He asked the secretary for Rabinowitz. He remembered what country folks always said about how to choose a lawyer.

"To find guilt beyond a reasonable doubt, you, the members of this solemn jury must by common law and the law of New Hampshire, determine, beyond a reasonable doubt, I remind you, that the evidence points incontrovertibly to the defendant on both *actus reus* and *mens rea*... For the offense of murder in the first degree, the State of New Hampshire must prove that the person killed another person; the person killed the other person with malice aforethought; and the killing was premeditated.

Twelve men, mostly eighth grade dropouts, had to know Latin beyond a reasonable doubt. One thought the murder had to be with a mallet; another waited for a translation of "premeditated," which he thought had something to do with drugs and poisons.

The autopsy showed some elevation in arsenic beyond that normally occurring from natural sources. Could it have contributed to her death or hastened her death? One part of murder seemed clear. The actions of the defendant—the *actus reus*—had to have caused the victim's death, at least to a large extent.

The prosecution wasn't easy on Dr. Francis for failure to diagnose stomach cancer until it was beyond hope, but undoubtedly stomach cancer alone would have, could have—in all probability did—cause Edith Taylor's death without any other causal factor. The defense lawyer called the evidence of stomach cancer a *cadit quaestio* (a matter admitting of no further argument), thus making it, he announced with a catlike grin a *res ipsa loquitur* (and open and shut case). The jury began to nod off *in situ* (in their seats), overwhelmed by Latin and by the aggressive cross examination of the defense lawyer.

The prosecution countered that if the evidence wasn't strong for *actus reus* of murder, then possibly *actus reus* of an attempt? Motive—the *mens rea*—was as easy to sniff out as a skunk under the porch. "My God, it's time for some women in the jury box, at least, if not on the bench," Mariah sputtered when she heard court reports.

The neighbor took the witness stand, a lovely old lady who spoke English very well even if she couldn't conjugate any Latin verbs. She told about Edith's despondency after the mysterious suicide of her father. Rabinowitz turned her train of thought around faster than a locomotive in a roundhouse by getting her to label Edith as "close to suicidal" when she last saw her. Casting doubt and conjugating plenty of irregular verbs in legalese left the jury and Mira in legal mumble jumble. Mira was not the only one with motive and means. By the time Rabinowitz got done with the old lady neighbor, despondent Edith became a prime suspect in her own death. After all, didn't poor, suicidal Edith have access to rat poison? Why, yes. It was out on a shelf in the shed. Closing arguments with smoke and mirrors led the jury to a verdict of "not guilty."

Mira had slipped through the crack of reasonable doubt and was out the courthouse door in a flash. Although still in mourning, Brad was out of trouble and in the money just when Mariah and most of America were deep in the hole. Despite the verdict, the good citizens of Plaistow were not about to forgive or forget. Brad and Mira found themselves *persona non grata*; in plain English, Brad soon figured out that the two of them needed to get out of town. If Brad could talk his mother into selling the business to him, he could escape judging eyes and fulfill his boyhood dream as well. Brad had always longed to follow in his father's furrows and help his mother right out the door, and now it was possible with what was left of Old Man Dayton's estate.

For Mariah, the temptation was great to let Brad have the place, but her nightmares painted a vermilion descent from Purgatory to Hell itself if she gave in and took Brad's blood money. She remained convinced, no matter what Rockingham County Superior Court concluded, that sins of commission or omission were involved in Edith's—and her unfortunate father's—demise.

Mariah moved dozens of jars of preserves from the pantry and stored them in apple crates against an interior kitchen wall to prevent them from freezing overnight. A paper bag of cookies sat by the door for Elmer Holt who gave her a ride to town once a week. Maybe in the spring she would have to break down and learn to drive.

For the winter of '32 she would become a coffee depot for the regular traffic on Brown's Ridge, what little traffic there was. Mariah offered the Ossipee plowing crew coffee and muffins; she even put up with Clyde Davis's nosiness just for a little more human contact. She felt as lonely as the Ancient Mariner surrounded by a wintry sea of white.

Some relief came in the form of a battery-powered crystal set Ed had given her. Better than radio was the daily mail. Dotty and her husband Andy would come up as soon as the weather broke. Mariah's first grandchild, little black-haired, dark eyed Susan, had turned three and had all the personality for the talking pictures. Little snapshots from a Brownie camera were tucked into the folds of the letter. But not all the letters brought good news.

Ed and Rita, who were married in the fall by a justice of the peace, had little work and no money. Occasional work at a sawmill, and his trusty aim brought home a scrawny deer he had poached plus a few rabbits. His mother's root cellar and the Schrafft's box would help get him and the Redhead through the nation's harsh winter of discontent. Ed promised he would not go back to bootlegging; besides, F.D.R. promised to repeal the Volstead Act as part of a program of "national recovery."

A week before wonderful news arrived in the mail about another betrothal—one that was long overdue. "Amos W. Brandon, Jr. and Eleanor Marie Cosgrove request the pleasure of your company at the Free Will Baptist Church…" Moze, long a bachelor plying his trade as a barber in the Town of Franklin, had found a woman who could stop his drinking. Eleanor, a spinster school teacher with years of experience in straightening out the wayward, had put off the wedding until Moze had been dry for a year. In Mariah's eyes, Eleanor was a belated blessing from God even if she did remind her of her mother.

A spring wedding, Mariah sighed. She was anxious to share the news, but there was no one to hear her voice in the drafty rooms of the farmhouse. Mariah's loneliness would have dampened her joy if it had not been for the second piece of news from Eleanor. Moze and Eleanor wanted to open up the long darkened family home in Sandwich. They couldn't afford to buy it for a few years, but if Florence and Mariah were willing, they would work out terms to buy his sisters out over time.

*Thank God. I'll be able to go back there without crying.* The house had been boarded up for fourteen years since the folks passed away. Florence, Moze and Mariah had resisted letting the place go as long as there was the faintest hope that someone from their generation or the next might buy it and bring the homestead back to life. Mariah imagined another generation diving from the perch into the pothole, another generation walking to the North Sandwich Store for penny candy, another generation working the land, and tapping the maples for sap. Now, once again, an Amos W. Brandon would sit at the kitchen table with his school teacher wife. Once again Brandons would listen to the voices of Cold River.

There was even more reason to celebrate. With some additional income for her share in the homestead, Mariah would not be forced by the poor economy to acquiesce to Brad's offer and turn over her business to him and that little moocher girlfriend of his.

Mariah looked around the kitchen. The ceiling was dingy from daily belches of smoke from the stove, and lines crisscrossed it just as she remembered at home in Sandwich. A kettle of hot water hissed on the back burner, and every once in a while a log collapsed into cinders in the stove. Her life was much like her parents' lives despite paved roads and automobiles, talking pictures and airplanes. Electric power and telephones had not made their way beyond Center Ossipee down Brown's Ridge Road.

Despite the Depression, Mariah was proud that she had never gone to the town or to a church or to anyone else for relief. *Relief comes with hard work, dammit, and hard work is no novelty for me.* The Democrats were promising a New Deal to the American people, but Mariah would rely on her own two hands. No "New Deal" could hide the shame of a government handout.

With this small blessing from the old homestead, she would survive. An old country farm was not the life she expected to live when she slept in Will Dunfield's arms, but she would survive. A light snow began to swirl against the windows, small, gritty flakes that pelted the windowpanes like sand. The bitter cold that frequently follows a storm tumbled the clouds southeastward and shook the remaining snow from them like a shifter.

Life in the country was hard, but George Washington Taylor was a proud man who never would have stood in a breadline. Nor would she, with God as her witness. Bristling when she read that Rita was urging Ed to go on relief, she found a poem by Florence Converse in *Atlantic Monthly* and slipped it into the mail to them.

What's the meaning of this queue,
Tailing down the avenue,
Full of eyes that will not meet
The other eyes that throng the street—
The questing eyes, the curious eyes,
Scornful, popping with surprise
To see a living line of men
As long as round the block, and then
As long again?
What is the meaning in these faces
Modern industry displaces,
Emptying the factory
To set the men so tidily
Along the pavement in a row?

On it she wrote, "Your father would turn over in his grave if anyone in his family ever took a handout. You can always work here if things get rough, and there's always food under my roof."

There were bread lines in Rochester, in Dover, in Manchester. Where men and women once queued up for work, now they queued up for a handout to feed their families. Those in the country could at least live off the land as before.

She finished a letter to Brad welcoming him for the spring planting, but telling him in no uncertain terms that Taylor's Preserves and the farm were not for sale. He would have to wait his time. She also told him of Uncle Moze's happy news.

As Mariah rose from the table, the gusting winds rattled the dampers on the stove, and occasional puff backs sent the smell of creosote into the room. Brad had not done his usual cleaning of the chimney in the fall, and winter was upon her before she could get Ed up on the roof with the wire brush. She opened the dampers to increase the draft. Taking four loaves of bread from the oven, Mariah placed them in a line on cooling racks with the rest of the baked goods to be boxed for Coursin's Store. Would to God they would sell at a nickel a loaf. Supply and demand had turned into scarcity and want.

Suddenly she heard a roaring in the wall. A dense, black smoke blew over the face of the late afternoon sun and cinders sizzled as they settled on the pristine snow. Mariah shut down all of the dampers, bundled herself up, and began throwing valuables out the door and into the soft snow. Chimney fire. She prayed that someone would come down Brown's Ridge Road before it was too late.

# CHAPTER 40

## Home Sweet Home

*W*hen he didn't get an immediate reply to his offer, Brad wrote a second letter to his mother a week later. Only four days after sending the second letter, Brad's impatience got the better of him and he decided to drive to Ossipee to show his mother he had the money and he was serious about buying the farm.

Brad's letter was awkward and mercifully short. His big hand was neat, but infantile with many misspellings. "He woud never regrat marring Edith," he wrote. Mariah knew he had no regrets that he inherited everything the Daytons had amassed. He was also sure that he was going to do "the right thing by Mira," as if he owed her a wedding ring for her good service to Edith during her long period of suffering.

He didn't mention his new car or Mira's new clothes, or his new refrigerator, or any of his other purchases that had taken a considerable bite out of the Dayton estate, never mind the fee to Rabinowitz. Brad still had a wallet stuffed with large bills, more cash than even Ed had seen at one time. Brad was eager to surprise his mother, but *she* had an even more stunning surprise for him.

Mariah and her sister worked side by side in Florence's impressive kitchen. Neal Coursin had called to warn that Brad was on the way, and none too happy at what he'd found. "You should have called him immediately. Here he is coming all the way up here to pay a visit and what does he get? The shock of his life, that's what," admonished Florence. "And he had to find out from a grocer that you were staying with me."

"Even Brad could have figured that out," retorted Mariah. "I couldn't tell him over the phone," said Mariah. "If he hadn't just decided to come right up here, he would have gotten my letter. I'm sorry he'll have to learn it this way, but maybe it's all for the best."

Florence went at her pie dough with abandon, her irritation with her sister playing itself out with the rolling pin. Florence was in baker's white from hair to hem; her black shoes with powdered white on the tops.

"My hair's turned white worrying about your children. It will just about kill him to drive up Brown's Ridge and see the place, and then wonder what happened to you. Would be a blow to anyone, but especially poor Brad. If I had known that he didn't know, I would have called him immediately."

"Yes, and I told you to stay out of it."

"And I did," sputtered Florence, "but I don't want to be standing here when he walks in."

"That's fine with me. I'll give him some pie. Two pieces, as a matter of fact. That will calm him down. Brad always has a good appetite."

"It's not right, it's just not right."

"I'll decide what's right when it comes to Brad," said Mariah as she took a damp cloth off a bowl of risen bread dough.

Florence had tried to intervene for Brad and Ed in the past, and it only caused friction with Mariah, and even though fortune had shone far more brightly on her, Florence would always be the kid sister who had to keep her place.

As she worked silently beside her sister on the soapstone countertop, Mariah felt a sadness sweep over her. Where had the years gone that they had suddenly become old? Mariah was sixty-four and as capable of a hard day's work as ever, but her hair, piled into a loose bun, was white and her figure stocky and square. Mariah's brows remained dark, and behind her rimless glasses, the black and fiery eyes were the last hint of the beauty that had been her pride.

Florence was fifty-seven, and her strawberry hair hid some of the gray. She was slimmer than Mariah, but still matronly. Her expression was gentler, her movements more fluid. She wasn't driven by the chronic frustration that showed itself in Mariah's brusque handling of everything from dough to farm animals. She seemed to be in a desperate struggle to bring control back into her life, and, by God, into the lives of her sons. At least she didn't have to worry about her daughter. Dotty's husband still had a job, and her little Susan was the family's Shirley Temple, cute and clever with all the personality, but topped with raven curls instead of golden ones.

Dorothy's middle position among the siblings, and the blessing of being the girl, gave her a detached objectivity about people, and a quiet determination to steer her own course, accepting others for what they were, but not allowing others to impose their will upon her. Dotty found that she and her mother got along very well as long as they were separated most of the time by about a hundred miles.

Brad had climbed Ayers' Hill at twenty miles per hour, babying his new Chevrolet coupe over frost heaves and around potholes. The January sun was bright, the air still. When Brad reached Brown's Ridge, the road turned into a tunnel of mature elms, vaulted like a big city church. The road was crisscrossed with bony shadows of limbs. He was dressed in a white shirt and tie, just as his mother would want to see him. Brad's big farmer's hands gripped the wheel exposing white wrists. Shirts his size never seemed to have sleeves long enough.

His hands looked artificial, like big pincers grafted onto a human body. Others might think him menacing, especially with his dark-browed, down under stare, but he was timid in the face of a strong will, malleable like a child who would never defy authority to its face.

Brown's Ridge Road was dotted with puddles of melted ice and snow. It was the January thaw, just the climate Brad hoped for when he talked to his mother about the business.

He stopped the Chevrolet coupe near the creek that ran under the road and down the slope by the abandoned Adams homestead. He got out a rag and dipped it in the creek to wipe the dirt off the windshield.

He smelled the moss kept richly green by the frigid mountain water. This was home. The longing came back. He would cut the brush back to the stone walls, and the fields would be back in full cultivation. Everything would be as it should be, as it was when his father worked elbow-to-elbow with him.

Brad felt alittle guilt that he sometimes wished his mother dead. He was all the more convinced that she was in league with invisible powers. Although he lived more than sixty miles from her and she knew no one in Plaistow, she tracked his movements nonetheless. Brad did not know his mother's secrets, but she knew his. She predicted consequences of his folly with uncanny accuracy. The cow he bought that gave no milk, the winter trip to the picture show in Wolfeboro with no tire chains—*You'll need chains for the black ice, I'm warning you*—that landed him in the ditch. He respected her prescience more than a sharp knife while at the same time he resented her for the control she seemed to be able to exert over him despite the expanse of time and space. Women weren't supposed to be as strong as men, but in her own way, his mother was stronger than most men he knew, even his prodigal younger brother.

When he finished cleaning the car, Brad reached for his billfold and took out a fistful of new twenties. He intended to flash them in his mother's face as the down payment for her business. Maybe a fan of twenty-dollar bills would surprise her and change her mind.

The Chevy purred to life. Brad was feeling more relaxed and more capable of dealing with his mother than he had ever before. Feeling confident that he would soon be the owner of Taylor's Preserves and his father's farm, he was on top of the world, at least for one short moment before he crested the hill where the house would come into view.

The sight before him took his breath away; he thought he would choke. The massive center chimney of the homestead stood solitary. Something like a seizure gripped him; the car veered and dipped into the soft sand of the shoulder. He brought the car to a stop with a metallic squeak of the brakes.

The chimney was blackened, like an obelisk memorializing a tragic loss. Flinging the door open, he ran to the granite doorsteps as though there was something he could do to bring the house back from the inferno that had consumed it. Piles of charcoal, a few blackened timbers oundation were all that remained of the 1732 house that Brad had expected to inherit one day.

The kitchen woodstove sat in the cellar hole in pieces; the smell of sodden ashes turned his stomach. Why had his mother not told him? Brad sat on a fallen granite hitching post and wept.

"Ed's going to build me a little place right across the street," said Mariah to Florence as she browned stew beef in a big pot for the guest's lunch.

"That son of yours certainly has potential," observed Florence who chose the word "potential" as her harping theme. She kept cutting vegetables, avoiding a glance at her sister who knew full well that the next words at the tip of Florence's tongue were about education and missed opportunities.

"Ed's learning from life, and those are the lessons that really count," said Mariah in rebuttal of Florence's unspoken thoughts. "Ed can do whatever he sets his mind to."

"Unless something stands in his way. He's never learned to be persistent." Florence peeled carrots with the speed of a machine.

Mariah's knife came down on her cutting board with a startling thwack into a beef shank and Florence jumped.

"I didn't tell you how to raise Helen, even though you spoiled her, but you always tried to tell me how to raise Ed."

Florence rested her hands and turned to her sister whose knife was at the ready. "I'm sorry you feel I'm interfering, but an aunt has a right to say something. Ed has tried cooking, but he doesn't have the training he needs to be a chef. He's worked as a mechanic, but he doesn't even have a high school diploma, and no bank is going to advance him the money to set up his own garage. He gets started in a direction, then gets frustrated. He's proven to be good at sales…"

"Don't say another word. I know where all this is heading," said Mariah, gesturing with the bloody knife still in her hand. "If I'd let him go to school, Ed would already be a success at something, something other than selling liquor."

Florence was not about to be cowed, even if her elder sister was punctuated her argument with a knife. "And it would be all the more gratifying if Ed succeeded at something *legal,* something that wouldn't bring disgrace to the family."

"That's what it's always been about, isn't it? I disgraced the family, and now my son is following in my footsteps. Was it my fault that I caught a disease from my philandering husband?"

"Mother warned you, and what she feared came true," blurted Florence in an angry fusillade. As soon as the words were out of her mouth, she regretted saying them. *"And the tongue is a fire, a world of iniquity: So is the tongue among our members…"*

Mariah read in her sister's face the horror of momentary loss of control. Florence had shocked herself with her rare outburst, the kind of candor that the world expected out of her dark sister, not from her. Mariah was punished many times for the excesses of her tongue. Florence normally set a cooler thermostat on her words, not so much out of humility, but out of pride in self-control. She was the favored daughter, obedient to a fault, and constantly rewarded for her compliant nature and her conformity to the rules. It had all worked for her. Her mother had adored her; she married well; she had social standing; she never suffered from the pinch of want. What an irony to develop such pride out of subservience to society's dictates, her sister thought.

Mariah retaliated with pregnant silence. A silence of slow cuts followed. Mariah dropped the pieces of beef into the heated pot for browning; Florence finished cutting up vegetables, her hand trembling.

The tension was broken when a new Chevrolet coupe turned into the driveway. It was to be a surprise, but Mariah already knew about the car. She put the teakettle on the burner and stood at the door ready to receive her elder son. "I'll call you down when the tea is ready," said Mariah as though she owned the place and her sister was a hired hand. Florence left the kitchen without arguing.

Brad didn't knock, and he let the storm door slam behind him.

"Why didn't you tell me?" he cried.

"A letter was on its way." Mariah responded calmly. I just couldn't do it over the phone," she said in an attempt to pour oil on troubled waters, but Bradley remained agitated and unforgiving. Mariah then resorted to what she knew best. Control. "Sit down there." She pointed to a seat at the kitchen table, and after a brief moment's hesitation, Brad obediently took the seat, cowed as usual by her authority.

"I told you last fall the chimney needed sweeping and pointing up, didn't I?" said Mariah sharply.

Despite everything Brad had done in the last few years, she wanted to put her arms around him, but she couldn't bring herself to do it as long as he was out of her control. "Here," she said as gently as she could. Mariah put a plate in front of Brad with two pieces of apple pie, each topped with a thin slice of cheddar, just the way he liked it, still warm, but not steaming. "Tell me which one you like better." As the kettle whistled, she walked out of the kitchen and called out, "Tea's ready!"

Florence came into the kitchen with a sympathetic half smile and gave her nephew a quick peck on the cheek and a pitying glance. Brad's mouth was full of pie. He mumbled a greeting.

"Well," said Mariah with a hint of irritation, "which one do you like better?" Mariah turned toward Florence with one hand propped on her hip and a look of absolute confidence. Reluc-tantly Brad point-ed with his fork to the pie on the right.

"Mine," said Mariah with a quick glance at her sister. Brad stopped chewing and looked apologetically at Florence. Suddenly, with the knowledge that he had been used to humble his aunt, he said, "There's really not much difference," but the choice had been made.

Mariah and Florence sat in silence sipping their tea, waiting for Brad to eat to his satisfaction. It would take an earthquake or an explo-sion to take Brad's attention off his food. Even life's high dramas were held in abeyance by a plate of food. When the plate was empty, except for the crust edges, he drew his tepid tea close and slurped a half-inch off the top. He never drank his tea hot, and he always finished the fluted crust with the tea.

"Ed's building me a little place across the street with some of the insurance money. He was there the day of the fire. Good to have a son who's there when you need him." The barb stuck into Brad's flesh. Mariah could read his face. *So Ed was there when the house burned down. And who run off and missed his own father's funeral? Where was he all those years since Pa died? Who was there most every day from plantin' time till harvest?*

Brad slid the plate back at his mother, wishing that he had chosen his aunt's pie, or wishing he had refused to eat anything offered by her hand. His own mother had not told him that the house had burned down, a total loss. His corner room on the second floor that caught the morn-ing sun, the kitchen where he steadied his father's trembling hands as he lifted his tea to his lips, the parlor where he helped light the candles on the tree every Christmas Eve and watched the candles burn down until his parents snuffed out the magic of the light; in all their years of childhood they went off to bed at Christmas with the smell of hot wax in their nostrils. The old homestead, built in 1732, destroyed by fire exactly two centuries later, and his mother laid the blame at his feet because he had not come home to sweep the chimney.

Mariah clanked dishes together as she cleared the table and carried the plates, cups, and silver to the sink. She still could not bring herself to comfort Brad. He had left her alone to manage the farm. He had married a woman almost old enough to be his mother, and he had gotten totally out of control and dragged the family name through the muck with folly that Mariah didn't even want to contemplate. She felt she had no choice but to come down on him hard, and to get him back under her watchful eye. No telling what trouble he'd get into if she didn't.

Taking advantage of the distance between mother and son, Florence sat down opposite her nephew and put her hand over his. "Brad, I'm so sorry."

Tears welled in his eyes. "I coulda saved the place if I'd stayed home, but I needed my own life, didn't I?"

"Of course you did," comforted his aunt.

He looked over his shoulder, wanting to know that his mother was listening, but not wanting to pour out his pain to her. Florence kept her hand on his and nodded, watching his down-turned face.

"You've had so much on your shoulders, Brad, what with Mr. Dayton's death and Edith's, I'd say you had your hands full. You have no reason to feel guilty about the fire. It was just an act of God, and God works in mysterious ways."

"That's for sure," said Mariah. "So I'm afraid "Taylor's Preserves" isn't worth much right at the moment." Mariah took a deep breath and softened the tone in her voice. "Brad, I sent you a letter. I'm sorry it didn't get to you on time." Mariah sat on Brad's left and put a gentle hand on his shoulder.

After his tears stopped, he decided he was going to say what he intended to when he started out from Plaistow in the morning. Brad stood up and took out his wallet, thick with money. He fanned out a fistful of bills to make his point. "You see, I was gonna pay you a down payment in cash for the place and sell the Dayton place. I was comin' home, but not now," he said, nearly reverting to tears. He appeared to be struggling in his mind to find something good to think about. He turned to his aunt. "Would you like to take a little ride in my new car?"

"I don't think the three of us can fit in that little thing," said Mariah.

Brad started to open his mouth, then thought better of telling his mother she wasn't invited.

"Maybe the next time you're up, you can give me a ride," said Florence. "So what are you going to do now, Brad?"

"I'm still going to sell the place in Plaistow and get a new start. In a while I'll get married again. Edith would want that," he said softly, almost morosely.

"That Chevrolet coupe cost you nearly eight hundred dollars, I understand. Why it won't cost me that much to build the cottage, and that's all it's going to be, just a little two bedroom house, but it will have a nice screened in porch, something I've always wanted. There'll be a room there for you when you decide to come home."

He nodded and managed a weak smile. Small comfort when the invitation was mixed with another one of his mother's implied predictions that he couldn't make it on his own. "Oh," he said, anxious to change the subject. "I almost forgot about the chocolates. Brad went to the car and returned with the box. "Sorry I ain't got a box for you, Aunt Florence, but I didn't know."

Florence smiled wanly and nodded.

"If I can help with the new place, just let me know," he said to his mother.

"You've got your hands full already," Mariah responded. Brad's expression sank lower. His mother was telling him that Ed would build the new place without his help.

Mariah put the boxed pie halves in Brad's unsteady hands. "There's plenty there for the rest of the week—for you and what's her name." Mariah, with a watchful eye on her sister, stepped closer to Brad and touched his arm. "I'm sorry. It's a pretty sad time for all of us."

Brad accepted a rare kiss on the cheek from his mother and welcomed a hug from his aunt. He looked back at the sisters behind the storm door—so much alike now in appearance, but as different as ever beneath the masks of age. He drove out of the yard in his eight-hundred-dollar Chevy coupe with an anxious and heavy heart.

Mariah turned to Florence. "He'll be under my new roof before too long." A weighty sigh and Mariah changed the subject. "You've gotten your letter from Moze by now. I guess we need to talk about the house in Sandwich." The sisters sat down for a second cup of tea.

# CHAPTER 41

## Pistol-Packin' Mama

Ed had put the finishing touches on Mariah's new house just before black fly season set in. The ground was still soggy with spring runoff, the maple trees tinged with red buds waiting for a few days of shirt-sleeve weather to unfurl them into leaves. Yesterday's Easter dinner was silver, linen and crystal at Florence's, the last holiday that Mariah would have to be a guest in another woman's kitchen.

They drove up to the new house with Ed's radio playing "Lullaby of Broadway" and the air still smelling of new lumber and turpentine. With dark green trim against cedar shingles, the cottage looked like a bucolic retreat of one of those fine New York families steeped in Thoreau and socialism and looking forward to a peaceful revolution under Franklin D. Roosevelt.

Ed stopped the car and shut off the radio. He and his mother sat in silence as she took it all in. The last time she came out to see progress, the house was just framed and roofed over. She got out of the Plymouth coupe with her wicker basket with fixings for lunch and walked a little closer. Ed got out and stood just behind her. "So camp's all set up; all you gotta do is build a fire in the cook stove," he said with a touch of humor in his voice.

"Wait a minute. 'Camp?' So you call it a camp? You make it sound like I'm going to live like a roving gypsy. This is no camp. It's a beautiful little house. Just look at that front door," she said as though Ed was just now opening his eyes to his own work. Through a screen door and across the porch was an elegant varnished paneled door with bull's eye glass and sidelights, a grand door fit for a Beacon Hill home. The door faced the Stevens's across the raspberry patch and made a silent statement that another lady of taste was in the neighborhood.

Mariah set her basket down and gave Ed a big hug. "When does my stuff arrive?" she said with an excitement he had not seen in a long time.

"Brad and Dot are coming over from Florence's this afternoon with a truck. They'll help move you in." After a walk through, Ed set up a card table and two folding chairs in the kitchen for his mother who busied herself in lighting a fire in the old cast iron wood stove salvaged from the house fire. The first puffs of smoke rose from the chimney and the house warmed quickly.

Mariah paid for all of the materials up front, and gave Ed twenty dollars a week with his promise that he could build the place in five weeks with Dot's husband Andy as a part-time helper. The money came none too soon. Congress had already voted to repeal the Volstead Act, and the ratification of the twenty-first amendment by three quarters of the states by December was virtually assured. Prohibition—the "noble experiment"—would be history by Christmas of 1933. Corks would pop all over America on New Year's 1934, but for Ed it would not be a time to celebrate. The legalization of liquor was not entirely welcome. He was now working at his aunt's boarding house, an even less welcome topic with his mother.

"So you won't need any help around here till the strawberries come in, is that right?" Ed gathered up remaining tools and paint brushes and put them in a box. Ed, who was twenty-four, dressed and groomed himself like a man who didn't normally do manual labor. He had dark good looks that inspired more than one of his girlfriends to call him Clarke Gable. He wore the same thin moustache.

"June bearers all come within two weeks, so I'll need as many hands as I can get to pick 'em and cook 'em." Mariah's business—Mrs. Taylor's Fine Preserves—nearly went up in smoke with the old farmhouse.

If it hadn't been for the insurance money, she would have had to live on Florence and Harry's charity.

"I don't know how much help Rita and I'll be with strawberries," Ed said without looking up from his brush-cleaning.

Just mentioning Rita's name cooled the kitchen down again. "She couldn't be much less help…"

"Now don't start on her, please, Ma!" Ed knocked over a coffee can with soaking brushes from the previous day's trim painting and some green-tinted turpentine splattered on his shoes. "Look what you made me do. And I was just about to spring our happy news on you." He took the broom out of his mother's hands to get her attention. Despite his mother's sixty-five years, she was as formidable in her bearing as ever.

"Give me that broom, damn it!" she shouted as she wrested it from her son's hand. The marriage to the Irish redhead Rita O'Brien had never set well with Mariah. Vain and temperamental, Rita didn't see why the Depression had to interfere with the lifestyle she ima-gined for herself, and Ed, in his bravado, had promised. She could get into a huff over chipped nail polish when her young husband was working at anything that put bread on the table

"Ma, Ma. Will you listen?" he said imploringly. "I got news, I'm trying to tell you."

Mariah stopped sweeping and looked at him. "All right, I'm listen-ing."

"Rita's pregnant. She's due this fall—mid-November if we counted right."

"I see, well." Mariah went back to sweeping, but with slow swipes of the broom. "That complicates things, now doesn't it?" *Just what I need. A little Catholic who'll grow up thinking her Grandma's going to Hell.* Ed stood silently watching his mother whom he believed had missed nearly every opportunity to smile since her children left home. "'Complicates it'? Is that all you can say, Ma?" with a tone that showed his disappointment without stepping over the line into disrespect. "I know it wasn't any easier for you when you had us, especially when I came along." Ed had learned from Aunt Florence how to play on her guilt.

As if the whole exchange had not taken place, Mariah walked over to the stove where a pot of coffee was percolating at the tempo of Ed's pulse. Mariah took a few deep breaths and said in an even tone, "How 'bout a cup of coffee?"

"Sure," said Ed who sat at the card table where his mother had laid out egg salad sandwiches wrapped in wax paper.

"You did a fine job on the place." She reached into the pocket of her apron and took a tattered envelope containing several bills. She counted out a ten and two fives. "That's for the last week," she said. She pulled out another bill and slid it to him under her palm like a trump card. "Here's something extra for that baby of yours," she said. Mariah took her hand away and Ed looked squarely into the eyes of Ulysses S. Grant.

Ed leaned over and planted a kiss on her cheek. "I haven't seen a fifty-dollar bill in a long time," he said quietly.

"Not since your delivery days, I bet." They both let out a little laugh. "You earned it, son. Your daddy used to think you hated to have to work with your hands. I wish he was here today to see this." Ed couldn't remember when his mother had been so effusive in her praise. She had always loved him, and although she could hardly admit it to herself, she secretly admired his rebel spirit and his reputation as a lady-killer. He was no common farm boy. But the proper townsfolks' label hurt: "unschooled, unskilled and untrustworthy," Neal Coursin had told Ed to his face.

"Just imagine Neal's face if I went up to the store and bought myself a Coca-cola and paid for it with this." Ed smiled and crossed his wiry, veined arms across his chest. He took out his wallet and put the bills in, hiding the fifty under the flap. "I'll be leaving soon, so I won't be seeing Brad and Dot. I expect to see Brad on Decoration Day anyway. He gets all worked up if I don't come to put flowers on Dad's grave." Mariah looked at him over her glasses with pursed lips. *And shouldn't he?*

"I wish you could see his reaction when he sees the place," said Mariah. "Remind me when we're at Coursin's to give him a call. I want him to bring me some day lilies and irises to plant right along there in front of the kitchen where they'll get good sun. Those came from my parents' garden, don't you know?" Mariah's younger brother whom she could not stop calling "Moze" even when his wife Eleanor repeatedly and pointedly addressed him as Amos, had welcomed Mariah to the house once it was opened up and dug up some flowers that would remind her of the home in which she grew up. It was a comfort to Mariah to know that she could go home any time and walk along the banks of Cold River again.

"Ma, let's have that cup of coffee," said Ed, taking his mother's arm. Ed's expression told her he had a piece of gossip that he had some doubts about sharing.

"So now what's Brad up to?"

"Nothing he shouldn't be, I guess. It was just a big surprise, that's all." He laughed at his older brother as he often had occasion to do. "Well, I never thought him capable of it, but he proved me wrong." Ed laughed again with suggestiveness in his tone.

"You don't mean…"

"Yup. Mira's going to have a baby, too."

"Well at least Mira's got a talent for *something*," she scoffed. Little fifteen-year-old scrawny Mira had apparently managed to relieve Brad of his burdensome virginity in addition to most of his inherited cash. "So when is *that* little package likely to arrive?" she asked.

"I'd say October, but I can't get much information out of Brad. Mira really opens up if Brad isn't around, but he keeps a pretty careful eye on her. She's the one to ask."

Mira was a straggle-haired waif who darted about searching for attention and diversion. Any man that looked at her and smiled could ignite an excited response. After years of neglect and occasional abuse, Mira fluttered into others' lives and would alight long enough to suck out the nectar of opportunity while the eyes in the back of her head watched out for the next swat. She was a caged pigeon pecking disks to get rewards and avoid punishments.

"A child raising a child," said Mariah as she went to the stove to refill their cups. "She's lucky to have a roof over her head, especially in these times." The unemployment rate in the country had peaked at twenty-five percent as people waited to see what impact F.D.R.'s whirlwind first hundred days would have on the disastrous economy. Mira was always looking for a new deal, but it wasn't from Franklin Delano Roosevelt.

"I'm afraid there's going to be some bad news about that roof over their heads before too long."

"Oh, God, don't tell me." Mariah's cup came down on the oilcloth-covered table with a thud.

"Well, you can't blame her entirely. Milk prices collapsed. She wants Brad to sell the place."

"She likes having the cash to play with. What else is she after?" asked Mariah who didn't like to admit that she was ever caught off guard with Brad's goings on.

"I think his name is Clifford." Ed pursed his lips and rolled his eyes.

"Clifford who?"

"Clifford who lives in a cabin down the foot of the hill. I guess he has a way with the ladies. Look, I don't know his last name and I don't want to. I think Mira's just waiting to turn the old Dayton farm into cash and then she'll be gone."

"If that's the case, I sure hope she takes the baby. Otherwise Brad is a father at thirty-one and I'm a mother at sixty-five!"

Ed couldn't suppress a laugh. "Ma, nothing about your life has been ordinary."

Mariah walked out onto the porch and listened to the rushing of the mountain stream pouring its bounty into the spring only a few yards from the north end of the house. She closed her eyes and listened again until voices of Cold River came back to her. Mariah had never wanted her life to be ordinary, and , for better or for worse, she had gotten her wish.

Ed joined his mother on the porch and motioned for her to sit in the lone rocking chair that she had managed to pull from the house fire. He sat on one of the sawhorses he drew up beside her chair. "What are you thinking about?"

"I'll need a lot of help this summer." An uncomfortable silence followed. "And I don't know where it's going to come from." All three of her children were married and gone, her house had burned down and she was starting a new life—an aged widow—with no income but what she could earn with her own two hands. The small nest egg from the remaining insurance money would not last over three years. Her business that had started up again, closed down after the fire, and it was more than Mariah could do to resurrect it by herself. Although Mariah had sacrificed much for her children, she knew that she had at times frustrated their dreams and interfered in their lives, especially after George's death. It pained her to realize that all of her children had reason to resent her. She had even tried to kill Ed in the womb, and for all of his life she struggled for ways to make it up to him.

"Look, Ma, there's lots of people in town who'll work for peanuts just to have something coming in. You know that." There was an edge of irritation to his words that he softened with a quick pat on her hand.

"I suppose, but can I trust them?"

"If they don't show up or don't do what you want, then don't pay 'em," said Ed. "That's all there is to it. The only thing you might have to worry about is the person who delivers the merchandise and collects money. But, hell, you know most of the people in town. Don't tell me you can't figure out who you can trust. And I have a feeling Brad will be back home before too long."

Ed was not about to be manipulated. Mariah could not conceal the motivation for her self-pitying appeal for help. Aunt Florence had hired him to work at the boarding house and was providing Rita and him room and board and a good hourly wage. The aura around Mariah's sulking expression was as green with jealousy as the freshly painted trim.

"I can't pass up the money at Aunt Florence's, you know that. And Uncle Harry just bought ten gallons of white lead and oil and he sure isn't going to paint that great big, fancy house of his himself. That's more money for me. Rita and I'll need every dime we can get."

"I see," she said in a huff.

"Don't worry. We'll get you to town when you need. I can help you find a few dependable workers. I got some friends with cars with lots of experience delivering merchandise that need work."

"I can just see it in the *Gazette*. 'Mrs. Taylor Gets Ex-Rum Runners Into Jam.'" Suddenly the ice was broken and Mariah and Ed had a good laugh.

"A year from now, things are gonna be a lot better." Ed got up from the sawhorse and took out a Chesterfield and lit it up. "You'll be making money again, but there's something I heard on the radio that's gonna make life a lot easier. Electricity's coming down Brown's Ridge."

"You don't say."

"Yup. Rural Electrification."

"Just a year away?"

"Ya, Ma. I'll be glad when you have a phone. You've got some money saved up and word gets around. You can trust the banks now, you know. They're insured."

"Now how am I going to run to the bank? I need cash to pay workers," said Mariah who still had a fear of turning over her money to a bank. The fact that Mariah was always home was an inconvenience to robbers who were unlikely to turn to violence, but desperate people might take desperate measures. The camp was shrouded in overhanging trees and backed up to White Horse Ledge. Just a few yards to the south Brown's Ridge Road crested and curved sharply. People could come unnoticed from that direction behind the house through the woods.

"I've got something I want you to have," said Ed who took a drag on the cigarette as he went through the screen door and out to his little coupe on the side of the road. He reached into his glove compartment and took out something wrapped in a white cloth. He came back onto the porch and placed a blue-black .32 snub nose pistol into his mother's hands.

"I hope that damn thing's not loaded," said Mariah who fumbled with it nervously.

"Holy shit, don't drop it! Yes, of course it's loaded. Wouldn't be much good if it wasn't." Ed took the gun from her hand. "I know you've fired rifles, but a pistol's different, so let's practice," he said with a wink.

"Right now?"

"Sure. Who's it gonna bother? The Stevens place is still shut up and Old Man Holt is two miles away." Mariah looked at her son and at the gun, hesitating to move. "Come on. And you carry it. I want you to get used to it." She got out of the chair and headed for the door holding the gun somewhat stiffly out to the side. She was careful not to have her finger on the trigger. Ed picked up a hammer and a few nails from his toolbox and followed her out to the north side of the house. He nailed a scrap piece of ten-inch wide floorboard to a maple tree several yards beyond the spring just where the land started to rise up the ledge.

"Here. Hold it straight out." Ed stood behind her and held her hand steady. "Now close one eye. Center the sight on the board. OK, now, squeeze!"

Bam! The gun kicked up and Ed grabbed it before it fell from his mother's hand to the ground. "God Lord!" shouted Mariah. "I could knock myself out with it."

"It recoils different from a rifle. That's why I want you to practice. Just stay calm and let's try it again." Mariah aimed again and Ed dropped his hand and stepped back with the confidence that his mother would show that .32 who was boss. He was not disappointed. Bam. Bam. Bam! She put three shots into the board at a distance of thirty feet, blowing the corner of it away.

Two sedans coming down Brown's Ridge Road from the north squeaked to a sudden stop just beyond the Stevens place. The driver of the first car got out, shading his eyes from the sun and looking toward the camp.

"Now look what you've done. Gone and scared the hell out of those folks," said Mariah half in irritation, half in pride.

"What's wrong with that? I hope they're local folks so the word'll get around town that Mrs. Taylor has a gun and she knows how to use it." Ed emerged from the cover of trees and brush and motioned the cars on. They proceeded slowly, gawking at the young man standing beside a matronly lady dressed in white who popped off two more shots at the target just for show.

# CHAPTER 42

## The Old Vanity

Mariah buried her face in the luxuriant lilac blossoms, thankful that the bushes had survived the flames of the previous winter. Just beyond the bushes that drooped with copious purple and white blooms were the charred remains of the old farmhouse, and beyond the old barn's cellar hole, Bradley stooped over verdant strawberry plants. Row upon row of plants were loaded with berries just starting to show their color. Although Mariah now had three hired hands, no one had the magical powers with plants that Brad had inherited from his father. The spring air was filled with fragrances of life and Mariah was thankful, thankful for her new home, and thankful that her first-born son had come back to help, even if only for a while.

The distance that had grown between them over the years was largely her own fault, but she didn't know what to do about it. Bradley managed in a small world with a firm hand, but once out in the larger world, he didn't know what to do with freedom. She was the firm hand who had often taken the rudder from her stubborn son and guided his craft away from the shoals just in time to avert disaster. But there were times when Brad needed a tender touch, and Mariah's hands, toughened by years of adversity, had failed her time and again, even when her spirit fought within her to reach out to him in his need.

Lifting a bolt of cheesecloth that she had laid on the ground in front of the lilacs, Mariah walked down the path to the strawberry fields and saw how the plants were all neatly weeded and mulched. The spring rains of had finally given way to two weeks of warm May sun, perfect conditions for a bumper crop for June-bearing plants.

When Brad saw his mother coming with the cheesecloth, his expression turned slightly sour. She thought she was helping him while he thought she was there to tell him what to do. "Don't need that yet," he said with enough curtness to erase the smile from his mother's face.

Mariah held back and didn't comment on his rudeness. "That's fine. I'll leave it to you to decide when we need to…"

"Not til the berries show more red than white," he said with a lecturing tone. "The birds don't start in peckin' at 'em till they've got some smell to 'em and they're soft and sweet." Brad looked down at the plants and his face softened with the love that he had for plants and animals.

Although Mariah was well aware when berries needed to be covered, she said, "I trust your judgment," and told her son that she would leave the cheesecloth out on the porch where he could find it when he needed it.

Brad looked up, puzzled by his mother's restraint. He had expected her to respond as she usually did. As she often had said to him, "If I give you an inch, you take a mile," but strangely enough, she had given him more than an inch.

Mariah left Brad to his work and returned to the lilacs. She took a pair of sheers out of her apron pocket and started cutting until she had a big bundle, first of purple and then of white.

She smelled the blossoms again. This May 30 was the warmest and most beautiful Decoration Day she could remember since the nation had started honoring the war dead after the Great War by decorating their graves. As the years went on, more and more people began marking the day as a time to decorate the graves of all loved ones. Mariah would honor her parents and the father of her children by dressing herself up as well as dressing up their stones with an abundance of homegrown flowers. She remembered the day when her parents gave her the plants from the banks of Cold River where they grew in profusion. Her father had helped George dig them up and bundle them in burlap for their ride to Brown's Ridge Road where they had flourished as a sign of her parents' continued presence in her life.

Once inside, she tied the lilacs in mixed arrangements and put them in water-filled crockery jugs. The wall clock reminded her that Ed would arrive in less than half and hour. They would all go to the cemetery together and have a picnic lunch near Cold River.

The new pastel lavender dress was her first dressy outfit in quite some time, but when she sat at the vanity, she was reminded by the reflection that there was nothing she could do to bring back the beauty she had once seen in the mirror. Will had purchased the vanity for her when they moved into the house on Wakefield Street. She had given it to her mother when she went to Iowa, but it had remained out in her parents' shed for years and eventually forgotten. When Dotty found it there, she insisted that Bradley clean it up and move it into their mother's new home. Sitting next to a lonely perfume bottle, a brush and a comb were pictures of her three children taken shortly before George died. On the right stood a photo of George dressed in his Sunday best out in front of the house that now lay in charred ruins across the road. The left side of the vanity was an empty slab of marble where a wedding photo once stood—a photo of Will with his arm around her waist.

Mariah ran the comb through her hair a few times and set it down. She picked up George's picture and could not stop the tears. *I'm sorry I dragged you back here. I was only thinking of myself. You weren't even home when your mother died. I hurt you time and again, I know.*

But she could smell the fragrance of the lilacs wafting through the house, and looked at the photo of her children. *I can't feel sorry about everything,* she thought. They had the children, the farm, and a business that had turned successful. Although Mariah often felt punished for her lofty dreams and her desire to steer her own course, she refused to feel guilt for hopes and aspirations that all human beings—women as well as men—had a right to. We were all made in God's image, she thought, and that image wasn't the tired old body that looked back at her in the mirror, but a person who was more than flesh and blood, gender and station, bound by time and place.

Mariah remembered the wedding photo from 1883 and went to

the bookcase to see if she could locate it. Dusty volumes from her childhood, some worm-eaten, had been moved from place to place from Sandwich to Rochester to Iowa and back. Newer books often went to family, but some meant too much to lose. *Maybe Tennyson,* thought Mariah as she fanned through books one by one, raising a cloud of dust. Suddenly she remembered the Emerson essays where she had once hidden the picture at the beginning of the essay "Self-Reliance." She smiled at the thought of her youthful exuberance for Emerson and ran her hand along the old leather-bound books until she found old Waldo's name in faded golden letters. *There.* She opened to the famous essay and found nothing. Her heart sank. She fanned the rest of the book. She shook it. Nothing. *It's the only picture I have.* Brad and Dot had moved her things here, but she couldn't ask them if they had found the photo. Mariah had never mentioned it to them and wouldn't even want to admit that she had saved it, especially to Bradley who knew how much that photo had pained his father. She felt the tears coming, but held out hope that maybe her memory had failed her. After looking through several more books, she finally picked up Longfellow's poems, another old favorite. She could see that there were three markers. Surely one of them was the wedding photo. The first was an old bookmark with a pen and ink sketch of a lady of fashion. She remembered making that when she was still in school and smiled at the sparkles she had drawn around a jeweled hairpin. *Diamonds.* And she thought of the vanity that filled her girlhood dreams and the only power that girls of her era possessed—their looks. Then she felt the thick edge of the next marker and knew it had to be a photo. When she opened the book, her heart was wrenched with pain and she gasped. The wedding photo had been torn in half. She stood alone with only Will's right hand visible around her waist. She flipped to the last marker hoping that it was the other half, but was disappointed to find that it was only an old business card from Meader Realty, the man who had sold Will and her the Wakefield Street house. The only picture that remained to testify to her youthful dreams and the beauty of the two young lovers had been destroyed. And the worst was that it could not have been an accident. It had to have been the vengeful act of her elder son expressing in a secret act years of unspoken grievances that had built up in his heart.

Mariah could do nothing at the moment but grieve. She had to go through the loss of Will once again, and yet she felt the guilt that her conscious attachment to him had driven a wedge between George and her and she had not worked hard enough to remove. George had died without hearing his wife pour out a contrite heart and without an expression of appreciation for all he sacrificed to bring her home. Her love for him was not exclusive, and he had resigned himself to the ghostly presence of Will Dunfield even after the handsome figure in flesh and blood had returned to the dust from which all flesh—common or exalted—is made.

As she looked at the torn photo through a prism of tears, she heard Ed's voice at the door. Before she could collect herself, he was looking at her anguished reflection in the mirror and at the torn picture in her hand.

"Oh, my God!" he blurted angrily. "I know who did that." Ed started for the door with one hand already made into a fist.

"No, no, don't do that!" Mariah implored. "You sit down for a minute," she said. "She dried her eyes and asked him to calm down. "You know that I never let Will go and I should have. That hurt your father, and since he died, I've never talked this through with your brother—with any of you, for that matter. Please. Just go get him. Ask him to come see me." She put her hand on Ed's cheek and tried to smile. "And would you wait out in the car for a little while?"

After a moment of intense struggle with his instincts, Ed complied, and Brad came into his mother's room. His eyes widened when he saw the torn photo. He looked at his mother with fear of an outburst. Instead of the expected anger, his mother asked him to sit on the bed beside her. She took his hand in hers and prayed for forgiveness from him and from God for love withheld, for words unspoken, for wounds that remained unhealed.

"I don't even expect you to forgive me, but maybe someday you will. As to this, I deserve worse." She got up and put the torn photo back in the book and closed it.

By then Brad was crying. "I'm sorry I did it," he said, but he couldn't bring himself to touch her until she came across the room and patted his hand.

After what seemed like hours, Ed saw them coming out of the house loaded down with lilacs and a picnic basket, but looking composed. He helped his mother into the car in silence. As they drove to the cemetery, Mariah asked Ed to turn on the radio and they drove without speaking until they came to a stop not far from the family plot. The marble stone was marked with Brandon on one side and Taylor on the other. Ed found it disconcerting to see his mother's name carved below his father's with her year of birth followed after a dash by an empty space.

Brad dug a hole on the Brandon side as his mother touched the carved names of Amos Brandon who had lain in that spot for over three decades, but whose face and voice came to Mariah's mind as fresh as the currents of Cold River. And she touched her mother's name and thought with a wry smile of the children's baptism day and how much she owed both of her parents, even though they had failed her at times, just as she had sometimes failed her loved ones.

At last the graves were decorated, but Mariah turned to see Brad holding a few lilacs that he had saved from the bundle. She and Ed gave him a puzzled look. "These are for Will," Brad said with his eyes averted.

When she hesitated, Ed gave her a nudge. "Go on. It's only right," he said. He and his brother watched as Mariah walked the hundred-foot distance between her two husbands and rested the bouquet in front of the lonely stone, one of the few left undecorated on the day of remembrance. When his mother stood up, Ed went to her. "Now let's go eat and listen to the river."

# CHAPTER 43

## *Blind Date*

*B*rad had taken the second bedroom at the camp soon after his divorce from Mira became final. His daughter Angeline's first birthday followed a few days later near the end of October. There was no more work to be done for the season with Mrs. Taylor's Fine Preserves, so Mariah got Brad a job at the Gulf Service Station on the north side of Center Ossipee square. Neal Coursin promised to keep an eye on him by day, and Mariah kept track of him by night. Brad saw very little of Angeline and even less of Mira. He would like to have gotten a bead on Clifford, in ambush, but would never have had the courage to challenge him to his face. A year had passed and Brad had a new lady friend, and this time, not a woman with a roving eye. In fact, Brad's new love interest was blind.

Vivian lived in Sanbornville, a town thirty miles south of Ossipee. Her parents ran an old inn near the Boston and Maine Railroad station. They kept Vivian busy in the kitchen where she had learned to do dishes, sort and fold linens and do many other tasks that did not require eyesight to accomplish. Vivian was thirty years old and had never had a boyfriend until she met Brad Taylor at his mother's booth at the Sandwich Fair on Columbus Day. Vivian fairly glowed with the attention, and that made Brad feel good.

Brad made the mistake of mentioning Vivian to the other men at Leighton's Gulf Station. One Friday night he asked to leave early to get himself cleaned up for dinner at the inn. When Mr. Leighton left the station for a few minutes to go over to chew the fat with Neal Coursin, the foul-mouthed grease monkey, Bernie McGee, got onto Brad's back. Bernie was a tough, muscular dirty blond lad who was proud of his endowments and none of them were cerebral. He had knocked up a Wakefield girl from a family with not enough money to send her away for the duration, and he refused to marry her. In his meanness he blamed her condition on the high school football team's victory party. He got a job in Ossipee where his reputation had not preceded him.

"So, Bradley, does your little Vivian have to feel around for your tools?"

"You shut your dirty mouth," replied Brad with his face turned away. Bernie moved two inches away from his face and slowly raised a big fist. Brad went silent and accepted the abuse that would continue as long as Mr. Leighton chewed the fat across the square.

"So," said Bernie, who reminded Brad of the German heavyweight champion Max Schmieling, "you got a blind date tonight?" Brad refused to answer.

"Well, you got a date, and your date's blind, so that adds up to a blind date, now don't it?" said Bernie who snapped Brad's nose with his finger. Although Brad was thirty-three years old and taller than Bernie, he had the hangdog look that attracted bullies.

"You goin' down and shackin' up somewhere?" asked Bernie. Brad didn't answer. "You said to Mr. Leighton you was thinkin' of stayin' overnight."

"I'm thinking of staying overnight, but my mother's going down to meet Vivian's folks." Brad had asked his mother, but she hadn't actually said yes. When Brad heard the bell ring for a gas customer, he happily answered the call. He spent extra time washing the windshield and checking the oil of the sleek new DeSoto sedan.

He stalled for as long as he could; finally he saw Mr. Leighton crossing the square. It was nearly five o'clock, already dark, and the lamps over the two pumps cast small circles of light on the ground.

The gasoline ran through the glass bulb on top of the pump, and a little propeller spun inside. At nineteen cents a gallon, the full tank rang up at two dollars and forty-seven cents. Brad took the three dollars into the office and quickly did the math on paper that he never trusted doing in his head.

Bernie was humming the new hit tune, "I'm in the Mood for Love." He broke it off early to help Brad with the math. "Fifty-three cents, you moron!" said Bernie who could see the final sale on the pump.

Brad ignored him, but was pleased that he had counted out the correct change.

Mr. Leighton made some small talk about Brad's mother and how well she had done in the summer season. Leighton respected Mariah Taylor as a widow who had learned to make a respectable living by her own hand, and he was willing to give her son a job for the off season even if he wasn't the quickest wit he'd met. Bernie hung around like the Cheshire cat, quiet and respectful to Mr. Leighton. "Good night, Sir. See you Monday. Have a nice evening, Bradley," he said. "What time are you heading out for the evening?"

"Soon as I get changed," said Brad coldly and without turning to look at Bernie who was being the ultimate phony gentleman for the boss's benefit.

"Your Mama keeps you real tidy, now don't she, Bradley?" said Bernie as another taunt.

Brad got his coat and hat on and kept quiet. Mr. Leighton shut off the lights on the big, round orange and blue Gulf sign, and the two lamps over the pumps, closed the door and locked the place up for the weekend. It was the slow time of year.

Things weren't moving so slowly elsewhere in the world. Mussolini had invaded Ethiopia, the Japanese had begun their inroads into China, and Hitler was preparing to show off the "super race" at the Berlin Olympics. The Federal government was putting Americans back to work through the W.P.A. and the C.C.C. and all kinds of public works from the Tennessee Valley Authority to the Golden Gate Bridge. The recovery was slow, and people begged for jobs. The alphabet agencies put money into people's pockets without the humiliation of "relief."

Mr. Leighton, like Mariah Taylor, expected people to work if they expected to eat. He handed Brad and Bernie their pay envelopes and sent them on their way.

November 12, 1935. Twenty-five cents an hour for forty honest hours of work. An hour's work for a pound of coffee; an hour for three loaves of bread. Bringing home the bacon took an hour and a half a pound. A one-bedroom apartment cost five dollars a week. All the money Brad and Bernie had to their names was in those thin envelopes. Brad was impressed to think that his mother's Schrafft's box was filling up again with the sweet profits from her fine preserves. Unfortunately for his mother, Brad had done some bragging about the candy box around Leighton's Gulf.

Brad pulled off his black and red checked cap as soon as he came in the door. He tucked the earflaps back inside and hung his hat and coat on a peg. Surprised by the smell of pork and beans baking, he called to his mother who was nowhere to be seen. In a moment she came in the back door carrying a flashlight she needed to guide her steps down the hill from the outhouse.

"What's this?" said Brad, upset and surprised by the sight of a meal ready to eat.

"It's supper, what do you think it is?" Mariah retorted.

"Don't you remember?" said Brad, his bottom lip beginning to quiver.

"Remember what?"

"You was goin' with me down to Sanbornville to meet Vivian's folks."

Mariah held a wooden spoon in one hand; the other rested on her hip. "But Brad, I never said I was going. You asked, but you never waited for an answer. I don't think it's a good idea courting a blind girl. That would be a big responsibility for you. You could get yourself into another fix and I just got you out of the last one," she said with a definitive puff of air and then went to stir the beans.

Sitting at the kitchen table, he started to blubber. "How am I gonna call her now? T'aint a phone I can get to in three miles." Mariah finally broke down and came over to rub his shoulder. "There, there, Bradley. You go right along if you want, but you think about what I said." She went back to her beans. He wasn't very clever about making up excuses for other people, but he'd had plenty of time on the road to think of something to explain his mother's absence since he seldom went over twenty-five miles an hour even on the best straightaways. "Well, I'm sorry, Brad, and I hope you have a nice visit anyway," Mariah added.

After Brad left, Mariah sat up until eight reading Fitzgerald's latest novel, but the flickering kerosene lamp strained her eyes. Rural electrification hadn't made it through Congress yet. It seemed to Mariah that she would never live to see country life change. When she married Will in 1883, she moved into a downtown apartment with gaslights, steam heat and indoor plumbing. She had electricity before she was twenty years old. Fifty-two years had passed and she was yet to enjoy the luxuries she knew as a young woman. She might die before she caught up to the lifestyle she had enjoyed a half century ago.

Mariah carried the lamp into the kitchen and loaded the woodstove for the night, closing down dampers to save coals for the morning. The moon was full, but heavy clouds were streaming across the sky from the west and the temperature dropped noticeably. "Maybe a little snow," Mariah said to herself as she shone her flashlight under her bed. Everything was in order. Her .32 was right within reach next to the Schrafft's candy tin and her bedpan was at the other end of the bed close to the outside leg. Mariah had been especially tired of late, tired and thirsty and light-headed. She wondered if her heart was weakening. She dreaded trips to the outhouse in the middle of the night.

Not more than an hour later when the bed was warm and the room had cooled down, she heard a sound at the back of the house. Twigs breaking, scratching. Not the sound of mice or squirrels, but something bigger. *Damn coon. Can't just scare it off. Brad isn't here to shoot the damn thing, so I'll have to do it myself.* Just as she threw back the covers and started to sit up, the rustling sound stopped. She pulled the covers back over herself and closed her eyes, hoping the critter was gone for good.

The wind rattled branches against the windows, and the gritty sound of wind-driven snow added to the disturbance of her sleep. A heavy thud against the back door, and another. Mariah's heart raced. Had she locked the door? Brad always locked every door and every window, but Mariah didn't live with his fears. She had lived alone after

Brad's first marriage in the old rambling rattletrap of a place with ten rooms and chunks of plaster dropping from ceilings. Mice scurried through the walls. It may have been a blessing that Brad didn't clean the chimney and the old place had gone up in smoke. Mariah was glad that she had much less to bother with. Her bones ached in the cold, and her ankles swelled when she spent long hours standing at the stove. She had enough to worry about with the four rooms she had.

Suddenly an explosion of glass. No animal but a bear could do that, but bears were already hibernating. Her feet touched the cold floor and she grabbed the pistol and the flashlight. In a frightening crash the back door flew open and Mariah saw light coming from under the bedroom door. She heard mumbled words between two men. No need to attract their attention with her flashlight. They either didn't know she was in the house, or they didn't care. In a second they would be through the door. Could she handle two men, armed or not, miles from any help? If she didn't shoot them, what would she do with them until daylight?

Mariah threw the flashlight on the bed, held the pistol with both hands, and aimed for the middle of the door. As soon as it started to open, she fired.

A scream was followed by a string of obscenities as she heard two men—young by the sound of their voices—stumbling over one another out the door and down the steps. They had shut off their flashlights to avoid making themselves easy marks.

Mariah's blood was up. Now that she was over her initial fear, she didn't want the bastards who had broken into her house to get away. She felt around for her flashlight and turned it on. As fast as she could, she went to the bedroom door and opened it. There was a trail of blood on the floor leading to the open outside door and running down the steps. They were thrashing through the woods and she followed a short distance and let off another round to make sure they knew she was in pursuit. She stumbled on slippery ledge as the land rose. A car started and tires squealed. Mariah wanted to see the car, even get the license number, but she feared that she might break a leg and die in the cold if she tried to run. But it didn't matter now. She had her moment of triumph over two robbers who lost to an old lady brave enough to shoot at two intruders.

Mariah was in slippers and had no gloves. The gun was still warm as she held it between her hands, prostrate on the ground. In a moment she got herself to her feet and picked up the flashlight. Feeling dizzy with a ringing in her ears, she made her way back to the camp.

The house was cold. Mariah opened the dampers on the cook stove and threw on more wood while she contemplated how to keep the cold air out. In her winter coat and hat, she swept up broken glass and searched for a hammer and nails. A spare blanket from the foot of her bed would do to cover the broken door glass. She folded it into quarters and nailed it over the shattered opening. When she was done, she marked her calendar with the time. As the fire warded off the chill, she thought through the details of the story she would tell her family and the police.

Through the night she sat by the woodstove, comforted by a pot of coffee, a good book, and a .32 caliber pistol sitting on the table. She wanted to be awake in case the bad boys came back.

# CHAPTER 44

## Cops and Robbers

The next morning was gusty, clear and cold with a thin shroud of fine snow coating the roads. By ten o'clock Brad had reached the southern end of Brown's Ridge Road. Since he was afraid to go over twenty-five miles an hour, he couldn't get his battered 1923 Essex sedan up the steep hill just beyond Old Man Holt's place. He rolled out a set of rusty tire chains in front of the rear wheels and pulled them over the cracked, bald tires.

He thought longingly of the beautiful Chevy coupe he had to sell to get rid of Mira. How he regretted getting involved with her. By the time she was done with him, he didn't have much left. It galled him that once again his mother had been right. And when Vivian's parents found out that Brad had been married twice before, they told him that it would be best if he didn't see Vivian again. He hated to face his mother with the news.

Just as he started up again, a State of New Hampshire highway crew passed in a dump truck with high sides and a tarpaulin stretched over the top. Two men stood in the back flinging shovelfuls of sand over the road. Near the crest of the hill at White Horse Ledge Brad saw tracks of a car that had apparently slid off the pavement and managed to get out of the ditch and back on its way. "Damned fools," he said under his breath, his dark brow rising and falling with disgust.

Brad followed the truck up the last steep incline. Finally safe at home, he drove onto the gravel and loosened his white-knuckle grip on the steering wheel. There were no footprints in the snow from the kitchen to the spring, a morning trek for water his mother always insisted on making herself. He looked up at the chimney—which he called a "chimley"—and saw only a bare wisp of smoke. Something had upset his mother's routine. Anticipating an "I-told-you-so" about Vivian, he hung his head as he approached the door.

*Still locked?* Brad looked through the lace curtain covering the kitchen door glass and saw his mother lying on the floor near the table. "Oh my God!" he shouted as he fumbled with his keys, dropping them on the steps, pulling his gloves off, fumbling again.

At last he swung the door open, and knelt to feel his mother's head. She was still warm, but breathing shallowly. On the table lay her pistol, a calendar, and a coffee cup. A book had fallen open on the floor near the stove. Brad froze in shock. He didn't have time to figure anything out because he heard the deep, brassy sound of Clyde Davis's horn at the mailbox. Brad rushed out and begged Clyde to help him. "Inside, Clyde. It's my mother!" Clyde gulped and straightened his bowtie. He left his Studebaker station wagon running and turned on the lights since he was still partly in the roadway.

Clyde took charge. Mariah Taylor hadn't shot herself or been shot, but there were only three live cartridges left in the gun. He dispatched Brad to the bedroom to get a blanket to wrap his mother in for the trip to the hospital. The mail on the south end of the ridge would have to wait.

"Jumped up Mike!" shouted Brad from the bedroom. "Come see this." Clyde moved with dispatch, but as usual, always under control. "Two bullet holes through the door."

Clyde looked up close and noted that the bullets had been fired from inside the bedroom. Brad was breathing so loudly that it finally unsettled the normally unflappable Clyde. "Now Brad, you set yourself down on that bed and collect yourself. We'll get your mother to Huggins in no time 't all."

Before Brad sat down, he looked under the bed and found the

Schrafft's box. He opened it and snapped it shut with his back turned toward Clyde, muttering under his breath, "Thank God."

Clyde opened the rear bedroom door. His eyes widened when he saw the blood and the broken glass, but he quickly figured out that Mrs. Taylor had driven off an intruder and was in good enough condition to cover the broken door glass and get herself back into the kitchen. He started to close the door to avoid agitating Brad further. He was too late.

"Oh, my God!" Brad shouted again. "Someone's been shot!"

"Yes, Brad, and it appears your mother did the shootin'. Now let's get her into the Studebaker. Get that blanket," he said, pointing to Mariah's rumpled bed, "and let's get movin'," said Clyde with a take-charge tone.

In the back of Davis's station wagon, Mariah was surrounded with U.S. mail, "out" up the left and "in" down the right. So much like the day his grandmother fell dead from her buggy, Brad thought. He sat on a tool chest behind the driver's seat with his knees almost chest high clutching the Schrafft's candy tin in a pillowcase. Brad was a lanky six-footer, but like his father, his height was mostly in his legs. His long arms ending in large hands gave him the appearance of Boris Karloff minus the Frankenstein scars and head bolts.

The station wagon swerved on some corners, and on the straight runs, Clyde pushed it up to forty, making Brad fear for his own life and forgetting for the moment about his mother's. Clyde pulled up in front of Coursin's and honked repeatedly until Neal rushed out.

"What's all the racket for?" scolded Neal who was still in his blood-stained butchering apron. "Is that you back there, Brad? Car trouble? What's that you got in there?" he asked, his eyes blinded by the sun.

"It's Mrs. Taylor," said Clyde. "Brad found her unconscious on the floor."

"Oh, no," said Neal. Coursin pushed back a thin covering of hair over his bald spot unstuck by a gust. "Is she going to be all right?"

"She's breathing, that's all I can say. Now I need you to call Huggins Hospital and let Dr. Douglas know we're comin'. Call her sister Florence, and she can find Ed. And call the police."

"The police?" said Coursin, his jaw dropping and his eyes widening.

"Yes, the police. Someone broke into her house last night and she fired two shots. Whoever it was got hit. We don't know how bad, but he left some blood behind. She's got a .32 caliber. Get the cops over there before the sun melts any tracks out behind the place.

The ride to Wolfeboro was a test of Mariah's heart, Brad's stomach, and Clyde's nerves. He was nearly as cautious a driver as Brad under normal circumstances, but when duty called, he could put the pedal to the floorboards. Within the hour Mariah was in room two fifteen with a clear view of her sister's guesthouse across the street, its huge elms glistening with a coat of ice and snow.

Mariah opened her eyes to see Brad sitting on a chair to her left and Ed holding her hand standing on the right. Florence looked down upon her with an expression of Christian compassion on her dignified, matronly face. Mariah realized that the ravages of age did not escape even those whose life circumstances were far easier than her own. She was amazed that she was thinking such trivial thoughts after the traumatic events of the night.

"You'll need a few days' rest," said Florence reassuringly, "and Dr. Douglas will get you on some medicines that will make you a lot better."

"A few days?" Mariah snorted. "I can't afford to be in here one night, and I gotta get to the police right away."

"The police are already over there, Ma," said Ed.

Mariah had stiffened her back and tried to sit up, but she didn't have the strength. "Well I ought to be there to tell 'em what happened."

"I got the candy tin," said Brad as though that was the most important matter to be handled.

"That money's been counted. I just want you all to know." Everyone laughed except Brad who took the remark personally. It was one of Brad's rare moments of insight.

"The police are coming over here before too long to get a report from you," said Florence who assumed the role of the lady of standing in the community to whom police, doctors, and other officials deferred.

"Ma, I bet you're glad I gave you a few lessons with that .32," said

352

Ed who glanced at his aunt with a look that implied that he had pre-empted her in importance in the situation.

"From what we heard from Clyde, you must have hit the bastard..." With a glare from Aunt Florence, Ed edited his remarks. "You must a hit the fella in the upper body. Not his head, not the heart, but you got him."

"Sorry I didn't get 'em both. There were two of 'em, both young. I fired two shots and I heard a scream, but only from one of 'em. You've never heard so many cuss words..." Mariah stopped to get her breath and looked up at Ed.

"Well, I suppose *you* have," said Mariah with a clearly audible whisper. Ed laughed heartily, Florence laughed uncomfortably. Brad snorted.

A nurse came in, starched and neat with her cap bearing two blue stripes, the only color in the entire room of white except for her rosy lips and cheeks. Ed smiled at the pretty nurse and made a remark about wishing he was confined to a hospital bed for a few days. His aunt cleared her throat to bring Ed's remark to an abrupt close. The nurse touched Mariah's arm and told her sweetly that Dr. Douglas would be in to go over her new diet and to start her on her medicines.

"He hasn't even told me what's wrong with me," she said tartly.

"I'll leave that to him, Ma'am," said the nurse who nodded to each of the relatives as she left, her last nod and longest glance reserved for the son with the Clarke Gable moustache.

Dr. Douglas came in and took the clipboard off the foot rail of the bed. He gave Mariah a quick clinical diagnosis, and a set of stern new rules Mariah would have to live by. He wanted the relatives to hear because he knew Mariah's distain for modern medicine and her confidence that her own will could triumph over the failings of the body.

"Now I *know* you're not a Christian Scientist," he said. "But don't get me wrong, Mrs. Taylor. The will to overcome illness is a powerful tool, and I would never discount the value of prayer."

"I pray with my eyes open," replied Mariah.

"All the better to see prayers answered," said Florence with a gentle smile.

"And to duck from the slings and arrows of outrageous fortune," added Mariah with a touch of hardness in her voice. "So good doctor, what is wrong with me that I don't know already?"

The doctor described in plain English what congestive heart failure was doing to Mariah's body. The right side of her heart was more efficient than the left. She had swelling in her legs and some inflammation of her liver. The right side was stronger, yet still compromised, and she had fluid in her lungs causing breathlessness. "Especially when you exert yourself to excess," the doctor noted.

"Such as last night?" Mariah added with a sly smile.

"Such as last night," said Dr. Douglas who allowed his lips a little flexibility.

He prescribed digitalis and diuretics and told Mariah to get rid of the saltshaker. Then the doctor let the other shoe drop. Mariah had developed diabetes mellitus. Her diet would have to control her sugar, and if she could not do so, she would end up having to inject herself with insulin every day. Brad almost fainted. Testing, diet, maintaining proper levels. All of it would be difficult, and if she could regulate her insulin with a strict diet, she might avoid the necessity of taking the shots.

Mrs. Taylor's Fine Preserves was built on a pillars of salt and a tower of sugar. Jams and jellies, pies and relishes. Sugar had made her business thrive. Sugar was like an old friend that one could never sacrifice for a selfish thing like one's own health. Mariah pouted and rolled her eyes through the entire litany of the new regimen she would have to observe.

At last the medical lecture was done. Dr. Douglas suggested that the family leave the room for a while to let Mrs. Taylor rest and think about what he had said. The doctor also wanted an opportunity to talk to the family in confidence about how critical the danger was to Mariah's life.

At age sixty-seven Mariah was to turn over a new leaf, tighten her dietary belt, sacrifice, and go without. All of the years since she left the warm embrace of Will Dunfield in the comforts of their steam-heated bedroom, Mariah felt that she had done penance for her sins and the sins of others. She had done hard labor, sacrificed and bowed to her duty. The last words she wanted to hear were the virtues of going without.

*How can I work with pounds of sugar every day and not eat it? My name is on the jars and pastry boxes. I have built my business with an iron will, elbow grease and sugar, and now this doctor is telling me to go without the sugar?*

Her sunken spirits were suddenly lifted when her daughter Dot and her six-year old granddaughter Susan came into the room. Susan, raven-haired like her mother and her grandmother in her youth, stood at the bedside with a warm smile. Her dark eyes and striking brows were a picture of the child Mariah, all the beautiful exuberance for life Mariah had once known radiated through the eyes of that child. "Let me kiss that beautiful face," said Mariah, struggling not to cry.

"I brought you a box of chocolates, but the nurse said you couldn't have any."

"Oh?" said Mariah. "Where are they?"

"Not on your life," said Dot, wagging a finger in her mother's face. "They told me everything out there before we came in."

"I asked for one," said Susan with an impish smile, then added a whisper in her grand-mother's ear: "but I didn't eat it." Susan was so adorable and sparkly that Dot allowed the chocolate to move by sleight of hand from Susan to her grandmother and into Mariah's mouth.

"You are an angel from heaven, my dear," said Mariah, patting Susan's cheek. "Much nicer than your mother," she said with a wink.

"Tell me all about the robbers, Grandma," asked Susan who bubbled with excitement and rubbed her hands together. "I heard you shot one of them." Then her smile disappeared as she switched her point of view. "I hope he didn't die."

"No, he didn't die, but I can't say I didn't try to kill him. It was kill or be killed, I thought as they broke down the door and smashed the glass," Mariah said, reciting the words like a Saturday morning cowboy serial that she would happily act out if the nurse would let her out of the bed.

Dot proceeded to urge her mother to be good. Mariah told Dot that sometimes she reminded her of her mother. Sarah Brandon indeed. Even though Dot's coloring was inherited from the dark Brandons and not the fair Sanborns, she had the serious, no-monkey-business personality of her grandmother. Dot had given into her wild side in her teen years, but when she had a child to care for, somethin her profoundly changed. She was fair, but strict. Her devil-may-care husband Andy gave her the nickname "Grunch," to mock her tendency to take life too seriously, but he valued his life too much to call her "Grunch" to her face.

"Now no more of this medical nonsense. Let me get back to my story," said Mariah. Her face lighted up at the prospect of telling her daughter of the night's terrifying event as a story that would go down in family lore with all the dramatic embellishments of legend or myth. Just as she was thinking where to begin, the nurse reappeared.

"Excuse me, Mrs. Taylor, but there are two police officers here. It looks like you're feeling well enough to speak to them," she said with a smile.

"You bet I am," said Mariah. "Crank me up straighter, dear," she said with a touch of gruffness that she seemed to adopt in preparation for telling the story from an adult point of view. The nurse bent down at the end of the bed and turned the left crank until the head of the bed brought her patient to a sitting position.

The two officers came in, excused themselves, and explained that the family could not be present while they took down Mrs. Taylor's story. Susan curled out her bottom lip. When her grandmother reassured her that she would hear the story soon, the usual charming radiance returned. The taller officer closed the door and began simply by asking, "Can you tell me what happened?"

She couldn't identify the young men except possibly by voice. One was much bigger than the other. "Fair haired and solidly built, I'd say, just seeing him from behind through the woods. The other looked small and thin, darker." The police told her they had taken her gun as a piece of evidence. "What am I going to do without it?" she complained. She had grown attached to her .32.

The police had the tires identified, and thought they might be able to track down the "getaway car" as they called it. They were just starting the investigation, but the lack of any useful description might make it harder to catch the culprits.

"Who do you need to crack this case, J. Edgar Hoover himself?" said Mariah with a mock snarl.

The nurse knocked on the door after the police had been in the room for twenty minutes or so, and the officers were beckoned into the hall. It seemed that a couple from over on the Moulton-borough Road had brought in their son last night with a gunshot wound in his shoulder. "The story goes," said Dr. Douglas, relating the report from a colleague in surgery, "this lad was with a friend. They got fooling around with a pistol and it accidentally went off," so they took out the bullet and lathered him up with iodine." The retrieved bullet was a .32 caliber. The boy had been dropped off at his parents' house, and his friend with the car sped away. They expected to get his name before the day was over.

Mariah was about to nod off when Dot and Susan came back in, kissed Grandma, and told her they had planned to leave for home, but it appeared there was a break in the case. The family rotated visits by twos. The hospital was strict, but not so strict that they didn't allow the adorable granddaughter in to cheer up a patient who had been through an ordeal.

Ed and his Aunt Florence came in with exciting news. Ed knew the young man with the bullet wound from some run-ins with local toughs a few years before. He also knew his burly, fair-haired, fair weather friend who dumped his wounded friend at his doorstep and fled.

Florence kissed Mariah's forehead and excused herself to get home to feed Harry. Brad and Ed resumed their places on the left and the right. After Mariah fell asleep, Ed whispered to Brad, "I think you better tell Mr. Leighton he's gonna need another grease monkey come Monday."

Brad mouth dropped open. You mean Bernie's the one...?"

Ed nodded. Brad smiled with satisfaction.

# CHAPTER 45

## *Sweet Sacrifice*

*D*ot and her two girls topped off their tin buckets with the last plump blueberries of the season. In the kitchen they poured all of their berries into one large pan and placed it on the scales. The yield for the summer of 1943 was not Mariah's best, and with war rations on sugar, there would be no more blueberry jam for the year. Clouds billowed inside and out as the pots boiled and a dark thunderhead obscured the sun in the western sky. Dot counted the seconds between flashes and distant thunder as she stirred the last of the berries into the pot.

"Mother, you better shut off that radio," said Dot who had come up from Massachusetts to help her mother get in the berry harvest. With the war on, help was hard to find. Even young women were lining up for jobs at the Portsmouth Navy Yard where ten thousand workers were launching more than a sub a month. Picking berries wasn't a wartime priority for anyone but the Taylors.

"Don't touch that dial," Mariah commanded.

" 'The Guiding Light' could be lightning any minute. I don't want to be fried just so you can hear the end of your soap opera," snarled Dot.

"A thousand one, a thousand two, a thousand three." Mariah counted out loud between lightning and thunder and pronounced it safe to hear the finale of Reverend Matthews' sermon on "lust of the eyes."

The minister's lamp guided another young woman from the edge of moral depravity just in the nick of time. Cracks and flashes penetrated the camp, and little Jane began to cry. Susan held her six-year-old sister on her lap, and stroked her long dark hair. The sky was a battlefield of celestial explosions and groanings. Still there was no rain.

When the organ theme music and the commercial for Dreft detergent signaled the end of the half hour, Mariah snapped off the radio to her daughter's great relief. "Oh, don't get all worked up about that storm. It's going to be all show and no go. It'll blow over," said Mariah with total confidence in her predictions. "Now, let's see what we have here," as she looked at the scales through her bifocals. "Six and a half pounds."

She lifted the lid off her canister of sugar to show how little she had left to finish the last batch of preserves. "The ration board won't raise my allotment," complained Mariah about the Carroll County board's arbitrary attitude. "They say I'm not a business because I don't have any papers. I showed 'em my papers," she snorted with a sarcastic laugh as she held up a handful of jar labels.

"Ma, I brought a couple of pounds of sugar just in case," said Dot who had been saving up her rations.

"You're a godsend," said Mariah delightedly. "I was going to send Susan over to the Stevens place to see if they'd swap some rations— sugar for butter."

"You're welcome to it, Ma. I don't do much baking in the summer," said Dot as she poured a little water into the pot of blueberries on the woodstove. Dot was only two inches taller than her mother, but she had the lean frame of her father. "I hope we don't have too far to drive to deliver the preserves," she said. "I need my gas rations just to get home. I cut way down on driving last month after Andy's destroyer left, but I'll need enough to get to work each day," she said. Dot worked in a textile mill that made fabric for army uniforms

The war effort demanded major sacrifices at home, and for some, real hardships. Pleasure driving was prohibited, and the roads were nearly deserted on Sunday afternoons. No new cars were being made for the duration of the war; it wasn't easy finding parts or tires to keep the old cars going. Some businesses were not considered priorities, and many raw materials were constantly out of stock in the stores.

The country had hundreds of thousands of men—and some women—overseas needing to be fed and supported, and if the Allies were going to bring down Hitler and the Japs, Americans would have to learn to live on less. For most of the one hundred thirty-five million Americans, they got top notch training in sacrifice from the Great Depression.

Mariah resented the comments by a member of the ration board that she should retire. "Look, lady, you're collecting social security." Some considered fancy preserves a luxury that shouldn't be encouraged in a time of war; others just thought it was foolish for a seventy-five-year-old woman to be working long hours running her own business. Dot agreed, but knew it was useless to try to bend her mother's will. Mariah had told her in confidence that she had to save as much as she could to provide for Brad. He was a burden she didn't want to pass on to the family without a little trust fund to help.

At least Brad was safe from the draft. He was soon to turn forty-one. With the military calling up nearly every able-bodied man thirty-five and under, Ed made the cut by one year and quickly volunteered for the navy. The separation from Rita was not the sacrifice most married men felt in leaving their wives and kids behind because they had already been separated for four years despite a few attempts at reconciliation. The marriage between two fiery-tempered, impulsive kids was doomed by family religious feud straight out of the Reformation and money management akin to the Crash. Ed and Rita tried to get along for the sake of their little girl, but darkness won out over light and each sought solace in the arms of one lover after another, coming up empty as they and the nation were swept up into another war.

As the blueberries began to yield their juices in the steaming pot, Dot complained about the poor cuts of meat she had to stand in line for an hour to get. "Believe me, I've been creative. A pound of shank can be a little 'chipped beef' on gravy poured over toast…"

"You mean S.O.S," added Mariah. Dot chuckled at her mother's reference and knew that her mother wouldn't say the "s" word with her granddaughters in earshot.

"Oh, I almost forgot. When we see Ed, remind me to ask him if he's located some tires for Brad's car," she added, shaking her head. Rubber was in high demand by the military because sources of latex were largely under Japanese control, so getting decent tires for the family car was not easy, even after American scientists developed synthetic rubber.

"Well, girls, this is probably the end of the line for me; this might be the last batch of blueberry preserves I ever make for sale." As the percussive sky played out its final measures, and the clouds moved on, the girls were surprised to see Mariah's prediction that it would be "dry lightning" proven true.

Mariah threw more logs into the stove and started cooking down the blueberries with the last of the five-pound bag she was allowed for the month. She would have to take Dot up on her offer for another two pounds to get her to the end of the month.

"What can *I* do?" asked Jane who was less talkative than her fourteen-year-old sister and didn't enjoy sitting around listening to adults gab. Her grandmother soon set her to work on mixing the yellow food coloring into the margarine. It took all of her strength, and she eventually had to ask Susan for help.

"Why don't they color the margarine at the factory?" asked Susan.

"The dairy farmers want to remind the public that it isn't butter. If it looked just like butter, folks might not mind so much that it didn't taste like butter," said Dot who was busy sterilizing glass jars that had gotten dusty in their storage box.

Finally the clouds were gone and sun lighted the distant fields and trees across the road with a golden hue. It was so dramatic that the girls laughed with delight and went outside to look for a rainbow.

"No rainbows without rain," said Susan as the girls headed out the door.

"No indeed," said Mariah with a sigh, "there are no rainbows without rain. You girls will learn that soon enough." The girls, ever hopeful, ran out to check the sky anyway. "Yes, they learn that even if the sky opens up on you, that doesn't mean you're going to be dancing under a rainbow while you're drying off," Mariah added with a slight tremble starting in her chin.

"Ma, what's wrong?" said Dot as she put the lid back on the simmering pot.

"A lot of doors seem to be closing, if you know what I mean." Mariah sat at the kitchen table. She took in deep breaths and put her hand over her heart. "Get me one of my pills, will you?"

Dot's hands were shaking as she fumbled with the top. She managed to get a nitroglycerin pill out and her mother placed it under her tongue. "Are you all right?"

"You know the answer already, dear. With diabetes and a bad heart, I can't say life insurance would come cheap." Mother and daughter laughed at the truth. "And I've got other things to worry about, but thank God you're not one of 'em."

"You never know, Ma. You were pretty worried when I was a flapper," said Dot with a smile that showed she was beginning to relax as Mariah's breathing returned to normal.

"If a kid's not a little crazy as a teenager, there's more to be worried about when life gets hard. No, it's your brothers. I guess I didn't do right by either of them. Brad will never really be independent, and Ed? If there's a rainbow out there, he's probably at the end of it digging for the pot of gold. Will he ever get settled? I haven't seen him really happy in a long time, and now he may be heading off to war."

"You never gave Rita a chance," said Dot. It was one of the rare times she directly criticized her mother. "I've always felt sorry for her, and I know, Ma, you had plenty of reasons. I understand all that."

Mariah's expression acknowledged the truth in Dorothy's words, and the two fell silent for a moment.

"But Ma, he's found a new girl. In fact, she's coming up to visit today."

"You don't say?" said Mariah with a mixture of hope and skepticism.

"She's really cute, of course. Ed always finds good lookers, but she's soft and gentle, a really sweet girl. I don't know if I'd call her naïve or innocent. That's the only part that worries me."

"Go on," said Mariah.

"She's in art school and she plays the violin. Comes from a very talented family. They met last summer at the Briarcroft Resort before he had to go in the service."

"You don't say. Well, it seems that Ed's taste in women has changed."

"Maybe so. I understand the divorce is final." Dot touched her mother's hand and got up to attend the preserves that had scented the whole house with a wonderful sweetness. "You know, Ma, if you go out of business, I'll miss these 'sweet moments'."

"I'm not so sure about that," laughed Mariah. "This isn't exactly a vacation in the country for you and the girls, now is it?"

As Mariah and Dot continued their work on the blueberry preserves, they heard a car pull up. Almost before the screen door slammed shut, Mariah asked Ed, "Where's this new girlfriend of yours?" He was somewhat taken aback.

Over at Aunt Florence's. Getting to know the family," said Ed offhandedly.

Mariah's face fell. So he thought it was more important to introduce his girl to my sister. Ed could read her better than a road map.

"Ma, Aunt Florence has a big boarding house. You can't put us up here. And Florence is making a big dinner for all of us and Liz offered to help. Now don't you go and get all offended. Liz is really excited to meet all of you, especially you." Ed gave his mother a hug and a kiss, and as she usually did, she was won over by Ed's charms as most women were.

Dot went to the door and called her daughters. "It's time to come in and get cleaned up, girls." They didn't need much coaxing when they saw Uncle Ed who always seemed to have a treat in store for them.

"Girls," said Mariah, "you go in and wash up and put on your best dresses. When Uncle Brad gets home, we'll be heading over to visit my sister. She's got a great, big house."

"And we're going to have the best ice cream you've ever had," added Ed. When the girls went to wash up, Ed's expression changed. Mariah knew, as was typical with her sister, that there would be some kind of news that wouldn't necessarily be welcome. Mariah couldn't think of too many times when there wasn't an agenda laid out with fine china and starched linen.

"Eleanor's going to be there, too," said Ed.

"Well, that's nice. I haven't had a chance to see her since…"

"I know, Ma, since Uncle Amos died."

Mariah nodded. She could hardly think about her little brother Moze gone before her. Just a few weeks before he had died suddenly of a heart attack. His hair was only beginning to gray.

"Eleanor's going to be moving in with Florence," Ed said. He was reluctant to say the rest. After looking down, he met his mother's eyes. "She's gonna have to sell your folks' old place."

When the girls came out, everyone complimented them on how nice they looked. Their grandmother kissed them both and then went to her bedroom door.

"Ma," added Ed softly, "Eleanor wants to arrange for you to go with her to the house. She says there are some things there that belong to you."

Mariah nodded before she turned the doorknob. "I'm going to lie down for a little while," she said, putting on her best face so she wouldn't spoil what was meant to be a family celebration.

# CHAPTER 46

## *Keepsakes*

$\mathcal{E}$ leanor, as formal and correct as a Puritan, let Mariah into the parlor. "I'll give you a little time in here alone," she said, and gently closed the door. Through the window Mariah could see Susan pushing Jane higher and higher on the swing hanging from one of the hearty sugar maples on the river side of the house. Although Moze and Eleanor never had children, he told his wife he kept the swing for any children who came to visit. The truth was he did his best to preserve reminders of his childhood wherever he could.

The parlor still had the dark round table in the center of the room with the same ornate lamp, now electrified, that used to fascinate him as a child. Moze would take one of the pendant crystals hanging around the base of the globe and chimney over to the window to cast rainbows around the room.

The mantel clock, with its deep, wooden sound, still counted the seconds that added up to minutes, and quickly enough, into decades. Mariah sat on the old horsehair Victorian sofa with a carved grape cluster on the trim. It was here that she sat, her mother on one side and her father on the other, when they prepared to go to Frederick's funeral. On the inside wall to the left of the parlor stove was the charcoal portrait of her father, his beard hiding his mouth, his eyes devoid of the devilish sparkle. No drawing or photograph had ever captured his humor and vivacity. Mariah began talking to the man in the picture, hoping to conjure her father's spirit back from the grave. Her eyes blurred with tears.

There on shelves to the right of the hearth were her mother's books. They had grown musty, and their leather bindings were brittle and dry. How she loved to read, and how she had passed that love on to her daughter. Sarah Sanborn Brandon had let the genie out of the bottle when she introduced Mariah to the broad horizons that beckoned from the pages of literature. Mariah sat in her father's Morris chair and closed her eyes. She heard the distant laughter of her grand-daughters and the steady ticking away of time.

After nearly a half hour had passed, Eleanor called gently through the closed door, "Mariah, are you ready for tea?"

Eleanor and Susan had moved an old trunk into the kitchen. Mariah recognized it immedi-ately as the trunk from the farm, a tin-clad trunk that had gone to Iowa and back with her. After George's death in 1924, she had locked the trunk and put it in the birthing room, the small room behind the kitchen chimney used in colonial times for newborns and their mothers. Mariah had turned it into a pantry. The trunk had been stacked with empty jelly jars for years. It had taken all of Mariah's strength to pull the trunk out of the house and into the front yard as the chimney fire began to ignite the roof.

"A treasure chest," said Jane. "Let's open it."

"Wait, girls," said Eleanor who saw ambivalence in Mariah's face. "Would you rather open it when you get home?"

"Oh, it's just a bunch of old stuff. Nothing valuable," Mariah said. In truth, it was Mariah's life and it was only fitting that it be opened here within sound and sight of Cold River and in the house where her life started and took shape. Susan and Jane were so excited at their grandmother's acquiescence that they immediately stooped down and undid the latches only to find that the clasp was locked.

"Where's the key?" asked Jane as though it would be simple to produce the key to a long-forgotten trunk that had been pulled from a fire.

"I have no idea where the key is after all these years. Eleanor, if you get me a hammer, I'll open the thing."

"Now watch out, girls," said Mariah who pried the clasp open with the claw. As Susan lifted the lid, Mariah prepared herself to ward off any ghosts that might escape.

The girls took out each item and handed them one at a time to Mariah who took each to the table and set it down. The girls clamored to know about each one.

"Let me do it my way," said Mariah who glanced at them and shook her head. They were to watch and wait until she was ready to tell the story that she laid out on the table like pictographs from an ancient tomb.

A hand-colored photograph of Mount Chocorua. *Some day, somehow, I'm going to see my mountains again.* "I took this picture with me when I moved to Iowa when I was twenty-five," explained Mariah.

"You moved to Iowa, Grammy?" asked Jane.

"I lived there for nine years. Can you imagine going away and not seeing your mommy or your daddy or your sister or brother for nine years?" said Mariah with her face close to Jane's and her voice soft.

"Why did you go?"

"When we get all of these things out, then we'll take a walk along the river path and I'll tell you more. Some day, when I'm gone, someone can tell you the whole story." Jane nodded without a word. Her eyes were big waiting to dig deeper into the trunk.

A yellow silk hat with a black ostrich plume. *I was just like a mail order bride and I never realized it.* The hat excited the girls, and Mariah allowed each one to try it on before putting it in its place on the table.

"I wore that hat with a matching dress for the trip out west," Mariah said as she held it up and noticed how crushed, stained and weak the fabric had become with time.

"Did you want to go out west?" asked Jane.

Mariah put her fingers to her lips. "Remember, the walk along the river."

The girls continued to lift treasures from the trunk. Eleanor watched from a distance looking pained, watching Mariah's reaction to tattered pieces of her life resurrected. Yet Mariah pressed on, handling each item reverently.

A brass button with the letters G.A.R: Amos Brandon's Civil War uniform, the Grand Army of the Republic. *Daddy, why won't you ever put on your uniform? Why are you so sad when you look at it?* An empty bottle of potato bug remedy. A cup and saucer from Dodge's Hotel. *Robbing the cradle, aren't you, Will?* An old photograph of a fair-haired boy on the verge of manhood. *Frederick, Frederick, keep your eyes open. Don't give up.* A hymn book from the First Baptist Church, Central City, Iowa. *Bertha's story, Jim's song, praising their savior all the day long.* A linen napkin with the monogram S.G.C. *I want you to be our guests. Stephen Grover Cleveland.*

A photograph of a team of workmen laying the first beam over granite bridge abutments. Mariah pointed to a man who looked much older than the rest. "That's Grampy Taylor." *George, you can't go through another season like this one. Next July you'll turn seventy-four. Look at your hands shake.*

Old tin cookie cutters from Great Grandmother Brandon, George's buggy whip, a palm-size gray granite stone, worn round and smooth by time and the waters of Cold River. "I kept that stone on my nightstand all the years I was away from home. When I rubbed it, I was in the Cold River again," she told the girls. Dress gloves, baby clothes, and some trinkets and mementoes lay on the bottom of the trunk.

Mariah opened the compartment in the cover. The old wallpaper lining the trunk flaked away at a touch. She withdrew a small packet of letters and a small, plain book with a marbleized cover. Mariah untied the string and opened the little book. A photograph of Mariah's father standing in front of a hay wagon with three young men atop the load. One of the young men immediately drew one's eye. It was Will Dunfield. Under it was a wedding picture of a raven-haired beauty with a curvaceous figure. Very young. A second wedding photo had survived. Mariah clutched it to her heart and was speechless. She thought of Will and she thought of George. *You never loved me the way you loved him, isn't that the truth?*

Mariah stared at the other photographs in silence, then placed them back in the book and retied the bundle. She took a deep breath and looked up into the faces of her granddaughters who could barely refrain from asking about the handsome man who stirred such a re-sponse. Mariah had said nothing about the letters or the picture, and from her expression, they knew that they should not ask.

Rising slowly, she walked to the kitchen window that looked down the old gravel road that she traveled sixty years before out of the notch. "Eleanor, if you don't mind, we'll put everything back after we get back from our walk. Girls, are you ready? Then let's go down to the river."

# CHAPTER 47

## *Tares Among the Wheat*

"Tt's been the story of my life," said Mariah to Neal Coursin. "Here I am giving up another house."

Neal, who was stooped with age and would soon turn over the store to his son, nodded sympathetically. "Once our kids are grown, life gets smaller with each passing year," he said.

Mariah had two big cardboard boxes on the counter. She was stocking her cupboards in the new house on the square.

"It's a cute little cottage," said Neal as he looked across toward the little house at the south end of Courthouse Square, just where Brown's Ridge Road began. "You're lucky to be all moved in before the holidays. No more lugging firewood and pails of water for you, Mrs. Taylor," he said cheerily.

"True, but that's the end of my business, too. Come the New Year, I don't know what I'll do with myself."

"Well, there's not many days left of 1947, but I bet you'll come up with plenty to fill your days." Neal beckoned a stock boy. "Mrs. Taylor, Sammy here will carry those boxes over to the new place for you."

The decision to give up the place rested on her chest like New Hampshire granite stones piled into boundary walls. In the stroke of

370

a pen she had converted land into cash to provide for herself and her eldest son, yet in signing the contract, she had struck Brad a terrible blow. It had to be—for her, for him, for her children and grandchildren. Duty spoke to her of acceptance; her will protested the heavy tread of fate. Once again in Mariah's life she felt guilty for circumstances beyond her control.

The fields across from the camp, tilled and seeded by Taylor hands for forty-five years, had yielded to weeds as it lay fallow. Saplings grew in the cellar holes of farmhouse and barn, a sight of abandonment and defeat. Mariah had managed fields and farm and business for twenty-three seasons. For each season there was a time and a purpose under heaven; Mariah felt it in her bones, in her heart; but her will refused to acknowledge the changes in earth and sky that whispered to her that it was nearing the season to die.

Ed had bought the camp, and on an overcast November day, had moved his mother out and his young family in. The farmland across the street went to some New Yorkers who saw it as a long-term investment. With only two bedrooms, the three children, all under six, would share a room with the two boys, Bobby and Ronny , in one bed and little Betty still in a crib. The worst adjustment for wife and children was the outhouse. Mariah saw the dread in Elizabeth's face as she made her first fearful trip with the boys to the privy. Growing up in a gracious suburban home with two full baths and all the hot water you wanted from gleaming chrome faucets, Elizabeth was not the pioneer used to adversity. The delicate hands of violinist and artist would learn to dip water from a spring, haul wood for the cook stove, and contend with wild animals outside and under the house trying to gnaw their way in. This was not the kind of romantic adventure she expected when she married Ed.

In the post-war recession, jobs were scarce. Millions of servicemen were back home and the economy struggled to adjust to peacetime. Rationing had continued for months after Hiroshima and the Japanese surrender. Ed had run afoul of the authorities in Massachusetts for selling tires and batteries on the black market. Playing it safe, he took off for the New Hampshire hills where he had the prospect of a job as a mechanic from an old buddy in Tamworth.

371

Mariah had already told Ed and Dot that she was leaving her little house on the square and any money she had left to Brad. She had already set up a trust with her brother-in-law Harry for an allotment over the next five years. It was the best she could do. But Brad needed more than money; it took a strong hand to keep him on the straight and narrow. Ed and Dot would have their hands full. Nothing weighed more heavily on Mariah's weak heart than the fate of her elder son.

Susan's wedding pictures arrived in the mail lifting Mariah's spirits. No one brought Mariah more happiness than her sparkling, loquacious, good-humored granddaughter. She had married a navy man, so she would never live nearby, but Susan always made the effort to visit her grandmother whenever she could. Mariah was about to turn eighty; there were only a few people in town that had reached her age. She looked at the smiling faces of Susan and Kent with the hope that they would make her a great-grandmother before her strength and will gave out.

"Brad, it's time." He dried his eyes with a handkerchief and looked at his mother with an expression of torment and anger.

"Papa wanted me to have the place," he said with a shaky voice as he walked across the square with the box followed by the stock boy who kept a good distance

"I'm sorry that life didn't turn out that way," responded his mother.

"That's what Pa wanted," he whined bitterly. "It just ain't right."

"What's right and what's wrong isn't easy to see, especially when you're in the middle of it. I did my best. I'm leaving it to God to sort it out in the end," said Mariah, hoping that her soft answer would turn away Brad's wrath.

"If you'd a loved Pa the way you ought to…"

"Don't say another word about love. No words can teach me more about love than eighty years of hard lessons."

"I could a made it with your business if you'd let me."

It was rare for Brad to answer his mother back. Mariah took stronger verbal measures than she wanted to. "You had a beautiful farm down in Plaistow, and what happened to it?" Mariah asked rhetorically. Brad began to weep. Giving them both a little time to calm the storm, she at last put her hand on his arm. "There, there. You can have a nice little garden behind the new place. You can walk to work right across the square." Brad could not be comforted. The land he had always longed for, now gone to weeds, would never be his.

"Brad, I'm leaving everything to you," she announced. "Oh, some little things—not worth much—I'm giving Ed and Dotty, but you're getting this house and what money I have. It's not a lot, mind you." Brad took out his handkerchief again and wiped his eyes. "Uncle Harry and Aunt Florence will take care of the money for you," Mariah added with a cautionary tone. It wasn't much, but she was doing this as much for George W. Taylor as for his elder son. She had dragged George back to New Hampshire, sold off much of his beloved stand of timber, and kept a part of her heart out of his reach. She could not surrender her heart or her will, but she could and she would do her duty and her penance. Brad would be provided for.

Brad collected himself and got the car started. Just as he got onto the road, he saw Ed driving up to his mother's new house. Ed hopped out of the car with a relaxed smile. He had done right by his mother and he knew she was going to do right by Brad.

"Ruth would like both of you to come over. She wants to give you a little sendoff."

Brad and Mariah looked at him coldly. "Your brother doesn't drink and I don't drink," said Mariah.

Ruth Luddington held court on Saturdays for summer folk and a select few natives who appreciated sherry and intelligent conversation: The Iron Curtain, Chiang Kai-Shek, the latest Hemingway novel. Ruth had been published a few times; she had traveled; she spoke French. The gay divorcee, raconteur, and connoisseur of Brown's Ridge Road found Ed wildly charming and his new artist wife, a delightful adornment in her cultured circle of friends. Ruth did not acknowledge the intelligence of a woman like Mariah who supported herself by menial labor. Mariah and Ruth had long been flint and steel; Mariah had no desire to set sparks flying.

"You can have a cup of tea. Some great food. Come on. Take the chill off in front of the fireplace." Ed's smile faded as he saw his efforts failing.

"I wouldn't set foot in that woman's house," said Brad who had forgotten that he had actually been lured into the witch's lair a few times years before and had emerged unscathed. He would not be able to stand being caught between his mother and Ruth Luddington, two women in league with evil spirits of various kinds.

"No thanks," added Mariah. "I'm pretty tired. I'm anxious to get into my new place," knowing that her tact would not rub off on Brad, but would spare Ed more discomfort. "This is your welcome party, so you go and enjoy it."

From the farm to the camp to the cottage on the square: Mariah's shrinking world. The new place was tiny, but a charming white clapboard New Englander with the front door on the left opening to a staircase and a hallway. Mariah's bedroom backed up against the kitchen on the ground floor with a living room on the front. She could look across the square to the post office and Coursin's Store on the right and the Gulf station to the left. All the houses on the square were white, just as she remembered the buildings on the Ring in Center Sandwich.

She told Brad to go up and see his bedroom, but he had little enthusiasm for the new in-town house on a tiny parcel of land. "Well, how about going out back and planning a garden?" she said with a forced smile.

"Hrumph," grunted Brad, slumped into a new overstuffed chair beside the big wooden Philco radio. Tired of the cold silence, Mariah turned on the radio to Edward R. Murrow news. "We'll see what Truman's up to," she said, "and after that, you can listen to 'Fibber McGee and Molly.' Get your mind off things." Mariah took control, as she knew she always had to. She braced herself against the archway into the living room to catch her breath and stop the swirling in her head. Mariah worried more and more as days came and days went, about who would take Brad under his wing when she was gone.

A day of concealing torn emotions, of enduring the pain of change. She willed herself to look for the silver lining. The house had hot water, central heat and indoor plumbing, luxuries she had last experienced as Mrs. Dunfield in downtown Rochester in the early 1880s. The kitchen had a white enamel gas range with four burners on the left and an oven on the right. No more lugging wood and seeing your breath when rising for morning chores.

The greatest luxury was a telephone. A 4-party line was affordable. She sat in a chair by the front door and lifted the receiver off its cradle. Immediately the operator said, "Number, please," and Mariah asked for Lakeside 5-3827 and after three rings, Florence answered.

"Mariah, I'm surprised to hear from you at this hour. Isn't Cours-in's closed?"

"Of course. I'm calling from my own phone and I want you to have the number." It gave Mariah satisfaction to hear surprise in her sister's voice.

After all of the news was exchanged, Florence mentioned Dr. Doug-las. "He's been expecting to see you for a checkup on your sugar. He suspects you're not watching it. Mariah, are you overdosing on insulin? You know that's not a cure, don't you?" chided Florence.

There was only the sound of rapid breathing on Mariah's end of the line. *Is it any of your business what I do and don't do?* "You can give Dr. Douglas my number, Florence." Said Mariah. "If he wants to check on me, he can make the call. You know as well as I do it won't make any difference."

"Because you won't do what the doctor says, that's why!" sputtered Florence.

Mariah's response was only slightly sharp. "It hasn't been doctors that have got me through these eighty years."

After she hung up, Mariah felt a release of pressure, and asked Brad if he'd like her to bake some cookies. She beckoned him to get down new bags of flour and sugar. Sweets always made her feel better.

# CHAPTER 48

## The Work of Water

Water does mighty works. It carves through miles of stone and carries mountains to the sea. It rises higher than the tallest peaks and sinks miles below the densest land. In its solid state it breaks gargantuan boulders apart and sends them crashing to the valleys below. It moves in massive glacial sheets to reshape continents. In its invisible state it blasts from deep within the earth and shows itself in plumes of vapor mightier than all the engines of human ingenuity. It hides the sun behind billows of ever-changing shape, and glories in its life-giving magnanimity in all the rainbow's hues.

Water, the universal solvent, paired with limitless time, dissolves anything and brings together dispersed elements into new and wondrous combinations. There is no life without water. It floats the leviathans of the sea and sustains millions of darting microbes in a tiny drop.

Water batters and builds, drowns and revives. It speaks to living creatures in many voices. It soothes and calms in its gentle courses; it rages in anger with deafening torrents; it rumbles as it crashes, grinding in ceaseless waves, withdrawing for rest, advancing again with whispered, eternal regularity. The voices of rising and falling water tantalize those who seek to conquer the sea, and mock the proud in parched irony with endless water all around, and not a drop to drink.

Water has power to cleanse, and living water, the water of belief, has the power to wash away sins. Mariah dreamed of the voices of Cold River and woke with her heart burdened by duty and her will troubled by regret.

The day before Thanksgiving Mariah rose deeply disturbed by her dreams, disturbed at herself for holding back love for the father of her children, and in other moments disturbed at God for denying her deepest desires. Throughout her life, whether she bowed to her duty or raged against the injustice of her fate, she was seldom at peace.

Why was a woman defined and confined by the boundaries set by men? Why was a woman given gifts and callings only to be punished for aspirations and dreams? When Mariah's prideful will rose on waxen wings to defy the limits of the established order of the universe, she was not the only one to suffer. She prayed that the opposing forces that had tormented her from her youth would be resolved in God's mysterious ways.

Tomorrow; Thanksgiving Day, Mariah's eightieth Thanksgiving. She longed to see her children together again around her table. So much had gone unsaid; she worried that the long string of days ahead, days that she would never see, would bring problems and sorrows as her legacy. Yet she had blessings to be thankful for as a wife and a mother; she would tell her children of her love and thank God for them. She would ask God for peace that eluded her in life.

In the early hours, before dawn, when the only lights on the square were four circles from street lamps scattered like giant golden coins on the dark ground, Mariah worked in her new kitchen. She mixed eggs and cream, sugar and spices. Scents of cinnamon and nutmeg filled the air steaming with cooking squash and slices of apple sautéed in butter.

Mariah's breaths were shallow and quick; her legs became numb and full; at times the room swirled and she sat to wait for it to still. She rose again and ran the faucet; she felt the warm water flow over her hands. Running hot and cold water was one of the comforts she had enjoyed over the past year. She was warm without building a fire. She could get to the store every day, and best of all, she could call anyone from her own home whenever she wanted.

There was much to be thankful for as 1948 came to a close. The nation was at peace, and most of the young people who had gone to war had come home, some profoundly changed, and some irreparably damaged, but all were lucky to be home. Her children were well and attentive to her needs, and she had grandchildren to tell stories to, stories they would carry into the next century and to generations yet to be born.

And the greatest joy of the year—a great granddaughter. Mariah never expected to live to see that generation. Her first child was born when she was thirty-four, her last when she was forty-one. Most women were grandmothers by the time she had birthed her second son. With great sadness she thought of George W. who was fifty-nine when his last child was born. He never knew the joy of grandchildren.

Susan had a little girl during the summer, and had come up early in the fall for precious pictures of baby and great-grandmother. Mariah looked forward to seeing the baby, bubbly and chubby. She delighted at the joy the child brought to Susan, the granddaughter who had always brought happiness in her wake.

Brad got up and had his coffee. Still upset over his displacement from the land, he could not engage in pleasantries. Mariah knew he needed time, but she knew she had little time to heal his brooding hostility. She dispatched him to work at the service station, and reminded him to go to a nearby farm for a fresh turkey right after work.

No, she was not feeling ill, and no, she didn't need to sit down. Why was he suddenly solicitous? It was very important to Mariah that she put Thanksgiving dinner together, and she was going to do it despite a little dizziness and shortness of breath. "I've gotten used to it," she said. "And the diabetes? I just take my shots."

By the afternoon the square was busy with cars stopping at the post office and at Coursin's or gassing up at the Gulf station where Brad would be until dark. Mariah listened to the news as she worked. The Berlin airlift was still underway, and the announcer said it was going to "hold the line against communism." Harry Truman was still in the glow of his victory two weeks before against Governor Dewey of New York, and now there was talk of integrating the races in the military. The most interesting news was the opening of the first television broadcasting stations in Boston. She had never seen a television, but some townsfolk had seen it demonstrated at the 1939 New York World's Fair.

When Brad returned with the turkey, he found his mother at the kitchen table pricking her finger and testing her blood. Her color was not good, and she was struggling for breath. What do you want me to do?" he asked.

"You go in and listen to Arthur Godfrey. Don't mind me. I'm just late on my insulin," she said, puffing between words. Brad left the room. He found it nauseating to see his mother give herself a shot.

Mariah had made chowder and biscuits and called Brad to the table. Her voice was too weak to reach him, so she picked up a cooking spoon and banged it on the table.

"What's the matter?" he said as he rushed into the room.

"Supper, that's all," said Mariah who tried to act as normal as she could. "I'm just tired. I've been at it all day. Brad sat opposite his mother and watched her labored breathing. Her eyes were closed. He touched her hand. It was cold. She didn't touch her bowl, and after Brad was done, she rose and walked to the living room and rested on the sofa.

Just before Mariah fell asleep, the phone rang. Dot and Susan had stopped at a store and wanted to know if Mariah needed anything for tomorrow's dinner. "No, no, no. I've got everything I need. Just seeing you is all I need. You've got your hands full with the baby," she said. Far be it for Mariah to ever ask for help in the kitchen. They would be there in about an hour, and Mariah was determined that she would be alert and aglow to welcome them.

Flesh struggled with will. Mariah was barely able to get up from the sofa by herself. As the clock struck six, the moonlit western sky was colored azure to black with scattered clouds of smoky pink. Mariah gripped the edge of the sink and gazed at the changing sky, fixated by its beauty, saddened by its evanescence.

As she stood and watched, Brad announced that Ed was driving into the yard. Mariah was content that Ed was settled into domesticity. Mariah turned to greet him. Her color was ashen and her eyes were glazed. Ed's heart sank at her appearance.

"Are you all right?"

"Just over excited, I guess. I've been cooking all day. Dotty..." she regained her breath, "Dotty and Susan...any minute."

Ed helped his mother into a chair and called to Brad. "Can't you see Ma's not well?" he said with an edge in his voice.

"She don't want the doctor," said Brad firmly. Brad had no more faith in doctors than his mother and considerable fear of their black arts, so he was quick to assent to his mother's commands.

"Get my digitalis." Brad located her medicine on her nightstand, and she took a dose. While Mariah rested, Ed slipped the phone outside the front door and called Dr. Douglas's home. He was out on a house call. "Can you give me the number there?" Ed asked Mrs. Douglas. The patient, Mildred Regan, had no phone. "I'm going to let Lizzie know what's going on. You keep an eye on her," said Ed, pointing his finger at Brad's face. "I'm coming back with a doctor."

After a quiet half hour, Dot and Susan arrived. They came in with big flakes of snow on their coats. "A mix of rain and snow," Mariah heard Dotty say to Brad. "Just started."

Mariah had gotten up moments before and stood at the kitchen table mixing stuffing for the bird. Dot kissed Mariah's cheek, and Susan held out baby Jackie for her grandmother to take. "Let me sit down." Before Susan could place the baby in her arms, Mariah slumped to the side. Dot braced her. "Brad!" Dotty called. They took her to her bed.

*Ample make this bed,*
*Make this bed with awe*
*In it wait till judgment break*
*Excellent and fair.*

Dot, Susan and Brad took turns sitting by Mariah's bed. Mariah labored against the water in her lungs for each breath. Breaking water, the harbinger of birth; collecting water, the harbinger of death. The freedom of water, defying gravity, Mariah was buoyed once again—young and confident, plunging to the sandy bottom for sparkling treasure, the laws of the land void in the realms of water. Mariah heard Cold River's voices again, exulting in possibilities, drowning out admonitions to conform to limits. Mountain water numbed the senses that warn of danger.

"What are you thinking about? Your eyes are busy under those lids."

*Seeing, not thinking.* "What? Is that you, Susan? Teach that baby how to swim, do you hear me?" *No marching. No cadence. The tremulous cadence slow. Drumbeats are eternal notes of sadness. Let her find herself in the freedom of water.*

*The siren allure of water. Parched Tantalus feels the water rise and fall, but always out of reach. I have thirsted like Tantalus, struggling to reach the water of my desire, only to have it withdraw. There are terrible prices to be paid for defying conventions.* "Be strict with her so she won't get hurt."

"Freedom or obedience? Tell me, which is better?" Susan touched Mariah's head and patiently waited. Air battled water in shallow breaths.

"Give her both." She must watch and listen. "I hear her cry. Go to her." Susan dried her eyes and traded places with her mother.

"Is there anything I can do?" Dot held her mother's cold hand.

"My dress. Dark blue." Her daughter, face contorted with worry, found the dress in the dim light by the feel of silk. "Hang it on the door." Mariah would have her favorite blue dress in sight. She wanted to be laid out in that dress, a fabric too delicate for life's daily slings and arrows. Mariah would be clothed in silk when she was called to the throne of grace.

Mariah asked for water and drank. "So many mistakes. Stubborn," she said as she opened her eyes to see Dot's face.

"We're all human," replied Dot with a whisper and a touch.

"My excuse." Mariah managed a gentle laugh that set off a spasm of coughs.

"We all say that," replied Dot. Girls in town had called Dorothy Taylor "the flapper" in her teen years because she wore her skirts short and her winter boots unclasped and her black hair bobbed. She painted her face when she got out of sight of the farm. How had such a crazy girl become so serious? "You took care of Papa. You seldom had words."

"I held back. Your poor daddy deserved better."

"I'm sure he knew you loved him."

"Just listen. I know my heart. God knows, too."

Dot's eyes filled as they seldom did. Mariah had toughened her against the barbs that one must pass through each day. In nature weak animals are quickly culled from the herd.

"God forgive me, I longed for Will for years after he died. That ate away at your father."

Dot stroked her mother's head and let her rest. When morning came, the family would thank God for new life, for the release of pain, for forgiveness that follows truth. They would give thanks for the strength that always seemed there when Mariah met hardship.

Ed returned after almost two hours; he came in exhausted. He ushered Dr. Douglas to his mother's side; Lizzie was with him. The doctor listened to her chest and hoped to avoid saying the obvious: Her lungs were filling with fluid; her heart was seriously weakened.

Mariah Taylor was not a woman to be lied to or manipulated with euphemisms. "I know I'm dying. Don't be afraid to say it, doctor." Mariah apologized for the unnecessary visit. "Go somewhere where you can do some good," she whispered with a faint smile.

"Is there anything we can do to make you more comfortable?" he asked as he packed his stethoscope into his black bag and snapped it shut. Mariah had spent much of her life worrying about her comfort and finding little. If doctors could have provided pills that would bring her acceptance of her lot in life, she would gladly have taken the medicine years ago. If modern science could sterilize the soul, purifying it of all contagion, she would have willingly accepted the treatment.

"It's out of our hands, doctor," she said, with a good humor and peace that surprised him. Dr. Douglas did not remember Mrs. Taylor as a religious woman. It was her sister Florence who attended church regularly and rose to prominence as a pillar of the community. Mariah might not be religious in the usual sense of the word, but at the moment she seemed to be on speaking terms with the Almighty. "Now what do I owe you?" she asked with a touch of humor.

"I wished you'd made me a pie," he said as he patted her hand and rose from the chair.

"There's plenty out there. You take your pick," she replied.

"Goodbye, Mrs. Taylor," he said. "You're a remarkable woman, let me tell you." She made a last request, and the doctor left the room and closed the door.

Eighty years, few of them gentle. Mariah Taylor, an ordinary farm wife and extraordinary businesswoman, unremarkable yet remarkable.

"All anyone can do now is make her comfortable," said Dr. Douglas to the family. "It may be an hour; it may be a day. She does have one request. She'd like you to wash her feet. Her circulation is poor, so the warmth and the massage will make her feel good."

Lizzie and Susan, who were both anxious to do something, volunteered. Susan held the basin and talked to her grandmother about her baby. Lizzie hummed a Brahms waltz as she washed Mariah's feet. The warmth and the massage were luxurious; the water made Mariah feel clean and free. Water of purification, water of healing. Faces swirled before her inner eye assuring her that time and death did not ultimately triumph. Her breathing was still slower, still shallower. Water claimed her while it brought her peace. Mariah was a young girl again listening to the voices of Cold River.

Brad, Dot, Ed each told their mother that they loved her and they kissed her for the final time. Lost in their own thoughts, they fell silent. Lizzie and Susan hummed a new love song they had heard on the radio. The family didn't know until the humming stopped that Mariah had left them.

# ACKNOWLEDGMENTS

Voices from Cold River was a story many, many years in the making. The book started as an interest piqued in my childhood from the stories I had heard about my grandmother, Sarah Mariah Tappan. It eventually turned into a literary reality in my retirement, as I found the time to devote to research and tracking down the people and places connected to Mariah's life, in order to do her life story justice on the page.

I have many debts of gratitude to the countless people along the way who helped with my research, who read my many drafts, and who provided words of encouragement at just the right times. I was fortunate to have been surrounded by many talented writers in the English department during my tenure at Oyster River High School in Durham, New Hampshire. I must specifically mention Elizabeth Dodge and Elizabeth Whaley who read my book and made very specific and wise suggestions which helped me to shape the novel into what appears here. Their wisdom and knowledge of the literary craft were instrumental in helping me to mold my characters into fallible, complex, and complete people.

My gratitude extends to the Durham Men's Book Club, of which I was a member. This group of men agreed to read my book in its raw state. They gave me valuable insight. Their positive comments gave me the courage to continue to press forward toward publication.

I do not have the space to adequately thank all of the people along the way who met with me at libraries and historical societies, giving me the information I needed to create a historically accurate novel. Their help was critical in establishing an authentic context in which my characters could exist. To all of my former students, I thank you for teaching me so much about the writing process.

Finally, my deepest gratitude is reserved for my wife, Sally, who has always been my steadfast sounding board. At every stage of this process, you listened and gave me encouragement and the freedom to write the story that I had long envisioned.

R.C. Tappan

Made in the USA
Middletown, DE
11 May 2017